IN A DISTANT VALLEY

ALSO BY

SHANNON BOWRING

The Road to Dalton
Where the Forest Meets the River

Shannon Bowring

IN A DISTANT VALLEY

A DALTON NOVEL

Europa Editions
27 Union Square West, Suite 302
New York NY 10003
www.europaeditions.com
info@europaeditions.com

First publication 2025 by Europa Editions

Library of Congress Cataloging in Publication Data is available
ISBN 979-8-88966-140-5

Bowring, Shannon
In a Distant Valley

Cover design and illustration by Ginevra Rapisardi

Prepress by Grafica Punto Print – Rome

Printed in Canada

CONTENTS

For everyone everywhere
who carries their own Dalton within them

" . . . and now instead of two stories fumbling
to meet, we belong to one story
that the two, joining, made."

—Wendell Berry, *Entries*

IN A DISTANT VALLEY

I.
Fate

Her

For the first time in the nearly seven years since Nate bought this property on Davis Road, the house is filled with people. Downstairs, adults nibble on appetizers; upstairs, kindergartners play hide-and-seek, shrieking with delight whenever they find each other behind toy chests or under beds. Someone has turned the radio to the Top Forty countdown, dropping Oasis and Blues Traveler into discussions about lumber prices and snowfall. Guests spill from the living room to the kitchen to the front hallway. Several young moms talk about the upcoming grade school Christmas pageant, their voices overlapping with those of Nate's parents, the Haskells, the Bests, every blond Lannigan. Vera Curtis is here, as well as Alice and Roger from up the road, and Arlene Nadeau, too, swooping in each time Nate refills the olive dish. Floating through the house are the mingled aromas of simmering tomato sauce, damp wool mittens on the woodstove, and a trace of someone's floral perfume.

"Quite the turnout for a six-year-old's birthday party," Nate's mother says when she finds him in a corner of the kitchen slicing cheddar for the cheese and cracker tray. "There must be nearly thirty people here."

"Thirty-two at my last head count," says Nate, speaking loudly to be heard over Leigh-Anne Buckley and Cheryl Fortin, standing next to him immersed in a good-natured argument about the best quilt pattern (Log Cabin; Flying Geese). The women are crowding Nate at the counter, but he doesn't mind—he's filled with a buoyant energy he hasn't experienced since he was in his early twenties, just starting out in marriage and in his job at the Dalton Police Department. The feeling began when the first guests arrived around noon and has grown stronger in the hours since as he has fetched sodas, restocked the toilet paper in the bathroom, adjusted the thermostat down, then up, then down again. He can't get over the giddy wonder of seeing so many people give up their Sunday afternoon just to celebrate Sophie.

"Bridget would have loved this, Nate."

"She did like a get-together."

In the five-and-a-half years since his wife died, he has learned grief doesn't follow a clear line like a road paved from one point to another. Grief instead is a river, raging sometimes, meandering others, advancing and then twisting back on itself, swirling in stagnant pools before rushing toward the next bend.

Nate's mother starts arranging the sliced cheddar on a platter. "How about that surprise party she threw for your twenty-first? She must have invited the whole town to the Aroostook Lodge, remember?"

"Yup. That was something."

"And Helen McGreevy got so boiled up about the noise she tried to call the cops and the fire department to shut it down?"

"Well, there were too many people there, Ma. It was against code."

"But the joke was on Helen, wasn't it? All the cops and firemen were whooping it up at the Lodge with the rest of us."

"I wasn't whooping it up."

"True. You never have been much of a whooper."

Across the room, several people explode with laughter in reaction to some punchline Bruce Rossignol has landed. Part of Nate wants to walk over and find out what's so funny. But most of him is content to stay right here, tending the snacks and waiting for the pasta water to come to a boil. It's better to observe from the edges than to be at the center of attention—he had more than enough of that in the months after Bridget's suicide. Everyone in town watching him as he pumped gas, bought groceries, mailed bills that might have been a day or a week overdue. All the mundane routines that make a normal life. All the motions to keep himself alive while his wife lay buried under still-fresh earth.

So the choice to stand off to the sidelines today is partly Nate's inclination to observe rather than participate. More than that, though, there's something profoundly comforting about letting the party unfold around him.

This is what he has always wanted—a house bursting with life and sound and laughter. Growing up, his wasn't an unhappy home. But his mother worked long hours at the retirement community, and his father was away a lot on trucking jobs. Nate often wished for siblings to add some noise, some depth, to their little ranch on Russell Street. When he and Bridget, as hopeful teenagers, would unspool their dreams of a shared future, they talked about two things above all else: Where they would live, and the number of kids they would have. They agreed on both subjects: It could only be the old Donoghue property at the edge of town—this beautifully dilapidated farmhouse with views of the North Maine Woods, Mount Katahdin, the Aroostook River, and Dalton, the buildings of their hometown scattered as if from some invisible, divine hand. And they had to have at least two children, maybe three. One was just too lonely.

"Dad?"

Nate turns to see Sophie squeezing past Cheryl and Leigh-Anne. Her copper curls are wild, cheeks flushed from the work of entertaining so many other kids (he insisted she invite all twelve of her classmates, so no one felt left out). Her dress, a birthday present Grampa Frazier FedExed north earlier this week, is already stained with grape juice.

"When are Adam and Brandon getting here, Dad?"

Nate's stomach swoops as if he's driving the police cruiser over the frost heaves on Route 11. Beside him, his mother's hands still; Cheryl and Leigh-Anne fall silent. When he answers, he's careful to keep his voice light.

"Rose is bringing them out here as soon as they're done visiting with their dad."

"Why can't they visit their dad another time? It's my party day."

"Remember we talked about trying to be more patient?"

"I'm not going to have any more fun until they get here."

"Don't you think your other friends want you to go back up and play with them?"

"If I have to be patient, so do they." Of all the things she inherited from her mother, her stubbornness is one of the most prevalent. That and those jewel-green eyes.

Before Nate can think of a response, Leigh-Anne leans between him and his mother to grab a slice of cheese, which she offers to Sophie. "Tell me, sweetie, what's your favorite subject in school?"

"All of them."

"My daughter works at your school, in the front office," says Cheryl. "You know those announcements you hear every morning, about the lunch menu and student birthdays? That's Sarah—you probably call her Mrs. Best."

Now Nate's mother chimes in, asking Sophie if she'd like to hand out snacks to her friends upstairs. Then the women ferry the girl away, expertly diverting her as only a group of mothers could.

Thank god for them all, thinks Nate, throwing a handful of spaghetti into the now-boiling water. Fate may have deprived Sophie of her own mom, but she has never lacked the love of ones who don't biologically belong to her. It's one of the best things about Dalton—all the surrogate mothers, always ready for any kid who might wander into their orbit needing a sandwich, a Band-Aid, or a lecture on the importance of manners. It was the same for Nate growing up in this town. He had his own mother, along with Jo Martin and Arlene Nadeau, Mrs. Kalloch and Mrs. Warren, Althea Morse and Hazel Cloutier . . . a small army of women helping him navigate childhood and adolescence, shaping him into the man he is today.

As Nate turns off the burner, he feels someone lightly smack his ribs, and he turns to see Trudy Haskell standing beside him, one fist balled on her hip.

"A man who cooks and actually enjoys it," she says. "You're a rarity, Nathaniel."

"I hope not."

Here is his best stand-in mom, placing the colander in the sink for him to strain the spaghetti before he can ask. Here is his mother's closest friend of two decades, adding basil to the sauce he made from scratch. Here is Trudy, one of his favorite people in the world, demanding he unplug the radio so she can talk to people for one damn minute without Mariah Carey interrupting her.

"And where's your mother? We have a deal never to abandon each other at parties."

Nate is about to answer when he hears the door open in the front hall, and his breath catches in his throat as he imagines that it's Rose entering the house. Is she wearing the burgundy sweater she wore that day in the clinic last week when he went in for his annual checkup? Is her hair pulled up loosely above her neck? Will she be well-rested, or will she be weighed down with worry?

But it's not Rose. It's Nate's father back inside from having a smoke, tossing the butt into the trash before turning to hear Bruce tell a story that involves a lot of rude gestures.

It's not until Trudy slaps Nate's hand away from the pot and steals his wooden spoon that he realizes how transparent his disappointment must be on his face. She laughs, not unkindly, as she stirs more salt into the sauce.

"Awful, isn't it?" she says. "Wondering when the person you want to see most will come walking into the room."

* * *

Growing up, Nate was vaguely aware of Rose Douglas—there were rumors about the girl whose mother spent most of her time at Frenchie's getting drunk and looking for men to bring back to her trailer out in Barren. But it wasn't until Chief Halstead hired Rose as the receptionist at the police station a few months after Nate started his rookie year that their lives began to intersect. He wasn't sure what to think of her at first, with her paperback romances and tendency to burn the coffee. But it didn't take long for him to see she was more than a ditzy twenty-year-old. Nate once watched her handle a phone call that should have gone to the emergency dispatcher, instructing a father how to give his son the Heimlich maneuver. Thanks to her, the toddler and his dad were back to eating Cheerios by the time EMTs got to their house. With her delicate features, brown eyes, and soft voice, Rose could easily be mistaken as weak. But Nate recognized something under all that, a strength that must have been the product of growing up as the daughter of someone like Peggy Douglas.

It took Nate a few weeks to notice the fading bruises on Rose's arms and the weariness she wore on her face in moments she didn't think anyone was looking. Maybe the decision to investigate rumors that her fiancé, Tommy Merchant, was selling drugs out of his uncle's autobody shop could have been mistaken as a rookie's desire to prove himself. But no doubt it went deeper than that for Nate.

"She's like family to all of us on the force," he confided to Bridget that fall of 1989. "We want to protect her." Bridget, who was pregnant with Sophie at the time, gave Nate a look he couldn't quite decipher before asking what he imagined would happen to Rose and her kids if he did manage to get Tommy arrested. “Do you think throwing him in jail will be better for that girl? Like all her problems disappear if he does?” Naively, that’s exactly what Nate had believed. He rushed to point out that removing Tommy from Rose’s life would, at the very least, stop the physical abuse. Bridget didn’t disagree with that. “Remember, though,” she said, “the damage doesn’t end once the bruises are gone.”

He arrested Tommy the following summer, but the whole thing was cursed from the start. Tommy was out of jail only a few weeks later. Rose quit her job at the station out of loyalty to him. And when Nate came home from the arrest, he found all the lights of the farmhouse off. Sophie screaming in her nursery. His wife still as a stone in pink bathwater.

By the time Tommy left town soon after Bridget’s funeral, Nate didn’t care about him—or much of anything—anymore. He let his parents take care of Sophie while he hid away inside the house he and Bridget had planned to fill with children. He quit the force. Some nights he drank enough to blur it all into something more bearable. He kept busy with projects. Refinishing cabinets, painting trim-work, replacing ceiling fans, attempting to figure out the use of the switch beside the staircase—no matter how many times he flipped it on or off, nothing ever happened. Months passed.

Shortly after Sophie’s first birthday, he ran out of projects. He cut back on the drinks. It got easier to wake up and move through the day. He started working at his father-in-law’s mill. Missing his daughter with a hollow sort of hunger, he brought her home. Five years passed.

Nate would regularly see Rose around town during that time, and he often wanted to talk to her, ask if she and the kids were okay. But it felt intrusive, so he kept his distance—until that June day when he ran into her, Adam, and Brandon out at Portman Lake.

All the hours added up, he and Rose probably spent less than a whole day together last summer. The kids ran through Nate's yard, swam in the river. On the Fourth of July, the five of them watched the parade together, Rose catching handfuls of candy and passing it to the kids. Nate felt a spark of possibility, one that burned brightest the August morning he invited Rose to help him repaint Sophie's bedroom. The way she gave him space to mourn the color Bridget had chosen for the walls filled Nate with a glimpse of potential into what his life could open up to become.

When they walked down to the river, he told her he was thinking about becoming a cop again. Resuming the life he had abandoned. They sat together watching the water, and Nate had an almost dizzying glimpse of a new future—endless days spent by that river with Rose beside him.

Then Tommy came back. And any future Nate had briefly imagined vanished.

Because even though Tommy is an abusive jerk, he is also the father of Rose's children. And like Bridget said, the damage doesn't end once the last bruise has faded. Maybe the abused is fated to always be loyal to the abuser, for reasons Nate may never comprehend.

He barely understands how his own allegiances can flow in so many directions at the same time. Bridget, Sophie, Rose . . . it seems impossible to choose one while still honoring the others. In a way, it was easier when Tommy came back to Dalton, because then Nate didn't have to make a choice—Rose did when she decided to help her kids repair whatever relationship they might have with their father.

Not everything fell apart this time, though. In the months since Tommy has returned, Rose hasn't let him move back into the trailer with her, Adam, and Brandon. She won't allow him to spend time with the kids unless she's there to chaperone. Biggest of all, she told Tommy he wouldn't interfere with the boys' friendship with Sophie. Nate doesn't know the specifics of that conversation, but whatever she said worked. A couple times a month, she brings the boys to the house, and while their kids play, she and Nate sip coffee and eat whatever dessert he has baked for the occasion.

So summer passed into fall, and then winter. Tommy stuck around Dalton and allegedly followed Rose's new rules. Outside the house where Nate and Bridget used to dream of a life bright with sound and color, Sophie, Adam, and Brandon chased each other among the flowers, jumped into piles of leaves, built snowmen with lopsided smiles. Being the kids they deserved to be, free and laughing beneath the wide blue sky, while Nate and Rose, sitting a safe distance apart, bore witness.

* * *

She arrives just as Nate sets Sophie's cake down on the table.

One second, he is laughingly asking everyone to give the kid room to blow out her candles. The next, he hears the door open and shut, and he looks above the crowd to see Rose smiling back at him.

She's wearing the burgundy sweater. She's gotten a haircut since the last time he saw her—the new bangs suit her.

All the other guests part for her, Adam, and Brandon, letting them squeeze up to the table so Rose can land a kiss on Sophie's cheek.

Then Adam starts to sing the birthday song, and everyone joins in.

Everyone, that is, except Trudy Haskell, who catches Nate's eye among the crowd and winks.

A mother, even a surrogate one, knows.

Hours later, after everyone has left the party and Sophie has had her birthday call with Grampa Frazier (he and Nana, still getting used to life after selling the lumber mill, are spending the winter down in Florida), Nate ushers his daughter to the front hallway and tells her to bundle up. They're going outside.

"But it's almost bedtime, Dad. It's a school night."

Moments like this when she sounds so grown up, Nate feels like he's been knocked into a wall—breathless, dazed. Then she wipes her nose on the sleeve of her pajamas, and she's back to being the kid she's supposed to be.

"Come on," he says, holding out her pom-pom hat. "I decided we're going to start a new birthday tradition."

"Since when?"

"Since now."

They step from the warmth of the house into the bracing night, boots crunching against snow as Nate, holding Sophie's pink-mittened hand, guides her across the yard and toward the forest. Above them are millions of pale blue stars, an almost-full moon. The air carries the smell of all the woodstoves working overtime on Davis Road tonight, sweetened smoke drifting on the breeze. Snow predicted tomorrow; could make for a busy shift for Nate—people driving too fast, believing they're invincible.

But that's tomorrow. Right now is only for Sophie, who, for once, isn't asking endless questions. *Who invented the alphabet? Why don't airplanes fall out of the sky? How do birds know when to fly south and where to go?* Nate had thought kindergarten would help satisfy some of this curiosity, but every day, she comes home from school wanting to know even more about the world. And he wants to give her the answers. But how do you explain millenniums' worth of history and physics and instinct to a six-year-old?

Every day, she becomes a little more herself. One day, she won't come to Nate with her questions anymore, believing she can figure out all the answers by herself.

Tonight, though, he can give her something she's been

asking for since she finished her last bite of pumpkin pie at Thanksgiving.

"When, Dad?" she says at least once a day. "When can we get our tree?"

And at least once a day, he tells her the same thing: birthday first, then Christmas.

When they reach the forest, he nudges her toward the juvenile white spruce he scouted yesterday while she was at his parents' house. It's the perfect Christmas tree—plump, evenly-distributed branches, just tall enough to graze the ceiling in their living room.

As soon as she sees the handsaw propped against the trunk, Sophie starts jumping up and down. "Finally! I thought it was *never* going to happen."

Nate is grateful she hasn't yet learned to hate the curse of a December birthday. Let it always be like this for her—one good occasion rolling into the next, always a reason to celebrate.

She was supposed to be born in January. Bridget was supposed to be here with them now. But nature, or maybe fate, had other ideas.

"Stand back, Soph," says Nate, waiting until he's certain she is clear from the fall before making the first cut.

Him

Motherhood, thinks Rose as she crosses the river and drives up Depot Hill, is a series of never-ending lies. *Yes, Santa is real, and magic and mermen, too. Monsters don't exist; bad things don't happen to good kids. Your dad wants what's best for you.*

She would like to believe these lies come from an urge every good mom has to shield her kids from all of life's meanness. But sometimes she worries her habit of prettying things up for her kids makes her like her own mother, who mostly lied for her own benefit: *No, I didn't bring anyone home from the bar last night; you must've been having one of your silly dreams again.*

How long until Adam and Brandon figure out all the ways Rose has deceived them? How long until they see the world for the cruel place it is and throw the blame back on her for hiding the truth from them?

Her mistakes will probably make a therapist rich one day.

For right now, the boys are smooshed next to each other in the backseat, poring through the Sears Wish Book under the dome light. Brandon wants one of those deluxe art supply kits with oil pastels and watercolors. Adam wants a remote-controlled car, or a Super-Soaker, or a bike.

"You hardly ride the one you have now," says Rose, turning onto Larch Street.

"This one has ten speeds."

"That's nine speeds too many."

"What does that even *mean*?"

"It means it isn't safe, Adam," Brandon says, and he sounds like such an old man Rose can't help but laugh. Her seven-year-old fuddy duddy.

She pulls into the driveway between her trailer and Marian Gallagher's—there's a glimpse of the old lady in the window, scowling at her television—and turns the headlights off quick so she doesn't have to see how depressing this place is: rusted metal siding, cracked cement slab where a set of steps should be. Not even the red and green Christmas lights strung around the windows cheer the place up.

"Okay," she says. "Bath, then bed. Hand me that; you guys can have it back tomorrow."

Before Brandon can give the catalogue to Rose, his brother lurches forward and grabs it away from him, crushing it to his chest.

"Mine," Adam says, and he sounds so much like his father Rose can't help but feel a jolt of dread. Her nine-year-old bully.

He almost always acts up after a visit with Tommy. She thought they had avoided it today—he was so good at the birthday party, teaching Sophie and her classmates how to create the perfect snowball. But now here he is, staring at Rose as if daring her to wrestle the magazine out of his hands.

"Adam. Give that to me."

"No."

"I'll count to three."

"No, you won't."

Brandon huddles against the seat, his eyes flicking between his brother and his mother. Not daring to pick a side.

"One."

Adam flips through the Wish Book, his almost-black hair falling across his forehead and into his eyes.

"Two."

Adam dog-ears the page with the cherry-red ten-speed bike.

"You know what comes after two."

Adam starts humming the song about grandma getting run over by a reindeer.

Tommy would probably leave Adam in the car, tell him to come inside when he's ready to stop being a brat. Maybe that's the answer. She could take Brandon into the trailer, tuck him in bed, and put her feet up for the first time since she woke up early this morning. Bust into the Tupperware of cake that Nate slipped into her bag as she was leaving his house, telling her she wasn't allowed to share it.

Nate would never leave a kid in the car, no matter how bratty that kid was being.

"Fine, Adam. Keep the magazine. Just come inside and get ready for bed, okay?"

It's unsettling how much he looks like his father when he smiles like that—as if winning a stupid argument is the same thing as claiming all the world as his own.

Later, when Rose peeks in on the boys after they've taken their baths and brushed their teeth, Adam is curled with Brandon on the bottom bunk, two sets of bare feet poking out from underneath the Lion King comforter as they flip pages in the Wish Book. He points his brother's attention to a bigger artist kit than the one he first had his sights on, grinning when Brandon's eyes light up.

Adam has always been like this, straddling the line between Good and Bad. Rose has watched him give his brother a toy truck just to yank it back one minute later, shouting at him for playing with it wrong. She's gotten calls from his teachers about how nice he is to the kids who get picked on the most, and she's gotten calls from his principal about Adam's roughness out on the playground (last spring, he pushed a girl off the slide). He cried for days when a baby robin died after smacking into the trailer window. Not long after, Rose caught him studying the carcass of a mouse mangled by one of Marian Gallagher's cats.

It's the uncertainty of whether he'll turn into a Good or Bad adult that leaves Rose with a queasy feeling in her stomach. What if she's raising a boy who will become like his father? What if all the love she gives her son won't be enough to stop him from inheriting traits that generations of his father's family have carried around with them? Violence. Addiction. Alcoholism.

"Imagine," Adam whispers to his brother, stroking his fingers against the pages of the toy catalogue. "All the pictures you could paint with an art kit like that."

Her boy. Her sweet, beautiful, possibly doomed boy.

After Adam and Brandon are asleep, Rose settles on the couch to call Vera Curtis for their evening wardrobe check-in, which started about a month ago after they inadvertently showed up at the clinic wearing matching outfits three days in a row. "We look like we're in a cult," Rose said the last time it happened, staring at Vera's skirt suit, an exact replica of her own. "This is what happens when the only halfway decent place to shop in a thirty-mile radius is JCPenney."

So now they take turns calling each other every night before work the next day. The outfit consultation takes less than twenty seconds, but they always find more to talk about.

Rose still can't believe how fast they became friends. Within days of Vera filling in for Dr. Haskell at the clinic after his heart attack last summer, she was treating Rose like an equal rather than just a secretary. Within a few weeks, they started getting together for drinks and viewings of *Unsolved Mysteries*; soon after, they were swapping books, recipes, and town gossip on a daily basis.

Sad, how Rose had to wait so long to find a real friend—twenty-six years is a long time to navigate the world without one.

They could have had their wardrobe chat at the party today, but Rose is glad they didn't. It's better this way, the two of them gabbing on the phone with nothing to distract her other than the hum of the dryer.

Vera answers on the second ring, not bothering with a hello. "Red cashmere sweater, the linen pants you want to steal, and flats. You?"

"Black shirt, wool skirt, tights, and those clogs you hate."

"I can't believe you wear those Pilgrim shoes."

"I can't believe you own cashmere."

Down the hall, Brandon coughs, and Rose stills, waiting to hear him call out for a glass of water. But it goes quiet again, and she relaxes even though it's cold enough here by the window to make her bones hurt.

"So," says Vera. "How did it go with Tommy this morning?"

When Rose closes her eyes, she's back in his apartment above the Diner. Half-broken blinds. Dingy wallpaper. Smell of fryer grease and the sound of dishes clattering downstairs. George and Arlene Nadeau were good to let Tommy rent the place, but the nicest thing Rose can say about it is that it's heated better than this damn trailer.

"It was fine," she tells Vera. "You know, more of the same. 'Look how good I been doing, they might promote me at the mill, I haven't hung out with Sully or Stu or any of them guys.' That kind of bullshit."

"Do you believe him?"

"I want to."

"How was he with the kids?"

"Not terrible. He and Adam played Crazy 8's. He got Brandon to talk about the Christmas pageant."

"Well, that's progress."

Vera always follows Rose's lead on conversations like this—if she wants to rage against Tommy's habit of smoking in the apartment while she and the boys are there, Vera nods along, talking about the link between indoor smoking and ear infections in children. If Rose is feeling generous and wants to give Tommy even the smallest bit of credit for remembering Brandon's allergy to strawberries, Vera is there for that, too, complimenting his thoughtfulness.

The dryer stops, leaving a screaming silence in the trailer. Rose feels emptied out, which could either be hunger or loneliness. She reaches for her purse, slung on the armchair next to her. Maybe cake will help.

"I saw it, by the way," Vera says.

"Saw what?"

"The way Nate was looking at you at today."

Rose's face warms at the sound of his name.

"He wasn't looking at me any kind of way."

Vera laughs. "You're blind."

* * *

Rose still can't believe how fast your best day can turn into your worst one.

That day last August out at Nate's house, painting his daughter's bedroom, then walking down to the river—that was her best day. The most perfect few hours she ever had.

She'd had a crush on him when she started working at the cop shop the summer of '89, but the obsession fell apart after he arrested Tommy and buried his wife. By the time Tommy left her and the kids, she didn't have time to think about any kind of romance, with Nate or anybody else.

Before Dr. Haskell asked her to work at the clinic, Rose juggled three minimum-wage jobs. Her mother helped for a while, until she pissed off downstate with one of her boyfriends. Adam and Brandon were always hungry, or sick, or angry, or bored, or filled with energy Rose couldn't match, or asking questions she didn't know how to answer.

She didn't want Tommy to come back, though. She might've been tired all the time and completely overwhelmed. But at least she wasn't constantly watching what she said or how she said it. She was alone; she was lonely. She was never afraid. These were the trade-offs. In the five years that passed,

Rose adapted to life as a single mom, resigned to doing everything herself.

Last summer, however, something shifted. At the lake when Nate asked Adam and Brandon out to his house for a playdate with Sophie, Rose knew it was about the kids. But sometimes she wondered. There were moments she caught Nate smiling at her in a way he never had before. In the years since Bridget died, he'd grown older and sadder, but in a way that made him seem more in touch with the world Rose knew all too well, one that could turn on you in a second. She hated that Nate had to lose what he loved most to see that world, but it made him seem far more real than he ever did back in those days when she would imagine him as a kilted hero on a white horse in one of those trashy novels she used to love.

What Rose felt that day with him at the river went so much deeper than some girlish crush. What she did feel, as she and Nate sat with their feet almost touching in the cold water, was a calm sort of hope. Maybe even faith. Nothing other than shit has ever come easy to Rose, but something about that moment made it possible to imagine there would be more days just like that one.

And then she got home that afternoon, and there was Tommy, and her perfect day turned into the one she had been dreading since he left town.

Seeing him step out of the trailer, understanding he'd taken Adam and Brandon from Marian's place, where the old crow was supposed to be watching them, made Rose feel like she was eight years old again, falling out of her favorite climbing tree. One second, she was safe under the green canopy; the next, she was dropping through empty air, ground rushing toward her. All she got from the tree, though, was a sprained ankle—nothing compared to all the hurts Tommy had inflicted on her since she was sixteen years old.

"I'm back," he said with a grin. Like she should be thankful. Like she should wrap her arms around him.

There were a lot of things Rose wanted to say to Tommy at that moment. *Fuck you* was top of the list, but that wouldn't have been okay with the boys right there—Adam hopping around, excited to have his dad home again, and Brandon, shy around strangers, pressing his face into her hip. *Go back to wherever the hell you were*, that was second of the list. But it was pointless to tell Tommy to do anything; once he made up his mind about something, that was it. *You look ridiculous*; that was the third thing Rose wanted to tell him, because he did, standing there in the fading heat of summer in his black jeans and leather jacket like one of those guys from *Grease.*

What she finally did say, after a long time of saying nothing as Tommy stared at her, his grin getting a little smaller every second, was, "Why?"

"What do you mean, why? I missed you. I missed the kids. Ain't that enough?"

She had a lot of other questions, but as her time with Nate disappeared quicker than the flash of Tommy's lighter as he lit a cigarette, she didn't bother asking any of them. She wasn't interested in his bullshit. What mattered was keeping Adam and Brandon safe. Tommy had never laid a hand on either of the boys. But Rose wasn't going to take any chances.

She sent the kids inside to watch TV—Adam whined about it, but he wasn't going to win, not that time—then turned to Tommy and stood as tall as she could.

"You can't stay here with us."

It was satisfying to see him look so surprised, to have proof he had believed she was going to let him come waltzing back in like nothing bad had ever happened between them.

"Where am I supposed to go?" he asked, a tinge of the old anger in his voice.

"Not my problem," she said, steeling herself for the clenched fist, the sharp knuckles.

Tommy blew out a cloud of smoke, which floated away on

the leaf-scented breeze, and stared at her for what felt like a century.

"Okay," he finally said. "I'll figure something out. But you can't keep me from seeing Adam and Brandon."

He flicked his cigarette onto the ground and smashed it under his heel. Then he said something in a voice so quiet Rose almost couldn't hear.

"Please don't take my boys away from me."

"You want to see those kids, you play by my rules," Rose told him. "It's over between you and me."

Tommy promised he would do whatever she asked, even though he looked like he was falling out of his own tree.

"I mean it," she said. "Nothing's going to happen between us. This is just for Adam and Brandon."

"I swear," he said. "I'm ready to be their dad."

Rose wanted to believe him. And so for the past three months, she has adapted to life with Tommy back in town, trying to prove he can be a good father, a better person. She hasn't believed him for one single second.

* * *

After she hangs up with Vera, Rose eats the cake, relishing every bite.

Once the piece is gone, she goes through her usual routine: Lock the doors. Pack lunches for school. Sort laundry. Fold laundry. Check the doors again. Brush teeth. Wash face. Check the doors once more.

By the time she gets into bed, it's started to snow outside, fine flakes that glitter in the Christmas lights around the window. Maybe tomorrow it will snow so hard and for so long that the boys will be released early from school, and she'll leave the clinic so she can be home with them, here to make cocoa with marshmallows for when they come back inside from building

Dalton's fattest, cutest snowman. Or maybe the snow will turn to nothing, and tomorrow won't have any sort of magic at all.

Halfway between awake and asleep, Rose remembers the way Nate smiled at her when she handed him a stack of plates smeared with chocolate frosting. They stood next to each other at his cast iron sink, elbows almost touching, him washing dishes and her drying, stacking them neatly in cupboards. All through the house was the chaos of Sophie's birthday, sugared-up kids and adults shouting to be heard over a radio that kept getting turned up louder and louder. But there in front of the sink, a perfect pocket of calm. Quiet. Everything else seemed far away, and not one bit of Rose felt lonely.

Borrowed & Blue

Bev can gauge what's going on up at the mill by the type of pastry Larry Briggs buys each morning. If lumber prices are up and the new owners are happy, it's one muffin. If the market is in flux and the white hats have been spending a lot of time in their office with the door closed, it's two donuts. And if the bosses are threatening layoffs or salary cuts, it's straight to the cinnamon buns, turnovers, and cream cheese Danish.

This morning, two weeks before Christmas, Bev greets Larry with a spirited hello when he walks into the Store 'N More.

"Back at ya," he says as he heads for the coffee machine (always, no matter what, half-caf with one cream and no sugar).

Bev breathes a little easier whenever Larry shows up like this, smiling while he peruses the muffins. He used to be Marshall's Number Two at the mill, before Marshall left town back in September. Now Larry is just another peon at the mercy of the new Canadian owners—not that there's anything inherently wrong with Canada, or with businessmen from that country. But these particular businessmen who represent Northwoods Lumber, a Subsidiary of Acadian Logging, Inc., are morons. Jackoffs. Word from the millworkers is that these damn Canucks can't even tell the difference between white pine and white spruce.

It's been a rough transition for Dalton, accepting that their town's biggest employer no longer belongs to the family who opened it a century ago. The Fraziers might have gotten a little out of touch over the years (just look at what happened to Annette last summer, with the drinking and the shopping and the fire), and there was always a bit of the tension that's existed between the haves and the have-nots since the beginning of time. But for most of the mill's history—which is impossible to separate from the history of Dalton itself—the Fraziers were regarded as decent people. They gave out holiday bonuses, accommodated schedules, donated money to local families whose children needed surgeries or medication not covered by insurance. Before he started long-haul driving, Bev's husband, Bill, worked at the mill for a couple years. He was only a forklift operator, but everyone in management made it a point to get to know him, and more than once, Warren Frazier helped him maneuver the forklift out of heavy mud. Not often you find a boss willing to get his hands dirty like that.

That's the biggest problem the workers have with the new owners—they only care about numbers and spreadsheets; they're disconnected from the lumber process, the daily grind of slogging through holding ponds, replacing wires in the boiling upper floor of the kiln, exposing skin, hair, eyes, and limbs to everything from sawdust to razor-sharp, quick-spinning sawblades. And if there's one thing the people in Dalton can't abide, it's that better-than-you, I'm-in-charge-so-I-don't-have-to attitude.

Larry holds this belief close, even though he might say one thing about it to the men who sign his paychecks and another thing to people like Bev here at the store. Today, as he balances his single muffin on top of his Styrofoam coffee cup, she chats with him while she stocks the deli with fresh veggies.

"You ready for Christmas?"

"Maureen does the shopping, so I assume so."

"You two going to the pageant tonight?"

"If we didn't, Carly would hold it against us till she got married and had her own kids. Two weeks, every night, practicing her kicks and twirls in the living room. If I have to hear that damn holly jolly song one more time, I'm gonna lose my mind."

Bev throws together a ham Italian for his lunch. She adds an extra pickle spear on the side, remembering well the long-ago days when it was her own third-grade son awkwardly learning those same moves for that same song.

"Stay strong, Larry."

At the counter, Angela Muse rings him up with a bored expression on her face. Bev still can't quite believe the girl managed to get out of bed and into the store on time—most mornings, she stumbles in thirty minutes late with knots in her hair and sleep-seeds in her eyes, smelling like weed and Aquafresh.

After Larry leaves, there's a steady stream of other men who pop into the store on their way to work. All of them fuel up on coffee and cigarettes; all of them say hello to Bev, ask how she and hers are doing.

"Good," she tells them. "We're good."

And she smiles when she says it, because for the first time in a long time, the words really feel true. Nate is back at the police department, and even though Bev can tell his confidence is nothing like it was before Bridget died, she has a feeling he'll be okay. Bill likes his new part-time gig as a school bus driver. Sophie is thriving in kindergarten. She misses her Grampa Frazier (not so much her Nana, and who can blame the girl), but the two of them write letters and talk on the phone a few times a week, which seems to stop her from feeling as abandoned as Marshall and Annette's house, still unsold, sitting high and empty on Rich Fucker Road.

So when the people of Dalton ask Bev if she and her loved ones are good, she can finally say yes. Yes, thank Christ, they're alive and healthy and doing the best anyone can, after all the loss they've endured. Yes, for now, at least, all the people she cares about most seem to be at peace. Settled. Even Trudy has been softer than usual these past few months, ever since

Richard took a step back from the clinic and delegated most of the one-on-one patient interactions to Vera Curtis.

Between customers, Bev finds herself glancing at the clock, counting the hours until the Christmas pageant. And afterward, for the first time since before Bridget died, a whole weekend alone together with Trudy. Just the two of them at Trudy's house, safe from the world. Thanks to Richard and his downstate bird convention; thanks to Bill and his promise to stay with Sophie out at the farmhouse while Nate's away until Sunday at a police training.

Halfway through the shift, Angela finds Bev in the walk-in sorting through packages of cold cuts.

"Can you watch the front for me?" she asks. "I need to take a walk."

"It's a little tough to cover both the deli and the register."

"I'll be quick, I promise. And next time we work together, I'll cover your break an extra ten minutes."

It's impossible for Bev to say no. Rumor is Angela got into some trouble while she was living downstate over the past couple years. Bev doesn't care about any of that. Angela might never be on time for her shift, but when she's here, she works hard—restocking supplies, feeding the fish in the live bait cooler, dusting shelves. She never acts like the job is beneath her, like so many other people her age would.

She takes Angela's place at the register, where she stands on sore feet and stares out the plate-glass window. The tint makes everything outside look a little bit blue. Blue trucks trundle down the slushy road. Blue cars idle at the gas station across the street. Blue snow falls from the sky; blue snow covers the ground.

Funny, the memories triggered by a color. Staring out at the aquatic-tinged world, Bev thinks back to a time maybe eight winters ago. Trudy picked her up at midnight, and they drove through the silent, sleeping town, down to the skating rink behind the Rec Center. "This is trespassing," Bev said. And Trudy said, "For Chrissake, our taxes pay for this damn place." The warming shack was unlocked, and they went inside to lace themselves into rental skates—the only ones that would fit Bev's feet were a scuffed pair from the men's wall that looked like clodhoppers. Out under the blazing stars, they couldn't stop laughing, drunk from the cold and the ridiculous, lawless thrill of it. Trudy traced looping figure eights onto the ice, which gleamed silver under a full moon. Their breath clouded the air, tasted like spearmint. And when they started to shiver, they went back into the shack and warmed each other up with a different kind of laughter.

The electronic *BING-bong* of the door startles Bev from the memory, and she pulls her eyes from the window to see Ron McCurdy walking into the store, beating his feet against the mat to shake the snow from his boots. Even before he approaches the counter, she's reaching for his usual pack of Marlboros.

"How we doing?" he asks. "How're you and yours?"

And Bev smiles, remembering Trudy's body pressed against hers under those endless blue stars. Imagining all the laughter that will be theirs this long-awaited, much-needed weekend together.

"Me and mine are good," she says. "Me and mine are perfect."

Richard is all a-flutter about his bird weekend, and Trudy can't stop thinking about food. His way of expressing his excitement is to babble nonstop, while she prefers to muse to herself as she sits on the bed and watches him pack more shirts than anyone needs for two days away.

"Should I bring spare binoculars?" he asks, fussing with the snaps of a suitcase he hasn't used in a decade. "If the first pair breaks . . ."

Should Trudy roast a chicken tomorrow, or should she make that baked ziti Bev loves so much? If they have pasta for their main meal, they'd have to go easy on the appetizers. But if she went with the chicken . . .

"Channel 2 is predicting clear skies all weekend, but should I bring my heavy jacket just in case? Though we probably won't go out for a sighting trip if the weather turns bad . . . "

Maybe over the next two days they should just graze on cheese and crackers and those smoked almonds Bev is so fond of.

"I'd love to see common redpolls," says Richard. "Do you know they tunnel into the snow to stay warm overnight?"

Trudy does know, because he has already told her. He's told her all sorts of things about the feathered world over the past few months—the mating habits of dark-eyed juncos, the preferred nesting materials for osprey, the various flight patterns of migratory birds. All the ways they follow the sun.

Maybe in the past, Trudy would have been irritated by this avian trivia. She spent too many years of their marriage irritated with most of what Richard said and did. But ever since all that time they spent together walking around town, making him strong again after his heart attack, she's softened toward him. Where he used to be the cumbersome spouse, the thing that kept her away from the woman she loved, now he is an endearing combination of partner, friend, and celibate roommate.

"We are who we are," Richard says when the guilt starts pecking at her organs for not giving him the marriage he expected or deserves. "We love who we love."

There's sadness with the acknowledgment; of course there is. But there is peace in it, too, acceptance of what can never change.

Trudy used to think you could will yourself into being in love with someone. Adapt to a relationship that, on paper at least, made sense. Ever since she met Bev, though, she has believed there's a stronger force behind what brings two people together. Not destiny, exactly, but something like predetermination—the instinctual pattern a robin or red-winged blackbird will follow because it has been passed down to her on a cellular level, woven into the fibers of her being.

As Richard flits from closet to suitcase, muttering about extra socks and eyedrops, Trudy settles against the headboard of a bed they haven't shared in years. Her own room is across the hall, shadowed now in the mid-winter afternoon. That room smells like lavender and well-loved books. This room, the one where Richard sleeps, smells of Barbasol, with an afterthought of the antiseptic he uses at the clinic to wipe down all the surfaces at the end of each day. Still loyally tending the business his father left him so many years ago, even though Vera tells him he's earned the right to relax and let her do the dirty work. For Richard, though, it's one thing to allow Vera, a nurse practitioner as capable as any MD, to handle the patients; it's another to assume she should have to do the cleanup herself.

"Did you know," he asks Trudy, "that unlike most other songbirds, cedar waxwings are considered non-territorial?"

"For Chrissake, Richard," she says, leaning forward to reopen the suitcase he's just snapped shut. "You didn't pack your best sweater. Don't you think you might get cold out there with all those birds? It's southern Maine, not Florida."

Half an hour later, they say goodbye to Mycroft, who meows irritably before going back to his nap in front of the baseboard, and step into the dark chill of December. Under the porch light, Trudy tightens Richard's scarf, and he tucks a lock of her hair under her earmuffs. Not the same kind of spark she gets when Bev does the same thing, but it's still a good feeling. Reassurance.

Boots squeaking on snow, they walk across the street and into the parking lot of the grade school, packed with cars and trucks. Ridiculous, how many people turn out year after year to watch kids dance around to godawful Christmas music. Already the line out of the gym snakes to the end of the lobby, decorated with glittery snowflakes and candy canes. The overheated space smells of cinnamon breath-mints and sawdust from the men who rushed from the mill to get here on time.

Richard spots Bev and Bill near the trophy case and leads Trudy toward them, pressing past dozens of familiar faces, unable to resist falling into the role of town physician. "'Scuse me, Marian; looking svelte, Dean, keep it up with that new treadmill."

By the time they reach Bev and Bill, Trudy is sweating under her jacket, cranky with the sheer number of people in the world. All this just to watch a six-year-old hop around on stage for three minutes. Crazy what you do for the people you love—she might not have any blood in common with Sophie Theroux, but Trudy would do anything for that girl. Can a childfree woman be a stand-in grandmother? Does she have the right to claim that title? She sure as hell believes so, given all the time she spent with Nate when he was growing up. He might as well be her son, and god help anyone who dares say otherwise.

While Richard and Bill start talking about the usual—weather, back pain, price of oil—Trudy presses close enough to Bev that they can entwine their fingers without anyone noticing. She smells of rosewater. Her blue sweatshirt is threadbare on the collar, and her hair curls from her head like a swarm of bees.

"It's too crowded, Bevy."

"It's good for you, Tru."

"A human stampede is good for me? Suffocation?"

"Quit being so dramatic."

They're smooshed between the Lannigans and a pack of Bergerons. Molly's only palomino is sick. Customers are loving the buy-one-get-two-free deal on cartons of eggnog. *Might be time I put Old Gus out of his misery. Maybe we should get the cranberry sauce on sale, move what's left over from Thanksgiving.*

Trudy would like to push her way through the throng and escape to the freezing relief of the parking lot. Walk home, curl up with Mycroft on the couch.

"You promised, Tru. No abandoning me here."

"You wouldn't be alone. You've got your husband, and I'll loan you mine."

She and Bev both know she won't leave, no matter how much she wants to. You live in a place long enough, you love a person hard enough, you build a family from something more than blood. Trudy might get annoyed with Bill's complaints about his sciatica, and she's not looking forward to sitting in a folding chair for the next two hours just because Sophie asked her to. But these people are her people.

After buying their one-dollar admission tickets from the new art teacher, the two couples head into the gym, where nearly every seat is taken. Bev is in the middle of trying to work something out (they could gather their courage and ask Helen McGreevy to make room) when Trudy spots gangly arms beckoning them from three rows back from the stage—Nate, standing high above the crowd.

"Ma!" he shouts over the horde of aunts and uncles, parents and grandparents, sulky teenage siblings. "Over here, Ma!"

It occurs to Trudy, sometime during Mr. Doucette's long-winded introduction in front of the red curtain, that they are sitting in the same order they've sat at nearly every function they've ever attended together—weddings, baptisms, graduations, Bridget's funeral five and half years ago in the front pew of the Congregational Church: Nate in the middle, Trudy to his left, Bev to his right; Richard beside Trudy and Bill beside Bev. If they were one giant bird, he would be the heart, and they would be the wings.

When the curtain opens and the kindergarteners come skipping onstage, everyone cheers as if it were the opening of the Olympics. Sophie is dressed in a green shirt and a gold sequin skirt that shines under the lights. Just before the music comes on, she spots her family—blood and surrogate—in the audience, and grins, waving wildly at them.

"There's our girl."

"Cutest one up there."

"She puts the rest of those kids to shame."

Halfway through the dance, as Sophie abandons the choreography and twirls to her own Jingle Bell Rock rhythm, Trudy decides to hell with it. She'll make the baked ziti tomorrow, and they'll eat that and the appetizers, too. Maybe she'll whip up a loaf of sourdough as well, which they can eat with some of the fresh butter she bought from the Best farm yesterday. And she'll make the chocolate cake, too, damn it. She and Bev will have it all, everything.

Legacy

That night, like every other night, Tommy paces alone through his dark apartment.

He wants to sleep. He can't.

He wants to drink. He can't.

He wants his kids here with him, but thanks to Rose and all her rules, he can't have that either.

In the kitchen, he smokes one cigarette after another as he stares out the window. Under the streetlights, in the falling snow, everything looks soft and silver. The church across the street has one of those manger scenes out in front, and the farm animals and wise men and baby Jesus are being slowly buried. If they were real animals and people, they'd be half-blind from weather like this. By tomorrow morning, they might be totally entombed so they couldn't see anything at all.

Not that there's a lot to see. Not in a place like this.

When Tommy left town five years ago, he had no end place in mind. All that mattered was getting the hell out of Dalton.

He'd been thinking of leaving ever since Rose admitted she'd lied about being knocked up just so Tommy would be nice to her. And then Nate Theroux tried to throw him in jail, which was complete bullshit (according to the lawyer who owed Tommy's uncle a favor). But the last straw was Nate coming onto Tommy's property and sucker punching him. It was harassment, police brutality, and Tommy could have sued. Should have. But it's not like any of the other cops in Dalton would ever take his side over Nate's. The whole town would say it was Tommy's fault, like he was asking to get beaten up.

Every bad thing in Dalton eventually got blamed on a Merchant or a Wilkins. Tommy's people. Trailer trash. Thieves. Junkies. Alkies. Wife-beaters. Like Dalton wasn't to blame for making all of them that way. His old man used to say it best: You turn into what people say you are.

Tommy loved his kids; he didn't want to leave them. But that wasn't enough to make him want to stay in a place where the chips were always stacked against him. That day he drove south out of Dalton, the sky was the color of that knock-off cleaner his mother used to use on the bathroom mirror in the shack on Poor Man's Road. Tommy was pissed at everything—Rose and Nate and all the cops everywhere and all the women everywhere who did all they could to stomp a man down.

It wasn't until he reached the stretch of Route 11 where the forest fell away toward Katahdin that he remembered the mirror in the shack had gold specks in it, just like the ones in Rose's eyes. That was one of his favorite things about her when they started up as teenagers—those sparkles in her eyes. That and the fact she actually listened to him and cared how he felt about things.

"This is who we are," his mother told him one day when he was eight or nine. She was drunk and sprawled on the lawn outside the shack. His father was screaming at the clipper that was too dull to clip any grass, his face the same shade of red it got when he was bringing the belt down on Tommy's back. The air smelled like dog shit. Log trucks kept driving past, making the ground shake.

"This is who we're always gonna be, Sprout," his mother said. "This is the life you're always gonna have, so you might as well get used to it."

He hated that nickname, but he believed what his mother told him. Even as a kid, he noticed the dirty looks he and his family got around Dalton, and he knew that no Merchant or Wilkins had a life like the kind he saw in movies he rented from the library. In those stories, no one bought government cheese; no parents stole vodka from the convenience store. That world of homemade waffles and sappy life lessons was a total lie.

But when he and Rose started dating when she was fifteen, Tommy started to wonder if a better life was possible. She was all the things he wanted and none of the things he was desperate to get away from. She drank sometimes, but she never went crazy with it. She didn't call him stupid when he had to read a sentence three times before the words stopped squiggling around and fell into the right order. She was gentle, but she was tough, too—she could change a tire, drag a four-wheeler out of the mud, smoke a bong without coughing. Didn't hurt that she was sexy, with curves in all the right places, or that she was always up for anything Tommy wanted to do with her.

He knocked her up when she was sixteen. He was two years older. At first, he begged her to get an abortion, but she refused, and before long, he was relieved. Pregnancy agreed with her—her round belly, the way her skin glowed. She was even sexier than before, and he loved her so hard it almost hurt. His father was dead, and his mother had moved to Fort Kent, and Tommy was glad he could focus all his attention on Rose. He held her hair back when she puked, bought her gallons of Giffords' ice cream, rubbed her feet whenever she wanted. Here was a chance, he thought, for him to have the family and the life he had never dared to believe he could get.

The day Rose gave birth, Tommy watched her split open. She hardly cried, just gritted her teeth and went on with the wreckage, and he couldn't believe it, how a person could be turned inside out like that and survive to talk about it.

"Your son," she said as she held the pink, blinking baby toward him. When she smiled at Tommy with a kind of gratitude he'd never seen before, he swore to be a better man for her. And for the tiny person they made together.

He wanted a Junior, but Rose loved the name Adam, so they settled on Adam Thomas. It was never a question of whose last name the kid would have, though. There was compromise, then there was tradition, the right way of doing things. Their son would be a Merchant. But they'd raise him to be different from the others.

Rose dropped out of school to stay home with Adam in the trailer on Larch Street, which Jo Martin leased to them for next to nothing. Uncle Stu hired Tommy at the autobody shop, paying him to pound dents out of fenders and replace broken radiators. He liked how physical the work was, how it kept his hands busy and his thoughts quiet. He felt like he was part of something bigger than himself, like he had a purpose. He and Rose would lie in bed for hours with Adam wedged between them. Things were good. Things had potential.

But there were times when Tommy would be struggling to twist a frame into shape and suddenly hear his old man shouting at him to pick up the pace, stop acting like such a wuss. Or he'd be at the bank, watching the teller's overplucked eyebrows rise at the pathetic amount in his account, and the need for a drink would get so strong that he would rush to Frenchie's, where he'd catch glimpses of himself in the mirror behind the bar, chugging down one vodka after another, and he would look so much like his mother that he'd feel sick to his stomach.

On occasion, Tommy would come home after a long day and find the trailer a total wreck. There'd be no supper waiting for him, and he'd say things he shouldn't, things like how lazy Rose was getting and how sloppy she looked in her sweatpants that were always stained with baby puke. And maybe a couple times, he might've called her the same words his father used to shout at his mother. And maybe he felt a little thrill when he saw how those words made Rose flinch.

But for the most part, they were a happy family, and Tommy felt like he was really doing it, spitting in the face of all the Merchant and Wilkins men who had come before him.

It wasn't until Rose got pregnant the second time that everything changed. Her morning sickness lasted all day. Adam, not as cute anymore, needed constant attention. Jo raised their rent. Stu cut Tommy's hours. The thirst for booze got stronger, and while Rose waddled around the trailer not doing the dishes or the laundry, Tommy spent most of his nights at the bar. Sometimes he'd do a little coke or molly with his cousins or his buddies from high school. By then, Rose wasn't giving it up anymore, and there were a few times he hooked up with random chicks in the bathroom, just to get what any hot-blooded twenty-year-old guy needed. The cost of everything was going up—gas, food, cigarettes, clothes, diapers, doctor appointments for Adam's never-ending ear infections—and Tommy needed cash, tax-free dollars no one could steal from him. And there was this guy in Prescott who had some stuff that needed selling. Not often. Not a lot. Just sometimes, just often enough to cover the bills Tommy had to pay for the family he'd sworn to take care of.

And then, the winter day Rose brought their second kid into the world, she held him to her milk-fat tits and stared at him while the doctors and nurses flitted between her legs, cleaning things up down there. She seemed to be thinking something secret. When Tommy asked to hold the baby, she said she needed another minute. When he told her he wanted to call this son Wyatt, she gave some bullshit story about how the name came to her in a dream one night, the baby himself whispering it to her. Brandon Geoffrey.

"That's a pansy name," Tommy said, but she wouldn't listen. All she would do was stare at that slimy, shrieking bundle like it was the one thing keeping the earth from spinning into the sun. Tommy might as well not have been there. After everything he'd done for her. All the sacrifices he'd made.

Selfish, ungrateful cunt.

Not long after that, he hit her the first time. He didn't mean to. He didn't plan on it. But it was late at night and he couldn't sleep and Brandon was crying and Adam was screaming and the trailer reeked of baby shit and dirty clothes and Rose was leaking milk all over everything and Stu had just cut his hours again and no matter how many beers he drained Tommy could still hear his father's voice telling him what a fucking mess he'd made of his life. What a failure he was. Then Rose asked him to change the baby's diaper. And something snapped like a dry twig inside Tommy. The bruise bloomed right away. She stood there holding her hand against her cheek, staring at him with the same stunned expression he'd seen a million times before—it was the same way his mother used to look at his father, after the rage exploded.

He knew at that moment he was no better than the man he'd feared all his life, and he swore to Rose he'd never hit her again. It was the booze, he told her, and he broke down in tears as he said it. Never again. He wanted to believe it, but he knew he was babbling out all the same words his father used to say after he slammed his mother against the wall. *I'm sorry, you know I wouldn't hurt you sober. Never.*

That was the moment Tommy saw it bright and clear. There was no escaping destiny, or the weight of his name.

You become what you're told you are.

For a long time, he was glad to be out of Dalton. He stayed in Bangor for a while. Waterville. Lewiston. But it wasn't until Portland that Tommy felt like he'd arrived somewhere. He liked the noise of the city, the sirens in and out of the hospital, the horns from boats out on the bay. He liked the glint of sun on tall steel buildings and the smell of seafood that curled through restaurant doors onto cobblestone sidewalks. It was a place where things happened, where people made things happen.

He felt like he'd found a place where life—where *he*—could really be something.

Sure, he missed his kids, especially Adam. He could've called more often—he probably should've—but it was too hard to hear his son's voice asking when he was going to come home.

He did miss Rose, even though he tried not to. There were nights Tommy felt like he was going crazy, he wanted her so bad. And he'd call to tell her that, to see if she was ready to ask him to come home. Maybe beg a little. But if he was playing a game, so was she, and she always pretended she wasn't glad to know he hadn't forgotten her.

That's how it went for a few years, and even though he had to work his ass off just to pay for gas and food and cigarettes and booze and rooms in extended-stay motels where he knew the guy who stayed there before him had OD'd, Tommy still loved the city. The possibility of it. The convenience of it—all the things he wanted were so close, so easy to find. Chinese food. Whiskey. Snatch. Everything.

Work was easy to get, too, even if none of the jobs he was qualified for were very pretty. Mostly he worked in warehouses, pressing buttons and loading pallets. He did a stint at the B&M bean factory, until he showed up late one too many times. There were other canneries, companies that mailed out flyers no one ever looked at. Life in the city was a hustle, which Tommy liked. The constant movement. The almost drug-like high of doing a job good enough until he found a way to fuck it up. There was always another one to replace the one he lost.

Somewhere around the four-year mark, though, the thrill started to fade. When he wasn't working, Tommy spent all his time alone. He tried for a while to make friends—some of the guys he met through his jobs seemed decent enough at first, and he'd go out to lunch or drinks with them. But before long, they all ended up laughing at him like he was just a Northern Maine redneck. They'd ask him if he ever rode a moose to school, or they'd ask him to drop into the St. John Valley accent he heard so much growing up, even though he never actually used it himself. More than once, Tommy had to set the assholes straight, knock them around a little to prove he wasn't some brainless hick they could fuck with.

He dated a few girls, never for long, and after a breakup was when he would miss Rose most—when he'd get drunk and call her late at night. They were still playing the game, and her disappointed sighs proved he was winning. Even from hundreds of miles away, he still had the power to crawl under her skin.

But then, out of nowhere last summer, she stopped answering when Tommy called. At first he thought there must be something wrong with the phone—maybe she screwed up and didn't pay the bill, which would serve her right. But the more he called, the more she didn't answer. And eventually the lack of response proved she'd forfeited the game. Or worse, decided silence was its own kind of win.

Suddenly the city was too loud, too crowded. The water tasted like chemicals. The rotting-fish air felt poisonous to inhale. The sirens never stopped. Every motel was worse than the last, filled with roaches and burn marks on the sheets. Tommy got fired from one job, then another, then another. It was all hustle, no reward. And Rose still wasn't answering his calls, not even to let him talk to his own kids.

The last straw was a bright August morning. Tommy was sober; he thought maybe calling her in daylight, without any booze in his system, would change his luck. But he stood there with the greasy phone pressed to his cheek, listening to it ring and ring, until he finally heard her voice on the machine: *Hi, you've reached Rose and the boys. Leave your name and number and we might call you back.*

Rose and the boys. Claiming them as her own. Sounding so damn cheerful about it, too. So proud of herself.

Tommy threw his stuff in a duffle bag and drove out of

the city, away from the possibility that didn't exist anymore, had maybe never existed. Maybe the joke had been on him all along, he thought as he watched the buildings and the ocean drop vanish behind him, maybe he'd been an idiot to believe he could live in a place like that. Maybe the only life a guy like him could ever have was in a place like Dalton, where everyone knew his name. Where things were quiet and the roads were empty. Where the mother of his children was waiting. Maybe she thought she had won the game, but Tommy wouldn't just let go of what rightfully belonged to him. Not without a fight.

Late summer crickets were whirring on Larch Street when he parked outside his trailer and slid down out of the truck that day, sore from nearly six hours of driving without even a piss break. The trailer was empty; no car in the driveway, and for a few panicked minutes, he thought maybe Rose had taken the boys and moved somewhere else, somewhere he could never find them.

Then he heard the laughter he recognized from his phone calls back home. Adam. He followed the sound to Marian's trailer, where he found his boys sitting in front of the TV. When they turned to look at him, Tommy felt like he might collapse on the cat-hair covered floor. They looked like Rose—dark hair, heart-shaped faces. If it weren't for Adam's eyes, the exact shade of hazel as Tommy's, he might have thought they didn't belong to him at all.

Adam let out a shriek of joy that made Tommy feel more like a man than he had in his whole life. Here was his firstborn, running at him with arms wide open. Marian blubbered on about how she shouldn't let the boys leave without their mother's permission. But these were Tommy's kids, he reminded her, and he took them to the trailer next door, where they sat inside and waited for Rose to come home.

Tommy didn't have some master plan to take the boys away

from her. He only knew that as he watched Adam show off his Matchbox cars while Brandon hovered close by, he didn't feel as alone as he usually did. And that, he supposed, was what hope felt like.

When she finally showed up at the trailer, clothes flecked with yellow paint, Rose held the boys close to her like Tommy was some kind of zombie about to eat their brains. It was over-dramatic, annoying. But it was her game now. Her rules.

"No booze," she told him. "No way you're going to spend time with my kids if you've been drinking."

"I'm a sober man now," Tommy lied. "I quit that shit for good."

In the old days, that would've been good enough. But this new Rose stared at him with the same suspicion his mother used to throw his way when she accused him of stealing cash from her purse.

"Don't think this whole town won't be watching you," she said. "Things are different now—I got a good job, friends, people who care about Adam and Brandon. You get one chance. The first I hear from anyone you're up to your old shit, I'll get a restraining order and make sure you never see those boys again."

Suddenly she didn't look like his mother anymore. Instead she was just like his father, pressing Tommy's face into the dirty plywood floor of the shack out on Poor Man's Road. And Tommy was that pathetic kid all over again, the weak little shit who knew the only way out was to tell the sole of the boot anything it wanted to hear.

"Whatever you say," he said.

Anything to crawl out from under the weight and get up off the floor. Stand tall. Walk away like a man, pretending nothing's been broken.

* * *

Nights like this, though, when Tommy sits by himself as snow comes drifting down, he doesn't have to pretend he's not in pain.

Much as he wishes the boys were here with him, maybe it's better this way, them at the trailer with their mother and Tommy here, no witnesses to see his eyes keep flicking over to the cedar chest by the couch, where, buried under quilts and sleeping bags he will never use, rests his father's old shotgun.

Tommy has carried it with him ever since he was twelve, when his father died. At the shack, it lived under his bed. At the trailer with Rose, he kept it in a locked safe. On the road, it lived in his truck, tucked between the seats and the floor.

He's never used it for poaching, like his father did. He's never used it for anything. But Tommy feels better knowing the gun is within easy reach. Here if he needs it, if all the other hurts get to be too damn much.

Nothing Here is Sacred

As snow falls outside the window of her childhood bedroom, Angela stares at herself in the mirror and considers giving in to the feminine urge to chop off all her hair. For as long as she can remember, she has worn it long, but maybe this is the moment to hack everything away. Turn herself into something new.

She grips the pair of scissors, holds it level to her chin. The idea of what she could do so easily is both a horror and a thrill—what would everyone down on the rez think of her cutting away what's supposed to be sacred?

"Baby girl!" her mother's footsteps, moving down the hall, getting louder, stopping just outside Angela's closed door. "What're you doing in there? I thought we was going to church together."

The face staring back at Angela in the warped glass doesn't belong to her. Something is off, like a blurred painting, or an image held underwater. The blades whisper against a strand of her hair.

Her mother's voice again: "If we don't hurry up, we'll miss the singing."

Angela lets the scissors fall onto the dresser, where they clatter alongside bottles of Bath & Body Works perfume and a framed Polaroid of her and Greg Fortin, taken when they were twelve years old. Their faces are pressed together, Greg's arms stretched out to hold the camera. After he took the picture, they rode their bikes in the parking lot of St.

Mary's until he got sick from the Skittles and Pop Rocks they'd bought at the Store 'N More. As Greg vomited a rainbow beside a dumpster that held a water-damaged picture of Jesus, Angela stared the dead icon in its sad blue eyes and tried to understand how something so insubstantial could be considered so holy.

"Ange, get your ass in gear!"

She doesn't know what in this life, or any of the lives before and after, might actually be sacred. Maybe everything. Or nothing.

* * *

When she left Dalton the summer she was sixteen to live with her father and his family on Indian Island, Angela hoped to find something there she'd never managed to find in Dalton. She arrived at his house with questions she had been asking herself her entire life: *Why didn't you fight harder to make things work with Momma when I was little? Why didn't you drive up north to visit me more than once a year? Why didn't you invite me to come stay with you sooner?*

When her father, during one of their weekly phone calls, had pitched the idea of her finishing her final two years of high school in Old Town while living with him, his wife, and their twin girls, Angela thought she must have heard him wrong. Other than visits over school vacations, she had never spent much time in that house on the rez.

"Why?" she had stammered into the phone.

"Might be good," her father said in a shy voice. "For you to try living somewhere other than there, you know."

It wasn't exactly the answer Angela had been hoping for. But it was enough. She was sick of Dalton at that point, bored with all the people who lived there. So, a month later, her mother drove Angela three hours south, dropping her off at her father's house with nagging reminders to thank Pam for every meal and to do her own laundry. *Nobody likes a moocher, baby girl.*

In the beginning, things were good. Her father gave her his old Chevy so she would have the freedom to get wherever she wanted. Pam, who ran a catering company, experimented with new recipes every day, tempting Angela with quiches and fruit tarts. Colie and JJ invited her into their private twin-sister world of Fisher Price playsets. Angela's father left the house early six days a week to get to his shift at the paper mill. After work, he went around the rez and nearby towns doing odd jobs—bleeding radiators, repairing leaky faucets, making engines run again. He seemed to have unlimited knowledge of how to fix any problem. Unless that problem was his own daughter.

Even after she got settled, things never felt easy between Angela and her dad. The silences that had once peppered their weekly phone conversations now existed in a solid space—more pronounced, and harder to ignore.

"How was school?" he would dutifully ask as they washed dishes together while Pam got the twins ready for bed.

Angela, afraid to bore him with details of proof geometry, would say school was good. School was fine.

"What about you, Dad? How was work?"

"Oh, it was good. It was fine."

She sometimes considered surprising him with an anecdote about her PE teacher's toupée or the floppy hotdogs they served in the cafeteria. But she always realized, just before she opened her mouth, that she didn't know her father's humor well enough to guess if he would appreciate her jokes. And if she couldn't talk about those stupid little nothings, there was no way she could gather the courage to ask him why he had chosen to build a new family rather than stay with her and her mother.

As difficult as it was to talk to her father, Angela found it that easy to talk to Mason, Pam's twenty-two-year-old nephew who lived in the apartment over the garage. She chatted with him about music, books, *Seinfeld*—everything. One night, several weeks after she moved in, she confided to him how far away she felt from her father.

"Maybe you should take his name," Mason said.

"Deacon?"

"No, his real name. Isn't that your middle name, anyway?"

"Different sort of Dawn."

"Still, though," Mason said. "I think your dad might like that."

So, around the time leaves began to drop from the autumn trees, she shed her first name, slipped Dawn over her shoulders like a thick new robe. The weight was heavy but convincing, almost comforting.

For a little while, anyway.

* * *

The Dalton Advent Church smells like a cupboard. The pews are upholstered in green wool, and a wooden cross hangs behind the pulpit. A Charlie Brown tree sits beside the organ, decorated with tinsel and cheap ornaments. The whole setup is tragic in all its staged ritual. What self-respecting god would want to hang around in a place like this?

"Pay attention," whispers Momma. "You might learn something."

Her mother's devotion to God didn't kick in until after Angela moved downstate. That also happened to be around the time Momma broke up with the creep from Prescott who carried around pictures of his dachshund in his wallet. Her mother has always needed someone to love, someone to love her back, and with so few options in Dalton—most of the bachelors her mom's age are either drunks, unemployed, or almost certainly secretly gay—Angela guesses God was the only remaining choice.

In the pulpit, Pastor Ray is stroking the pages of a Bible. "Virgin Mary," he says to the small congregation of mostly old ladies and their husbands. "Given a miracle of life, a Son who would save the souls of our entire world."

He has a nice voice, Pastor Ray, like a teacher talking to a class of little kids, which Angela guesses he is, in a way. Seems like his job isn't all that different from leading children through their ABCs and 123s. Spell a word and get a gold star. Do this and go to heaven. Do that and go to hell.

"Imagine! The news she would bear the Child of God Himself. The honor, the wonder—but what about the burden? We never talk about the burden, do we?"

Momma is leaning forward, her hair sweeping across her cheek like a wave of molasses. She's listening to every word Pastor Ray says, and Angela wonders if he, instead of God, is the one her mother is actually devoted to. He's not terrible looking, if you don't mind weak chins. But he has a wife and kids, and Angela can feel in her gut that even without the threat of eternal damnation, he isn't the type to screw all that up for a chain-smoking single mom.

"I suspect Mary was, in many ways, like any mother," says Pastor Ray. "Protective, loving, no doubt. But any mother—any parent—is imperfect. Who among us hasn't given our kids some candy to get them out of our hair for a few minutes? Now, I don't know the ancient version of a lollipop—"

On cue, the crowd laughs.

"—but I'm certain even Mary had moments while Baby Jesus was teething or throwing terrible-two tantrums when she wished she could quiet him with some kind of sweetness. Have a moment to herself. But this was the Son of God. Both immortal Savior and flesh-and-blood infant, requiring all the necessities every child needs. *Imagine.* The great privilege, and the great responsibility—the burden—of treating Him as both a human thing and a holy thing. Navigating the line between mothering him and worshipping him."

Momma's eyes are glassy, her hands clenched in her lap. Angela has the urge to run up to the pulpit and tear the cross off the wall.

"And in that way, is Mary all that different from any mother—any parent—here in this room today? Is parenthood not a constant balance between guidance and adoration? Example and adulation?"

Momma sighs with relief, as if unburdened of a secret she's been holding onto all her life. Angela wonders how much that cross weighs, if she's strong enough to hurl it through the windows, through stained glass and snowflakes.

"So this Christmas season," concludes Pastor Ray, "let us give thanks to our Almighty Father, to Jesus, and to Mary. That good woman, the selfless mother whose burden became our saving grace. Let us pray."

A collective silence. And then the endless singing. Do you hear what I hear? Tidings of comfort and joy. Do you know what I know? Fields, floods, rocks, hills, plains. Do you see what I see? God and sinners. Rejoice.

As soon as the service is over, Angela slips between the blue-haired old ladies making a beeline for the basement buffet and heads outside. She lingers beside her mother's van in the parking lot, watching snow swirl through the pines and around the steeple that reminds her of a sewing needle.

She feels dizzy and breathless, like she's leapt from one universe to the next, which is what used to happen to her after a hit or two of molly. It's been months since she took any kind of drug (other than weed, which barely counts), but she sometimes still has these out-of-time moments where she feels like she's in the middle of a bad trip, the sky dripping like candle wax, the ground rolling as if the world is made of nothing more than water.

"Angela?"

Turning toward High Street, she sees a figure walking toward her through the snow—no, not walking, more like gliding; the thing is *gliding* towards her, and she has a moment of panic, or maybe it's elation, when she is certain it's Jesus himself, dropped down from heaven to deliver a message.

"Shit, Angie, it's really you."

And of course it's not Jesus, or any kind of god at all.

Instead, it's Greg Fortin staring back at her, and there's a lot less of him than she remembers. When she left before their junior year, Greg was—there's no other, more polite word for it—fat. Now, four years later, he's thin and tall like a willow sapling. No more acne; no more double chin. His hands are covered by bright yellow mittens, which seems like an odd choice, but then again, he was never concerned about wearing whatever "in" thing everyone else in their class was wearing.

Before she can think of what to say, Greg pulls her into a hug. Through their jackets, she can feel the muscles in his arms, and it's easy, but also slightly absurd, to imagine he has spent time building that strength on purpose, one rep at a time.

"Mom told me you were back in town," he says. "I didn't expect to see you here, though. Have you finally given your heart to our Lord and Savior, Angela?"

He stares at her, bright-eyed and biting back laughter, while she fights her way past the shock of him.

"I haven't given my heart to anyone," she says, then immediately regrets it, worried he will read more into the statement than she might like. "What about you? Aren't you supposed to be down at college?"

"Home for winter break. Just had to leave the house for a bit, you know, take a walk."

His smile slips a little, and she wonders what private ghosts he might be lugging around. The burdens he might carry.

There's a squeaking of hinges, and they turn to see Angela's mother stepping out of the church, doors swinging shut behind her. "Shit on a shingle!" she yells, running across the lot, throwing her arms around Greg's neck, pecking his cheeks like a deranged chicken. Annoyance pricks in Angela's belly. Why does the woman have to be so embarrassing? It's been like this since grade school, when Momma insisted on attending every one of Angela's classroom parties, obliviously handing out cookies and Valentines to the same kids who made a game of pushing Greg and Angela off snowbanks during recess.

"How long's it been? How's Orono? You kicking ass and takin' names down there?"

"Too long, Cindy, it's been too long," says Greg, and he's laughing again, a sound that softens some of Angela's animosity. "School's great, way better than it was last year. I switched my major—dropped the business bullshit, and I'm going for horticulture instead, with a focus on landscaping."

This makes sense to Angela. She had never really been able to picture Greg following in his father's footsteps and running the hardware store like his parents wanted. Especially not after he started working in Trudy Haskell's garden their freshman year of high school. Who knew a fourteen-year-old boy could get so excited about fertilizer and perennials?

"So what're you doing back in town, Greggie?"

"School break."

"How long till you go back?"

"Twenty-seven days. Not that I'm counting."

"Oh, sweetie, I know. You get feeling at home somewhere new, it's hard to feel right in the old places."

Suddenly, without her permission—that's the worst part, the swooping unpredictability of these moments—Angela hops another universe, and she's back on an unfamiliar riverbank, the sound of late summer crickets shrieking in her ear. Smell of dirt. Sunset sky. The weight of something enormous and eternal pinning her down to earth.

A sharp breeze against her cheek brings her back to the church lot, dropping her into the middle of a silence as Greg and her mother stare at her.

"What do you think, Ange? Sound like a good idea?"

"Does what sound like a good idea?"

"Having our guy here come over for supper before he goes back to school." Her mother turns to Greg. "I been craving steak—you aren't a vegetarian now, are you? Is that how you keep yourself so skinny?"

"Shit, no."

"Thank God—vegetarians freak me out, So how about it, Ange?"

"Sure, Momma," she says, because she's tired of the snow and the cold and the echo of those clean white hymns, and all she wants is to climb into bed, forget this world and all the ones beyond it. "Supper sounds good."

Refusing her mother's invitation for a ride home (he knows as well as she does that Momma is an absolute terror behind the wheel), Greg hugs Angela again before he gets back to his walk through the snow.

It's not until his yellow mittens are halfway down the street that she wonders if she should have told him how good he looks, how new and familiar at the same time, like the self he was always meant to grow into.

Hours later, after she has smoked a bowl of her mother's finest indica, she curls under the sheets Momma bought her when she got back to town a few months ago. That September morning, she showed up in her father's truck and found her mother out on the porch smoking a cigarette, waiting for her even though Angela never called to tell her she was coming.

The sheets, which were supposed to make her feel better about what brought her crawling broken back home, are nicer than anything she grew up with, silky-soft and the color of springtime sky, and Momma washes them every Saturday night while Angela robots her way through another shift at the Store 'N More.

Outside the snow is still falling, and the sky is so heavy and so gray, and maybe all that gloom is punishment; maybe Jesus has decided to take all the light back up to heaven as an early birthday present for himself, pass glowing slivers of it around to all the dead white men, white women, white children. Angela's mind is scattering; her limbs are water-choked pylons. Her skin smells of woodsmoke even though her mother's house is heated through electric baseboards. Her father, though—he burned logs to keep his family warm, trees that once drew breath and lived; it was the natural way of things, that's what Angela said to him when she helped him chop firewood that first autumn she lived in his house, and he looked at her funny and asked what she meant. "How the ancestors did it," she said, or something like that, something that meant the same thing. And her father threw his head up toward the sky and laughed.

Fantasy

Greg has barely stepped into the house and taken off the mittens he borrowed from his mother when he hears his mother calling him from the kitchen. The snow hasn't yet melted from his hair, and the image of Angela standing among snowflakes in a ruby-red coat still burns in his brain. A church parking lot, of all places. There she was.

Stepping into the kitchen, he sees his family sitting at the table exactly as he left them half an hour ago, as soon as he finished his obligatory participation in Sunday brunch. Sarah picks at a bowl of blackberries while her husband, Ian, shovels forkfuls of cold frittata into his mouth. Aimee, who recently traded her Kurt Cobain flannels for black clothing and skull-shaped jewelry, sips a glass of juice. At either end of the table, Greg's parents stare at him, his mother with a look of pained apprehension, his father with what has become a permanent scowl over the past few months.

"Nice walk, son? Get the air you needed?"

"Oh, Jim, don't pester him."

Greg decides it's safest to pretend he hasn't heard them—prey survives when it blends in with its environment—and lowers himself into his chair. "What'd I miss?"

"A rousing game of charades," says Aimee. "Followed by a deep discussion of religion and world news. Ian here has been so shocked by that Princess Diana interview a few weeks ago he can barely focus on anything else."

Pinching the bridge of her nose, their mother asks Aimee

to please, just this once, keep the sarcasm to a minimum. "It's almost Christmas, dear," she says. "Consider your restraint a present to all of us."

Everyone around the table falls quiet enough to hear every terrible note of a holiday special playing on the TV in the living room. Leave it to Greg's parents to cling to these outdated traditions—sickly-sweet variety shows, mistletoe in every doorway, a tree heavy with sentimental ornaments (if Greg has to hear one more time about Sarah's clothespin reindeer, he will lose his freaking shit). It's been clear, since he arrived two days ago, that no one in his family has any Christmas spirit this year. Why can't they drop the act, rip down the garland, punch a hammer through Lawrence Welk's creepy face, and go off to hide in their separate rooms?

"Because," his mother snapped when Greg made this suggestion earlier this morning, as she scrambled around trying to pull together a meal no one had asked for, "Christmastime is for family." And then she dropped an egg on the floor and let out a waterfall of swear words that was both shocking and impressive.

Finally, after what feels like approximately forty-two years, Ian finishes eating, and Sarah announces it's time they head back to their own place.

"But it's snowing out there," their mother says.

"We can drive in snow." Sarah slips into her coat as Ian ferries an armful of dishes over to the sink. "And we promised Gareth and Louise we'd stop in for a visit today. You're not the only parents anymore, remember?"

There's a moment when the double, unintended meaning of her words floats like invisible shrapnel around the room.

"Sarah's right, Cheryl," their father says. "We can't hold them hostage here."

After rounds of hugs, the newlyweds make their exit. Outside the window, Greg catches a glimpse of them in the driveway. Ian opens the car door for Sarah, then kisses her forehead. If she hadn't had the miscarriage, they would be bundling a brand-new baby into the backseat right now. Greg wonders if it would have been a boy or girl. What they would have named him or her.

Aimee skulks up to her bedroom while their mother goes off to take a "good long bath," leaving Greg and his father alone at the table—the very disaster Greg has managed to avoid since he got back home.

It had to happen eventually, though; you can only run around a maze for so long before you come up against a wall. So it's horrible, but no surprise, when his father adjusts his gold-rimmed glasses and tells Greg, in a tired voice, "About the store . . . "

As he starts droning on about monkey wrenches and copper wire and the cost of tuition and promises broken by ungrateful sons, Greg closes his eyes and thinks of dandelions.

Taraxacum officinale. They get a bad rap, dandelions; everyone thinking they're weeds that need to get mown down as soon as they pop up from underground, but Greg loves them. Their sunny faces. Their spent, fluffy petals morphing into children's wishes blown away on the breeze.

"It's a family business," says his father.

Taraxacum, derived from the Arabic word for a bitter herb.

"Fortin and Sons."

The term may be related to the Greek word ταράσσω, meaning to disturb.

"We had a deal."

Dandelions are a natural diuretic. The flowers can be turned into wine; their roots and leaves essential in traditional medicine to treat everything from kidney disease to inflammation to high blood pressure. Every part of the plant has a use, if you know how to use it.

"Damn it, Greg, you could at least pretend you're listening."

A person should avoid dandelions if they are allergic to

ragweed, yarrow, marigold, chrysanthemums, chamomile, daisies, or iodine. A person should avoid their father if they intend to study dandelions and other flowers the rest of their life, rather than spending their life stuck inside a fluorescent-lit store that sells monkey wrenches and copper wire.

The speech ends with a sigh—the oldest sound of betrayal, a father's wishes scattered to the wind.

After the one-sided argument, his dad heads down to the cellar, where he will spend the rest of the day channeling his anger into his model railroad. As Greg washes the dishes, hot water stinging his knuckles, he wonders how pissed his mother would be if he left for another walk around the block. Or would she understand that, after dandelions, those solitary walks are the best way Greg has to avoid his father's disappointment?

Actually, the best way to avoid his father's disappointment is to not be around for it at all. This method worked all the way between August and now, months Greg spent deliriously immersed in his new botany and landscaping courses at UMO. The first semester as a sophomore, he was still riding the high from the late summer days he had spent driving alone around the coast, discovering native plants he never could have found up in the County. Beach vetchling, pit-seeded goosefoot, herbaceous sea-blite. And during that heady time back at school, it was easy not to think about his father—well, *easier*. Because Greg still thought about his father every time he saw a hammer or a Stanley tape measure. But when he was remembering the sunrise above the ocean or focused on memorizing the Latin names for his favorite flowers, he could leave the world of hardware behind. Inhabit one of his own choosing. He could almost forget that by telling his father he wouldn't return to Dalton and take over the store after he finished college, he had destroyed every dream the man had ever had for his only son.

That store and that life, passed down from one male Fortin to the next.

Greg's mother had begged him to come home for Thanksgiving, but he got out of it by sending her a strongly worded letter about Pilgrims and Indians, smallpox and massacre. He would have tried the same sort of thing for this holiday—he could've come up with something against Christianity or rampant consumerism—but his mother made it clear, in a strongly worded telephone call earlier this month, that if he didn't show up for winter break, he could consider himself formally exiled. *And don't you want the molasses cookies, sweetheart? Don't you want to watch our favorite movie, like we always do? And don't you miss it here?*

The truth was, Greg did miss Dalton with something that swung between homesickness and existential dread. Anytime his roommate, David, who grew up outside Boston, asked about life in the County, Greg fell back on his favorite lines about the rural landscape and the town that raised him. It was the place dreams went to die, he said, and that was true; the majority of people born in Dalton remain in Dalton forever, few aspiring to more than a job at the mill or on their family farm. It was a place where nothing happened, Greg told David, and that was also true; there was little in the way of entertainment, unless you liked to shoot wild animals or ride snowmobiles through the woods. Where he came from, Greg laughed, was barely a blip on the map. Hardly worth a mention.

Each time he said something like this, though, he felt a sense of betrayal akin to throwing his own mother under a log truck. True, Dalton didn't have much going for it. But didn't he still daydream of those moments, on Rich Fucker Road last summer, when he would pause during his morning run to stare out over the forests and fields? And wasn't Dalton the official, if not mythical, gateway to the North Maine Woods, where people went for clarity and transformation? And didn't Greg have an abiding respect, even gratitude, for the men and women who toiled their whole lives at the mills and on the farms just to keep their families fed? And—maybe most importantly—didn't his love of the natural world begin in this place, during those days in Trudy Haskell's garden, flowers bright with life? Or maybe his love began long before that, when he would play with his sisters in the yard and eat blackberries straight off the bush, the sweet taste of sunlight bursting on his tongue.

Greg never would have had any of that if he'd grown up in a city. And yet his first instinct, when asked about Dalton, is always to denigrate it. Tear it into little pieces of a throwaway joke he'll likely be telling all his life.

He figured he owed it to the town, or at least to his mother, to come home for Christmas. Eat the molasses cookies. Watch Jimmy Stewart and Donna Reed dance their way backward into a swimming pool. Make small talk with the old ladies at Bergeron's; drive the familiar streets. Count the days until he can return to the life he has made for himself in Orono—which could be argued is its own version of a nowhere-town, a stopover largely populated by students and visiting professors, nobody who plans to stay very long. A halfway place between one life and another. But for Greg, compared to what he comes from, Orono is a mecca of opportunity and entertainment: There, he can walk out of his apartment and be at the movie theater within five minutes. He can shop at the IGA or the chain grocery store that plays pop Muzak all day, every day. He can eat a one-dollar cheeseburger from a fast food joint or wander to the local bakery when the urge for an éclair is too much to resist.

Probably the best part about Orono, though, is that Greg can drive east from there and be at the ocean within an hour. And doesn't he still daydream of that morning three months ago when he drove along that coastal road and saw the first glimpse of sea peeking through the firs? The sun hadn't quite risen; the sky was the color of cantaloupe. He rolled the windows down and tasted salt on the wind. The air felt different than anything he had ever felt before; on either side of the road, there were unnamed ferns and flowers silvered with dew. An entire new world. And Greg, impatient, had pressed his foot to the gas, set his eyes on the blue beyond the trees, and headed right for it, as suddenly and desperately in love as any nineteen-year-old could be.

Not that he's ever actually been in love, Greg has to admit to himself as he lies in the dark of his room later that Sunday evening. These past few months, though, he has finally gotten closer to some approximation of it.

Early in the semester, he sat next to a girl with purple hair in his microbiology class. Her name was Renee, and she had a precise, delicate way of handling slides that made something inside Greg hum. On their second date, she gave him his first kiss. On their third and final date, she kindly told Greg she liked him, but she liked her ex-boyfriend more. There were a few intense make-out sessions with Valerie, who worked at the Hilltop Commons. And there was the guy at that club who danced with Greg under the strobes and grabbed his hand without hesitation on their way to the bathroom. It was hurried yet tender, intense but also gentle—a perfect combination of magic and inelegance. Greg left with an unfamiliar taste on his breath and a thrill resonating through every nerve of his body.

At college, he has met a few others like him, some closeted, others out and proud, or at least not completely ashamed. Other than David, no one really knows about Greg—even though Orono has more to offer than his hometown in ways of entertainment, it still isn't exactly a haven of progressive thinkers. He admires the people brave enough to claim their identities, the ones who flock to underground clubs like the one he went to in Bangor.

He remembers it often, not just the thrill of that boy, but the joy in all of it. The space was small, and everyone made room for each other. The dance floor smelled of sweat and Day-Glo. "Greg," he told anyone who asked for his name. "Bi," he told anyone who wanted to know, but he was surprised by how few people actually cared about the specifics of his desires. "We're not here to therapize each other, baby," a guy with painted nails shouted over the pulse of Depeche Mode. "We're just here to dance." The longer Greg was there and the looser he allowed himself to become—not with any of the drugs other people were passing around; he wasn't ready to feel *that* free—the more he wondered if Fingernails had it wrong. Maybe dancing and therapy were the same thing. What else would you call the shining rush of a crowd under a mirror ball, dozens of bodies dressed in all colors moving in synchronous rhythm? And why would a person even need drugs in a place like that, where the prism of all those bodies, so awake and so alive, created its own high?

That was over a month ago, but Greg can close his eyes and be right back there again amid the pulsing music and crush of bodies dancing under those neon lights.

In her bedroom on the other side of the wall, Aimee starts listening to a Mariah Carey song, singing along with the lyrics in a sweet, clear voice. Hard to imagine a Goth chick singing about being in heaven with her laughing boyfriend, but that's Greg's sister. Strong enough to be whoever the hell she wants to be at any given moment.

Down the hall, the murmur of his parents' voices—they sound defeated, and Greg feels the usual shock of guilt, knowing he has contributed to their exhaustion.

Six months ago, his family had everything to look forward to, an entire future mapped out in a series of all the usual milestones. Their oldest daughter newly married and pregnant with their first grandchild. A son who would one day take over a store built generations ago. Another daughter prone to mouthiness and horrific fashion sense, but at the top of her class.

And now Sarah spends her time off from work watching soap operas; Aimee, failing geometry, looks like Wednesday Addams; and Greg, a semi-closeted bisexual, has ended a legacy that began with his great grandfather. No more high honors. No more Fortin and Sons. No more unnamed grandbaby.

Greg wonders how much more depleted his parents would feel if they knew that at this moment, he is thinking about not just the one guy at that bar, but all the other people, male and female, gay and straight, he danced with before he went into the bathroom.

"So you play for both teams," David said when Greg came out to him last fall after they smoked a joint to celebrate getting out of the dorms and into their own apartment. "Whatever. If you bring someone home, just hang a sock on your door, okay?"

It wasn't the reaction Greg was expecting, the one he'd been afraid of. Maybe it's easier for people from big cities—maybe they're exposed to more ways of living. Different ways of loving.

But Greg isn't from the city. He's from the County, where boys date girls and men marry women. Period. And for the next twenty-seven days, he's stuck here.

On the other side of the wall, Aimee starts the song over again. *Hectic inside. Darling if you only knew.*

Greg closes his eyes and replays his encounter with Angela earlier today outside the Advent Church.

He was sure it was some kind of dream or vision when he spotted her through the snow. In the whirling white, her red jacket was like the flash of a cardinal. Her hair hung down to her waist in loose, dark waves, and Greg watched as she tilted her face to the sky and held her arms out, palms up, as if trying to catch snowflakes.

He hadn't seen her since she moved away to live with her dad. His first year at college, Greg looked for her everywhere he went in Old Town and Orono and Bangor, hoping to run into her at the mall or a random gas station. He thought he saw a glimpse of her once at the movies, but by the time he worked up the nerve to shout her name across the lobby, whoever the girl was had vanished into the crowd. A stoner from his landscaping class who had a friend who grew up on the rez said he'd heard some shit about Deacon Muse's daughter, something about her getting sent off to rehab. But Greg didn't really believe the guy, who was only taking the class to try and learn how to grow his own weed.

Not long after that, Greg's mother called to tell him the news. *Guess who found her way home?* He didn't know what to say. He was surprised Angela would go back to Dalton—she complained all through their childhood how much she hated the place.

When he saw her today, Greg felt his heart stammer as he remembered all the times he had imagined kissing her back in high school. Wondering what it might feel like to trail his fingers along the graceful curve of her spine.

He thought the desire for Angela had disappeared along with the pounds he shed before college—but seeing her again woke something, a want that surged through his blood like the waves that lapped at his feet as he stood on the beach that August morning, watching the sun rise over the ocean. Breathing in the tang of seaweed; hearing the gulls laugh. Feeling, for once in his life, completely still. Completely right.

And then he stupidly agreed to have supper with her and her mother, and now Greg might as well be fourteen again, stressing out over what he should wear, how he should act, who he should be.

He closes his eyes and tries to drown out the music behind the wall as he reaches under the quilt, finding the warmth of his own skin. His thoughts float everywhere: Dance floors, strobe lights, long fingers, pleasant tickle of stubble against his cheek. Crash of wave on ageless granite, tide that brings sea glass pounded smooth by salt and wind and water, perfect alchemy;

and her dark eyes, and her coat bright against snow, and the shape of her underneath, gentle rise and gentle fall. Sway of hips under jeans, pelvis pressing against his when he hugged her, still disbelieving she was there. Angela. Her name like a prayer with every quickened breath. Angela, Angela, Angela.

Policework

White banks flank the tote road, traveled almost daily by 18-wheelers loaded with timber. In a few months, mud will run from all the furrows, collect in the hollowed ruts. But today, two days before Christmas, everything is frozen. Lifeless.

Steering wheel in one hand and a Hostess pie in the other, Bruce maneuvers the cruiser down the road, suspension squeaking each time he hits a frost-heave. Crumbs are sprinkled down to his stomach, which pushes against his DPD jacket. The car smells of burnt coffee, sugar, cigarette smoke; on the radio, a Dire Straits song is playing. In the passenger seat, Nate tries not to make it obvious that he's pressing his foot to an imaginary brake pedal.

"Been driving worse roads than this since I was ten, Boss. Don't worry 'bout it."

A dozen yards in front of them, a bull moose lumbers out into the road, and Bruce slows to a stop as the massive creature considers the vehicle, its head hanging low under the weight of its antlers.

"Are you going to tell me what we're doing out here?" asks Nate.

"Molly Lannigan was out snowshoeing the other day, saw a pickup that didn't seem to belong. Says she saw it once before in the same spot, few weeks back."

"What do you think? Teenagers out parking?"

"Or poachers."

Bruce hits the horn, and the moose bolts off into the trees.

"Are we on Phil and Molly's land right now? I figured this belonged to the Fraziers like most of the other tote roads."

"Lannigans' property runs up against it. Maybe they had some kinda agreement? Hell, you'd know better'n me. It's your family."

Sometimes it still catches Nate off guard that he will forever be associated with the Fraziers. Even when Bridget was alive, she was so separate from her parents and siblings. She and Nate fulfilled their obligations by going to family reunions and holidays, but neither of them enjoyed it. When they were in fourth grade, Bridget confided to Nate that she suspected she was an alien dropped into that house on the hill, that she didn't actually belong to any of the people who lived inside it. It's not that she disliked her siblings; she just felt different from them. (Nate hears sporadically from Will, Craig, and Penny, all of them living far south of the County. He knows when they call to check in on him and Sophie that they're looking for a way to feel connected to their youngest sister, counting on him not to bring up the fact they rarely tried to do the same thing while she was alive.)

Ironically, Bridget always felt closest to her father, who spent most of his time at the mill. But Marshall has been a good man—hardworking, committed to his family and the business, proud of everything his kids did. While Nate sometimes wishes his in-laws would have stuck around Dalton for Sophie's sake, he also thinks the distance makes Marshall a better grandfather. As if the man feels so guilty about his absence that he finds other ways to compensate for it—not with money, though he's told Nate there's a sizable account waiting for Sophie when she's old enough—but with postcards and letters and phone calls. Sophie loves going with Nate to the post office every Thursday afternoon and opening the box, seeing the cards from New Hampshire, Vermont, DC, New Orleans. Their twice-weekly phone calls often last hours, Grampa never tiring of stories about art projects and backyard birds. Nate knows it's the same way Marshall used to listen to Bridget talk about her latest painting or her favorite books when she was little. Some people just instinctively know how to make a child feel special.

Bridget's mother, though . . . Annette can either be falsely sweet or downright venomous. She expects too much from everyone, especially her kids. Until a few months ago, Nate thought of Annette as selfish, even narcissistic. He still thinks she can be those things, but he feels a little softer toward her now, knowing how deeply Bridget's death hurt her. You don't become an alcoholic and a compulsive shopper unless you're trying to bury intense grief. You don't drag your belongings onto the front lawn and set it all on fire if you're in your right mind.

When Bruce pulls up to a snowplow turn-around on the tote road, they unfold themselves from the cruiser doors—Nate with his crane-like legs, Bruce with the heft of a bear—and step into the morning. Bright sun with little warmth.

The men walk a few yards in either direction, boots crunching. "Did Molly give a good description of the truck?" asks Nate.

"Dark, older model Chevy. Didn't get close enough to read the plates—guess she was afraid some psycho was gonna jump out and steal her snowshoes or something."

Nate thinks of the nightmare Bridget once had about a masked man chasing her down, shoving her into the trunk of his car. Nate told her it was impossible for something like that to happen to someone here in Aroostook. "It could happen to any woman, anywhere," she said. "And every woman everywhere knows it." While she said it, she gave him a look filled with something between pity and frustration. *The boy lacks imagination*, his second-grade report cards used to proclaim.

"You never know about people," Nate says to Bruce. "Molly was right to be cautious."

"Prob'ly should go talk to her. See if there's anything she forgot to tell us. Or hell, maybe we time it right and she'll feed us lunch."

"Isn't that kind of rude?"

Bruce laughs, the sound booming off snowbanks and evergreens. "You might not be a rookie anymore, Boss. But you still got a lot to learn."

In the Lannigans' kitchen, two brown dogs sleep on the floor. From upstairs come the thumps and exclamations of what sounds like an entire wrestling team; a Whitney Houston song plays in the living room. Beside the table, a window offers a view of the paddock, where several blanketed horses stand in the snow.

"So it's like I told Bruce over the phone," says Molly as she kneads a ball of dough on the counter. "I didn't get a good look at the truck—seemed familiar, but I couldn't place it. Honestly, I felt a little ridiculous calling it in. God knows I did plenty of parking on tote roads around here when I was younger."

Bruce's mustache flicks up in a boyish grin. "Didn't we all?"

"Rite of passage, wasn't it?" Molly slams the heels of her hands into the dough—push-push-pull. "Anyway, something about the truck just seemed off. Poachers, maybe, scouting out a good spot."

"On private land?"

"Thing about poachers, Boss, is they don't usually give two shits about fancy things like land ownership."

Just as Molly puts the dough into the warming drawer of her stove, her husband, Phil, enters the kitchen, bringing the scent of cold air and manure with him. When he moves toward the table, he walks with one hip thrust slightly in front of the other—the result, Nate assumes, of spending a couple decades driving over the County tending to sick and wounded farm animals. "How we doing today?" Phil nods at

Bruce and Nate as he drops into a chair. "You two sticking around for lunch?"

"They are." Molly hands bowls of soup to each of the men, along with plates of grilled cheese sandwiches. "Now brace yourselves, I'm summoning the wild ones."

She calls them all as one, five separate identities rolled into a singular being.

"*BEN-JULIA-ROBBIE-KATY-ETHAN!*"

The music ends. Footsteps crash down the stairs from the second floor. The dogs jolt awake and hop around the kitchen, toenails skating across the floor as they greet each Lannigan child entering the room.

Twenty-year-old Ben plops into his seat first. Next is Robbie, sporting heavy orthodontia, and then Ethan, small for seven, clambers onto a dictionary on his chair so he can reach his plate. Katy comes bounding in dressed in a leotard, legwarmers, and neon tights.

"Where's your sister?" Molly asks her.

"I don't know, in her room, I guess."

"Or on the throne," says Ethan, then he and Robbie start making fart noises on the backs of their hands.

"Boys, that's enough. We have company."

Before they can apologize, Bruce pushes up the sleeve of his shirt and blows a high-pitched, freeping blast into the crook of his elbow. The kids rush to mimic his strategy.

Molly turns toward the stairs and takes a deep breath before yelling again. "*JULIA, GET DOWN HERE OR YOU'RE ON HORSE-MUCKING DUTY THE REST OF THE WEEK!*"

On the floor above, a door slams shut; moments later, Julia, seventeen, slumps into the kitchen, her gold hair swinging in a ponytail.

"I was wrapping the Christmas presents you made me buy with my own babysitting money," she says as she takes the last open seat at the table. "Am I really going to be punished for that?"

"Don't be moody, dear, it's not becoming," says Molly. "And kids, those noises better stop right this instant or I'll have all of you out in the stalls mucking. That includes you, *Sergeant* Rossignol."

"Why're the fuzz here, Mom?"

"I asked them to check out the tote road where I've been seeing that truck."

"What truck?"

"None of you guys would know it. Anyway, it's probably nothing."

"How would you know if we know it or not?"

"Honestly, Julia, you get so confrontational when you're menstruating."

"Ohmy*God*, Mom, why are you such a—"

"Don't speak to your mother like that."

Nate and Bruce glance at each other, agreeing silently it's time to make their exit. They offer to wash their dishes before they go, but Molly won't hear of it.

"Don't be silly," she says. "Why do you think we had so many kids?"

After briefly being blocked by the dogs, they're back out on the front porch, letting the storm door wheeze shut behind them. Bruce, lighting a cigarette, mumbles something about being thankful for an infertile wife. As they walk down the steps toward the driveway, Nate can still hear the Lannigans in the house—the wild ones and their loud laughter boiling over, pushing through all the unseen cracks and crevices that make a solid home.

Back at the station, Bruce hands a sheaf of paperwork over to Nate. "You've got prettier handwriting than me, Boss."

There's no point in arguing. Bruce is like the big brother Nate never had—a decade older, a hundred pounds heavier, and almost always right. He hikes his gun-belt higher on his hips and saunters off toward the coffee pot, boots squeaking against the tile floor.

What both of them know is that Nate would rather handle paperwork all day than go out on the beat to do the hard policing. The past few months back on the force have been stressful, so much time spent brushing up on current law, renewing his CPR certification, shooting bullets into paper torsos at trainings like the one down in Augusta last weekend. There's so much to remember, so much he has allowed himself to forget.

The hardest part about returning to the job, though, has been reminding himself how to deal with people who are depressed, angry, broken. People stuck in a cycle of poverty, which goes hand in hand with drugs and alcohol and violence. Seems like one generation makes a series of bad choices, and the next, having no other example, repeats those same choices. Over and over and over again, until all the bad, ugly things take root in the blood. Nate hasn't lost the urge to help people, but he has started to doubt he can do anything meaningful for the folks who need it most. Who is he to heal a century or more of hurt?

There have been instances when he feels almost like he did when he donned his DPD uniform for the first time nearly seven years ago. There was the rainy day he helped Ollie Levasseur wrangle his dog from a culvert, and he watched as man and animal were reunited, Ollie wrapping his jacket around the shivery bundle of fur. It was a glimmer, a reminder that the job isn't always doling out punishment or witnessing people at their worst. There was also a full-moon night in November when Nate pulled over a car driving erratically on Poor Man's Road. He was ready for something terrible—one of the Wilkins, high again—but it was Mrs. Taylor, his middle school English teacher, suffering from low blood sugar. He sat with her in the cruiser, feeding her Rolos from Bruce's stash in the glove compartment, until she felt clearheaded again. They talked about what they were reading—*Jane Eyre* for her; *Maine Criminal Code 1995* for him.

If only Nate could pare the job down to those shining moments and to this thankless but necessary paperwork. If only he never had to chase a speeder down a dark road again.

He fills out a report of today. Make and model of the truck Molly reported. Location. *No vehicle found on premises. Follow up & monitor area as needed.* With that done, he checks in with Bruce, who has made himself cozy in Chief Halstead's office while Peter and his wife Betty are off on one of those nightmarish ocean cruises. Bruce has his feet propped on the desk while he reads a week-old *Bangor Daily*. Christopher Reeve released from physical therapy, the newspaper says. What a world—Superman brought down by a horse, confined to a life in a wheelchair.

Nate files his report in the cabinet near a window that offers a view into the staff room, where Jan Shapleigh, Town Councilor, is picking her teeth near the microwave. The joys of a shared municipal building.

"Any other paperwork you can foist off onto me?" he asks Bruce.

"How 'bout all of it?"

Nate feels the familiar pull between wanting to prove himself worthy of this job and wanting to run out of the building as fast as he can, straight for his parents' house, where Sophie is waiting. He promised her they'd make cookies today, cut the dough into shapes of stars and snowmen and sprinkle them red, green, and gold. He promised they'd set the best ones aside for Santa's visit tomorrow night.

Seeing Nate glance at the clock on the wall, Bruce chuckles. "Quit standing around looking cute and get the hell out of here, Boss. Shift's over."

Stepping into the kitchen of his parents' house, Nate is hit in the gut by a red-haired tornado. He lifts Sophie into his arms, as always surprised by how heavy she's getting, how her legs and arms just keep growing. Hopefully she never gets as tall as Nate, who's spent his whole life ducking under doorways and ceiling fans.

"I missed you," he says, squeezing her tight before she jumps down and skips back over to the table, settling into the same chair he used to sit in for every meal of his childhood—the one by the window, for a view of the lawn.

"Dad, guess what? Bampy's teaching me how to play poker."

"Don't worry, Nate. We play a clean game. No cash."

"So what do you bet with?"

"Jellybeans," says Sophie, holding up a handful to demonstrate before shoving them into her mouth at once.

Nate should say something to his father about sugaring her up. But it's hard to criticize anything his parents do for him or for Sophie—no way he could navigate being a single dad without them. His mother works the early morning shift at the Store 'N More so she can be around anytime Nate needs her, and his father recently took a job driving the school bus so he could spend more time with Sophie before and after her half-days at kindergarten. Sometimes after he has dropped off all the other kids, despite his bad back, he takes her for joyrides around town, pretending the yellow bus is a limousine.

"Ma at the library with Trudy?" Nate asks.

"It's Saturday, ain't it?" There's a sandpaper grit to his father's voice, a sound that only seems to come when he's talking about Nate's mother and her friendship with Trudy. Nate has never understood it, though he thinks it has something to do with loneliness, or jealousy—his dad isn't exactly the type to go out and make friends. He's more of a stay-at-home-with-a-beer-and-the-TV kind of guy.

After one more round of cards, Nate tells Sophie it's time to go. "Tally up your jellybeans."

In the truck, he checks twice to make sure she is buckled

into her booster seat—"Dad, *come on*, I'm in"—then he turns around in the driveway, careful not to bump against his mother's lilac tree. Dead now, but it will be bursting with purple in a few months, making the spring air smell sweet and new. Hard to believe on an afternoon like this, barely ten degrees, the world steeped in the dismal gray of December.

At the end of Russell Street, Nate heads down High. He slows near the Diner to let Dean Buckley pull out in front of him, and that's when he sees it: Tommy Merchant's truck parked beside the Dumpsters. Brown, older model Chevy.

Nate pulls into the lot and parks behind the truck.

"What're we doing, Dad?"

"Just checking something out. Give me one minute, then we'll be on our way."

He takes his pen and notepad out of his coat pocket to jot down the plate number. 8401 DB. Registration and inspection stickers up to date. Mud, salt, and slush flecked all over the tires and running boards.

"Can we *please* make cookies now?"

"Okay, okay, we're going."

Before he drives away, Nate glances up at the windows in the apartment above the Diner. He thinks he sees a flash of movement behind the glass—but maybe it's just a trick of the winter light. Maybe there's no one there at all.

Later that night, Nate finishes up the chores as quietly as he can. Quiet dishes. Quiet sweeping. By the time he finishes wrapping the presents from Santa, it's nearly nine o'clock. The house is still, but there's a familiar feeling of a presence beyond his own and that of his sleeping daughter. Sometimes, like now, Nate finds himself wandering through the house half expecting to find someone around every corner. Unseen ghosts all over the place.

Though his eyelids are heavy and he's craving the weight of a quilt tucked around his shoulders, when Nate goes upstairs, he finds himself pulled to Bridget's studio rather than his bed. He steps into the room, closes the door, clicks on the lamp. Surrounding him are Bridget's paintings, all the color she left behind. Emerald forests and cobalt rivers; sunflower fields golden under pink-morning skies.

It never stops being a marvel, the ways she captured the wonder of this land she loved as much as Nate still does. He used to avoid this room. But sometime last summer, around the time he and Rose repainted Sophie's bedroom, it got a little easier to come in here.

Outside, a pickup in need of a new muffler speeds down Davis Road, and Nate cringes, worried the sound will wake Sophie. He waits a few moments after the truck has faded away, listening for her movements through the walls. But it's quiet in her room, and he breathes easy again, knowing she's asleep.

He turns off the lamp and pulls aside the curtains to stare at the starlit snow. He wants to go out walking under that sky, amble down to the frozen river and find Rose there, waiting for him. He wants to hold her hands and ask if she feels loved, if she feels safe. Maybe he could even ask her, under the guise of Official Police Business, if she knows anything about what Tommy does at night, where he goes. If she, like Nate, suspects that Tommy drives out to logging roads and parks in the darkness, waiting for animals to wander out of the forest and into the sights of his rifle. Because it would be just like a Merchant to do such a thing. Prey at night. Take the unfair advantage, fire a clear shot at the unsuspecting target. The way all poachers do.

Coward of The County

Christmas Eve morning, Tommy wakes up early.

He showers, dresses in his Dickies and steel-toed boots, smokes two cigarettes instead of scarfing down a bowl of the cereal he keeps around for when Rose brings Adam and Brandon over every Sunday. They should be here today. But Tommy drew the short straw at the mill, and he's got to work while nearly everyone else in town gets to lie around eating sweets and thinking about all the presents wrapped under their trees.

At least Rose agreed to have Tommy over to the trailer tomorrow for Christmas morning, even though she probably won't let him or the boys out of her sight while he's there. It's like that every time Adam and Brandon are here on Sundays.

Chaperoned visits, Rose says. Like Tommy is his child-molesting uncle. Every time she comes over with the boys, she hovers, watching Tommy play Legos or Matchbox cars with them, correcting everything he tries to say or do. *No, don't roughhouse with them like that. No, don't be so impatient with Brandon, he's sensitive. No, don't put on* The Simpsons, *they're too young.*

Just one no after another since Tommy came back, even though he's been following all her stupid rules. Sometimes it makes him so mad that he gets in his truck at night and drives out to Milton Landing to fire off a bunch of rounds from his father's old shotgun. Not shooting at any living thing, just aiming at the dark, *BANG-BANG-BANG*, one after another until most of the anger is gone and all that's left is a thirst for the one thing he can't have.

When he told Rose he quit drinking, he thought he'd be able to at least sneak in a few beers when she wasn't around. How would she ever know?

But she was right—everyone in Dalton has been watching Tommy close. Arlene knows what time he leaves for work and comes back home every day, making comments whenever they see each other in the Diner or out in the parking lot. *Got in late last night. Hot date?* All the old-lady cashiers at Bergeron's eye his groceries like he might be buying stuff to make a pipe bomb. One day he went to the library to rent some movies for the boys, and the librarian asked him outright if he was planning on borrowing the VHS tapes or stealing them. Not a bit of respect for him and the nice thing he was trying to do for his kids. It's like Rose dispatched a cooze army to monitor his every movement.

Worse than any woman, though, is Nate. Driving around in his pigmobile, thinking he's so mysterious whenever he slows as he passes Tommy going the opposite direction. Pretending it's an accident when they run into each other at the post office or hardware store. *Crazy how expensive stamps are getting, don't you think? Here for a plunger, huh?* Like Tommy is dumb enough to believe in that kind of coincidence. Like he doesn't know Nate is trying to get rid of him so he can move in on Rose.

If Nate's crush on her wasn't obvious already, it sure was last week at the pageant. Bad enough Tommy had to suffer through all that music, all those dances. But then, after the lights came up and the kids rushed backstage to change out of their costumes, he had to listen to Rose and Nate while they gushed a bunch of bullshit about how great the show was. Nate couldn't take his eyes off her. And Rose was loving it, soaking it all in.

Tommy might have been able to deal with that, though, if it weren't for what happened after the kids came bursting into the gym. Because who did Adam and Brandon run to? Not to their father. No. They, along with Sophie, bolted right for Nate, desperate to hear what he had to say. *You three were the best ones up there. I'm so proud of you.* Grinning at the kids like all of them belonged to him. It wasn't until Tommy put his hands on his boys' shoulders that Nate got the hint and stepped back.

Gulping down the rest of his morning coffee, Tommy glances at his watch. Only 4:30. The Canuck bosses at the mill have busted him twice in the last month for coming in late without a good excuse, but fuck them. There's enough time to make a quick detour before he has to punch in.

It's not a long drive to Davis Road.

One early November afternoon when Tommy was twelve, his father asked if he wanted to go for a ride around the backroads of Dalton. Driving lessons, he said, which was another way of saying he wanted his kid to ferry him around while he sat in the passenger seat drinking Schlitz and smoking joints. Tommy didn't mind—they didn't take these trips a lot, but when they did, his old man was usually in a good mood.

That day, brown leaves were blowing in the breeze; the sun hung low. Tommy's father sang along with Hank, Waylon, and Merle. He had a voice like skeleton fingers raking pavement, or maybe Tommy still had Halloween on his mind. He and Sully Dozier had dressed up like vampires that year, complete with fake blood painted from the corners of their mouths down to their chins. They egged old ladies' houses. Stole candy from stupid kids. Crept up to the windows of the Rec Center to watch teenagers dancing to music they couldn't hear and to take bets on what color underwear Carrie Bergeron was wearing under her short nurse's costume.

"Mama tried, Mama tried," Tommy's father mumbled. Smoke curled through the cabin of the truck.

Tommy craned his neck to see over the dashboard and concentrated hard on the road—there wasn't much traffic on Route 11, but you never knew when a moose might step out from the woods.

"Take a right," said his father, laughing when Tommy cut the wheel so hard that some of his beer sloshed out of the can and onto his grease-stained jeans. "Easy, kid, you're doing good, you got plenty of room."

He drove out behind the back of the lumberyard, where timber was stacked high, across the bridge, and past the Pentecostal church—"Idiot brainwashed Bible-thumpers."

After a few miles, his father said, "Stop here."

Tommy pulled onto a dirt lane that bordered a field, some kind of grain he couldn't name. In the summertime, whatever it was grew high as a man's waist. The field ended in forest, which rolled on for miles. It was clear enough to see Katahdin far off to the southwest, its top dusted with early-season snow.

Instead of taking in the view, his father stared across the road at the old Donoghue house. No one seemed to be living there at the time—the lawn was scraggly, the windows like the blank eye-sockets in the leftover Jack-o-Lantern Tommy had kicked the guts out of yesterday, alone in the yard while his parents fought inside the shack. Or maybe they'd been doing the other thing. Whatever it was, it was loud.

"Ever tell you this place coulda been mine?" said his father, nodding toward the two-story farmhouse. "Donoghues were thinking of selling it a few years ago."

Tommy, who knew saying the wrong thing could ruin one of these good moods fast, told himself to stay quiet. Just sit there behind the wheel, Kenny Rogers singing on the radio, and don't be stupid.

Finally, though, he couldn't take the silence anymore.

"What happened?" he asked. "Why didn't they sell it?"

His father rubbed his hand over his lips, calluses scratching against his stubble. For a second Tommy could almost read his face, all the stories that lived behind his mud-colored eyes. All the things he never talked about.

Then a gust of wind blew hard enough to rock the truck, and his father's face closed shut again. He rolled down the window, flicked away his joint, rolled the window back up.

"Too long a story."

"Just tell me, Dad."

"For fuck's sake, kid. Trent Donoghue and his faggot brothers don't like me too much. Okay? That's what happened. That's why I didn't get the place."

Then his father slapped the radio silent, and Tommy understood driving lessons were over for the day.

A month later, his old man did some blow, got behind the wheel, and sped the truck into the guardrail of the bridge near the idiot brainwashed Bible-thumping church. A lot of adults tried to tell Tommy it was an accident, but he was never sure he could believe that. He thought maybe his father knew exactly what he was doing, how much to snort and how hard to press the gas to the floor.

He wondered if his father drove past the Donoghue house before the end, if he slowed down long enough to stare at the empty windows and imagine himself inside them, living some whole different life.

At the funeral, they played Merle Haggard. Tommy's mother wouldn't have it any other way.

It's still dark when Tommy slows his Chevy to a stop across from the house on Davis Road, all the eaves draped in Christmas lights. Of course Nate weaseled his way into this place—it's the kind of shit that always happens to Tommy. You want one thing from the world, and the world decides you can't have it.

What if he had grown up in this house instead of in that

uninsulated shack? Maybe his parents never would've fought. Maybe his father never would've hit him or Tommy's mother. Maybe his mother would've been sober and kind, and not so damn weak.

Three miles away, Adam and Brandon are sleeping. He gets to be with them tomorrow. Watch their faces light up when they see the bikes he bought for them, even though Rose asked him not to. Looking at him like they can't believe how lucky they are to have him as their dad. Or he'll tell the boys the bikes are from Santa. Either way, Tommy will know he was the one who made them smile like that.

Since he got back to Dalton, he's had better luck connecting with Adam. They've played catch in the parking lot outside the Diner (Rose watching), and Tommy's been teaching him about cars—how to check the oil level, use a pressure gauge. It's easy to talk with Adam, who likes math just like Tommy when he was that age, because numbers never jumped around a page like letters did.

It's been harder with Brandon. The kid's afraid of everything—thunderstorms, spiders, the sound when someone drops a pot lid on the floor. The boy's too soft for his own good; if he's not being bullied already, he will be soon enough. Then what? Is he going to cry his way out of it? Run to his mommy? Sometimes Tommy blames himself for Brandon's weakness—maybe if he'd never left, the boy would have a better idea of what it is to be a man. The ways you have to fight sometimes, for pride if nothing else.

As Tommy idles across the street from the farmhouse, he sees a light come on in a second-floor window. A shadow moves behind the curtain, pausing, and for a second, he feels the same animal fear that would flood through him when his old man reached for the belt.

Then the fear rushes out and the rage rushes in, and Tommy imagines himself getting out of the truck, busting down the door, and beating Nate senseless. He would leave bloody gaps where Nate's teeth should be. Bruise the jerk's face so bad Rose won't even recognize him.

But Tommy can't. If he ever wants to see his kids again, he can't.

He speeds off down Davis Road, fishtailing on the icy pavement. He hates that feeling when the tires can't find their grip—it's the worst kind of weightless. The space between one breath and the next.

He pulls into the employee lot at 4:58. Time for one cigarette before putting on his hard hat and starting another eight-hour shift stuck in a glass box above the kiln, where he hits a button about twelve thousand times a day. Flame on. Flame off. Flame on. Flame off.

He probably shouldn't complain about the job, which some guy quit just about the same time Tommy got back to Dalton. The Canucks could've given the job to one of the old-timers. But they wanted to hire new guys who'd work for cheaper prices, so he caught a break. For once.

On his way across the yard, Tommy runs into Larry Briggs. They get to talking about the usual crap—the weather, the potholes no one ever does anything about, Christmas.

"You believe they're making us work on a holiday?"

"It should be illegal. It just ain't right."

While Larry heads for the admin building, Tommy heads into the main mill, where the saws are already screeching, gnashing their teeth. It's not until he's halfway up to the catwalk he remembers he forgot to clock in.

Walking into the break room a couple minutes later, he sees Larry again, this time sitting at one of the tables with half a donut clutched in his hand. When Tommy nods at him, the bastard looks away, hiding behind his *Bangor Daily*.

There are two other men in the room, hovering beside the

time clock. One of them is the younger, thinner boss, and the other's the chubby guy from HR who gave Tommy a lecture two weeks ago about the importance of punctuality.

"Merchant," the boss says. "You're late again."

"I was right on time. I got distracted is all. I'm here to punch in."

"And the clock will show you're eleven minutes late."

"I wasn't, though. Ask him."

Tommy points to Larry, who drags his eyes away from his newspaper, his beady eyes flicking between him, Skinny, and Fatso.

"Tell them, Larry. Tell them we was talking out in the yard and I was here when I was supposed to be here."

"Sure, Tommy, we said a quick hello, but I don't know what time you got here."

"You cocksucker . . . "

"Is that the best tone to take?" asks Fatso in his thick Quebec accent.

Tommy's fists are clenched. He's sweating under his armpits.

"I'll take whatever goddamn tone I want."

Skinny raises his eyebrows at Fatso, who brandishes a wad of paperwork like some kind of sick magician.

"Mr. Merchant, you have now been warned twice about your failure to report to your shift on time. This is your third strike. We at Acadian Logging Incorporated, reserve the right to terminate any employee not in compliance . . . "

Tommy can't swallow. Can't move.

Steady income, gone.

Decent job, gone.

Chance to prove he can be a good father. Gone.

" . . . Sign here, clean out your locker, and leave the premises immediately. We will mail you your final paycheck."

Everything. Gone.

But why should Tommy be surprised? This is the way it

always goes for him. You ask for one thing from this world, and it's not enough for the world just to say no. It has to push you down, too, shove your face into the ground hard enough for the gravel to scrape your teeth clean.

Princes of Larch Street

The shag carpet is covered in wrapping paper, snowmen ripped to shreds. Adam insisted on listening to The Chipmunks tape while he and his brother opened presents, and the squeaky voices are starting to feel like tiny crowbars prying apart Rose's brain. She burned the first batch of pancakes. There's glitter everywhere from the cards Brandon made in art class. Half a candy cane is stuck to the coffee table.

A perfect Christmas morning.

Rose had been afraid Adam would throw a tantrum when he ran down the hall and didn't see a new bike under the tree. But when she explained they didn't have the money for it this year, he acted like such a grownup, even though he couldn't hide the disappointment on his face, still imprinted with the folds from his pillow.

"It's okay, Mum," he said. "Maybe for my birthday."

She hates not giving him something he wants so much. In a different family, Santa would have worked some magic and brought the bike. But in this family, Santa only brings stocking stuffers. Any other presents come from Rose (and, when she's feeling generous enough to write his name on the tags, Tommy). Maybe that's not the right way to talk about Christmas, but it seems better than letting her kids believe some fat guy from the North Pole deems them unworthy of nice things.

While Rose was growing up, her mother gave her exactly three gifts every Christmas: underwear, a toothbrush, and whatever toy was on sale at K-Mart. When she returned to kindergarten after winter break, Rose was stunned to hear about all the presents her classmates had received—Barbies, roller skates, board games, dollhouses, books, Easy Bake Ovens.

"Am I on the naughty list?" she asked her mother that afternoon. "Is that why Santa didn't bring me anything?"

Her mother barely looked up from painting her nails, "Santa is just a story."

"What do you mean?"

"He's not real. It's parents who give their kids presents, and some parents don't have the kinda dough it takes to buy all the stuff they might want."

"And you. . ." Rose paused. "You're one of those parents?"

"What do you think?" asked her mother. "Look at this dump. We got blankets on the windows instead of curtains. We use space heaters because kerosene's too damn expensive. You know that whole week you got to skip bath night? That's because I couldn't pay the water bill."

Rose had heard the word *poor* whispered between teachers at school. They said it as if it was some kind of sickness you could catch just by breathing it in. But this was the first moment she realized she was one of the people those teachers were talking about.

"I'm sorry, baby," her mother said. "I wish Santa was real. I wish I was a queen and you were a princess so we could rule the world. But that's not how it works."

It might have been the only time she was completely honest with Rose, and one of the only times Rose wished she hadn't been. Because that was the moment she understood poor kids didn't get to believe in the same lies normal kids did.

For her own boys, Rose has tried to soften the truth about this holiday. Give them partway lies. Santa exists, but only to bring stocking stuffers. The Tooth Fairy is real, but she can only give out quarters. The Easter Bunny can't afford the good kind of chocolate. As for God, she leaves that one alone—let the boys decide for themselves if they want to believe in any of those stories, though as far as she's concerned, the Noah's-ark, Jonah-swallowed-by-a-whale, Eve-cursed-us-all crap the pastor's wife used to force on her in Sunday school is the biggest myth of all.

"Mumma."

Rose looks up from her cup of coffee to see Brandon proudly displaying the picture he just drew with the oil pastels from his new art kit (the smaller, cheaper one). It's Captain Planet, green-haired and blue-muscled, dressed in his weird little red tankini. The cartoon creeps her out, but Brandon's drawing is surprisingly good. Somehow, he got the anti-litter superhero's chiseled jaw just right.

"Sweetie, it's perfect. How'd you learn to do that?"

Brandon's one dimple deepens when he grins. "Mr. M. taught me."

When Rose met the new art teacher at the grade school Open House back in September, she liked him right away. She could tell he was nervous by the way he kept pushing a sprig of dusty-blond hair out of his eyes. There was something comfortable about him, reassuring, and he has brought out a confidence in Brandon she's never seen before, an interest in something she never could have given him herself. Methods of drawing lion kings and superheroes, creatures half-man, half-horse.

Those are the kinds of myths she wants her kids to believe in.

Brandon stares at the picture, then glances up at Rose with worry in his eyes. "Do you think Dad will like it?"

"Of course he will."

"When's he gonna be here?" asks Adam, smashing two Tonka trucks together to the beat of the Chipmunk Christmas song. *We've been good but we can't last.*

As if summoned, Tommy drives up the gravel driveway, honking the horn until Adam and Brandon jump to the window.

Rose joins them, pushing the curtain aside to see Tommy standing beside his truck. He's in his usual black jeans, black jacket. Beside him is a huge box wrapped in shiny green paper. The boys turn to Rose, wiggling with excitement like puppies. *We can hardly stand the wait.*

An almost perfect Christmas morning.

"Jackets and boots," she says. "Mittens, too."

They dress fast, then they burst through the door before Rose has even zipped her coat. By the time she steps into the cold, they're tearing the paper off the box, Adam shoving his brother aside so he can rip off the biggest pieces.

"What is it, what is it?"

"Who's it from, who's it from?"

"It was Santa," Tommy says, grinning around his cigarette. "The old guy just got a little confused, you know, left it at my place instead of bringing it here."

"Santa gets confused?"

"The man is ancient."

Rose walks slowly toward the truck, blinking in the harsh light that reflects off the snow on the ground. After Brandon pulls off the last piece of paper, Tommy stoops down to slice his Leatherman through the tape holding the box together. The sides of the cardboard seem to fall away in slow motion, revealing first only dark space, emptiness, and then one set of handlebars. Two sets. Two seats. Two steel frames, one cherry red, one electric blue. Four wheels with shiny silver spokes.

Adam lets out a shriek of joy, then drags Brandon to the bikes, talking about all the places around town they can ride together next summer. The puddles they can splash through, the hills they can climb.

"Why'd you do this?" Rose asks Tommy as soon as she's sure the boys are too distracted to hear anything she or their father might say to each other.

"I didn't do anything. It was Santa."

"Don't bullshit me."

"Don't you think the boys deserve nice stuff, Rose?"

"But neither of us can afford nice stuff, Tommy. Especially not now."

She heard the news from Larry Briggs' wife yesterday when she went into Bergeron's. Linda, dressed in a hideous sweater, was blocking the milk. "Too bad about Tommy," she said, and when Rose asked what she was talking about, she didn't even try to cover the smug look on her face. "Getting fired on Christmas Eve. But it's like Larry said when he called to tell me, you can't just show up to work whenever you want and think that's okay."

Rose wasn't surprised by the news. In a way, she was actually relieved—she had been waiting months for something like this to happen, wondering when and how Tommy would find a way to screw up. But to hear about him losing his job from a woman who wore her jeans way too high was embarrassing. He should have been the one to tell Rose. He should've strapped on a pair and got in touch with her the second he got back to the apartment after it happened.

Part of her wanted to call him and lay it all out in the open to show he couldn't hide anything from her. But another part of her wanted to see how long he would push it, how far he would carry the secret. Hours or days? Longer? Back when he was selling coke out of his uncle's garage, he'd lied to her for months.

"Let him come to you," Vera said when Rose called her for advice. "If he wants to prove he isn't the same guy he used to be, this is a good chance."

So she watched *Emmet Otter* with the boys and waited. She cooked a pot roast and waited. She told stories about red-nosed reindeer, tucked Adam and Brandon into bed, wrapped their presents, and waited.

Finally, a little before 9:00 last night, Tommy called to tell her.

He would've told her earlier, he said, but he needed to sit with it a while; let it sink in. He said it was Larry's fault, not standing up for him. He said they all had it out for him from the first day he started at that shithole. Those fuckers, he kept saying, the word beating through the phone like fists against Rose's ear. Fuckers, fuckers, fuckers.

"We had an agreement," she said, trying to sound steadier than she felt. He could so easily break her. "If you want to keep in contact with the boys, you need to stay clean and have a decent job."

After that it was all sweetness and promises. Give him three, four weeks at most, and he would find another job.

"A better one," he said, "somewhere people appreciate me."

None of it was his fault, he told her, but he was sorry anyway, sorry shit like this was always happening to him.

"It's like I'm cursed, Rose," he said, and he sounded so much like a little boy that she felt all the fight fall right out of her.

"Two weeks," she said.

"Promise."

She didn't believe him last night and she doesn't believe him now as they stand watching Adam run his hands over the chrome handlebars of the red bike while Brandon stands back a little, pretending not to be excited about the blue one. He outgrew his old bike over a year ago, but he didn't complain once this past summer when he pedaled the thing around the street, his knees nearly smacking into his elbows. Every time she watched him, Rose felt like such a shitty mom. Her boys deserve new bikes that come from a real store rather than secondhand pieces of crap she finds at the thrift store.

But she should have been the one to buy them. Or at least the one to give Tommy permission to buy them.

"Can we ride, Mum?"

"Bikes aren't meant for wintertime," she says, though as soon as the words are out of her mouth, she knows they sound ridiculous. There's no reason they shouldn't enjoy the moment. For once, they will go back to school after winter break and talk about the amazing presents Santa brought them. Tell the kind of Christmas story Rose never got to when she was their age. And shouldn't she be grateful for that, no matter who made that story possible?

As the boys take off down Larch Street, tires humming against cracked pavement, Tommy turns to Rose. He's smiling, but there's something mean in his hazel eyes. It's the same way he used to look at her when he'd come home from Frenchie's reeking of yeasty sweat and cheap perfume, swearing he hadn't done anything with any other girls, knowing Rose had no way of proving he wasn't telling the truth. Both of them knowing if she tried to fight him about it, he would knock her down and bruise her up until she was the one saying whatever he wanted to hear.

But that was a long time ago. Maybe now she can find her own way to win the fight. "I'm sorry about what happened," she says. "I know you were trying real hard to make that job work."

His eyes soften, and suddenly she's staring not at Tommy the man, but Tommy as he was at seventeen—before the kids, before the hurt, before the leaving. Handsome and vulnerable, soft and sweet.

As the boys speed past the driveway, bicycle gears clicking, his eyes harden again. Under faded acne scars, his jaw clenches.

"Like I told you," he says as he exhales a cloud of smoke in her face. "It ain't my fault. Whole fucking world's against me."

And now she wants to win the fight his way, wants to shove that starry ember deep down his throat.

But at the sound of Brandon's laughter rolling down the street, Rose's anger collapses into something else, a cool sensation that might be pity.

Tommy's lies, she sees with the same sudden clarity she felt that day her mother told her Santa didn't exist, are never told to shield someone he cares about. He only lies to get what he wants for himself out of any given situation or person, even his own kids.

There's a difference between lying to soften the world for someone you love and lying to make the world soften for you—and if there's something so wrong inside Tommy that he can't see that difference, then there's nothing Rose can do except feel sorry for him. It must be lonely to live like that.

"You did a good job with the bikes," she says. "Thank you."

She can tell by the way Tommy stares at her and lets his cigarette burn down to his knuckles that he expected an argument. Probably even wanted one. But he's unfixable, and she has nothing left to say, and it's Christmas, and her boys are flying down Larch Street like they own this whole sorry town.

So she stands beside Tommy, both of them silent, and they watch as Adam and Brandon pedal up and down for so long that her toes inside her boots go numb.

Next door, Marian's toad-like face appears in the window of her trailer, and she scowls out at them for a while, then stares beyond them, all the way to the empty plot of land across the road.

In the summer, that land is a field, open and green; a perfect place to catch fireflies in jars and watch their lights blink on and off. Not long after Tommy left town, Rose brought the boys outside and told them they could wish on fireflies the same way they did on coins tossed into the river. Every time they caught one of the insects and set them free again, she said, they were sending their wishes out to the world, up to the sky.

Maybe that's the kind of story they will realize was a lie but forgive her for, anyway. Maybe one day they'll even tell their own kids the same stupid thing.

Right now, the field on the other side of Larch Street is nothing but a sweep of snow under the December sun, and Marian can't seem to pull her eyes off it, as if all that glittering white has put her in some kind of trance. Rose has half a mind to go into the old woman's cat-piss trailer and drag her away from the window. A person could go blind, she should tell her, staring at so much brightness for so long.

Crickets

Angela's father's truck lives in her mother's garage, because one of the only useful pieces of advice he gave her in the time she lived with him was to hide a good vehicle away from the elements. "Rust is cancer," he said.

Momma was happy to let Angela take over the garage, even though it's where she used to store her junk—headless mannequins, encyclopedia sets (missing volumes *H-J* and *Z*), Thigh-Masters, Joni Mitchell records . . . basically a shrine to all the things her mother tried to become but never did. She's not a seamstress, or a fountain of knowledge; she's strong but untoned, soft in the middle. And when she sings, it's more like Elmo than Joni.

"The point isn't to conquer the world," Momma said once after catching her thumb in the sewing machine yet again. "You just gotta give things a try."

Angela was twelve at the time, right on the edge of still believing her mother was perfect and finding everything her mother did as obnoxious as the itchy tags in her sweaters. She wanted to believe trying was good enough. But she doubted it was that simple.

That September day they moved Angela's truck into the garage, Momma hauled the junk out to the driveway and displayed her dead dreams for the whole town to see. She sat in a folding chair, beckoned everyone to come look. Angela watched from the kitchen as the people of Dalton walked away with her mother's discarded hopes—there went Mrs. Clark with one Thigh-Master; Arlene Nadeau took the other. Jerry Curtis claimed the mannequins for his wife, one tucked under each arm. One of the Lannigans took the Joni Mitchells. No one wanted any of the encyclopedias.

"You shouldn't just give it away," Angela said. "You could make some money."

"I can't accept money for this crap. That would be like stealing."

"But you're cool with all these other people essentially stealing from you?"

"It's not stolen if it's freely offered."

That's her mother, who gave away all her dreams as easily as if she were passing out Halloween candy. Take this one; this one; this one, too. Her mother, who likes to get to church in time for singing, so she can add her Elmo voice to the words being tossed up to heaven, or at least to the paint-peeled ceiling. Her mother, who drives Angela so ungodly insane that sometimes she has to leave the house, take her father's truck, and drive.

It's been months without anything stronger than weed, and Dalton at night gives her a hint of the high she still craves. Flying down empty roads, a nameless entity under the black and endless sky; its own kind of drowning. Seatbelt tight as steel across her chest. The radio playing songs with too many drums, but the noise is necessary; it swallows the sound of crickets. The memory of all sorts of unwanted things.

It was Mason who got her started.

Angela had been at her father's house nearly a year, and things hadn't gotten better. Some of the people on the rez looked at her mistrustfully, as though the pale complexion she'd inherited from her mother proved she wasn't one of them. She was wearing a name that didn't fit; no matter how hard she tried, she could never find the right thing to say to her father, the key that would get him talking to her as easily as he laughed and joked with Colie and JJ. Or maybe it was easier to hold a conversation with four-year-olds than your teenaged daughter.

"Nah, that's just Deacon," Mason once told Angela. "Good guy, but you can never tell what he's thinking."

"But I should know. I'm his daughter."

"Not really, though."

"Screw you."

They were on the roof of her father's porch, passing a joint back and forth under the stars, surrounded by the sounds of spring peepers singing from a pond nearby.

"It's like with me and Pam," said Mason. "She's *technically* my aunt, and that's why she lets me live here. But we don't really know each other. I don't know what she thinks about; she sure as shit doesn't know what I think about."

"So what are you saying?"

"That you can be related to someone and still be strangers."

Angela believed everything he said, because she was seventeen and he was twenty-two. She told herself it was okay to notice how cute he was, with his shoulder-length hair and sleepy eyes, because he wasn't *technically* related to her. He read Bukowski, listened to bands she had never heard of. He played guitar. A steady stream of girls slunk out of his apartment above the garage on weekend mornings, and sometimes he smiled at Angela like she could be the next one, if she played her cards right.

So that night on the roof when he reached into his pocket and brought out two pills, handing one to her, she took it. Something to relax, he said, something to let the night melt a little. And soon the night did melt; the stars came dripping down like warm vanilla icing, pouring onto her clothes and skin and hair, and the peepers gave their chorus just for her, and everything was indigo, perfect, sparkling.

"What is this shit?"

When he asked if it mattered, she laughed. She said no.

No, it didn't matter, because for the first time in her life, she didn't give a fuck about who she might be or what she might have come from. She didn't need her father's companionship or approval; she didn't need definition; she didn't even need a name. It was enough to let the night keep sliding from the sky.

After the haze cleared the next morning, it all made more sense to Angela—why Mason didn't have a steady job, why he was a grown man living rent-free above his aunt's garage. It also explained the silence that filled the house sometimes, the loaded glances between Pam and her father. Not that they ever said anything about Mason to Angela, or to each other in front of her. But even without any out-loud acknowledgment, there was often a feeling in the house like someone had dropped a glass and everyone else was holding their breath, waiting for it to shatter on the floor.

What didn't make sense to Angela was how she could recognize this kind of existence for what it was—pathetic—and still take whatever Mason offered her. Was it because he was good-looking? Was she trying to seem cool; was she that shallow? Or did her acceptance of his poison go deeper, as deep as the sky that night when all the stars dissolved?

She started to crave the anonymity of sinking into whatever substance he gave her. As soon as the liquor kicked in or the drugs took hold, she could be anybody or nobody at all; she was nothing, everything, all at once. Unlike the real act of drowning, which nearly happened to her when she was fourteen, this submersion was calm. Clear. Desired. Unlike Greg, who had pulled Angela from the water, Mason was happy to join her beneath the surface, and sometimes when she was really loaded, she could close her eyes and imagine herself and Mason floating together in some dark watery space, weightless.

The more Mason gave her, the more she wanted. When she wasn't on something, she felt like a piece of string pulled too tight. When she wasn't with him, she felt thirsty, feral, alone. He smiled every time he saw her. He listened to every word she said. He loaned her dog-eared copies of his favorite novels. He played guitar for her and taught her words to Led Zeppelin songs. He was so damn beautiful; she wanted to climb inside his skin; she didn't need a name or an identity if she could only inhabit his.

That spring of her junior year, the more Mason gave Angela, the less she cared about anything else. She would cut out of school early to be with him or skip entire days. Pam and Deacon had some idea of what was happening—they weren't that stupid—and more than once Pam suggested Angela not spend so much time with Mason. But by then they had no control over him or over her. The most Angela's father could do was threaten to call her mother, which would never happen, because that would mean he would have to admit to Cindy that things had fallen apart on his watch, just like she was afraid might happen when he suggested Angela move there in the first place.

And then.

Hot, sticky night. Late summer. Crickets singing. Mason led her to his favorite spot by the Penobscot. Tall trees shielded them from buildings and houses. The only light the stars, the moon. "Try this," he said. He gave Angela two pills, instructed her to wash them down with warm whiskey. She didn't question him; she trusted him more than she had ever trusted anyone, except maybe Momma. Soon she was floating, and she waited for him to join her underwater, but something was wrong. She was untethered, but he was solid and sober, his hands roaming over all the places she had dreamed of his hands being. But she didn't want it anymore, not like that, with the river and the sky low enough to strangle her and the forest laughing and the crickets screaming. All of it was wrong, and she said wait, she said no—but sometimes words have two meanings.

When she walked through the front door twenty minutes

later, Pam was standing at the oven stirring a saucepan of half-melted ganache. Her father was at the table, tinkering with an old mechanical clock.

"Sweetheart," said Pam, turning to look at Angela. "What happened? You're a mess."

It was only then she noticed the grass in her hair, the dirt under her nails. There was a long span of time—or maybe it was only a few seconds—when she considered telling them what Mason had done.

But if she told, there would be a trip to the hospital, the police station, maybe eventually a courtroom. There would be questions and judgments and other invasions of privacy to more than just her body. Assuming anyone even believed her.

"I fell," Angela said. Whatever drug Mason had given her hadn't yet faded, and she felt like the light above the bathroom sink back home, the one that fizzled and popped at random intervals.

"Are you hurt?" asked her father, in a voice filled with the concern Angela had always craved from him and never gotten. He wanted to protect her, she understood. But the time for that had passed.

"I'm fine."

Pam returned to her ganache, lifting the spoon so a waterfall of chocolate poured down into the pan. Her father continued to nudge the clock's hands from one number to another, back and forth. And that was the worst part of everything—not that they didn't believe Angela when she told them she was all right, but that they did.

Sometimes on her drives through Dalton, the music on the radio isn't enough, and she needs the thick, deep silence of the wild.

The best place for that is on the logging roads that crisscross the North Maine Woods, largely untraveled at night. When she sits in her father's truck and stares out the windows, all she sees are looming giants, bowing close as if about to tuck her in for the night. All she hears is the wordless language the trees whisper to one another. There in the forest, she is irrelevant and nameless.

She thinks a lot about Bridget Theroux. Their paths didn't cross much in life, but what about in the afterlife?

Say Angela sent herself away. Overdosed. Chose to swallow her own name forever. Would she meet Bridget in some sort of endless universe? Would they float together through clouds, spy on the people they left behind on earth? Angela imagines viewing Momma from afar, watching as she pumps other people's gas and smokes her cigarettes and prays for signs her daughter, gone too soon, is safe with Jesus. Maybe Bridget and Angela could toss pennies down from heaven, send cardinals to land on windowsills, knock on bedroom walls in the middle of the night—all the classic ways the dead supposedly communicate with the living.

It would be easy to disappear in this wilderness. Leave the truck, walk into the trees. Never walk back out again.

II.
Nurture

Fine Linen

The day before New Year's, Greg agrees to drive with his mother and Aimee out to Sarah's place in Milton Landing.

The cottage at the edge of the Best Family Farm, which reminded him of something out of a fairy tale when he was here last summer, looks depressing surrounded by winter. No ivy climbing the walls; no flower boxes under the windows. Just snow and ice. Inside, the house is overheated, the air uncomfortably dry. All the floors and cupboards are clean, but there's a rotten smell coming from the kitchen sink.

"I don't get it," says Sarah, squeezing a lemon down the drain. "I scrub and scrub, I use baking soda and vinegar, I scrub some more, and still . . . "

Their mother leans over the sink, wrinkling her nose. "It's got to be a deeper issue," she says. "Ian should have a look in the pipes, see if . . . "

"Ian's busy today, Mom, he and Gareth . . . "

"Soon, then. Though his parents do keep him awfully busy around here . . . "

Since his sister's miscarriage, she and their mother rarely finish a spoken thought to each other. Every conversation between them ends in ellipses, their words hanging in the air like half-frozen laundry on a clothesline.

Sarah throws the lemon rind into the garbage. "Forget it. I think I've got some leftover Yule log we can have, unless Ian . . . "

As she, Aimee, and their mother talk about the upcoming

high school Winter Formal—which Aimee insists she'd rather plunge her face into a hornet's nest than attend—Greg stares out the window at acres of snow. Hard to imagine these fields will yield thousands of potatoes in the fall, Ian and Sarah walking the rows to collect any tubers missed by the combine.

Greg picked rocks out here one year to make some extra cash, stooping and sweating for hours under the sun. There was merit in the work, a sense of satisfaction each time he heard the thud of a rock tossed in his bucket. But the idea of handling potatoes all his life like his brother-in-law's family makes Greg feel almost as claustrophobic as the thought of standing at his father's cash register. He is meant to work with the earth, but not on a farm.

"Greg?"

His mother is staring at him with her hands clutched at her chest the way she always does when she thinks she has a Great Idea.

"Sweetheart. Tell Aimee why she needs to go to the Formal."

"Why would I do that?"

"Because you went when you were her age. And you had fun, didn't you?"

Fun isn't exactly the way Greg would describe standing off to the sidelines and watching Angela and Henry dry hump under a disco ball. Sweating into his polyester shirt. Eventually he did share a slow dance with Shelby Wilkins, the two of them shuffling along to a Bette Midler song.

"It was the best experience of my life," he tells his little sister. "You have to go."

For the first time since they got to her house, Sarah's eyes light up. "We could get her all dressed up. Make her look like Molly Ringwald."

Aimee glares at them under a thick layer of eyeliner. "I will kill you both."

"Not if we kill you first."

"With *fashion*."

"Kids, don't talk like . . . "

Their mother keeps glancing at Sarah for too long, as if worried any mention of death will send her into a breakdown. But Sarah is laughing, a sound so much like their childhood that it's like they've all been kicked back in time to one of those rainy weekends they would spend playing dress-up and Red Light, Green Light.

"Greggie, why don't you teach Aimee how to foxtrot? Oh, or the jitterbug."

"This kid can't jive. Maybe a nice polka."

"I will turn you both into blood sacrifices. There's a full moon coming up."

"*Enough*," says their mother, slamming her hand on the table—a move that might have intimidated them when they were kids but now just makes the whole thing funnier. Even Aimee has started to giggle, her cross-bone earrings quivering.

After their mother stomps down the hall and slams the bathroom door, Sarah wipes tears from her eyes. "Oh my god, I needed that. I love her, but she's been driving me nuts."

"I don't know how you do it," says Aimee. "Deal with her up your ass all the time. She brought the fabric, you know. It's out in the car."

"What fabric?" Greg asks.

Sarah peers at him in a near-perfect impersonation of their mother. "For the curtains, sweetheart, the *curtains*."

"Mom is convinced gingham drapes and paisley Roman shades are going to fill the void in Sarah's womb."

It's the first time since Greg's gotten home that anyone has mentioned the miscarriage directly, and for a moment he thinks he should tell Aimee off for being insensitive. But Sarah surprises him by laughing again.

"Seriously," she says. "As if paisley *anything* ever helped anyone."

His sisters share a look so loaded with understanding that

he feels awkward witnessing it, as if he's peeking in on something not meant for him. Aimee and Sarah used to fight about everything from misplaced sweaters to who had dibs on the last bowl of cereal. This friendship between them must have formed while Greg was at school—or maybe before that, in the weeks right after Sarah lost the baby, while he was on the road south to the sea.

Their mother returns to the kitchen, frowning under her new glasses. Purple with cat-eye frames, they're nothing like what she would normally wear. The style suits her, though, makes her look younger and more awake. She claims she only bought them because they were on sale, but Greg wonders if she admired herself in the mirror at the optometrist's office, angling her face this way and that until she recognized the eighteen-year-old she used to be.

"If you kids are done being foolish," she says, "I want to bring in some fabric samples for Sarah, see if maybe she'd like . . . "

They burst into laughter, three siblings united against their mother while she stares at them from across the room, hands balled on her hips. It must be lonely, standing on the edge of a joke like that, and maybe it isn't totally fair. But what in this world ever is?

That night, Greg climbs the steps of the Muses' front porch and knocks on the door. While he waits for someone to answer, he stares at the swing where he and Angela used to sit for hours watching people stumble out of the Tavern across the street. One summer night, they sat in the dark listening as a drunk guy used the pay phone outside the restaurant to call someone and complain about how frustrated he was. *Not just mentally, man. Sexually, too.* Even though Greg and Angela couldn't stop giggling at the confession, he couldn't bring himself to look directly at her, afraid of something he couldn't name.

Just when he's about to knock again, Angela opens the door. She's wearing crushed velvet pants and a sweater that falls from one shoulder, revealing a black bra strap. Her hair is twisted into a thick bun.

"Fair warning," she says. "Momma is losing her shit. She burned the steaks."

"I'll tell her I like them well done," says Greg, hanging his coat on a peg by the door.

Nothing in the kitchen has changed from the last time he was here a few years ago. Vinyl tablecloth, orange-shaded lights. Cindy still has her salt and pepper shakers lined up on a shelf: mushrooms, windmills, tiny Coca-Cola bottles—so many ways to sprinkle flavor into life. The room smells like charred meat and boiled vegetables.

When Cindy comes fluttering over from the oven, she's already apologizing. "I don't know what I was thinking," she says. "When's the last time I made a damn steak? We're not big on homecooked meals in this house. Lot of sandwiches around here. Lot of soup from the can. But don't you look handsome? Look how handsome he is, Ange."

He spent half an hour staring at the clothes he brought home for break before settling on jeans and a gray sweater.

"Girls must go crazy for you down at school, Greggie. You turned into a real hunk."

"Calm down, Momma. He's too young for you."

"Not for you."

Greg stares at the floor, terrified of the expression he might see on Angela's face. He wasted so much time in high school imagining what it would be like to kiss her. Playing a mediator role in her on-again, off-again relationship with Henry—who he also fantasized about—was a unique sort of torture. He wonders if she ever intuited any of the muddled, jealous thoughts that raced through his mind every time he had to watch them nuzzle up together in the school cafeteria.

"What can I do to help, Cindy?" he asks.

"Don't be ridiculous, you're the guest. Sit. Get him somethin' boozy, Ange—trust me, he's going to need it. And don't worry about the legality, there aren't any snitches here. Twenty-one's just a guideline, anyway."

Greg accepts the glass of red wine from Angela, who gives him a look that clearly says what she so often used to proclaim about her mother when they were younger. *Momma's a maniac.* Maybe it's the familiarity of that look, or the first sip of alcohol, that eases the knot in his stomach.

Soon, the three of them are sitting around the table just like they used to when he would come over to do homework, he and Angela beside each other with Cindy across from them. She used to smoke one cigarette after the next while they struggled to figure out algebraic equations, promising them they would never have to use any of it in their real lives. Sometimes, as far back as middle school, she would let them take sips of coffee brandy, which made them feel adult and important. Maybe Angela thinks her mother is a maniac, but Greg always thought she was the epitome of a Cool Mom. Or at least cooler than his own mother, who keeps her Zema locked in a cabinet above the fridge.

Cindy asks about his classes, his friends, his love life ("I just can't get over what a cutie you are"). Greg talks about the orchids he's been nursing in the university greenhouses, David's tendency to leave towels on their bathroom floor. He pretends he has nothing to say about dating. The longer the conversation unwinds, the more relaxed he feels. Not enough, though, to talk about anything like that.

The green beans are watery, the steak like leather. But unlike Greg's mother, who frets when she leaves too many lumps in the mashed potatoes, Cindy just laughs it off, marveling at what a failure it turned out to be.

"We all have our talents, and mine sure as hell isn't cooking. You know what I am good at, though?"

"Momma . . . "

"Nothing like that, Ange, get your mind out of the gutter. I was gonna say I'm good at taking whatever comes at me. Some people, they kick and punch against all the crap that gets thrown their way." Cindy pauses to pour herself another glass of wine, then continues. "Me, I hold my arms open and let it stick wherever it wants. That's the secret. Let the shit pile up and make you stronger."

Greg wants nothing more in this moment than to sit here listening to all the stories Cindy could tell them about her life before she was a mother. But he's guessing Angela doesn't want him hearing it. Maybe she's heard it all too many times herself. She hasn't had any wine, and Greg wonders again about the rumors. Did she really go to rehab? What was her life like at her father's house?

When Cindy starts to clear the table, Angela raises her eyebrows at Greg and jerks her head toward the hall—their old silent code for him to follow her and abandon her mother.

On their way out of the room, Greg insists Cindy leave the dishes for him. But she waves him off.

"You two go do what young, pretty people do," she says. "Enjoy it while you can. Just be sure to use protection."

"I swear to god, Momma, you should be medicated."

"There are some Trojans in my nightstand if you need them."

Every part of Greg wants to run screaming out of the house, but Angela grabs his elbow and drags him down the hall, into her room. When they were younger, they spent a lot of time here together, listening to Madonna, playing Clue, talking about the places they might go once they grew up and left Dalton. The room looks the same as it did back then—dusky rose walls, secondhand furniture—but the feeling has changed. There's something heavy here now, a sense of expectation.

"You want some?" asks Angela, reaching for the baggie of weed and some rolling papers on the nightstand,

Greg, clutching his glass of wine, considers the offer, wondering what kind of things he might be bold enough to say or do under that double influence. Maybe it's the magic potion that could take away all his self-doubt, turn him into a sweet-talking lothario. Or he could collapse into a useless puddle.

"I'm good," he says. "But if you want to, go ahead."

"Don't need your permission, but thanks. I will."

She rolls a joint, seals it with the tip of her tongue, and lights it before lying back against pillows dressed in blue.

"Honestly," she says, "I just needed to get away from her for a few minutes."

"You're too hard on her. She's great."

"You don't have to live with her. For god's sake, don't just stand there, Greg. Sit."

With a pile of clothes balanced on her desk chair, the only place left is the bed. He settles tentatively at Angela's feet. He tries to get comfortable, resting his spine against the wrought iron bed frame so he can face her. Why does he feel like such a creep? They've sat here before like this countless times—without the wine and the weed, though. Maybe that's the difference. Or maybe the difference is Angela's slender ankles, the purple polish on her toes.

"Nice sheets, right?"

He doesn't realize until she says it that he's been rubbing his hand across the soft fabric.

"Wicked nice," he says. "Cotton? Linen?"

"Fuck if I know."

She plops her feet onto his lap, flexing her toes into the top of his thighs like a cat making bread. This is new; they've never done *this* before.

"So, tell me. What kind of college romances have you actually had?"

"Nothing interesting enough to tell," says Greg.

"Bullshit. Momma's crazy, but she's right—you really have

turned into a looker. I bet you have a whole freaking fan club on that campus."

"I guess I'm just not that kind of person."

"You're sort of a prude, aren't you? God, you always acted like you were witnessing a murder or something every time Henry and I used to make out in front of you."

Now Greg's nerves are mixed with irritation. What's he supposed to say? What does she want from him? Gently, he wraps his hands around her ankles and moves her feet off his lap, setting them back down on the bed.

"Are you gay?"

The weird thing is, earlier tonight, as Greg sat at the table with Angela and Cindy, he thought he might be able to finally tell them the truth. Or at least Angela. The way she's looking at him now, though, waiting for his answer like he owes it to her, makes him feel as though he's in the middle of an interrogation. He doesn't remember her being a homophobe. But who really knows about these things?

"I should go home, Angie."

In his rush to stand up, Greg drops his glass on the bed, the crimson wine soaking into the sheets.

"Shit," he says. "I'm sorry. Do you have any club soda? I don't know if it will help, but we could try . . . "

Angela stays where she is even as the stain creeps toward her. There's a look on her face that could either be amusement or disgust. She dabs out the scorched butt of her first joint and starts to roll another.

"Don't worry about it," she says. "It's already too late."

He wants to pull her off the bed and yank the sheets away from the mattress. They should be washed, given a halfhearted chance of rescue. But Angela only lies there on the ruins as smoke swirls around her.

"Just go, Greg."

What else can he do but leave her to the destruction?

As soon as Greg slumps out of her room, Angela wants to call him back so she can fix everything she screwed up. She shouldn't have been so mean; he didn't deserve it. No other guy would have offered to wash her bedding, now beyond salvageable.

But Greg has never been like other guys. When most of the boys in their class were snapping girls' bra straps, he was carrying his Walkman through the halls, bobbing his head to the B-52s. In high school, he looked at girls' faces when he was talking to them, not their boobs, and he never accepted an invite to one of the pit parties where other kids their age treated sex as casually as a kiss on the cheek.

"Dude's a queer," Henry's asshole friends sometimes said.

Angela would try to defend Greg, but she did often wonder the same thing. Then again, she had caught him discreetly looking at her curves. She always wanted to ask Greg the question, but she was afraid his answer—whatever it was—might change their friendship forever.

So why did she blurt it out tonight? And why did she sound so angry when she asked it? She doesn't have an issue with people being gay.

Maybe it was jealousy instead of anger. Because if Greg *is* gay, that would mean Angela has no chance with him. And sitting here with him tonight, feeling things she hasn't felt since high school, she wanted a chance.

There have been times when she's wondered how her life

might have been different if she'd dated Greg instead of Henry back then. Henry was good to her, but he was nearly as boring as he was cute. Clingy, too. And a little dumb, sometimes in a way that charmed Angela and other times in a way that made her want to throw a dictionary at his head (how many times did she have to correct his pronunciation of *supposedly*?). Their relationship had its thrills—they lost their virginity to each other on Henry's ping-pong table—but Angela spent a lot of time those first two years of high school wishing she had never tricked him into dating her.

And it *was* trickery, the way she befriended his friends and then schemed with them to get him to break up with Missy Cyr. She didn't even like his friends. But they—They, as Greg would say—were the ruling clique at school, and to be part of Them was to be part of something bigger than Angela ever could have been on her own. It was ninth grade; she was sick of being a loser. A loner. She wanted to belong to something. Someone.

Before Henry, she was the Muse girl, or Cindy's girl. With Henry, she was The Girlfriend, all-important and all-knowing. No one got to him except through her. No one demanded his attention the way she could. It felt good for a while, fitting in with Them, being wanted and needed by Henry. But by the end of sophomore year, Angela was sick of the whole exhausting charade.

She had thought that by leaving town, fleeing to her father's house, she might find a way of belonging somewhere else, but here she is alone again, wrapped in smoke, adrift on wine-soaked sheets. She doesn't understand what came over her. She'd noticed the moment she opened the door for Greg how attractive he looked, and a rush of heat had swept up her neck as she watched him sip his wine, imagining his lips on her skin. But it's not like she lured him into her room with the idea of seducing him, much as Momma would have encouraged that. She did try to flirt with him, but even that came out wrong, like mockery. It's as if every instinct she used to have about anything remotely related to sex or dating or even basic human interaction was shattered the second Mason put his hands on her.

She asked the question, and Greg ran from her like she was a predator.

Angela knows a thing or two about predators. And about running.

* * *

After the night by the river, things fell apart. With no warning or explanation, Mason moved out of the garage, and Angela had to pretend like she didn't know why—she never learned exactly where he went, but there were rumors he'd gone to another relative's house down in Skowhegan. Pam kept feeding her pastries; Colie and JJ kept begging her to play Barbies; her father kept asking how school was going, unaware that Angela had started skipping two or three days each a week. While other kids in her class were prepping for SATs and filling out college applications, she was sleeping all day and breaking into her father's booze cabinet at night.

She missed her mother so much it was like a physical ache, but she couldn't bring herself to call and tell her what had happened.

She was desperate for poison, erasure, and soon enough, she realized there were plenty of other things that could help her forget—booze, coke, molly, pills in all colors. It was easy to get if you knew where to look. Things fell apart faster. The winter of Angela's senior year, she was expelled for too much truancy, which felt like something out of an Alanis Morrissette song.

Pam and her father told her if she wasn't going to go to school, she had to get a job. She bagged groceries. Got fired. Flipped burgers. Got fired.

"What do you need?" asked her father.

"What are we doing wrong?" asked Pam.

Everything, Angela wanted to say, but she knew how difficult she had made things for them—sometimes at night she heard them arguing through the thin walls, Pam's voice panicked; her father's voice resigned. Even with Mason bumming around their house, they had had a good life together before Angela came along.

"I'll try harder," she promised.

A few weeks later, she lost her job at Rite-Aid after showing up stoned one too many times. Then she stole a fifty from the cash Pam kept on hand for catering supplies. Then she scared JJ and Colie half to death one morning when they walked into the bathroom to find her high and half-dressed on the floor beside the toilet.

There was an official Sit Down after that, the adults on one side of the table, Angela on the other.

"Sweetheart," Pam said. "We can't have this sort of thing here."

"I'm sorry," said her father. His eyes darted from the twins' *Little Mermaid* placemats to the vase of daffodils on the windowsill. Never landing on Angela. "But your stepmother's right. It's not good for us. For our girls."

Our girls. Dropping her from the list of children he wanted to claim. It didn't matter that she had left her entire life behind in Dalton to be here with him; it didn't matter that she had given herself the same name as him, only spelled differently. She was no daughter of his anymore. She was just an accident he had made with a woman he was married to for about four seconds. A mistake he wished he could take back.

When Angela called her mother to admit that her father had kicked her out of his house, Momma didn't ask for explanations. Just said, "Let me come get you." Angela considered it—going home. But running back to her mother felt too easy and too shameful at the same time, and she wasn't ready, yet, to be saved.

She was desperate for something, though—forgiveness, maybe, or some kind of grace. She tried praying to her mother's God, to Buddha, Allah, Zeus, Athena, snow, rain, thunder, ancient alien overlords. She even accepted Pam and her father's offer to pay for a stint in rehab. None of it worked.

She became a wanderer; floated between Old Town, Orono, and Bangor, sleeping on random people's couches and spare mattresses. She accepted whatever drug these people gave her. Pepper-sprayed perverts who tried to take what wasn't theirs.

Then one night last September, Angela was cutting through the unlit mall parking lot on her way to the gas station that never carded her. Near the JC Penney, a shadow detached itself from the concrete wall and lurched toward her. Something about his floppy hair and the way he walked—overconfident—convinced her it was Mason, that he hadn't gone away after all but had in fact always been right there, waiting for her. She bolted, and it wasn't until the man called after her, asking her to give him a smile, that she understood he was a stranger.

From the gas station, she bummed a ride to the rez, where she spent a sleepless night in someone's woodshed. The next morning, she borrowed her father's truck—it couldn't be considered theft, she reasoned, if he had once offered it to her—and drove the long road back north. Because what else do you do; where else do you go when you're nothing, when you've fucked everything up?

You go home to your mother, who loves you anyway.

* * *

Angela rips her ruined sheets off the bed and throws them in a ball on the floor. The red spots on the blue fabric look like lonely desert islands.

As her mother snores down the hall, Angela lies on her bare mattress under fading glow-in-the-dark stars she stuck to ceiling when she was eleven and imagines Greg in his own bedroom. Not wanting to lose whatever academic edge he had before winter break, he reads a textbook in a circle of lamplight. He's probably changed out of what he wore to supper and put on something comfier—sweatpants, or gym shorts if his mother, always cold, has cranked up the furnace.

Maybe he's lying in such warmth that if Angela were to climb under the covers beside him, she would be able to feel the heat radiating off his skin, pulsing out toward her. They could lie there together while he murmurs to her names of his favorite flowers. *Peony. Hydrangea. Amaryllis. Marigold.* A floral lullaby.

Hide & Seek

Sophie sets the rules of the game. The cellar is full of cobwebs and smells like dead mice and is therefore strictly off limits. All other rooms are fair, except the kitchen, because that's home base. The seeker has to count to ninety-nine, no more, no less, and they only have five minutes to find the person hiding—if they fail, they forfeit the round. Three failures means the loser gives up all rights to the last bowl of ice cream, and the winner can have all the hot fudge they want.

"You drive a hard bargain," Nate says. "But I accept your terms."

"Close your eyes," says Sophie, backing out of the kitchen. "And don't peek, Dad, that's breaking the rules."

He covers his face with his hands and begins to count out loud, pretending he can't hear her lingering in the doorway to make sure he doesn't cheat. Finally, she runs out of the room and up the stairs. For such a tiny human, she can make an extraordinary amount of noise. He can tell by her pounding footsteps that she's headed for her room, where she will roll under the bed and tuck herself into a ball, as if shrinking herself down can also turn her invisible.

How many times have they played this game? Nate knows all her hiding places, and she knows all his (not that there are many spots a 6'4" man can disappear in an old farmhouse). The rules are always the same, with small variations—sometimes the seeker counts to one-hundred-fifty; sometimes the prize is the final brownie. But the fundamental principles apply. No peeking. Three chances. Sweet reward.

When Nate lifts the dust ruffle under Sophie's bed with four minutes to spare, she shrieks with fake surprise—this is always her first hiding spot, and he's pretty sure she does it to make him feel good about himself. When it's his turn to be found, he does the same for her, crouching conspicuously behind the couch so the top of his head peeks out.

In the second round, Sophie gets more creative. Nate has discovered her under piles of laundry, at the back of the linen closet, and in the dryer—even though it was off at the time, that one caused a panic as he imagined all the disasters that could have happened had a random spark ignited and set the machine going with her trapped inside. He usually resorts to pressing himself between doors and walls. Easy prey.

At the start of the third round, her competitive side comes out. The gleam in her eyes, the hardened set of her mouth—it's the same expression Bridget wore when she was determined to beat Nate at Monopoly. Whatever edge Sophie had earlier in the game vanishes, her patience overwhelmed by a ferocious desire to win. She races through her counting so she can catch Nate before he tucks himself away somewhere. She peeks. When it's her turn to hide, she gets sloppy, letting her feet poke out under pillows, neglecting to close doors behind her. Sometimes Nate lets her get away with all of this, but he doesn't think any kid should win every game. She needs to learn how to lose and how to be gracious about it. He feels guilty each time he pulls back a cover to reveal her pouting face, but he tells himself it's good for her. Necessary.

Usually, though, Nate forfeits on purpose. Life has already taken away enough from his girl.

Today, he throws the last round by "accidentally" knocking a shampoo bottle onto the floor of the downstairs shower. Sophie pounces on him seconds later, grinning.

"You're not very good at this, Dad."

"Maybe you're *too* good."

In the kitchen, she pours about half the bottle of fudge onto her ice cream while Nate puts away their dishes from breakfast this morning. Winter sun streams into the room, kept cozy by the woodstove. It's only noon; the rest of the day stretches ahead of them. Nate will owe Bruce for taking the New Year's Eve shift, but that's a problem for another day.

"Dad?"

He turns to see Sophie staring at him with the serious look she always has before she asks a question he won't know how to answer. *How do bees choose their queen? Where do rainbows go when we can't see them anymore?*

"What is it?"

"If you're so terrible at hide and seek," she says, "how can you be good at being a please-man? Aren't you supposed to find bad guys?"

She's pronounced it this way for as long as Nate can remember—not policeman, but please-man—and he's never been able to correct her. For one thing, it's an adorable mistake. For another, he thinks she might subconsciously be onto something, the idea that law enforcement should be made up of people trying to appease or even elate the population they're meant to keep safe.

"My job isn't all about finding bad guys. Most of the time I'm watching over good guys, making sure they're okay."

"Are most people good or are most people bad?"

"What do you think?"

"Well, I know a lot of people," says Sophie, stirring the melted remains of her ice cream. "You, Mimi, Bampy, Grampa, Nana, Rose, Brandon, Adam . . . The kids at school, all the teachers . . . And Trudy and Dr. Haskell and Vera and Alice down the road and the old lady at the Diner who gives me extra pickles and that boy who planted our flowers, I forget his name. And they're all good."

Maybe that's the trick to shining an optimistic light on the world. Keep your own universe small. Ignore war, greed, injustice, poverty, pollution, bad weather, unclean water, crimes against women and children. Leave out the Tommys—pretend they don't exist, surround yourself only with love.

Nate used to believe it could be that uncomplicated. He doesn't believe that anymore.

A couple hours later, while Sophie watches cartoons, the phone rings. Nate pauses in the middle of balancing his checkbook to answer.

"Can you believe a whole year is gone?"

Even though it's typical of Rose to plunge into a conversation like this without a proper greeting, it makes Nate feel a little off-balance every time.

"I know," he says. "Remember how slow things happened when we were little? Summer was endless. And wasn't it about a decade from December first to Christmas?"

"Right? I swear kid-time is different than adult-time," says Rose. "So, listen. This is usually the boys' day with Tommy, but for God-knows what reason, his mother just showed up out of the blue—"

"How long's it been since she last came around?"

"Not long enough. Anyway, Adam and Brandon are cute, don't get me wrong, but they're starting to drive me nuts out here by myself. You feel like an impromptu New Year's Eve party?"

Nate hasn't seen Rose since a couple days before Christmas, when she stopped by the station to give him a loaf of banana bread, still warm from the oven, and a big book of science facts for Sophie. He's thought of her every day since, wondering how she's coping with Tommy losing his job (news spreads fast in Dalton). A couple times, he considered calling to ask if she wanted to talk about it. But he was afraid that would be one step too far over the invisible line that has existed between him and Rose since Tommy came back to town.

"Of course you can come over," he says. "Sophie will be thrilled."

"How soon?" Rose asks.

Nate can imagine her so clearly in her kitchen—she's almost certainly wearing two pairs of socks, because the trailer is always cold. He wants to sit her down in front of his woodstove with a quilt wrapped around her shoulders. She's more than capable of taking care of herself, but he wants to do what he can to make life easier for her, even for a few hours.

Bridget is dead; Tommy is a ghost of a different nature. The world is filled with horrors and complexities Nate will never understand, and sometimes he lies awake for hours both terrified of and fascinated by the secrets his friends and neighbors keep hidden.

But maybe there are some things that remain simple.

"Now," Nate tells Rose, hoping she can hear in his voice all the words he isn't saying out loud. "Come now."

Resolution

His mother is like a spider, all skinny limbs and big dumb eyes. She slurps her coffee. She smells a little like old vodka and a lot like menthol cigarettes. Since Tommy last saw her, she's lost a couple teeth, and there's an irritating whistle behind every word she says. She keeps digging her nicotine-stained fingernails into the oily veneer of the table.

"You hear about your great-uncle? Got caught spying on some teenage girl in Prescott. His first wife was always saying what a creep he was, guess we shoulda listened." Slurp, scrape, spitty exhale. "And Aunt Lucinda. That bitch. If she really thinks she can fuck around on Ronnie and still get all his money, she's got another thing coming . . . "

Tommy would throw himself out of the window to get away from this woman. Why did he let her into the apartment? He's supposed to be with his kids right now. They should be sitting in the living room watching TV, the whole day ahead of them. He was going to make mac and cheese with Vienna sausages, the boys' favorite. He was going to let them stay up until midnight to watch the ball drop, and they were going to love him for it.

"And this is good, I heard this when I called Darla the other day. She told me, she says, 'Wanda, you'll never believe it, our cousint's been going to church, getting right with Jesus.' You know the rest of us could never stand that Cindy, especially not after she got knocked up with that half-breed . . . "

The worst part of this whole shitty day is that when Tommy

opened the door to see his mother on the landing, his first instinct wasn't to push her down the stairs or tell her to fuck off. Instead, he wanted to press his face into her neck the way he did when he was too little to know better.

The next time she pauses to take a breath, Tommy jumps at the silence.

"Why are you here?"

"Since when does a mom need a reason to visit her son?"

"Since she pissed off a decade ago."

"For fuck's sake, you were eighteen, you didn't need me around no more. Didn't want me, neither. And I only went forty minutes up the road. You could've come to visit me just as easy as I could've come to visit you."

She's always been able to do this, knock Tommy flat on his ass with cruelty that doubles as unarguable logic.

"Anyway," she says, pushing her stringy hair out of her face. "I'm on my way downstate, and seeing's how you can't get there without going through Dalton, I figured I might as well swing by and say hello."

Tommy doesn't bother pointing out she could have avoided Route 11 entirely by driving over into Houlton and hooking up with I-95 there.

"What's downstate?"

"My old friend Shirley. You remember her, she used to watch you when you were little."

"I got no idea who that is."

"Sure you do. She had parakeets. You carried them around on your shoulder."

"You're making this shit up."

"I ain't a liar."

Which is the biggest lie of all, but Tommy decides to keep quiet. Anything to make her get to the point and leave.

"Anyway," his mother says. "Shirley's got this cute place close to the beach. She says I can stay a while, get away from the County. It's really starting to bother me, these long winters. Maybe I got arthritis or something. She says it's not so bad down there on the coast."

He remembers the city perched at the edge of the dark blue sea. Hundreds of miles away, surrounded by thousands of strangers, and still he couldn't escape the curse this woman dropped on him when she squeezed him out into the world.

"Maybe you should leave Maine entirely," says Tommy.

"You'd like that, wouldn't you? Me parking my ass in Florida like all the other demented old people?"

He should probably tell her she's not old—she's only a couple years shy of fifty—but he likes the idea of her imagining herself as something ancient, useless and decaying. She stares at him hard as she lights a cigarette with shaky fingers.

"Darla tells me you got yourself fired."

BANG, just like that. A blow hard enough to knock him flat on the floor.

"It wasn't my fault."

"You got something else lined up? How's a man s'posed to pay the bills without a job? You got kids, you know, you can't just sit around doing nothing."

"Drop it, Ma."

From downstairs, they hear the infuriating, happy sounds of people eating scrambled eggs and hash browns. Tommy hasn't wanted a drink this bad in months. Maybe he could steal a nip from the can his mother is hiding in her purse.

Before he can recover from the first blow, his mother's rearing back to throw the next one, cigarette dangling out of her nasty mouth.

"You know what today is, Sprout?"

"I ain't so dumb I can't read a calendar."

She always made such a big deal about Tommy's father being born on New Year's Eve. Like it was a sign he was some kind of god.

"We should do something for him," she says. "Mark the occasion."

"Screw that guy."

"Show some respect. *That guy* was your father. He fed you, took care of you. Put a roof over your head."

"Some fucking roof," says Tommy, remembering the corrugated metal that perched on top of their shack. The way the rain railed into it like shrapnel, so loud he woke in the middle of stormy nights convinced the house was going to collapse and bury him alive.

"You were always so ungrateful for everything."

"What was there to be grateful for? You and Dad being drunk or stoned all the time? You sitting around doing jack-fucking-shit while he beat the piss out of me?"

He feels a jolt of satisfaction when his mother flinches. She finally falls silent as she turns toward the window.

After a while, she says, "It wasn't easy for me, neither. Living with a man like that."

Tommy has the same hot, itchy sensation underneath his skin he used to get whenever his father started curling one end of the belt around his fist, the other end slapping the air like an animal tongue tasting for fear. His mother almost always ran away before his father could bring the belt down on Tommy, who held in his own cries of pain as she sobbed under her covers in the other room.

Sometimes after his father left to go rage-driving around town, his mother would slink out of her hiding place and lie with Tommy on the kitchen or living room floor. She would be sticky with tears and boozy sweat, but there was something nice about it, her so close and so quiet.

Sometimes his father would come back to find the two of them curled up together, and he'd lift Tommy's mother off the floor and carry her to the bedroom, and even with the door closed, Tommy could hear everything that happened in there, the pain and the pleasure, and he would close his eyes and wish himself smaller and smaller until he was a speck of dirt on the floor—and everyone knows dirt can't hear. Dirt can't feel any kind of hurt at all.

"Why'd you marry him?" Tommy asks his mother now.

"I was pregnant with you," she says. "I didn't want to raise a baby alone. And it wasn't till after we were married that he turned mean."

"But once he did, you could've left. You could've taken me and left."

"Maybe I was stupid." She stubs out her cigarette and lights another. "Actually, no, maybe it's not that simple. He wasn't only terrible all the time, you know. He could be the sweetest man when he wanted to."

Tommy thinks back to the driving lessons. The way his father would show him over and over again how to work the stick shift and the clutch, never losing patience even though it took so long for Tommy to understand.

But those were blips, brief interruptions in the life of a drunk tyrant.

"You're right," Tommy tells his mother. "You were stupid."

"At least I had enough sense to get myself fixed so I'd never make more than one baby with him."

She's staring at a photo stuck to the fridge, a shot of Adam and Brandon holding slices of watermelon, their faces stained pink. Summer sun peeks down from the corner of the photo like one of the boys hung it there. Every time Tommy looks at it, he can feel how hot the air was that day, even though he wasn't there when Rose took the picture, which he swiped from her own fridge.

Then Tommy's mother gives the last blow, probably the one she's been gearing up for all along.

"You ever going to let me meet my grandkids?"

When she wasn't crying or moaning behind closed doors,

when she wasn't lying beside Tommy on mud-caked floors, his mother was on the couch or in a folding chair out on the lawn with a bottle of vodka clutched in her hand. She drank it like water, like she could never get enough, and the more of it she drank, the more pathetic she got. One time when Tommy was seven or eight, she made a big deal about taking him to the movies for a Mommy/Son Date Night. She carried a dozen tiny, clinking bottles in her purse and drank them one by one in the darkness of the theater. They were barely halfway through the movie when she let out a yelp like a mouse being stepped on. *I had an accident, Sprout.* She tried to whisper, but it was more like a scream. *You're gonna have to sneak me out of here.* He can still remember the pissy reek as he led her down the aisle and into the lobby, where a silver-haired woman asked kindly if he needed her to call someone. Tommy knew she meant the cops, or the government people who took kids away from their parents, and he almost said yes. Almost begged to be stolen by strangers just to get away from the stench of his mother. But in the end, he gave the woman their number, and she waited with him and his mother, passed out beside the popcorn machine, until his father showed up to bring them home.

Tommy stares at the woman sitting across from him now. She might not be old, but she really is demented. Useless.

"I'd never let you anywhere near my sons."

She leaves not long after. No goodbye hugs or wishes to drive safe. She could roll her car into a ditch for all Tommy cares.

There are hours to go before the ball drops at midnight, more than enough time for Rose to bring the boys over so the whole day doesn't have to be a waste. When he calls down to the trailer, though, all he gets is the machine. *You've reached Rose and the boys . . .* Tommy lights a cigarette and tries again. Still no answer. He finishes his smoke, tries again. No answer. He putters around, eyeing the world outside from one dirty window to the next, and calls again. No answer.

Standing in his kitchen, staring at that picture of Adam and Brandon, Tommy feels a flash of certainty. He dials another number, one he doesn't want but Rose insisted he have in case of emergencies. It rings twice before a familiar voice comes on the line.

"Hello?"

Tommy ignores Nate and closes his eyes, concentrating on the background noise.

"Anybody there?"

The sound of kids' laughter ripples over the phone lines. And in some ways, Tommy might be as stupid as his mother, but he's not a complete idiot. He'd know that sound anywhere. It's Adam and Brandon. There at that house with *him* when they should be here in this apartment with their own father.

"Hell—"

Tommy slams the phone down. That burning itch is rippling all along his body; his skin is too tight. He can imagine it so clear—his father's gun beneath the blankets, in the chest behind the couch. He can feel the weight of it in his arms. The cool metal against his fingertips. The click of the safety turned off.

He scrubs the mug his mother used. Buries her cigarette butts in the trash. When he opens the freezer to grab a TV dinner, Tommy's rage turns to something else. Fear, maybe, or dread, but also the same sort of excitement he used to get when they served bikker-batter bread in the school cafeteria. The lunch ladies only made it a few times a year, always as a surprise, and he knew to make the warm, sweet, pillowy dough, topped with cinnamon-sugar glaze, last as long as he could. That sort of goodness can't just be scarfed down. It's got to be savored.

The bottle of vodka is standing tall in the middle of the freezer. His mother must've left it there for him when he went to the bathroom. Her sick way of apologizing? Or her even sicker way of getting revenge on him for not giving her what she wanted?

Whatever the reason, it's here now, and Tommy is alone in an apartment growing dimmer as the sun plummets behind the rooftops, the trees, the far-off hills. An icy breeze rolls out of the freezer, kisses his face.

If Rose finds out, that's it. He'll lose everything.

But how would she ever know? No one is here. It's only him, and this bottle, and all the light, disappearing.

Beneath the stars, the snow on the ground is tinted a bluish-green color that reminds Rose of oceans she will never visit, warm water lapping against palm trees and sandy beaches. Weird, to think of tropical places far from here, where it's so cold she can blow her breath like smoke rings toward the evergreens that border Nate's yard. Even weirder to imagine herself on some island while Adam, Brandon, and Sophie screech into the night as they chase each other up and down snowbanks.

Seated on the porch beside her, Nate nudges Rose with his shoulder, the slippery material of their jackets rubbing together.

"I thought they would've tuckered themselves out by now," he says. "Maybe we should make them go in and get warmed up."

"Or we go inside and let them stay out here, get as wild as they want."

"They'd love that. No adult supervision."

"Who do you think would take over? Adam or Sophie?"

"Is that really a question?"

To illustrate his point, Nate nods toward the snowbank that Sophie has claimed as her own. Every time Adam or Brandon tries to join her at the top, she proclaims herself Queen of the Mountain and demands they slide back down to the bottom.

"It's a good thing for girls to be assertive," says Rose. "Adam and Brandon have to learn to respect that. Their dad sure as hell never did."

As usual when she mentions Tommy, Nate's jaw squeezes

shut, as if he's trying to hold back all the words he could say against the father of her children.

"Do you mind keeping an eye on them while I go inside and make hot chocolate?"

Gentle as his voice is, it feels like rejection when he walks into the house, leaving a space beside Rose so cold and empty it might as well be one of those black holes she read about in the book she gave Sophie for Christmas. *When matter gets too close to a black hole*, the book said, *it is squeezed and stretched in opposite directions, turning into something resembling spaghetti.* The idea seemed ridiculous to Rose when she read it, but now, sitting on Nate's porch without him, she feels as brittle as the dried noodles that stick to the bottom of the pot when she doesn't get it soaking fast enough.

Why did she have to bring up Tommy? Bad enough he's tainted her own life; why does she have to spread the infestation to Nate's house, too?

Suspicious as she was when Tommy called this morning to say his mother was in town, Rose was relieved the boys wouldn't have to spend the day with him. There was guilt, too, though, especially after Adam and Brandon asked if they did something wrong, if their dad didn't like them anymore.

She tried to make the day better for them. She gave them the same over-sugared cereal they would have had at Tommy's apartment. She let them sit in front of the TV for as long as they wanted. She watched them push toy cars through the shag carpet. None of it was enough—Brandon barely spoke ten words all morning, and Adam kept smashing tiny vehicles into the walls, pretending all the pretend people inside were dead-dead-dead. He kept saying it like that, *dead-dead-dead,* in a hollow voice, until Rose thought she might scream.

It wasn't until she told the boys they were coming out here to Nate's that Brandon started talking again and Adam abandoned his fake murder spree.

She might be feeling spaghettified, but at least her kids are happy, Rose thinks as she watches them bring armfuls of snowballs up Sophie's mountain. The pompom on Brandon's hat is barely hanging on, Adam is growing out of his coat, and it's only a matter of time before they realize their father is a piece of garbage. But at least they're smiling now, laying those snowballs at Sophie's feet. No black holes for them here under the stars on Davis Road. Only offerings to their Queen.

In the kitchen, Nate pours hot chocolate into five mismatched mugs, adding marshmallows to them all. When he hands Rose a cup from the Store 'N More (*Live bait! Fresh food! Good coffee!*), she watches the tiny white clouds disappear into the steaming drink, turning it all the sweeter.

"Wait," Brandon says. "We have to cheers."

"What's cheersing?" asks Sophie.

"It's what you do on holidays," Adam says. "And other special times. Right, Mum?"

Rose, who taught her boys the tradition over plastic cups of milk on Brandon's second birthday, feels pride bubble inside her chest. Moments like this, she can almost let herself believe she hasn't ruined them completely.

Adam and Brandon teach the ritual to Sophie, who loves it so much she insists they all clink their mugs together one more time, and another, and one more. Finally, Nate convinces her to bring the boys into the living room to watch a movie.

"They're the guests, Soph, so you let them choose."

"Okay, okay."

Then it's just Nate and Rose standing at the counter, where they pretend to be fascinated by the shiny red skin of some apples sitting in a Pyrex bowl. After a few moments, she can't take it anymore.

"Come on," she says. "Let's sit."

They settle at the table. From the living room comes the familiar introduction to *Beauty and the Beast.* Even without glimpsing the television screen, Rose can see it perfectly, the slow pan through a fairy tale forest doomed to turn dark and twisted. She has never understood why the enchantress had to punish everyone else who lived in the castle—it wasn't their fault their king-to-be was an asshole.

"Guess Sophie steamrolled them with the movie choice after all," says Nate.

"Actually, it's Brandon's favorite. He's been wanting to watch it for weeks, but every time we go to the library to try and rent it, it's been checked out."

For the first time since they all came back into the house, Nate smiles at her.

"It's one of our favorites, too," he says. "I love how excited Sophie gets about that room full of books. Gives me hope she's got her priorities straight."

Thanks to small-town gossip, Rose knows that Nate's father, just like Tommy's, grew up poor with parents who were no strangers to the belt or the bottle. Yet Bill Theroux found a way to rise above that crap and raise his own son right. Rose can't puzzle it out, how the blight in one family tree can contain itself to only a couple limbs while the rot in others spreads from the roots to the tips of branches.

"I'm sorry about earlier," says Nate, running his thumb around the mouth of his cup, emblazoned with the Frazier Lumber emblem. "I shouldn't have walked away like that when you brought up Tommy."

Usually, Rose would let this go with a shrug and an assurance that Nate doesn't have to worry about it. No need for them to talk about her ex-fiancé, her history of shitty choices, or any other bad thing.

But something in the house has shifted—a softening of sound, a different light.

"So why did you?" She asks, even though she's pretty sure she knows the answer. Or at least she hopes she does.

Nate stares at his clasped hands on the tabletop. "You deserve so much better, Ro."

From any other guy, it would be a line. From him, it's everything—confession, apology, question.

He's so close. All Rose would have to do is scoot her chair an inch to the left, and she could lay her head against his chest, let herself collapse into him. Just one movement, a simple letting go, and they could transform themselves into their own sort of island. Create a new universe.

"Mum?"

Spooked by Adam's voice, Rose jumps in her seat before looking over to see him standing in the doorway. He's staring at her and Nate the same way he stared at his cars earlier as he bashed them into walls. The same way Tommy would always look at Rose whenever she wore something he didn't like or breathed too loudly or spoke too softly or asked too many questions or burned the toast or spilled the coffee. Hollowness in hazel eyes. Cold, blank space. *Dead-dead-dead.*

Nate must notice the look on Adam's face, too, because he turns his attention to him in a subtle way Rose guesses he learned during one of his police trainings. Or maybe knowing how to soften someone's anger is something natural.

"What's going on, kid?"

Her son pinches his mouth the same way his father does right before horrible words spill out. Before he can speak, however, Nate rises from the table and reaches out to take his empty mug. He pours the remains of his and Rose's cocoa into the cup, zaps it in the microwave, sprinkles fresh marshmallows on top, and hands it back. Adam blinks up at him for a few silent, eternal moments; moments where Rose is sure they are hovering at the edge of a black hole, about to stretch apart into nothing.

Finally, Adam says, "That movie is for babies. Can I hang out in here?"

"Of course you can," says Nate. "Your mom was just saying she wished you would."

"That's right," says Rose, reaching for Adam's hand across the table. "I want you right here with me."

Little Talks

Trudy has never understood the frenzy around New Year's. The idea that anyone could go to sleep on the last night of December and wake up the first morning of January transformed into something new is ridiculous. You are who you are, whatever the date on the calendar. You can change your behavior, adjust your reactions to the world, but there are things that can't be altered no matter how many resolutions you make.

"Don't go getting profound on me," says Bev when Trudy shares these ideas as they unpack books at the library while the rest of town is counting the hours until midnight. "We haven't even opened the champagne yet."

"I'm just thinking out loud. And I don't know why you brought champagne. You know I hate the stuff."

"It's tradition. Don't be such a buzzkill."

Truth is, Trudy is annoyed with herself—why can't she simply be here with these books, with this woman, and let the rest of the world go on unconsidered?

But while they work, she can't stop thinking about cows. More specifically, the hay-like smell of fresh milk sipped before the sun has come up. As a child, Trudy hated everything about living on a dairy farm. Her parents were always overworked and over-worried; all her shoes were constantly caked in manure. No one expected her to carry on with the farm once she was old enough—that life was for her brother, Eddie, who didn't mind getting filthy or rubbing bag balm on cracked udders. Yet forty years later, both their parents gone, Eddie having quit the business a decade ago after a heifer dealt a swift kick to his skull (no serious brain damage, though he does sometimes forget his birthday, and how many weeks make up a month), Trudy still wakes every day expecting to find a glass of fresh milk waiting for her in the kitchen. Almost hoping for it, disappointed when it isn't there. And she doesn't even like milk. She can only assume that the strange thirst must be a wired-in reaction, an intrinsic part of herself established nearly from infancy—maybe if she'd grown up on a potato farm, she'd wake each day craving hash browns instead. Either way, it proves her theory: there are things you can change about yourself, and things you can't.

"Quit thinking, Tru. Start drinking."

"When did you turn into a lush on me?"

"Somewhere around the time you turned into a philosopher."

In the light from the desk lamp, champagne mist tendrils toward the ceiling. Bev drinks straight from the bottle—of course she forgot to bring glasses—then hands it over to Trudy, who takes one sip, then another.

"That's right," says Bev. "Fuel up for this box of psychological thrillers."

She knows how Trudy feels about most of the titles she adds to the library collection each month—one white male author after another. Sure, there are plenty of books written by women, but the ones that circulate most are in the same vein as those written by men: Cheap thrills, unsurprising mysteries. Is it such a sin that she doesn't want to read tales about muscled heroes saving the world from communism or aliens or cloned dinosaurs? Maybe she would prefer a novel about the private lives of women. Maybe she wants sex scenes that don't use terms like *throbbing member* or *pendulous breasts.* Maybe she and all sorts of other readers are desperate to read of imaginary landscapes similar to their real ones, places with recognizable people and language.

"You're getting too fired up, Tru. Take another sip."

"Are you trying to get me drunk?"

"Was that unclear? And do we really have to work right now? It's a holiday."

With each mouthful of champagne, Trudy feels lighter and fuller at the same time. They are safe here in the library, which smells of books and the memory of sunshine caught on pages, cast on words written by people who died long ago yet still live on.

Bev takes another swallow. "I'm calling it. The books can wait."

Usually, Trudy would argue—she, the steward of these books, bears the responsibility of getting them sorted, cataloged, and organized on the shelves. But Bev's right. Some things can wait.

They shift closer in the lamplight, surrounded by stories written by men who would never imagine it could be like this. Easy. Joyful. Completely unremarkable, in the best possible way. Outside, snow is falling, silver flakes caught under streetlamps; beyond the library's brick walls, cars and trucks drive down the street, tires hushing against pavement—a sound like a whisper, or a heartbeat. All over Dalton, in houses, in parked cars, at Frenchie's, people are lamenting the end of one year and welcoming a new one, making promises that won't be kept. All over town, people are singing old songs and new songs, dancing and drinking to music that might drown whatever sorrows they hold inside.

But all of that belongs to the other world, the one out there.

In here with Bev, where the world can't enter, there is only the best kind of silence—and laughter, always laughter.

There are some things you can change about yourself, and some you can't.

A few days into the new year, Bev is at the Store 'N More, in the middle of assembling Larry Briggs' usual lunchtime sandwich, when all the lights go out and the hum of the coolers abruptly shushes.

"Power's out," Angela yells from the cash register, and Bev has to suppress the Trudy-like urge to shout back that there's no need to state the obvious.

"What the hell happened?" asks Larry, clutching his bag of pastries—two donuts and one cream horn today.

"No idea."

"Jo ain't got a backup generator in this place?"

"Apparently not a working one."

Larry brings his stuff to the register, where Angela tells him he might as well take it for free, since she can't run credit cards without power. He drops a wad of cash on the counter, insisting she keep the change, and heads into the still-dark morning.

After he's gone, Angela wanders down to the deli, where Bev is already on the phone with Jo, sleepy-voiced and unusually foul-tempered.

"What do you mean the power's out?"

"I mean it's out."

"How can it be out?"

"I don't know. That's why I'm calling."

While Jo grumbles about old wiring and circuit breakers, Angela sways from one foot to the other, fussing with the hem of her blouse.

"So?" she asks the second Bev hangs up. "What do we do?"

"Jo's coming in. She says it'll be about an hour."

"Should we close in the meantime?"

Bev considers. Larry was the last of the mill crowd today, marking the beginning of the usual lull before other eight-to-fivers come in for their coffee and cigarettes.

"I guess we stay open," she says. "If anyone shows up, they can either pay with cash or come in later after the power's on to settle their bills."

She can tell by the disappointment on Angela's face that she was hoping this meant she could go home and crawl back into bed.

"Let's have some coffee before it gets cold," says Bev. "Might as well settle in and relax for a bit."

They sit in Jo's office, which has a clear view of the front in case any customers wander in. Jo hasn't put up a new calendar yet, and Bev stares at the final days of 1995, wondering how time can go so quickly and so slowly all at once.

This coming summer will mark six years without Bridget. Over half a decade, even though it often feels like it was just a minute ago Bev was visiting with her daughter-in-law out at the farmhouse, sipping iced tea on the front porch. They could talk for hours or sit for long stretches comfortably saying nothing—exactly the relationship Bev would have wished for had she ever had a biological daughter.

"Want to hear something dumb?" says Angela, nodding toward the calendar. "Momma says it's bad luck to change the pages too late. Or too early."

"My mother used to say the same thing."

"Mine would probably say this power outage is some kind of omen, too. Like it's a sign 1996 is destined to be a crappy year."

"Do you think that's true?"

"I think it's ridiculous."

Bev sips her coffee and remembers the tarot reading she and Trudy went to decades ago over in Prescott. It was a lark; neither of them believed in that sort of falderal, as Tru called it. The psychic wore a gauzy shirt with no bra, providing a clear view of her nipples under the dim red light of a room that reeked of patchouli. *You're both seeking a soulmate*, she told Bev and Trudy, who laughed when they said they were married. The psychic peered at them with sharp eyes. *People marry the wrong people all the time*, she said. *But I'm not telling either of you something you don't already know, am I?* Less than a year later, during a Girls' Weekend down in Bangor, Bev and Trudy kissed in a corner booth of a low-lit hotel bar, and finally they saw it all so clearly.

"Ridiculous things can be true," Bev tells Angela.

"Like God? Because Momma believes in him, too."

"I can't speak to that."

Angela falls quiet, seeming to consider this as she stares at the scuffed toes of her clogs. After a couple minutes, she throws her empty cup in the trash, then starts digging through the paperwork and catalogues on Jo's desk until she finds the beach-themed calendar for 1996. She pulls the old one from the wall, hangs the new one in its place.

"Just in case," she says.

Something on Angela's face—desire fighting against what might be despair, or fear, or loneliness—makes Bev feel the same protectiveness she experiences whenever Sophie grabs her hand during the scary parts of her cartoon movies. The same way she used to feel during Nate's childhood whenever he would ask if lightning could strike the tree outside his bedroom and send it crashing through the roof.

Bev wishes she could give Angela a hug. Sensing that would be the wrong thing right now, she decides instead to ask her something she didn't ask Bridget enough before she died.

"Are you okay, dear?"

A ripple of surprise moves through Angela's eyes, as if no one else in recent memory has asked her this simple question with endlessly complicated answers. Maybe it's the soft shock of it that makes her reply with what sounds like the truth.

"Not really," Angela says.

Not knowing the girl's story well enough, Bev doesn't feel entitled to give any advice or opinions on it. She thinks hard under the battery-operated security lights as she stares at the new calendar, trying to imagine what she would want to hear if she were nineteen and facing another seventy or eighty years of living in a world as cruel as this one can be.

Finally, she channels Trudy and comes up with something far from poetic, but hopefully helpful. Or at least not completely unhelpful.

"Life," she tells Angela, "can be a real son-of-a-bitch."

Proof of Life

When Nate goes into the store before his shift begins, he's surprised to find all the lights off and no other customers anywhere in sight. For a moment, he wonders if he should panic. The eerie silence, the abandoned market. Something bad could have happened here.

Then he hears his mother's throaty laugh from the rear of the store.

"Ma?"

"Nate?" Her head pops out from behind the pizza case, not revolving as it usually does, all the slices shriveled and sad. "Come on back, sweetie."

He walks to the deli, where he finds his mother and Angela Muse on either side of the counter, playing a round of Crazy 8's. When a burst of swear words echoes up from the cellar, neither of them appears bothered.

"What's going on, Ma?"

"Something screwy with the circuit breaker."

"Jo's working on it," says Angela.

Nate's first instinct is to help. There might be some magic fix he can offer to turn the lights back on. But electrical work has never been his strong suit—the last time he tried to rewire something at the house, he gave himself a shock that filled his mouth with the taste of pennies and sent sickening waves from his fingertips to the soles of his feet.

"Don't worry," says his mother. "If Jo can't figure it out, she'll call Jim Fortin, have him come take a look."

"Does seem like a good job for a hardware guy."

"Speaking of hardware guys—have you seen Greg since he's been back home on school break?"

"Just in passing," Nate tells his mother. "I cornered him at Bergeron's and asked him to come back to the house next year, plant more of those hydrangeas."

Angela's cheeks redden as she shuffles the cards, and Nate wonders if she and Greg are still friends. Maybe more than that? They're almost twenty, an age when anything is possible. He remembers so clearly pulling them both to safety that day at the river six years ago.

When Angela steps away to use the bathroom, Nate's mother turns to him. "Was Sophie excited to go back to school today?"

"More than Dad was to get on that bus, probably. I don't know how he does it, all those potholes and frost-heaves."

"It might be bad for his spine, but it's good for his spirit."

She doesn't have to say more for Nate to understand. If it weren't for Sophie, his father would sit around the house all day with nothing but televised car races and cans of beer to keep him company.

When Nate was young, his dad would take him outside whenever he could, gracefully paddling canoes and jumping over tree roots as they hiked through the woods. He was like a child himself, holding onto his enthusiasm long after Nate was tired of blackflies and sunburns. *Pretty good, kid*, he'd say with a grin as he stepped back to look at their crooked tent or after each first bite of a hotdog barely roasted over the fire. *We got it pretty darn good.*

But with each mile his father drove for the long-haul trucking company, his spine slipped into further ruin. By the time Nate was in middle school, his dad was in so much pain he had to cut back to part-time. When that became too much, he started only taking local jobs. When that was too much, he shamefully applied for disability and shut himself away on Russell Street. No more camping trips. No more river paddles. Nate started doing the work his father once did, feeling like a traitor whenever he cleaned the gutters or shoveled the driveway while his dad slumped in the recliner with a heating pad pressed to his back.

Sometimes the old Bill would shine through—he'd eat a piece of pie and proclaim it perfect; or he would watch the Fourth of July fireworks with unabashed awe—but for a long time, he was a diminished man. It wasn't until he held Sophie soon after she was born that Nate's father seemed to spark back into the person he remembered from his childhood. *Pretty good*, his dad said, grinning when Sophie squeezed her hand around his pinky. *Pretty darn good.*

More curses fly up from the store basement, and Nate has to once again fight the urge to see what he can do for Jo.

"Stop fretting," his mother says. "We've got Jim on speed-dial. Now go to work and do some actual good for this town."

That phrase keeps turning itself over in Nate's mind later as he sits in his cruiser on the side of Route 11, speed-gun at the ready.

What is considered *actual* good? Is it waving at the familiar people who drive down the road, tires spewing slush from the pavement? Is goodness tied up with tedious departmental paperwork? Or is it something more cliché and heroic, like rescuing teenagers from hypothermic waters?

Lately on these solo patrols, Nate has started to imagine Rose sitting in the cruiser with him, riding shotgun. If she were here right now and he spoke these jumbled ideas out loud, he's almost certain she would tell him he thinks too much.

Well-known vehicles pass by at responsible speeds—there goes Eddie Dawson; Dean Buckley with a load of scrap plywood in the bed of his truck; Molly Lannigan. Nate is tempted to throw on his flashers so he can get her to pull over, ask if she's seen any more suspicious activity in the woods around her house.

But imaginary Rose tells him that would be an overstep, and Nate knows she's right. He'll stay where he is, parked here on the shoulder in plain view so people have plenty of time to slow down. Is that actual goodness? Giving folks a chance to correct their behavior so he doesn't have to do it for them? Or is that just Nate's way of avoiding hard policework?

On the radio, world headlines: United States deploys troops to Bosnia. Betty Rubble is the newest Flintstone vitamin. The Motorola StarTac goes on sale.

Imagine being able to call whoever you want from wherever you are; an ongoing conversation not bound by landlines. According to reports like this, that's exactly what will happen just a few years from now. To Nate, who thinks of the twenty-first century as something that exists an eternity away, this idea of instant connection feels like something out of science-fiction, both thrilling and strange.

On the road, a dark Chevy truck: Tommy, doing exactly the speed limit as if to taunt Nate.

Leave it alone.

He turns to look at the passenger seat, expecting to see her sitting beside him. But of course the seat is empty. That's not the only reason his coffee is halfway up his throat, though. It's because the voice didn't belong to Rose.

The lilt of her vowels, the almost sing-song rhythm . . . it was Bridget. All Bridget.

He has heard her voice like this before, so clear it's as if she is pressing her lips against his ear. Talk about conversations not bound by physical distance. Until she died, Nate didn't put any stock in the idea of ghosts or hauntings. But when he hears her like this, or when he wakes in the middle of the night with the sensation of her body settling onto the mattress beside him, he has to wonder. Maybe it's her actual spirit, or maybe it's a sort of echo, the reverberation of her presence on earth. Whatever it is, Bridget lingers. Somehow, she breaks through that invisible veil between life and death to tap Nate on the shoulder and remind him to look up. Look again. Reconsider.

He lets Tommy pass by. Stays where he is, parked in the snow, until it's time to head back to the station, to document all the good nothing he did out here today.

Counsel

Sunday morning, Greg sets out on a walk through gently falling snow to the Haskells' house. The world is glittering and quiet, hardly any traffic, and if it weren't for the torment inside his brain, it would be a beautiful morning.

It's been over a week since the disastrous dinner at Angela's house. Every morning, Greg wakes up determined to call her and make it right, tell her he's sorry for freaking out on her. Every night, after not calling her, he turns off his bedside lamp feeling like he used to in high school—a lonely loser.

Maybe it wouldn't be so bad if he weren't dealing with his family on top of everything else. With Dalton's winter break over, Aimee is back in classes, leaving Greg alone at the house with his mother most of the day as she cuts and sews curtains Sarah doesn't want. "If you're bored, you should go to the store," she keeps telling Greg. "Spend some time with your dad." But the only thing worse than helping his mother reorganize pin cushions is the idea of standing in that store restocking loose screws.

When he gets to the Haskells' house, Greg pauses to examine Trudy's rose bushes, frozen but well-pruned and waiting for spring. Her entire garden is in purgatory, buried beneath snow.

"You look like the village idiot out here, Gregory."

He turns to see Trudy standing on the porch. Even though it's closing in on noon, she's dressed in a bathrobe and slippers.

"You should look in a mirror," he says.

"No respect for your elders."

Where would he be without Trudy? She basically adopted

him when he was fourteen; taught him everything she could about plants and flowers. They've spent countless hours together pulling weeds. Who knew a teenager and a librarian in her forties could be so well suited to each other? Who knew this cranky woman would change the trajectory of Greg's life, offering an alternative to what he used to believe was his destiny? Instead of hammers and nails, he will now have living, growing wonder.

In the kitchen, Dr. Haskell is sitting at the table with a pile of journals and bird books. He doesn't look much better than Trudy; both of them keep dabbing their noses with tissues and coughing into their elbows.

"Have I walked into a plague house?"

"It's just a cold," says Dr. Haskell. "We always get one this time of year."

"My husband brings it home to me from the clinic like some sort of belated Christmas present," Trudy says, sounding more amused than annoyed. "Sit down, Gregory. What do you want for lunch?"

"If you're sick, you should be the one sitting. I can make something for both of you."

"We're not dying."

"Not today, at least," Dr. Haskell says cheerfully as he marks a page about the nesting habits of redwing blackbirds.

"At least let me help."

Trudy grumbles but settles at the table while Greg pulls egg salad from the fridge. While he makes sandwiches, he listens to Dr. Haskell tell her about a seabird-spotting cruise he wants to take this summer, all the way down the coast.

"From what I've heard, we're pretty much guaranteed osprey sightings. Cormorants and gannets, too."

"Sounds good, Richard."

"Better than good."

"If you say so."

While they eat, they chat about lots of little nothings. Greg feels himself relax more with each minute that ticks by—it's so different from his own house, where every word he says is over-analyzed by his mother and every glance from his father is loaded with disappointment.

After lunch, Dr. Haskell takes his books into the living room, leaving Greg and Trudy at the table with two mugs of peppermint tea. Snow ticks against the windows. Mycroft pads into the kitchen and hops on Trudy's lap, purring while she scratches his ears.

"Okay, then, Gregory. What's got you all scrunched up?"

"What do you mean?"

"Don't pull that shit with me. I can tell when something's bothering you."

She's the only adult who knows that Greg likes girls and boys.

Greg takes a sip of tea before answering. "Angela."

"Are you still obsessed with that girl?"

"It was never obsession. I'm not a stalker."

"Fair enough. So what about her?"

Greg tells Trudy about the dinner, everything from the burned steak to the awkward chat in Angela's bedroom—without too many private details. He wraps up by mentioning how fast he ran away from Angela when things got too intense.

"I don't know why I panicked like that."

"For Chrissake, we both know you can be a bit of a drama queen. But I doubt it was as bad as you think."

"I haven't talked to her since."

"She hasn't called you?"

"No."

"You haven't called her?"

"No."

"Both of you are foolish."

They go quiet for a while, Trudy letting Greg stew in his anxiety. Why did he bolt from Angela like she was trying to attack him? That's something the fourteen-year-old version of him would have done. He thought he'd gotten better with this sort of thing—the dates with Renee, the nameless boy in the club bathroom.

"You'd think being bi would double my chances at romance," he says. "But it apparently means I get to make twice the mistakes."

"So what do you want from me?" she asks. "Life advice disguised in some clever analogy about flowers, or some straight, cold facts?"

"Cold as you can get."

"Stop being an idiot."

When Greg steps out of the house, nearly two inches of fresh snow has piled up on the ground—if it keeps going at this pace, they could have a foot or more by nightfall.

In no hurry to get back home, he walks down to the thicket of woods that separates MacGregor Field from Main Street. When he was younger, he used to come here a lot. It was the perfect spot to escape, an in-between place that separated him from the world while also keeping him firmly rooted to it. He would stand among birch trees and scrub-brush, listen to the tweet of chickadees, and let himself pretend he was someone else.

Today, the woods are snow-silent; white-silver. Trees creak in the breeze; in the leafless canopy, blue jays flit from branch to branch. The cold numbs the tips of his fingers. He breathes in, lets it fill his lungs with sweetness.

Six years ago, he came to this very spot with Angela and Henry as part of a scavenger hunt for their biology class. They were searching for owl pellets and abandoned nests. Angela found a blue egg, empty and light as air, and she cupped it in her palm, staring at it with a mix of intensity and wonder. She carried that egg as tenderly as if it were the baby bird that once slept inside it.

How could Greg ever be afraid of somebody so gentle?

He leaves the woods, walks home through snow that clings to his hair, eyelashes, and lips like tiny, icy kisses. At home, he ditches his boots and jacket in the mud room and steps into the kitchen, relieved to find it empty. Everyone must still be out at Sarah's.

His parents were pissed when Greg said he wouldn't go this time, that he was overdue for a visit with Trudy. But the thought of sitting in that silent swelter was intolerable. Let them be angry. He'll deal with it later—or he won't, and they'll just keep on going like this, nobody happy and nobody talking about it.

Stop being an idiot.

Greg reaches for the phone and dials. When Angela answers, his stomach lurches, but he makes himself stand firm.

"About the other night," he says. "I'm sorry. I don't know why I flipped out like that."

"No," says Angela. "I'm the one who should apologize, I was too pushy. I don't know why."

They have been friends for so long, but there's so much about her he doesn't understand at all.

"Do you think we could hang out again before I head back to Orono?"

As soon as Greg asks, he worries it was a stupid thing to do. He should leave her alone, forget the whole thing.

"How about tonight?"

Too stunned for any other reply, he says yes before asking if she has anything particular in mind.

"Maybe," she says.

After they hang up, Greg stares out the window, watching snow drift down from a gray sky, marveling at how fast something as insubstantial as a few thousand snowflakes can gather on the ground, turn a recognizable landscape into something new.

Stopping By

Tommy is going to ruin everything. Rose is as sure of that as she is of the existence of gravity.

She shouldn't have left Adam and Brandon with him; he'll forget to make them eat their vegetables, or he'll let them watch one of those bang-bang-shoot-em-up movies, or he'll leave them alone at the apartment while he goes out to buy cigarettes. He's not ready. She should just drive over there and—

"Breathe."

She looks up from the box of dishes she's unpacking to see Vera watching her from across the kitchen. It's an unfamiliar room for them both, empty cupboards and blank walls.

"You've got to breathe, Rose."

"I'm being selfish."

"You're not. And it's not like you're unreachable—we're two streets away."

"I'm a bad mother."

"You are not a bad mother," says Vera. "You've said it yourself. He might not win any Father of the Year awards, but he's never hurt them."

Rose still isn't sure how Tommy convinced her to leave Adam and Brandon with him while she helps Vera move. Maybe she's overwhelmed by PMS and a long week at the clinic. Or maybe it was the way Tommy suggested they use today as make up for the time he lost with the boys when his mother came to town—none of the usual hardness in his voice. What sealed the deal was the excitement on Adam's and Brandon's faces when Rose asked them if they wanted to spend a whole day with their dad.

But should she have left them? Can she trust him?

He has an interview lined up for tomorrow, a janitor gig at the biomass mill. "It's a sure thing," he told Rose. "Sully works there, he'll get me in no problem." She doubts this, but he looked so hopeful about his prospects that she couldn't bring herself to argue with him.

Vera's right—they're on Winter Street, not the moon. If Adam and Brandon need her, they can call, and Rose will be there in two minutes.

"I just worry about them," she tells Vera, who nods thoughtfully before giving her a sly smile.

"You'd be a pretty shitty mom if you didn't."

For the first time all morning, Rose laughs.

Vera's new house is small, but she bought it herself. No linoleum, only hardwood floors and plush, cream-colored carpet she can sink her toes into. Double-paned windows overlook a fenced-in lawn. The fridge has an icemaker in the door; there are two bathrooms, one with a soaking tub, and a closet big enough for all Vera's clothes. There's even a sunporch, perfect for her potted plants.

"I just don't get why you need trees in your *house*," says Rose, lugging something with spiky leaves into the corner.

"I'm giving myself oxygen for all these winter months I'll be stuck inside, wallowing."

"You're not a wallower."

"Thank god. Move that over a bit, so it gets the sunlight."

They admire all the green inside the space. Maybe Rose is imagining it, but the air does feel cleaner in here.

Declaring the room good enough, Vera leads Rose back into the kitchen, where nearly every surface is covered with boxes labeled with the contents inside. *Pots & pans. Dishware—DO*

NOT DROP. Cooking utensils. Rose never knew one person needed so many different spatulas: flat, plastic, metal, long and skinny, short and wide. But that's Vera, equipped with everything she might need. She's the same way at the clinic, where she has reorganized all the cabinets in the exam rooms, shuffling things around so the most practical, important items are easiest to reach. She's overhauled Dr. Haskell's ancient filing system, too, abandoning the "pink charts for women, blue for men" model and putting everyone's history into the same matching maroon folders.

While Vera slices bread for sandwiches, Rose places dishes into the designated cupboard. All the plates and glasses match. The only real glass Rose owns is a chipped one she found at the thrift store—the rest are jelly jars covered with Looney Tunes characters and those plastic cups Brandon likes, the ones with the attached swirly straws she can never get clean.

At a blast of car honks from the driveway, Rose looks out the window to see Alice O'Neill climbing out of her Volvo, her dopey St. Bernard clambering after her. The dog rolls in the snow, eating mouthfuls of it, while Alice points her finger, scolding. A few seconds later, the two of them burst onto the sunporch—"Shake off out here, Willie, not inside"—then they step into the kitchen, bringing the smell of cold with them. The dog rushes over to Rose, thumping his head against her belly.

"Sorry I'm late," says Alice. "Nora just *had* to have me iron her sheets as soon as they came out of the dryer. Who the hell irons their sheets anymore?"

"Who the hell irons other people's sheets? Make the old bag do it herself."

"I would, but Roger worries she'll set herself on fire. Hey, Rose, don't give him so much attention, you're only reinforcing his belief that he deserves it."

"But he does," says Rose. To prove it, she gets down on the

floor with Willard and wraps her arms around his wet fur, feeling his body shake with joy.

While she scratches the dog's ears, Vera and Alice assemble sandwiches, talking about the storm (could be a big one), plans for Vera's spare bedroom (personal gym, or maybe a home office) and some of the other ways Alice's mother-in-law has been irritating her (do they make soundproof knitting needles?).

When Vera started inviting Alice to hang out with them a couple months ago, Rose felt panicked, sure the two other women would get hip to what a loser she was and kick her out of the pack. That's how it always happened when she was in grade school. She'd be certain she had finally made a friend, and then that friend would disappear into another group of girls—the popular ones who played sports, or the weird ones who pretended to be dinosaurs at recess—and never talk to Rose again, unless it was to say something snotty in the cafeteria line.

"Relax," Vera said when Rose admitted her juvenile worries. "You're still my number one. I just got talking to Alice when she brought Nora in for a checkup, and I think she's kind of in the same boat we're in—she doesn't have a lot of other friends here in town."

It didn't take long for Rose to be convinced. She likes Alice's competent yet slightly frazzled energy, which Alice blames on her work as a writer. She also swears she used to be nicer before her mother-in-law moved in with her and Roger, which Rose believes—she's had a few run-ins with Nora McGowan, and the woman is more bitter than old coffee.

Alice clears boxes off the table, and they sit down with their lunch. Vera and Alice each have a beer, but Rose sticks with Sprite—she'd feel shitty drinking while Adam and Brandon are with Tommy. If something happens, she needs to be sober; she needs to be ready to whisk her boys away from that piece of . . .

"You're doing it again."

She looks up to see them staring at her. Vera's shirt has a

splotch of mustard on the sleeve, but she still looks more put together than Rose does on her best days. Alice, too, with her shiny hair and emerald eyes. They're in their thirties, older than Rose, but with their unlined complexions, you'd never know it. Maybe that's what you get when you're childfree by choice and happily married—or, in Vera's case, happily unmarried.

"What's she doing?" asks Alice.

"Imagining all the bad shit that might happen but probably won't."

"Damn it, I'm the writer. That's my job."

"No. I'm the mom. It's my job."

It comes out meaner than Rose intended, and it stops the other women's laughter. Usually, she would rush to say sorry, but dread is chugging into her bloodstream, in time with her heart. The boys are hurt, or hungry, or lonely—she doesn't know what it is; she just knows something is wrong.

"I'm calling them."

Nearly tripping over Willard, Rose gets up and grabs Vera's cordless phone, which she carries into the living room. Pacing between piles of boxes, she dials the number.

On the fifth ring, Tommy answers. "Yeah?"

"What's going on? How are the boys? Are they okay?"

There's a long exhale, and she imagines him smoking in the apartment even though she asked him not to.

"Everything's cool," he says. "They're watching TV."

She wants to believe him.

"No problems at all?" she asks. "Have they been fighting?"

"They got a little rowdy after you left, but then they calmed down. We're good."

She doesn't believe him.

"Put them on the phone."

Both boys promise everything is fine. They're excited to go downstairs for lunch—Adam wants onion rings, but Brandon thinks he'll stick to French fries.

When Tommy comes back on the line, he uses the voice that always used to convince Rose of anything she wanted to hear. That she was sexy, that she was right, that he was sorry for every crappy thing he'd ever done.

"I got this," he says. "I can do this."

She so desperately wishes she could believe him.

It's a little past 6:00 when she parks outside the apartment. The Diner is closed for the night, and it's strange to see all the second-story windows blazing with warmth while the first floor sits dark and silent.

Stepping out of the car, she hears a faint tapping and looks up to see Brandon's face pressed against the window. Even from here, Rose can see the gap in his smile from his missing teeth. Adam jumps up beside him, balancing his arm across his brother's shoulders, and the sight of them together like that, happy to see her, makes her feels like she's on one of those Tilt-a-Whirls, spinning and spinning.

Then Tommy steps behind Adam and Brandon and stands there with an expression on his face equal parts *I told you so* and *Look, Baby, look what we made*, which makes her feel another, different wave of vertigo.

Upstairs, after Adam and Brandon gush about their day—lunch in the Diner was definitely the highlight—Rose tells them it's time to get their coats on so they can head back home.

"Do we have to? Can't we just stay until our movie is over?"

"Please, Mom? It's still early. Please?"

Up against their united front, she gives in, and the boys settle on the couch in front of the television, where two dogs and one sassy cat are setting out on a cross-country adventure.

"Want something to eat?" Tommy asks Rose. "I can fry you up a bologna sandwich or something."

"I'm not hungry."

"Coffee?"

Telling herself it beats watching this movie for the thirty-eighth time, Rose follows him into the kitchen, where he pulls a jug of creamer from the fridge—French vanilla, her favorite.

"You remember?"

"Course I remember. I known you how many years now?"

Tommy brings the coffee pot and two mugs over to the table. He pours the perfect amount for Rose, adds exactly the amount of cream she would have added herself. After he hands the cup to her, he reaches for the cigarettes in his shirt pocket. Then he stops and gives her an apologetic smile.

"I swear I didn't smoke inside this time," he says. "Which is maybe why I'm craving one so bad right now."

"Hard habit to break, I guess. Go ahead."

He lays the unlit cigarette in an ashtray on the table.

"How's work?" he asks. "Still liking the clinic?"

Caught between the suspicion he's trying to manipulate her and the desire to brag about how much she loves her job—she's needed there, respected there—Rose decides to play nice but keep things cool.

"Good, you know. Not bad."

"What do you do there all day?"

"I don't know, the usual office stuff—answer phones, make appointments."

"You don't get bored? Aren't sick people gross?"

"No grosser than when I was waitressing and touching other people's ketchup-covered plates. And it's not boring. I like seeing all the people who come in."

They sip their coffee under the ticking clock. She can smell his cologne, and she feels oddly comforted by it, like it points to some kind of permanence about him. Maybe he isn't beyond repair. He's looking for a job. He's not drinking. He didn't screw up with Adam and Brandon today, and they need a father, and isn't that what Rose always used to dream of? The four of them together, the strong family unit she and Tommy never had when they were young. Something whole.

When she finishes her coffee, he asks if she wants more. "We could play some rummy," he says. "Or maybe talk, you know, like we used to?"

Rose knows what the invitation really means. It would be easy to say yes. She misses the comfort of a body against hers, the pleasure of hands that aren't her own.

Something out the window catches her attention, and she turns to see snow glinting under the streetlights. Her eyes drift toward the darkened church across the street, then further, all the way to the just-visible roofline of the police station. She imagines Nate inside manning the front counter, disappointed to work the night shift but ready for whatever might happen on his watch. She hasn't seen him since New Year's Eve, when he helped her carry her sleeping kids out to the car after midnight. She wanted to kiss him. She wasn't brave enough. He looked so tall it was like his head brushed right up against the stars.

She pushes her empty cup across the table.

"It's a school night," she says. "As soon as the movie's over, the boys and I will head home."

Tommy doesn't argue. But he's not smiling anymore, either.

Woods

Cunt, Tommy thinks the second Rose pulls the door shut after her as she steals his boys away from him.

It was the same thought he had when she dropped them off this morning and told him about sixteen times not to smoke in the apartment. The same thought he had when she called to nag him about how the day was going. The same thought he had when, down at the Diner over a plate of onion rings, Adam told him about catching Nate and Rose in Nate's kitchen all over each other.

"What do you mean?" Tommy asked. "Making out?"

"What's making out?"

"Kissing."

"Oh. Then no. No kissing."

"So how were they all over each other?"

Adam got weird then, like he felt he was supposed to lie for his mother. "I guess they weren't," he said.

When Tommy asked Brandon if he had seen his mom do anything with Nate that night, or any other night, the kid pulled one of those faces like he was holding back tears, so Tommy dropped it quick. The last thing he needed was Brandon calling Rose and telling her his dad made him cry.

Other than that, it was a good day. Sure, within an hour of being dropped off, Brandon spilled his cereal all over the floor, and Adam, angry about not being able to find the remote, threw his plastic cup across the room. And more than once Tommy got so pissed about wiping orange juice off the wall and fighting the urge to tell his kids to stop arguing about who was the best Ninja Turtle that he thought hard about that bottle of vodka his mother left in the freezer, which probably had just enough left, after what he drank on New Year's Eve, to take the edge off a little.

But Tommy kept himself together, even after finding out about Rose slutting around at Nate's house with the kids in the other room. He didn't drink; he didn't lose his patience. More than once, he got both kids to laugh, and holy shit that was a good feeling, seeing their little faces light up from something he said.

Then Rose showed up, bursting into the apartment like she expected to find Adam and Brandon duct-taped to chairs. She didn't try to hide how shocked she was to see them undamaged. Tommy could have called her out on that, but instead he made her coffee. He was nice to her; he asked her questions about her boring-ass job even though what he really wanted to ask was how often she was fucking Nate.

If she'd give it up to a pussy like that, why wouldn't she give it up to her own ex-fiancé? The father of her own children?

But when Tommy put the invitation out there for her to stay longer, maybe all night—he wasn't even gross about it, he asked like a gentleman—she rejected him. He did everything right, all day long, and it still wasn't good enough.

Bitch.

As soon as she and the boys are gone, Tommy takes the vodka out of the freezer.

He tried not to drink it that night his mother left it behind. He tucked the bottle, sealed, behind the tater tots—out of sight, out of mind. When that didn't work, he buried it in the trash can under coffee grounds and banana peels. He put himself to bed. After not sleeping for a long time, he went back to the kitchen, took the bottle out of the garbage, and opened it. Maybe the smell would be enough, he thought. Maybe it would turn him off.

But it smelled like medicine, like something that could make all the other things better, and before Tommy knew it, he was chugging it from the bottle. It was still slightly cool from the freezer, and it was like snow sliding down his throat and turning to fire as soon as it hit his belly. After it felt like enough, he put what was left back in the freezer, collapsed on the couch, and fell asleep.

When Tommy had woken up, even though his brain was buzzing and he had the post-booze sweats, he felt better than he had in months.

Now, bottle in hand again—just a sip or two, just enough to calm down—Tommy wanders into the living room and stares at the city Adam and Brandon made from scratch. Plastic skyscrapers, plastic people. He's about the smash the whole thing under his heel when the phone rings.

For a second, he's sure it's Rose calling to apologize for all the ways she's made his life miserable. But it's Uncle Stu, who Tommy hasn't seen since he got back to town.

"So listen, kid. I gotta favor."

"What kind of favor?" Tommy wonders if this has to do with a certain guy who needs to move a certain product.

"We need another man for poker tonight," Stu says. "Paul's wife won't let him come play."

"I don't know," says Tommy, both relieved and disappointed it wasn't the other thing.

"Oh, come on, princess. We won't keep you out too late."

He used to go to Stu's poker nights a lot. But he's been keeping away from it, mostly because Rose told him he had to.

He's done everything she asked. He might've lost his job, but by this time tomorrow, he'll have another one lined up. He kept the kids safe and happy today. He bought them bikes. And still Rose keeps giving him more rules and no rewards.

Screw her. She can't control every part of his life. He deserves one night for himself.

"Okay," he tells his uncle.

He finishes the bottle. What was left was barely anything, less than one quarter. It doesn't even count.

Stu lives alone in a cabin out on a dirt lane not far from the mill. He built it after Aunt Dolores left him nearly ten years ago, and he likes to brag that no broad will ever set foot in the place unless it's one of the lady EMTs come to collect his dead body. It's a man's house, the walls dressed in antlers and hides of dead animals. No seashell-shaped soap in the bathroom; no ruffly curtains or potpourri.

At the card table is a sampling of Tommy's twisted family tree: Stu, his mother's half-brother; Daryl, his father's uncle; and Rick Sturgeon, who's screwed enough women on both the Wilkins and Merchant sides that he's considered an honorary cousin.

Tommy hasn't felt this at home in years. Finally, he's among men who don't apologize for being men. When one of them needs to belch, they belch; when someone comments on Mellie Martin's tits, they all chime in with examples of better racks around town. The cabin is filled with the smell of cigar smoke and beer, which Tommy is drinking only because it would look pretty fucking weird if he didn't drink around these guys. It should be safe—not like they're going to tell on him to Rose.

"Why don't we see more of you?" Daryl asks Tommy. "You been like a ghost since you got back to town."

"His baby mama's a ballbuster," Stu mumbles around his cigar.

"Like a bitch prison guard," adds Rick.

Ignoring a weird urge to defend Rose, Tommy joins in with their laughter. "You know how it is. If I don't pretend to play her game, she'll try and take away my boys."

"Those kids are lucky to have you," says Stu. "Imagine if it was just her raising them. She'd turn them both into faggots."

His sons' faces flash across Tommy's brain—Brandon's

gap-toothed smile, Adam's hazel eyes, so much like his own. No one should get away with hinting that his boys might grow up to be queers, and he has an urge to clock his uncle across the jaw. But these are the men who helped raise him, and lifting a hand against them would be more than disrespect. It would be a sort of betrayal.

"I'm doing what I can," he says. "Showing them what they need to know."

"Good for you, man."

They play for a while. Tommy wins one hand, then two, then three. He feels good, the beer is cold, and when he lands a full house, it's like the whole universe has finally turned in his direction.

"So, I heard something interesting," says Daryl after losing another hand. "I got Phil Lannigan talking over to the bar the other night, and he let it slip his wife called the fucking brass in because she's been seeing a truck out near their place. Parked on the tote road, you know."

"Molly might be fuckable if she'd wear a bra and brush her hair once in a while."

"Shut up and listen," says Daryl. "I got Phil talking over to the bar the other night, and he let it slip she called the fucking brass in because she's been seeing a pickup out near their place. Parked on the tote road, you know."

"Probably just poachers."

"Seriously," says Tommy, counting his chips—if things keep up like this, he could walk out of here with over a hundred bucks. "Who cares?"

"I think you should care." Daryl points to the window, through which they can see Tommy's Chevy parked in the driveway. "Seems like we found our poacher."

"Half the town owns a truck like that."

"That's why it's the perfect crime. You'd blend right in."

"I got nothing to do with it."

"It's okay, man, we'll keep your secret. Just get us some deer meat so we don't have to wait till fall."

"It's not me."

"Don't get hysterical, sweetheart."

As they laugh at him, rage builds inside Tommy. A minute ago, he was happy, everything was going his way, and now these men are mocking him just like his father used to do. Shit, if his old man were here, he'd be laughing, too, telling Tommy to untwist his panties, plug a tampon up his hole. Not that his mother would be any better—that *I'm-smarter-than-you* gleam in her eyes she used to get whenever she caught him stealing change from her purse. She looked at him the same way as she sat in his kitchen the other day.

He has two choices: Fold or fight.

With his father, it was only ever fold. But he could often shut his mother up with one hard stare and a few choice words. *You're just like your daddy, Sprout. Built out of nothing but mean bones.*

"You're a bunch of assholes," says Tommy, laying down his cards. Four of a kind. "And you suck at this game."

Then Daryl reveals his hand. Royal flush. He's still laughing when he reaches across the table and scoops all the chips away from Tommy, claiming them as his own.

A couple hours later, he drives alone with the windows down. Snow flies into the cab and slaps him on the face. His wallet is empty and he's floating on three or six beers, plus the vodka he drank before he left the apartment.

Think we found our poacher.

Probably the whole town believes Tommy is the one who's been parking his truck in the woods at night, waiting for deer or moose to step out from the trees. For all he knows, the poacher really is somebody from his family. But it isn't him.

He turns down an unmarked path that follows the border

of a potato field. He drives about a quarter mile, then parks and turns off the truck. His ears are ringing. There's a beer in the cupholder; he should cut himself off, but it's too late; he's past that now. He reaches for the gun behind the seat, feeling something settle inside him as soon as he grips his hand around the wooden stock.

Tommy finishes his beer and steps into the swirling snow. A guy could die in cold like this, curl up in a snowbank, close his eyes and sleep forever. Maybe it wouldn't be so bad, buried out here under the sky. Nothing but mean bones.

If they all think he's out here shooting, he might as well do it.

Tommy holds the gun close to his heart and waits until his breathing settles—his father taught him this, the importance of stillness before you pull the trigger.

Once his pulse has slowed from a gallop to a jog, he aims the gun toward the edge of the field, the start of the forest, and starts shooting at it all.

The snow.

The trees.

The dark.

On a Snowy Evening

When Angela picks up Greg at his house that night, he walks through the falling snow toward her truck. Seeing him in the beam of her headlights, surrounded by all those swirling flakes, Angela feels one of her bursts of disorientation, as though she's been picked up, spun around, and tossed down into another dimension.

"You look nice," says Greg as soon as he's in the cab. "The red jacket, I mean. It's a great color on you."

Angela senses that if she doesn't say something back, he will worry he's crossed the same kind of line she did the other night with all her misguided attempts at flirting. It's not hard to think of what to say to him, sitting here in a green sweater under an unzipped blue coat. His hair is slightly damp, as if he's just taken a shower.

"You look good, too. Nice shirt."

"Better than the band tees I used to wear?"

"So much better. You're like a real grown-up now, Greg."

He laughs and clicks his seatbelt before asking what she has in mind for the night.

"Do you trust me?"

"As long as you don't drive like your mother."

Careful to avoid the hedges, she backs out of the driveway and heads down High Street. Where the sidewalks should be is a sweep of clean snow. The road crews haven't been out with the sand and salt for a while, and the pavement is slick, but with her winter tires, Angela feels safe.

It was such a relief when she picked up the phone earlier and heard his voice on the other line. He said he was sorry, but what happened the other night is her fault, and it was an even bigger relief to admit this to him. Even though she couldn't see him, Angela knew everything between them was okay again. Maybe the world hasn't given her much grace, but Greg always has. The day she slipped through the ice into the river, the first thing he did after pulling her from the water was to tell her not to worry about it. He made it sound like it was as easy as breathing for him to keep her safe, to drag her, mostly unharmed, away from the edge.

Angela drives out of town. On Route 11, they follow a snowplow for a couple miles, its orange lights illuminating sleeping farms and snow-topped fields. Approaching the Lannigan property, she slows, squinting through the snow until she finds the turn-off onto the logging road.

This is her favorite place to go, easy to access but seemingly untraveled by anyone else—all the nights she's parked out here, she has never seen another human soul. It's as if this spot in the woods only materializes when Angela comes near it. Like it exists just for her.

And now for Greg, too.

The road is unplowed, but less snow has fallen here under the canopy of trees, and she's able to maneuver the truck about half a mile into the forest. Greg cranes his neck to watch the woods slowly envelop them.

"You still trust me?"

"Trying to."

She parks, turns off the ignition, and cranks down her window. "Go ahead," she says. "You, too."

"It's a little nippy."

"It's not that bad."

Once his window is down, Greg turns to look at her with a *what now* expression on his face. Maybe he's expecting her to break out some weed so they can smoke a bowl. But Momma smoked the last of Angela's stash this morning, claiming it was good for the cold that hit her hard and fast a couple days ago.

"What are we doing out here?"

"Just listen."

And that's what they do. They sit together, close enough to touch but not touching, and they listen to the silence of the forest—which isn't a silence at all, but a sort of singing. Groan and rattle of tree limbs, swish of wind, tinkle of snow through branches.

"Unbelievable, isn't it?" he whispers after a while. "A place like this living right up against ours."

He doesn't have to explain for her to understand. She has often thought the forest is more than a different world—it might be the only real world. Here, life goes on as it should, in a cycle, in a rhythm. Here, animals take only what they need and nothing more; the only hurt they inflict is if it's necessary for their own survival.

"Did you know I was in rehab last summer?" Angela holds her breath, unsure if this is too intense a conversation to have now, here.

"I heard rumblings," says Greg. "But I don't put a lot of stock in rumblings."

"You'll never guess who I ran into there."

"Who?"

"Annette Frazier. You know, Bridget's mom."

"So that's where she went after she set fire to all those things on her front lawn." Greg shifts so that his arm is slightly closer to Angela's. "Nate was sort of vague about it when I'd go out to his house to work on the garden."

"Like he was embarrassed?"

"More like he didn't seem to think it was his story to tell."

Angela doesn't know what to say to that idea. She wonders if there is a definite line separating one person's story from another's, or if it would be more accurate to say that everyone's stories, everywhere, are constantly overlapping.

"So what happened?" asks Greg. "With Annette, I mean?"

"She didn't remember me. I thought she was pretending at first—you know, the hoity-toity rich person thing—but after a while I realized she really had no clue who I was. Like we'd never even met before, let alone lived in the same town. She was so far gone."

By then, though, Angela was the same way. She clung to the name Dawn during rehab, but that time it was a way to remain anonymous. She didn't want to be there, and Annette clearly didn't, either—she barely talked to anyone, spent most of her time watching the eagle nest outside her window. She wrapped her grief around herself and strutted around wearing it like a cashmere sweater.

"How long were you at the hospital?"

"Probably not long enough."

One day, Angela got so pissed off about Annette's shitty attitude and group therapy that didn't fix anything and recurring nightmares filled with the sound of crickets that she packed her bag and simply walked out of the hospital. It wasn't a locked ward. She'd gone there of her own free will, and she was allowed to leave that way, too.

It wasn't long after that the creep in the mall parking lot scared her enough to convince her it was time to give it all up and go home—so maybe in a screwed up way, rehab actually did work for her.

"Do you think," asks Greg, "you'd ever want to tell me why you went? The whole story?"

Angela stares at the snow, letting it blur her vision, and considers. This is already more than she's told anyone else, even her mother. Greg is a safe place; he won't think less of her for the drugs or anything like that. But what happened on the riverbank . . .

"Maybe," she says.

"Okay."

They sit in the singing silence until they can't stand the cold any longer, then they roll the windows back up. Angela turns the ignition on to get the heaters running.

"So you tell me something, Greg. Who decides the names of trees?"

"Shit. That's a huge question. I don't even know where to start."

"Try."

It's a precise system, he begins, an intricate history of identification. But when you get past the science and the bureaucracy, he says, here in the wild, words have no meaning. Names are nothing. None of these trees, or any trees anywhere, care about whatever names humans have assigned to them. Trees don't call themselves or each other anything. They just keep growing, centimeter by centimeter, toward the sky. Maybe someday they'll reach it, or maybe the true nature of trees is not to care if they ever do, but to simply keep on climbing.

III.
Nature

Night Shift

Never again, thinks Nate as he pours himself a cup of coffee under the fluorescent lights of the police station. Never again will he ask Bruce for a favor if it means trading one day off for three night shifts in a row.

It's disorienting to work in the dark and sleep in the light. Not exactly a healthy schedule for a kid, either, so Sophie has been staying at her grandparents' house since Thursday—an arrangement more difficult for Nate than for her, who has been loving all the movie marathons with Bampy and baking lessons from Mimi.

"We watched Lion King and ate cookies," she announced when Nate called her after supper. "I got some eggshells in the dough, but Mimi says it happens even to the best chefs. Maybe I should be a chef when I grow up."

"What happened to whale doctor? Or zookeeper?"

"There are no whales here, Dad. Or zoos."

He had one of his familiar heart-bursting moments, caught between wanting to tell his daughter she doesn't need to confine her future self to this town and begging her to never leave here. Never leave him.

Hard to believe that conversation belongs to another day entirely. It's nearly 3:00 A.M. now; all the world sleeping. Nate doesn't trust nights like this, when everything seems so still and quiet. It reminds him too much of the night Bridget died, the airlessness in the house when he opened the door to hear Sophie crying from the nursery. No baby cried like that unless something was deeply wrong. No mother was silent like that unless she was no longer there to make a sound.

Nate finishes his coffee and settles back down at the desk, where he has spent the past several hours reading old reports in an effort to stay awake.

Even without looking at the names of the assigned officers, he can tell by the handwriting and language who jotted down each note. Dyer always gives too much detail: *On Tuesday, October 18, 1994, at approximately 5:56 P.M., I, along with the Fire Department, responded to a report of an unusual odor at 12 Linden Street, belonging to Larry Briggs. After a thorough investigation, odor was traced to corpse of raccoon under the back porch.* Bruce, unconcerned with grammar or spelling, gives only the facts, with an occasional attempt at humor: *Sun 7-11-93 just past noon fender bender corner Main & High H. McGreevy on the loose again suggest new glasses or showfer.*

Every time Nate's eyes tire from staring at the pages, he glances at the window to watch snow drift down under the streetlights. Bert Junkins has been plowing sporadically all night; each time he comes down the street outside the station, Nate sees the orange lights flash off the hardware store a few seconds before the plow itself comes into view.

Ten to four.

In two hours, Chief Halstead will relieve Nate from his post, waiting for a phone that hasn't rung all night—and that's a blessing, this drawn-out boredom, because it means no one in Dalton has needed any help. Nothing terrible has happened.

To ease the strain in his back, Nate gets up and paces around the station. Coffee counter. Lobby. Closet-sized bathroom, where he refills the toilet paper and gives the sink a scrub because someone should, and he can. He avoids the break room, where the on-call EMTs and firemen often spend their night hours playing cribbage. Not a bad way to waste time, but Nate doesn't want to stray too far from the phone. Just in case.

On his fifth lap, he pauses to stand at the window. He could fall asleep here, forehead pressed against the cold glass. He misses Sophie. He's craving some of those cookies she and his mother made. He wishes he could pick up the phone and call Rose—something tells him she's awake right now, sitting at her kitchen table in a fluffy yellow bathrobe. He's not sure if she actually owns a fluffy yellow bathrobe, but it's easy to imagine. Her hair is mussed; her eyes still starry from dreams already melting away from her memory.

Does she, like Nate, dream of ghosts?

With no one around to witness his lapse in duty, he sinks into a chair and allows himself to think of Rose in ways he rarely does, mostly from a sense of loyalty to his dead wife, or to his daughter, or for no reason other than his own insecurity. Here he is, thirty-one years old, and he's only ever slept with Bridget. Only ever kissed Bridget, too. In some ways, he might as well still be a virgin.

He might be barely awake at the moment, but he's still alive.

Maybe Rose isn't sitting at her table. Maybe she's lying in bed with the blankets pulled up to her chin, staring up at the snowy treetops swaying in the wind. Maybe she's thinking of the mundane things that make a Monday morning—homework tucked into backpacks, PB&J sandwiches cut into triangles and loaded into brown paper bags.

Or maybe she's lying under the blankets musing over less tangible things, her thoughts churning like the snow outside her window. Imagining the soft pressure of Nate's mouth against her own.

A deep-throated rumble and a strobe of lights jolts Nate out of his half-doze. Strange, he thinks, watching the plow push another inch of snow out of the street and onto the sidewalks. Strange to think of Rose thinking of him, to feel as if he is inhabiting both his mind and hers, his body and hers, at the same time.

He returns to the desk, skimming more reports as the light outside shifts from black to gray. Somewhere above the snow and the clouds, the sun is rising as it always does; the earth just goes on spinning.

Forty more minutes, and he will drive to Davis Road, walk into his house, lock his gun and badge in the safe he keeps in the front hall, climb the stairs, and fall onto the bed still in his uniform. Sleep away the morning and half the afternoon.

At 5:50, the phone rings. Even though it's a sound Nate has been girding himself for all night, it hits him like a shock to the chest.

"Dalton Police," he answers. "Is this an emergency?"

"Nate?"

For a wild, hopeful moment, he thinks the voice belongs to Rose, that she's calling to tell him she's been thinking of him, too.

"Can you hear me, Nate? It's Molly."

Trying to ignore the disappointment flooding his body, he says, "Yup, I hear you. What's going on? Everything all right?"

"Oh, we're fine out here, don't want to cause a panic. But I knew it was you on duty, and I wanted to call and tell you Phil and I saw the truck again, last night. Same one that's been parking out in the woods."

"Was it parked out there again?"

"No, someone kept driving it up and down the road in front of the house." Molly pauses to tell her dogs to sit down; she'll feed them in a minute. "Must have been three or four times, right around midnight—we were checking on the horses; they get a little morose in weather like this."

"Are you sure it was the same truck? Did you see who was driving it?"

"I'm sure. It was Tommy Merchant."

The thudding in Nate's chest could be fear. Or vindication. Or both.

"How certain are you?"

"I'd know that weaselly face anywhere," says Molly. "But if you need to do your police thing and check everything out, Phil managed to spot the plate. 8401 DB."

Nate flips back through the pages of his notepad to the information he jotted down a couple weeks ago as he idled behind Tommy's Chevy at the Diner. Same plate. Same truck. Same person.

"You might also want to know that not long after we saw the truck the last time, we heard some gunshots."

"How close?"

"Hard to tell. Not close enough to spook the horses at least."

"Why didn't you report this last night?"

"We didn't see him schlepping a poached animal out of the woods, and it's not exactly breaking the law to go tooling around, is it?" says Molly. "Plus, if you cops were called out every time someone hears a gunshot in a woods town like this . . . "

It would be easy to be annoyed with her, but what she's saying is true enough.

"The last time you saw the truck," Nate asks, "was it headed toward town, or away?"

"Away."

"I'm going to look into this. Please don't mention it to anyone in the meantime."

"I'll keep my mouth shut," she promises. "But you and I both know you don't have to say something in this town for everyone to know it anyway."

A few minutes later, Chief Halstead walks into the station, bringing the smell of wet boots and acidic burps in with him. Nate, so tired a few minutes ago, is fully alert. He needs to get out of here, drive out along Route 11 to see if he can find the truck and catch Tommy in the act of whatever he's doing.

When he lays out this plan, however, the Chief looks at him as though he has lost his mind.

"Forget the fact it's snowing like a sonofabitch," he says. "If Merchant really has been out there poaching, you know it's up to the game wardens to investigate."

"But . . . "

"Write the report, leave a message at the warden's office, and go home to get some sleep."

"I just . . . "

"It's an order, Nate."

Bruce might argue with the Chief. Dyer might pretend to give in and then go rogue as soon as he leaves the station, hauling ass out to the tote road to prove his own instincts. Nate writes the report. He leaves a message at the warden's office. Then he gathers his things and steps into the morning, where snowflakes fall on his cracked lips, reminding him how desperate he is for a sweet, cold glass of water.

At the blinking yellow light on Main, he has a burst of rebellion. Bridget wouldn't take no for an answer. Rose, either. Both of them would do *something* even if they had been told by someone they couldn't. Maybe he can't push it so far as driving out to the Lannigans', but he can make a detour past the Diner, just to see if Tommy is there.

Odd, Nate thinks, when he sees the parking lot covered in over a foot of undisturbed snow. He expected to feel satisfied, or at least validated, at the absence of Tommy's truck. But as he idles on the side of the road staring at the empty lot, the buzzing adrenaline in his chest is replaced by a queasy ache in his stomach.

What would a good cop do with this proof of possible wrongdoing?

Keep the details to himself. Follow protocol. Don't bring emotion into play.

Nate's eyes ache from the blur of flakes falling around him. He doesn't know how anyone manages it, this relentless balance of right and wrong, good and bad, love and law. He starts the slow drive home, still trying to understand.

Storm Day

Rose wakes up as snow tumbles down, glittering in the Christmas lights Adam and Brandon won't let her remove from the trailer no matter how many times Marian Gallagher tries to say the season of joy is over.

The clock on the nightstand reads 4:48, too early to get out of bed and too late before the day begins to fall back asleep. Rose doesn't mind, though—she's always liked this time between true night and new morning, these dream-drenched moments all to herself while the boys sleep down the hall, floating in their own imagined worlds.

Rose's bedroom, located at the farthest end of the trailer, is always the coldest in the house, and things are no different today, even with several quilts piled on top of her. If ever there was a moment to crave another warm body curled around her own, it's now. Not just any body, though.

Nate.

She usually tries to keep these thoughts far away—it's better to ignore the things you can't have, to pretend you don't want them. But in her half-awake state, she lets herself imagine the way he might mumble her name in the dark.

When the screaming jolts her out of the limbo between dream and reality, Rose's first thought is that something is wrong; one of the boys is hurt or sick or dying or dead. Or Tommy, still angry she refused his offer last night for another cup of coffee or a longer conversation, is here to steal her kids from her, and they are begging her to rescue them.

She has never moved so fast before, out of her room and down the hall, and then there is blind panic when she sees both Adam and Brandon missing from their bunk beds. But the screaming continues, and where is it coming from, what has happened, what has Tommy done; what has she let happen?

Running into the living room, Rose finds both boys jumping in front of the TV with grins on their faces.

"Snow day, Mum!"

"Mumma! Snow day!"

"It's on the news. They rolled it across the screen. Brandon, didn't I tell you they were gonna roll it?"

They continue to hop around like frogs on speed, making plans for their suddenly wide-open day—snowmen and snowball fights and a snow fort big enough to stand up in.

Rose's heart is going to explode out of her chest like the thing from *Alien;* all that will be left of her will be bones and slippery intestines. She could shake their perfect beautiful little bodies for scaring her so bad. She could yell about inside voices and give a lecture on the need to respect mothers who leave up the damn Christmas lights even though she secretly agrees with the mean neighbor lady that it's time to take them down.

Rose crouches on the shag carpet, feeling the soft give of the trailer floor beneath her knees. "Get over here," she says, opening her arms to gather them in.

While the boys eat cereal and hold a serious debate about who would win in a fight, Captain Planet or Inspector Gadget, Rose calls Vera.

"I just saw it on Channel 8," Vera says before Rose can finish saying hello. "Don't worry about coming to work today."

"Are you going to keep the clinic open?"

"I think so. Even though the roads are a mess and most people will probably cancel their appointments, there are always those few who decide they're smarter than the weather."

"To be fair, people do have to go to work. The world doesn't stop for a little snowstorm, you know?"

"Work is one thing," Vera says, "but driving twelve miles on unplowed roads to hear me confirm you have a cold that will resolve on its own? Anyway, if patients do come in, I'll have Richard there to help me keep things on track."

"Just don't let him reorganize my desk. The last time he covered for me, I couldn't find my stapler for two days."

"I'll do my best. See you tomorrow."

"Tomorrow," agrees Rose. "I'll wear what I would've today—black tights, red dress."

"Gray pants, pink sweater for me. Now go, spend some time with your boys. Tell them I say hello."

Rose turns to see Adam and Brandon standing behind her. The Crunch-Berry cereal milk has turned both their lips faintly blue. She knows what they need from her—permission to play in the snow, promises to bring them back in to fill their bellies with soup and cocoa, things that will heat their blood and give them energy to go back out to build more snowmen, more snow forts. It doesn't matter if their father is mad at her, because he's not here. For now, it's just her and these boys, here on Larch Street.

"Bundle up," says Rose. "We're going outside."

Enjoy the Silence

Greg can't see the forest. Not as it should actually exist, anyway.

A forest should never be only one thing, but many things—pine, spruce, cedar, birch, oak, maple; bushes and bracken and last year's leaves littering the ground, giving shelter for next season's pollinators. You should be able to trace individual branches of trees from trunk to tip. You should see evidence of a million little lives that call this place home.

But right now, all Greg sees is a world turned monotonously white. Snow has covered every tree, every branch, every bush. Trees of all species are draped in white cloaks like behemoth wizards. No peek of sky. The road is gone, replaced by a white ribbon stretching far ahead and far behind the truck.

"We are so fucked," says Angela, fists clenched around a steering wheel that isn't going to steer them anywhere anytime soon.

"It's okay," Greg says, even though he's never felt less confident that things will be okay. "We'll figure something out."

"How?"

"I'm just trying to stay positive."

"Do you know how annoying that is?"

The warm intimacy that existed between them the night before disappeared the moment they woke to find themselves stranded in the middle of the wilderness. Greg wants to point out it was Angela who drove them here in the first place, her idea to go into the woods in a snowstorm. But he went along with her plan, unquestioning, and though he should have woken her up when she dozed off last night, her head on his shoulder, he let himself drift to sleep. So maybe it's his fault, just as much as hers, that they're stuck here now, out of gas.

"Try the ignition again."

"It's useless, Greg." Angela zips her coat up to her chin.

Their words turn to clouds the moment they hit the air. Both of them are dressed in several warm layers, but neither of them has a hat or mittens. Angela is wearing boots; Greg only has an old pair of Nikes, worn thin at the sole and about as effective at heat retention as a piece of construction paper.

"I'm supposed to be at work right now," says Angela.

Hope flares in Greg's chest.

"That's good," he says. "Bev will call your house, ask Cindy where you are. That will get people looking for us."

"Momma's probably in a NyQuil coma as we speak. But your parents are home, right?"

"They called yesterday to say they were going to stay at Sarah's last night. Aimee, too. And with the snow, I don't know when they'll make it back to town."

"When they do, though, they'll see you're gone and send someone out."

"Except I didn't tell them where we were going since, you know, I didn't know where we were going."

"So you do think this is my fault."

"I didn't say that."

Last night, the truck felt like a cozy den, just big enough for the two of them. Now, the cab has turned fetid, filled with the smell of stale mouths.

"Do you have any food in here, Angie? In your purse, maybe?"

"Do you see a purse in here? Have you ever in our whole lives seen me with a purse?"

"What about water? Is there a bottle in the glove compartment, or—"

"Do you seriously think I wouldn't have brought out some water if I had some? Jesus."

"You don't have to be so mean."

"You don't have to be so . . . whatever you are."

It occurs to Greg with something between hysteria and hilarity that they could actually die here, taken by hypothermia before the next log truck rolls through after the storm is finally over later today or tomorrow. Or maybe this is an untraveled road, and no one will discover the vehicle or the bodies inside it for days, or weeks, or months.

"I'm sorry," Angela says. "I'm being a total bitch about this whole thing."

"Don't be so hard on yourself. I'm feeling bitchy about it, too."

She hugs her knees to her chest; in her red jacket, she looks like a bird folding its wings around its torso, trying to keep a frail heart warm and beating.

After a few minutes, unable to watch her shivering so violently, Greg asks, "Can I?"

He waits until she says yes before wrapping his arms around her and pulling her closer, right against his body.

"I have a lighter," she says, teeth chattering. "We could start a fire."

"No firewood. It's all buried out there."

"We could use it to melt snow, then. You know, for drinking water."

"What do we use to drink it? I'm assuming you don't keep any mugs in here."

"You're right," she says. "You are getting a little bitchy."

For the first time since they woke up to find themselves marooned on this white island, they almost laugh. Angela shifts in Greg's arms so her head is tucked under his chin.

"Do you remember that day at the river?"

"Hard to forget."

"Why'd you do it? What were you thinking, coming out there after me?"

"Honestly, Angie, I wasn't thinking at all."

"Weren't you terrified?"

He remembers the terrible pain of his arms plunged into a river made of frozen knives, the terror in her eyes as she screamed, desperate for safe and solid ground. And then the horrible, helpless feeling after he pulled her out and they lay on the ice, neither of them able to move back toward land.

"Not terrified, exactly," he says. "It was more . . . disbelief. Like none of it was real. Like we were stuck inside some stranger's dream."

"Yeah," says Angela. "I know that feeling."

He wants to know what her life was like after she left Dalton, what it is now, what she wants it to eventually become. He longs to know about the drugs and the booze and the rehab and anything else that might have broken her a little bit at a time, or made her stronger day by day, breath by breath. Last night, she seemed to want to tell him at least some of it. Maybe now, as they sit here waiting for almost certain death, is the time to ask again.

Or maybe now is the exact wrong time to mention these things; maybe it's too cold to go so deep. They're not here to therapize each other, Greg thinks, almost laughing again at the absurdity of it all, how life finds ways to echo itself on and on infinitely, in a thousand strange ways.

Huddled together, they fall into silence thick as the snow that now completely encases the truck. Every muscle shivers, and their teeth clack out a desperate SOS no one outside this tomb will ever hear. That's the thing about winter dens—they are built to be private, made to stay hidden.

Interrogations

Sully's wife can't cook for shit, and her haircut makes her look like a dyke.

Shame, thinks Tommy, who remembers Tanya from high school, when she was a whole lot thinner and a little bit prettier. Hard to believe it was only ten years ago he was feeling her up under the bleachers at a pep rally as a way to get back at Rose for flirting with Keith Bergeron. Now Tanya is just a tired, angry mother yelling at her three kids to pick their toys off the living room floor. The kids, two girls and a toddler with a butterfly-shaped birthmark spread across his face, ignore her as they watch cartoons at high volume.

"Leave them alone," says Sully. "If it's bugging you so bad, do it yourself."

"Like I do everything else around here? Like I got time to cook for you and your lowlife friends and clean the whole damn house, too?"

Tommy wants to tell them, and the kids, to shut up. His head feels like it's being squeezed between two slabs of concrete, and he was nauseous even before he tried Tanya's yolky eggs. How much did he drink last night? He remembers standing at the edge of a field, shooting at the forest. The memory of how he got here is cloudy, though—flashes of snow, Merle Haggard on the radio, Sully's face blinking behind a front door window. A lumpy couch, cushions damp with what smelled like curdled milk.

Tanya is slamming cupboard doors, clanking dishes, tossing utensils into drawers. The kids turn the TV even louder.

"You ready for today?" Sully asks Tommy.

"Today?"

"Your interview."

"That's not till Monday."

"That's today."

"But your kids are here," says Tommy, feeling the same sort of confusion he gets when he wakes up in the middle of the night, not sure where he is. "If it was Monday they'd be in school."

"Storm day, idiot." Sully points at the window, where snow comes down in swoops and whirls. "Don't tell me you're too fucked up for this. I put my ass on the line for you. My boss didn't even want to give you the interview, but I told him you was a changed man. Reformed and shit."

"I won't screw it up," Tommy says, wishing he had another beer in front of him instead of Tanya's bitter coffee. "Just remind me . . . "

"Eleven-thirty. You got less than an hour."

Back in grade school, he used to be afraid of Sully, who had a talent for knowing when he could throw rocks at kids during recess without any teachers noticing. More than once, Tommy's face was the one he pelted with stones, which smacked painfully into his teeth. The only way he finally got Sully to stop was to join him, the two of them tossing pebbles at anyone who looked like an easy target.

Tanya throws the frying pan into the dishwater, suds spraying onto the counter. Her pajamas are tight in all the worst places. Tommy remembers the stink of her when he lifted her skirt under the bleachers all those years ago, the tangle of hair between her thighs. Maybe she was more attractive back then, but she's always been sloppy.

"So are you gonna be there on time or what?"

Tommy wishes he had a fistful of rocks right now. Sharp ones.

"You should buy your wife some clothes that fit," he says.

The roads are a mess; he nearly skids into two snowbanks. The Diner is closed, and the parking lot hasn't been plowed; the snow is so high Tommy has to park on the street and wade his way over to the outside stairs that lead to his apartment. Halfway across the lot, his leg gets stuck, and he has to yank it free, leaving his shoe behind him in the snow. By the time he gets to his door, his wet foot is frozen.

It's quarter to ten when he gets inside the apartment, which still smells of the coffee he made Rose the night before. *Bitch.* If she'd just said yes to another cup and stayed a little longer, he wouldn't have finished the vodka or gone out to Stu's poker night or driven to Sully's place and fallen asleep on that couch just to wake up this morning hearing Tanya's shrill voice in his ear demanding to know who the hell he thought he was, coming into *her* house and sleeping off his bender dressed only in his boxer shorts in front of *her* kids. *You some kinda pervert*? she kept asking, until Sully stumbled into the room and told her to shut up.

In his bathroom, Tommy takes off his clothes, both disgusted and comforted by the smell of his own boozy sweat. He turns the shower to full blast, but the spray never even gets warm—when he steps inside, the shock of it jumps his balls up inside his body. How many times has he told George and Arlene there's something wrong with the water heater? Aren't they supposed to be landlords; aren't they supposed to fix shit when it isn't working?

His razor is dull; he nicks his cheek and has to spend too many minutes pressing toilet paper to the cut. By the time it stops bleeding, it's 11:05. It takes ten minutes to figure out what to wear to an interview for a cleaning job at a biomass plant—he isn't even sure what biomass is. Eventually he lands on his nicest flannel shirt, jeans, and his least-scuffed pair of steel-toed boots. Another few minutes wasted looking for his keys, still in the pocket of the pants he wore last night. Then back down the stairs, into the parking lot, through his tracks in the knee-high snow, nearly tripping on the shoe he had to abandon. In the time he's been inside, the plow has made a sweep through the street, barricading Tommy's truck behind a wall of clumpy, hard snow. It's 11:20 now, no time to walk back through the lot to grab the shovel George keeps in the shed behind the dumpsters, so Tommy gets in the truck and floors it, propelling himself out of one bank and into another on the opposite side of the street. This fucking town, he thinks, these fucking road crews who can't even keep a road clear.

And still the snow keeps falling down.

He skids into the plant lot at 11:26. None of the geniuses who work here have shoveled a path to the employee entrance, where Sully told him he should go, so Tommy slogs through more snow, this time up to his thighs. By the time he pushes his way into the lobby, his jeans are soaked. But the clock on the wall says 11:28—he did it, he's here on time, it'll all work out now, easy.

"Help you, darling?"

Tommy glances over to a small office, where an older woman with fake red hair is staring at him from beside a filing cabinet. She looks vaguely familiar—maybe a cousin or sister of one of his middle school teachers.

"Looking for Chuck," he tells her.

The woman bumps the drawer closed with one big hip. "Chuck doesn't work Mondays."

"No, he's supposed to be here. I got an interview with him."

"For the engineer position?" she asks, eyeing Tommy up and down.

"Do I look like an engineer?"

"What's an engineer supposed to look like?"

"That's not what I'm here about."

"You don't mean the supervisor job, do you?"

"Janitor," Tommy says through clenched teeth. "I'm here about the janitor job."

"Oh, we filled that position."

"If they already hired someone, Chuck would've called me. Or he would've told you to call me—isn't that what you do here? Make calls?"

"I'm not a secretary."

"What the hell are you, then?"

The woman spreads her arms wide as if showing off a kingdom rather than a dinky office. "Can't you tell?" she asks. "I'm an engineer."

Tommy can't figure out if she's joking. His mother used to pull this crap all the time, say something she knew he wouldn't understand just to make him feel stupid.

"This ain't fair," he says. "Do you know what I been through to get here?"

"Nothing's fair, darling."

"You stupid cow—"

Before he can say anything else, the woman laughs, staring at Tommy with a look in her eyes that tells him he might not know who she is, but she sure as hell thinks she knows him. And then she shuts the office door, leaving him seething and alone on the other side.

A whole morning wasted, Tommy fumes as he speeds onto the road.

Fuck biomass. Fuck that cunt. Fuck Sully and Chuck and Tanya and Stu and Daryl and Ricky and Rose and Nate and all the other people in this town who love to steal his money and laugh in his face.

Main Street is almost unrecognizable—the whole world is nothing but a wash of white and gray; he can only see a few feet ahead of his truck. Until, pulsing out of the snow like some kind of beacon: neon light flooding out of the window at Frenchie's. OPEN, the sign screams. OPEN, OPEN, OPEN.

His body relaxes as soon as he steps into the bar. It's just as he remembers it, moose head on the wall, classic rock on the jukebox, floors that stick to the soles of his boots. Men he has known his whole life sit in booths and at the bar; a few raise their bottles in his direction.

Mellie Martin is tending bar. She's wearing too much makeup and not enough clothes, just like always. When Tommy settles onto a stool, she doesn't look disappointed or surprised to see him—there's not much expression there at all, really, under those eyebrows plucked too thin.

"What can I get you?"

He looks at the bottles lined up behind the bar like multicolored jewels shining under red and green Christmas lights tacked up on the wall.

"Vodka," he says. "On the rocks."

Tommy watches, almost mesmerized, as she pours two fingers' worth of Smirnoff over ice. He can barely hear the music—it might be Pink Floyd, or Zeppelin—and if anyone in the room is watching him, he's unaware of it. All he sees is that glass sliding toward him over the stained bartop, closer and closer.

Interruptions

Bev is halfway through cleaning the pizza oven when there's a sizzle and a pop, and then the sudden silence of a store with no electricity, immediately followed by a string of Jo's irritated curses.

After throwing her sponge into a bucket of greasy water, Bev makes her way up to the front counter, which Jo has been manning since Angela failed to show up this morning.

"Is it just us?" Bev asks, looking out the window and squinting through the snow to find any sign of life. "Or did the whole street get knocked out?"

"Just us. See the light over at the gas station? I bet we tripped a damn circuit again."

"How?"

"Hell if I know."

While Jo, flashlight in hand, heads down to the basement, Bev remains at the register. The weather is making her restless and gloomy, and she can feel a hot flash coming on. She wants to be home with Bill and Sophie; it seems like a personal affront that he gets to spend a day off from school with their granddaughter while she's stuck here, hands reeking of oven cleaner and sweat trickling between her breasts.

Maybe once Angela comes in—if she comes in—Jo will take pity on Bev and send her home. Though they've already tried calling the girl twice, Bev picks up the phone again. With each unanswered ring, she feels clammier and more frazzled. Being constantly late to your shift is one thing, but not showing up at all, with no explanation . . . Bev doesn't know if she should be angry or worried.

Jo stomps back upstairs, her flashlight flickering and then dying out completely as she reaches the front counter.

"I have no idea," she says. "I tried to fix it the way Jim showed me, but I can't figure out what I'm looking at down there."

"Maybe we should call him again?"

"It's just so damn humiliating. I shouldn't need a man to come rescue me."

Another day, Bev might try to give some assurance that Jim being a man has nothing to do with it—if they knew a woman with electrical skills, they would be forced to call on her, too—but as her hot flash becomes a searing wave, she can only nod in understanding. For the first time in months, she wishes she still smoked cigarettes. The act wouldn't lessen her discomfort, but it might at least distract her from it.

While Jo dials the number to the hardware store, Bev fans herself with one of the deli menus they keep tucked behind the register. The tiny bursts of cool air aren't enough; she might just be desperate enough to run out into the storm, tear off her clothes, and roll naked through the snow.

"Shit," says Jo, hanging up. "He doesn't usually close in bad weather, does he? Should we call up to his house?"

"Worth a shot."

When that call also goes unanswered, Jo slams the phone into its cradle.

"Screw it," she says. "We're half-dead here anyway. Let's just lock things up and call it a day."

In the pale storm glow seeping in through the window, Jo looks devastatingly frail, her silver hair coming loose from an alligator clip. She's run this store for over thirty years, half of that as a widow. She longed for children, but her husband, couldn't give her any. She has arthritis; she's beaten cancer twice. And yet this is the most distraught Bev has ever seen her.

It would be easy to go home to Bill and Sophie. They could romp through the snow, make a fort of blankets in the living room and watch one of the Disney movies Sophie can't get enough of. A grandparent's dream.

"Let me take a look," says Bev, walking away before Jo can stop her. Down Aisle 2, she yanks a new flashlight off the shelf, along with a pack of batteries.

The basement is refreshingly cold, drying Bev's sweat as she sweeps her beam of light across the fieldstone floor, cinderblock walls, an overhead tangle of pipes and wires. It smells damp and foul down here, like vermin bodies trapped in hidden nooks and crannies.

Bev remembers Nate as a nine-year-old gazing at a lifeless mouse cupped in his palms. He'd found it at the bottom of the bin where Bev stored her birdseed, which she had forgotten to close the night before. The sides of the bin, made of steel, proved too high and too slick for the mouse to make an escape. *In school, we learned that mice can sing,* Nate told Bev. *Not with real words, though, I don't think.* She couldn't decide if it was a small comfort or an absolute terror to think of that creature singing itself to death alone in the dark.

She has no idea what she's looking at on the circuit breaker; some of the switches are labeled but most aren't, a puzzle beyond her comprehension. Nobody tells you menopause can boil your blood and also turn you stupid. She's been collecting her own stories of these female injustices, passing them on to Trudy as she falls into The Change herself. "At least we won't suffer alone," Tru said after her first round of night sweats. But that's not much of a consolation prize when your brain grinds to a halt like a train stopped on a track.

After Bev randomly pulls a switch and the power hums back into order, she stares at the chaos before her for several moments. She has no idea what the switch is attached to or why it should have fixed the problem. No idea at all.

It doesn't seem right, when she returns upstairs to Jo's grinning gratitude, that she should take credit for such an accidental thing.

As a general rule, Trudy keeps the library open on occasions when school is cancelled due to weather—those days are often when parents are most desperate for a place to bring their kids, somewhere warm and bright and full of stories they don't need to invent themselves. But when she woke up this morning and saw the announcement on the news, she decided it was as good a sign as any to stay home and rest, let her body heal from all its recent coughs, sneezes, and sniffles. She finds it slightly embarrassing that something as insignificant as a cold should tire her out so much, but maybe that's just part of getting older. Not that forty-seven is old. But apparently, it's old enough.

"You're doing the right thing," Richard said as he tucked a blanket around Trudy where she sat propped up on the couch. "It's good to take care of yourself."

"And what about you?" she asked. "Is it good for you to drive to the clinic today? Is that you taking care of yourself?"

"It's so close, Trudy. It's not like I'm driving miles and miles."

"Accidents happen close to home, Richard."

He smiled as he handed her the remote, knowing without having to ask that she was too tired to concentrate on the novel she'd brought home from work last week.

"I'll call you when I get there," he said, and he did just that less than ten minutes later, once he was safe inside the clinic—Trudy heard Vera's bright voice behind him, asking if he'd like some coffee.

Hours have passed since then, and she's still in the same spot on the couch. Mycroft has settled on her lap, occasionally muffining his sharp claws into her thighs through the loose weave of the afghan. Her brain is mushy from talk shows; her nose is so congested she's forced to breathe through her mouth. She should eat but has no appetite. She wishes Bev were here, not to talk or entertain but to simply sit and stare out the windows as billows of snow fall to the thick white carpet already covering the ground.

When the phone rings around noon, she has just started to doze off and almost doesn't answer. It might be Richard, though, or Bevy, and if they're calling, it's because they need to tell her something. She's lucky, Trudy knows this. Lucky to have not only one partner who wants to take care of her, but two.

So, much to the cat's disappointment—he stalks away with his tail held high in the air—she lunges forward to grab the cordless off the coffee table.

"Hello?"

"Trudy?"

"Who else would it be?"

"I'm sorry, you just sound all snotty or something, and—"

"Who the hell is this?"

"Me," says the girl, as if the answer should be obvious. "Greg's little sister."

The last time Trudy saw Aimee Fortin was at the library a few weeks ago—she was tired of the books her English teacher kept assigning, she said; she wanted to read something different. Trudy loaded her up with James Baldwin, Margaret Atwood, and Edward P. Jones.

"Why the hell are you calling here? Did Gregory put you up to this?"

"Well, that's the thing," says Aimee. "See, Mom and Dad and I, we stayed out at Sarah's last night, because of the weather, you know, and we just got back to the house and Greg isn't here even though his car is. And we thought maybe he was at your place. But obviously he's not."

It takes a minute for the onslaught of words to pass through

Trudy's ears and join in her mind to form a coherent, unsettling thought: Greg should be home, but he isn't.

"Did he leave a note?"

"Well, that's the other thing—he did, but it's not super helpful, because all it says is *Went out with Angela*. Like it doesn't even say when he left. We called Angela's house, but no one's answering."

The uneasy feeling starts to ripple into something bigger, even as Trudy tries to assure herself everything is fine; this is just some misunderstanding that will turn anticlimactic when Greg inevitably walks into his kitchen with a logical explanation for everything.

"Wherever he is," she says, "I'm sure he's okay. Your brother's a smart young man."

"No shit. But what about her?"

Trudy has heard the same rumors about Angela Muse everyone else has, though she doesn't find any of the stories particularly incriminating—what kid that age hasn't experimented with drugs and alcohol? You only figure out what you need by learning what you don't want.

"Mom and Dad are freaking out. I don't know what to do with them." Aimee pauses for a moment. "I guess I'll call Sarah and see if she and Ian have any ideas. Sorry to make you worry, or whatever."

Too late, after they've hung up, Trudy realizes Aimee wasn't simply stating a fact about her parents being so upset by Greg's absence—she was asking what to do, hoping an adult would step in and lift this responsibility off her teenage shoulders.

Maybe it's an overreaction, or a fit of immunocompromised panic, but Trudy can't shake the sense that something isn't right. Something is possibly very wrong.

She calls Aimee back and tells her to sit tight, let her take care of things. Then she nearly calls the police department before changing her mind—she needs someone she trusts. Bruce

Rossignol and the Chief might be perfectly adequate policemen, but this is Gregory.

She dials Nate's number. She knows he worked the night shift, because Bev told her, and she knows that he'll be sleeping. She also knows he will answer anyway.

Relay

Nate is stuck inside a dream, the only passenger on an old Pullman train. The drapes and upholstery are a deep velvet the color of rubies; mahogany woodwork glows from a sun he can't see outside the windows. He's dressed in a tuxedo and holding yellow flowers. The clickety-clickety-clack of the train is ceaseless. When a porter appears, Nate asks him where everyone is. "Look around," the porter says. "You're surrounded." Suddenly the car is filled with strangers talking and laughing, none of them looking at him. The flowers in his hands crumble to a fine golden powder as the train rolls forward, sounding a long and lonely horn that goes on and on until Nate, waking, understands it's the phone ringing on his nightstand.

Fighting against tangled sheets, he sits up in bed and answers.

"Nathaniel," Trudy says. "I've got something that might need your attention."

As she goes on to explain her call from Aimee Fortin, the absence of Greg and Angela from their respective houses, Nate feels more alert. Snowy light leaks through the windows; the bones of the old house groan and settle.

"It probably isn't serious," says Trudy. "But just in case . . . "

Nate agrees with what she isn't saying out loud: Two nineteen-year-olds unaccounted for could either be nothing at all or the worst thing. He grew up staring into the eyes of missing children on milk cartons—it astonished him then and still does now, the idea that kids could just vanish like that. Here and gone, no explanation. No good explanation, anyway.

"Let me get in touch with some folks, Trudy. I'll see what I can find out."

Because it feels wrong to conduct any sort of policework from bed, he gets up and dressed before heading down to the kitchen. Taking his notepad from the pocket of his DPD jacket, he settles at the table and writes out everything he knows so far, which doesn't amount to much: *Call rec'd from Trudy Haskell 12:15 P.M., Mon., 1/8/96. Possible missing teens, Gregory Fortin & Angela Muse. Fortins unable to make contact. G. last seen by T. Haskell afternoon of 1/7. A. last seen ???*

Nate wills himself to ignore his panicked thoughts about all the horrible endings Greg and Angela could have met.

He calls the Fortins first, noting the relief in Aimee's voice when she agrees to pass the phone to her parents. Cheryl gives Nate too many details—what Greg ate for breakfast yesterday, what she left for him to eat last night for supper before she, Jim, and Aimee went out to Sarah's house—while Jim stays mostly quiet, only speaking when Nate addresses him directly.

"We should have made him go with us . . . " he says toward the end of the call. Then Cheryl takes over again, saying Greg has been a little upset about the B– he received in his astronomy elective.

"It was more math than science," she says. "I think that's probably why he was so . . . Do you think that's important?"

"Anything you want to tell me is important."

"He's such a good kid. Such a beautiful boy. A few times after he left town last August, I drove out past your place just to see the garden he planted for you. And it's really something, isn't it?"

Wishing he could see flowers under a summer sun instead of the blank white nothing currently outside his window, Nate tells Cheryl yes. What Greg did here, bringing all that color back into his life, is more than something. It's everything.

The next call is to Angela's house—no answer.

Remembering she works at the Store 'N More, Nate calls there, feeling the same relief at the sound of his mother's voice now as he did as a kid, calling her in the middle of the night from sleepaway camp to confess how homesick he was.

"You know, it's funny you ask," his mother says. "Angela was a no-show for her shift this morning. We've been trying to call her, too. No luck."

"Do you know where her mother is?"

"You could try the gas station. I don't know if she's working today, though."

"Where else could she be?"

"I'm not sure, sweetheart," his mother says, and he senses she is closing her eyes behind the deli counter just like he is here in his kitchen, both of them wishing they were magic enough to solve a potentially unfixable problem.

"My shift's almost over," she says. "When I get home, I'll give Sophie an extra big hug from you. Your dad and I have everything we need for her, so don't worry about us."

Nate, craving caffeine but forging ahead, calls the gas station. Ollie Levasseur answers, shouting into the phone as if it's fifty years ago and they're speaking from two different ends of a transatlantic cable.

"Cindy? No, she ain't here. She's home."

"She's not."

"Is too. I seen her myself just a few hours ago, she come in for some medicine and she told me, she says, 'I'm goin' right back home to sleep off this goddamn cold.' And Cindy, she's a lot of things, but a liar ain't one of them."

Worry is starting to nudge out any semblance of rationality by the time Nate hangs up. Where could they have gone in a storm like this? What have they done; what has been done to them? And there's nothing he can do about any of it, stranded here outside of town while the snow keeps falling, never slowing, never stopping.

He does what he should have done from the start—how have only ten minutes passed since Trudy's phone call woke him up? He calls the station, unexpectedly ecstatic when Bruce picks up after the first ring.

"Calm your tits, Boss," he says after Nate passes on all the information. "I'll head over to Cindy's right now. Stand by."

While Nate waits, he paces between the kitchen, living room, front hallway, and back. Over and over. The dimness in each room is eerie. The house is colder than usual. Greg and Angela could be anywhere; like Bridget used to say, there are killers out there, in places you'd never think to look. But there are other dangers, too—icy roads, frozen rivers, hundred-pound branches suddenly let loose from treetops.

On his sixth pass through the kitchen, the phone rings, and Nate rushes for it, pressing it hard enough to his ear to hurt.

"Cindy's fine," Bruce says. "I'm here with her at her house. She just knocked herself out with some NyQuil is all, didn't even hear the phone."

Nate squints out at the snow, thanking the silence for this one good thing, Cindy safe and sound.

"Here's the thing, though, Boss. She says—shit, she wants to talk to you herself."

There's a rustling noise, the honk of someone blowing their nose, and then Cindy is on the line, talking so fast Nate has to ask her to slow down and start from the beginning.

"Angie left last night around 8:00," she says. "She told me she was picking up Greg and they was going for a ride—I should've said no, not with the snow, but she's an adult now, isn't she? I got no power over her. I tried to wait up for her, but I fell asleep. And when I woke up this morning, I was so desperate for some cold medicine that when I didn't see her in the house I just assumed she was at work. Only then Bruce shows up and tells me all this about Greggie being missing, and . . . "

When she sputters to a stop, Nate doesn't try to rush her.

"I got a bad feeling," Cindy finally says. "I got a bad feeling about my girl."

When she starts to cry, Nate hears Bruce murmuring in the background. There's the sound of water splashing out of a tap and into a glass. Then there's another rustling noise, and Bruce comes back on the line.

"Here's what we'll do, Theroux. I know you wanna help, but the Chief says you're off duty, so just stay home and sit pretty."

Nate's first instinct is to argue—he's awake, he can be of service; put him to use and let him find those kids, wherever they are. But as he stares out at the snow, gratitude washes over him. Maybe it makes him a coward, but he doesn't want to go out in a storm like this. He doesn't want to put himself in danger when he's the only parent Sophie has left.

"Should I call the Fortins?" he asks Bruce.

"I'm gonna head over there now. Then we'll reach out to the wardens, if any of them are sober, and come up with a search plan."

Maybe it's that word—sober—that reminds Nate of Molly Lannigan's phone call into the station earlier this morning.

Hours ago, he was so certain. Now, he feels like he's back in second grade, unable to tell the difference between one shape and another.

"What kind of truck does Angela drive, Bruce?"

"Uh, let me check with Cindy . . . Yup. 1982 Chevy. Black."

"Does she happen to know Angela's license plate off the top of her head?"

More mumbles on the other end, incoherent words like an alien language. Then Bruce comes back on the line.

"8104 BD."

Nate doesn't have to look at his notes from this morning or from the day he jotted Tommy's plate number down to understand what happened. Either he didn't hear her correctly, or Molly reported it incorrectly—whatever the case, the assumption it was Tommy driving back and forth in front of her house last night was wrong. Or at least not all the way right; it's possible she and Phil saw both trucks and assumed they were the same, belonging to one, as Molly put it, weaselly-faced Merchant.

"I might know where Greg and Angela are," he tells Bruce. And he explains it all. His mistake; the truck Molly has seen on the tote road.

"Could be a false lead," he sums up. "But it's a lead worth following."

"Try not to get yourself all riled, Boss. We been doing this a lot longer'n you. It'll work out."

But they both know nobody can make a promise like that.

Personal Jesus

If the silence of a church is holy, as Momma says it is, can the same be said about the silence of a winter forest? Are Angela and Greg becoming more and more blessed the deeper they get buried under all this sparkling silver snow?

"Angie."

She's lost track of how long they have sat here; impossible to count the hours without any way to track the sun's progress through the sky. She's beyond cold; she could close her eyes and give it all up; the only thing keeping her awake is the misery of a full bladder.

"We can't just wait here for someone to find us."

If she were alone, she might do it. Let the snow cover her up. No need for an identity if you're not alive. No more memories of screaming crickets and bodies pressing you to the ground. Buried, all those things disappear, go away with you. Or maybe after your last breath, those things separate and disperse, like fluff blown from dandelions and sent reeling on the wind, lifted to the sky or drowned in the gutters. Absorbed into the universe, and then forgotten.

"Angela. I think we need to start walking."

She's not alone. Greg is here with her, holding her tight. For minutes or hours or days or a lifetime, he hasn't let her go.

Somehow, suddenly, they are out of the truck, the passenger door yawning open. They're standing in snow up to their thighs; it's seeping around the edges of Angela's boots, turning her feet to frozen blocks. The shock of it wakes her up; for the first time in a long time, she looks at Greg, really looks at him, and she sees him shivering so violently she's afraid he might shatter his teeth.

"Don't look," he says, turning to face the trees.

The sizzle of his piss into the snow is all it takes. Before Angela can unzip her jeans and squat, her own bladder lets go, and the warmth down her thighs is like heaven, just for a second, until it freezes as it hits her ankles.

When Greg turns back to her, his eyes flick down to the stain, the dribble of yellow in the snow.

"Don't worry about it, Angie."

She knows what he actually means: don't worry about a little pee, because soon we'll both be dead anyway.

"I'm so sorry," she says. "I never should've brought us here."

"It's okay," says Greg, holding out his ungloved hand for her to take. "We're just going to walk out the same way we came in."

She follows him through the snow, stepping into the deep footprints he leaves behind. All around them, trees creak and whisper and growl in the wind; there is the occasional crack of a branch surrendering to the weight of snow, crashing to the earth, where it lands with a heavy, wet *whump*.

No birds are singing, but sometimes Angela thinks she sees a flash of red through the flood of snow. Here and gone. Momma says cardinals are spirits, dead people come to visit with those they left behind, which Angela has always thought is total bullshit. If a dead person could return to earth, why would they want to be a bird? Why not something with a longer lifespan, something impervious to all the other predators in the sky and on the ground?

Time turns meaningless inside the storm. Everything is

swallowed by the snow. The world is freezing, and small, and it is built only of layers of white.

They walk on.

Her bones are heavy as cement. Even in the silence, she can hear the crickets, and she can feel the pain and panic of Mason ramming himself into her. *This*, she thought while it was happening and still thinks now, far away from it, *is how you desecrate a temple*.

And they walk on.

"I need a break, Greg."

"We can't stop, Angie. We need to keep going."

"It's too far."

"We're closer every second."

The light could belong to morning or afternoon or early evening. The snow is relentless; it has always been snowing, this is all the world has ever been or will ever be, and all they can do is keep slogging through it. Miles and miles to go; what a relief it would be, to drop down where they stand and sleep.

Something tells her Greg is leading them in circles. In a forest like this, all the trees look the same, but she's almost certain she has seen this particular tree several times before.

Not long after she arrived at her father's house, he took her out bow-hunting early one autumn morning. The forest was cool, kissed with dew, light lifting slowly into the sky. They sat in the blind a long time until finally there was the snap of a twig, the scent of animal lifted on the wind. Angela saw her before her father did—the hooves, the white spots that marked her as no longer a baby but not yet an adult. They watched silently as the doe stretched her delicate neck to nibble from low-hanging leaves. It would have been a clean shot. But they didn't even reach for their bows. When Angela looked at him after the deer had walked back into the forest, her father was looking back at her. And he nodded, and she nodded, and that was enough.

"Fuck."

Greg shouts the word into the void, which crushes it to nothing rather than bouncing it back. He has stopped walking and is staring down at the bare foot he holds in his hand. It takes Angela too long to realize the foot is his, and that it's still attached to the rest of his body. Even after she understands, she still sees it as something unconnected, an offering held out on the palm of his hand like the stale bread Momma eats at church.

"I lost my shoe," Greg says, his voice weird and hollow. "And my sock."

"So put them back on."

"They're gone."

She slogs through the snow to stand beside him, and he leans on her, still holding his bare foot, as they search the ground. He's right. No shoes or socks anywhere to be found.

"What am I supposed to do?"

Angela has never seen his brown eyes so round or so horrified, not even that day at the river when he grabbed her before the water could whisk her away and turn her to nothing but memory. She remembers him as the eight-year-old boy she decided would be her best friend the day she saw him alone at recess, searching for four-leaf clovers at the edge of the playground. *You can't find them if you look too hard*, she told him. *You have to kind of glaze your eyes and let them find you.*

"Fuck, Angie, I don't know what to do. I don't know where we are. I don't know how to keep going."

She lifts his arm and wraps it around her shoulders, accepting the weight.

"Like this," she says.

No, she said.

Not like this, she said.

Stop, she said.

As it was happening, all she could do was try to catch glimpses of the sky above Mason's head. He blocked nearly the entire cosmos, but a few times, she was able to see a patch of sunset colors—pink and ruby and tangerine, clouds the color of her mother's favorite lilac tree. When she concentrated hard, she could smell those clouds—sweet scent of springtime—and when she closed her eyes, she could hear Momma's voice.

Miracle, her mother said*, the way it comes back every year. Even after a shitty winter, these flowers just keep blooming.*

"I can't, Angie."

"You can."

"My foot's going to fall off."

"Don't be dramatic."

"Just leave me here and go find help."

"I'm not fucking leaving you, Greg. It's just a little further."

The forest doesn't end. The forest keeps on going.

A long time ago, when she was still a child, her father told Angela that a tree does not view itself as a single tree, but instead as the entire forest.

When she was a little older, while out on a walk around Dalton, her mother told Angela to pull her eyes off the ground so she could see the sky and all its evening colors.

"Hold on," Angela says to Greg. "Let's take a break."

She can feel all his muscles shaking. He's bitten his lips so hard they're cracked and bleeding. His foot is turning purple.

"We're going to die out here."

"Shut up."

She thinks he's probably right—the odds are against them. Every part of her hurts; every part of her has been hurting for a long time. But it's one thing to go into the forest alone to let it bury you, and it's something completely different to let it claim one of the only people you've ever cared about.

Ignoring Greg's ragged breath, Angela looks up to see a sky not quite as white as it was a century ago, or a second ago. The trees look a little thinner. And maybe it's a hallucination, but it seems like the snow has started to slow.

In a birch tree about a dozen yards away, there's another red flash as the cardinal reveals itself. It lands on a low branch and cocks its head in their direction.

And then it sings, just a little. A few notes, repeating and repeating and repeating.

"Break's over," Angela tells Greg. "We have to keep going."

"I'm so tired."

"We're almost out."

"I can't."

Without thinking, she presses her lips against his and breathes what little warmth she can into his shivering mouth.

"Yes," she says when she pulls away. "You can."

They haven't walked much further when she spots something solid through the trees—a house, maybe, or a sugar shack. She nudges Greg to a halt and squints toward the snow-robed trees where she saw it.

"Angie," says Greg. "I need to stop."

"Hush," she says, and she watches the forest, every nerve heightened and waiting. Her hair has frozen into ropes that crackle in the dry air. Her fingers and toes have gone numb, all the blood pooling somewhere in the cage of her chest.

Jesus, Mason said to her that night the crickets screamed. *Stop fighting it.*

Eventually she did stop fighting. But Jesus had nothing to do with it.

It was the smell of lilacs, and her mother's voice, and the memory of a deer kissing apple blossoms, and something else Angela couldn't name, some kind of stillness that rippled down from the sky like invisible waves of light, breathing for her when she couldn't remember how. Expanding, contracting, working her lungs like bellows, keeping her alive.

A few more steps. A little bit further.

Suddenly the trees end, and they're standing outside a wooden fence that stretches to the left and the right. On the other side of the fence is the structure Angela saw before. It's a stable, massive doors ajar wide enough for her to hear the snorting of horses inside their stalls. Though the sky is still low and gray, the snow has stopped falling. If her instincts are right, dusk will fall soon—any longer, and they would've been in that forest at night. Wouldn't have lasted until the next morning.

"We're okay, Greg," says Angela, not quite believing it.

Out of the corner of her eye, she sees another flash of color, yellow this time. She turns to see a long coat attached to a woman with hair the color of morning sunlight. Nothing about this woman, who Angela understands by degrees is Molly Lannigan as she emerges from the stable and runs toward them, looks anything like Momma. But in all the ways that count, this figure in the deep sparkling snow is her mother, has always been her mother, lunging over the fence to open her arms and welcome Angela back to the world of the living.

Sprout

She's working at it, Tommy will give her that much, but it isn't going anywhere. Maybe it's the Joan Jett song he can hear through the thin walls of the bar. They've been in the bathroom too long, Tommy crammed between the toilet and the sink, slippery with soap from the broken dispenser. The girl's hair has fallen to the side, and the mole on the back of her neck is freaking him out—when she moves just right, it looks like a dead spider curled up on her skin.

"That's it," she says every time she stops to rest her jaw, pulling him with her hand like she's milking a cow. "You got it, baby."

When she first sat down next to him at the bar, Tommy thought he might know her. When he asked if they went to school together, she laughed. *Like you could forget*, she said, and he laughed, too, because fuck if he was going to admit he had no clue what she was talking about. Especially not after she started pushing her tits against his arm when she leaned in to talk. *Remember that pit party with Harvey and Stacey and all them?* And Tommy could only drink and nod along, pretending to understand. She wore too much mascara, but he liked her smile, and the way she smelled like some kind of flower.

In here now, though, she only smells like sweat, and neither of them is smiling.

"That's it, baby," she mumbles, jerking her wrist to the rhythm of the song—he wonders if she's doing it on purpose. "Come on."

"It'd go a whole lot quicker if you'd just let me fuck you."

"I already told you, no. This is what I want to do."

She squeezes, a little too hard, then takes him back in her mouth. But even as she does, he feels himself go soft, and she lets out a sigh through her nose before spitting him out and rising from her knees.

"Can't say I didn't try," she says.

Then she starts fixing her hair in the mirror above the sink, singing under her breath and staring at herself with a stupid smirk. She doesn't look at him—it's like he's not here, and it will always go like this for him, lonely even when he's close enough to inhale someone else's breath.

As she turns on the faucet to wash him off her hands, Tommy comes up behind her and wraps his arms around her waist. He forces himself to kiss her on the neck even though that mole makes all the afternoon's vodka creep back up into his throat.

"Come on," he says. "Let's try again."

When she tries to squirm away, Tommy tightens his grip, and there's a moment where they stare at each other in the mirror, neither of them sure how this might go. If he wanted to, he could hurt her, take whatever he wants, and the little bit of fear in her pale blue eyes tells him she knows it.

"You really don't remember?" she asks.

"What's there to remember?"

"I was a couple years behind you in school. We were at that pit party when I was, like, fourteen?"

"There were a lot of pit parties."

"Well, at this one, I drank too much, and that pervy cousin of yours tried to drag me off to the woods. But you stopped him."

"I did?"

"You did."

Tommy drops his arms from her waist and steps away, zipping his fly. Her hair has fallen to the side again, and the mole is staring at him harder than ever. She has no idea what she's talking about. He's never saved anyone from anything.

"You don't know my name, do you?"

"Don't matter now, does it?"

He needs to puke, or maybe he needs another drink.

"Weird," says the girl. "For so long, you were kind of my hero. It was, like, the biggest story of my life. And you don't even remember."

When she leaves, he lets the vomit come up, watching from a million miles away as the mess splatters into the chemical blue water of the toilet. That smell—sour vodka and last night's beer and other unknown stomach contents—that is the smell of his childhood.

This is who you are, Sprout. Who you're always gonna be.

When Tommy steps out of the bathroom a few minutes later, he's surprised to see so many people milling around the pool table and up near the bar. Couples and groups are crowded around tables and booths, everyone laughing and talking loud enough to almost drown out a new song on the jukebox, one Tommy can't name even though he's heard it a thousand times before. Something about thunder. Some of the people look familiar—the old doctor and his bitchy wife, Ollie Levasseur, the lady from the post office—but all the other faces blur into one big blob in the neon beer signs. Under his feet, the floor feels like it's made of ocean waves, rolling on and on until he's so dizzy he could puke again, if he hadn't already puked everything out the first time.

Why are there so many people out on a Monday night, during a snowstorm? Was the crowd this thick before he and the girl went to the bathroom and he had too many drinks to notice, or did they all show up while she was failing to get him off?

Tommy stands at the edge of the room, sure the girl is

somewhere at the center, telling anyone who will listen what he could have done to her in the bathroom. Making the story bigger, telling lies—*He forced me*. Or maybe they're laughing as she tells them other things—*Couldn't stay hard*. Any second now, they'll all look at him, point their fat fingers in his face and call him a faggot or worse.

For a second, he sees it so clear it's like it's really happening: Everyone turned against him, surrounding him until he's a speck of nothing at their mercy. There's one way out of an angry crowd like that, only one thing that can blast away so much hate stacked against him, and he was dumb enough to leave it out in the truck. He hears his father's voice in his head like the crack of that shotgun itself.

Show them some goddamn teeth.

And in that moment, Tommy is ready to fight, ready to raise his fists against the whole fucking world.

Then a guy with a mustache—another name he can't remember—turns to him and grins.

"Great news, isn't it?"

"What news?"

"Those kids."

"What kids?"

"Greg Fortin and the Muse girl. Molly Lannigan found them out behind her house. They've been missing."

Tommy doesn't understand any of it—not the idea of kids gone missing, or being found, or that girl claiming he saved her from something terrible all those years ago. What pervy cousin was she talking about? He has too many to count.

Shouldering his way through clumps of people, Tommy makes his way back to the bar, where his jacket is still draped on a bar stool. Someone else is sitting there now, a blonde woman with beer foam caught on her upper lip.

"Hey," says Tommy. "I was sitting there."

The woman ignores him.

"That's my spot."

The woman keeps talking to the man beside her.

"Move your ass, you stupid cunt."

The woman laughs and leans against the back of the stool, pressing herself into the fabric of Tommy's jacket.

Tommy wonders if he's become invisible, which is the power he used to wish for when he was a kid. Invisibility meant safety. But now, his brain a half-inflated balloon and the floor trying to pitch him off his feet, surrounded by all these people talking and laughing and raising toasts to kids who made it out of the woods, Tommy realizes invisibility is just another kind of hurt. Because suddenly he's slipped past a world where everyone hates him and into one where nobody sees him at all.

He needs another drink, but Mellie is standing all the way at the end of the bar, handing out champagne to a pack of women like they're royalty, and Tommy could kill them all. Wring their necks. It's no good in a place like this. He needs another drink; he needs air; he has never felt so desperate just to breathe before.

He needs to go somewhere he can't be ignored. Somewhere people who matter might see him. Somewhere he used to be loved, or at least shown a little respect.

Hopelessly Devoted

A house made of snow is surprisingly warm—this is what Rose thinks as she sits huddled with Brandon and Adam in the igloo they have spent the past several hours building. This snow-house might actually be warmer than the trailer, which is pretty depressing if she lets herself think about it too much.

"It's good, isn't it?" asks Adam, voice hushed as he curls his body against hers.

Brandon's head falls heavier on her shoulder. "Do you like it in here, Mumma?"

Red and gold flickers from the Christmas lights outside the trailer peek through the cracks of the igloo, splashing across the boys' cocoa-stained faces.

"It's perfect," Rose says. "I love it in here."

"Could you live here forever?"

"Would it be with you two?"

"Obviously."

"Then yes. For sure, I could live here forever."

The snowy ground is more comfortable than any bed she has ever slept on. She is warm and sleepy, belly full of the grilled cheese she made for lunch. No wonder bears choose to sleep inside their dens all winter. It's a sort of magic, she thinks. Hibernation.

"Mumma?"

"Yeah?"

"I have to poop."

And the spell is broken.

On their way across the yard, Rose hears the phone inside ringing—she's heard it several times over the past few hours, but no way she was going to leave the kids unattended in a house that might collapse. If it was important, she told herself, watching the boys build walls out of snow, the caller would leave a message.

As they step into the kitchen, though, whoever is on the other line hangs up before the machine can click on. She should get one of those caller IDs, she thinks as she helps Brandon fight his way out of his hand-me-down snowsuit.

"Do a dance, do a dance," sings Adam. "Baby's gonna poop his pants."

"Don't talk to your brother like that."

"You should've given him diapers for Christmas, Mum."

"Enough, Adam."

Brandon is crying, his face red from cold or shame or panic or a combination of all three. Rose can't untangle his feet from his boots, so she picks him up under the armpits and runs to the bathroom, for once grateful for the sure footing of shag carpets.

"It's gonna fall out, Mumma, hurry!"

Just in time, she gets him on the toilet.

Adam, blocking the bathroom doorway, is still singing about diapers as Brandon, perched on the seat with his feet dangling inches off the floor, covers his face with his hands and sobs, and this, thinks Rose, is motherhood, an endless string of scenes that might be hilarious if they weren't so completely miserable and defeating.

"Poopy butt, poopy butt—"

"Damn it, Adam, go to your—"

"Guess our mom is just a slut."

Adam is glaring at her with something beyond rage.

"Where did you learn that word?" asks Rose, even though she already knows.

"I don't remember."

"When did your father teach you that word?"

"After New Year's," Adam says after a few moments. "I told him about you and Nate being boyfriend-girlfriend."

She thinks back to the night in Nate's kitchen, the way they might have been close to something, until they caught Adam watching them.

"Nate isn't my boyfriend," she says. "And even if he was, you can't use words like that. Do you know what that word means?"

Adam squirms, looking nervous. When they had a watered-down version of The Talk last year, it involved a lot of other words he found funny, but this wasn't one of them.

"Dad said it means a girl who has a lot of boyfriends." The anger in his eyes is gone now, replaced with worry. "He said, 'If your mom's screwing Nate, I guess she's just a slut now.'"

Rose doesn't know how she will ever contain it—the damage their father can do and has already done to her children.

On the toilet, Brandon cries so hard it hurts her ears. He needs to clean himself up, or she needs to do it for him, and Adam looks like he's about to cry now, too, and it stinks in here of shit and the mold that keeps growing in the hideous green tub no matter how often she scrubs it with bleach.

The front door of the trailer bursts open.

Even before Tommy shouts her name, Rose is moving for the hallway. From some deep, dark space inside her, a place beyond thinking or planning or fear, she knows exactly what to do, because she has always been ready for this—ready to greet the violence head-on, in the vain hope she can stop it before it reaches her boys.

"Stay here," she tells Adam and Brandon in her firmest Mom voice. And then she leaves the bathroom, pulling the door shut behind her.

Tommy reeks of booze and is so drunk he can barely stand upright. He's staring out the living room window at the igloo his kids made, and when he casts a blurry smile toward it, he looks almost like a child himself.

When he held Adam and Brandon after they were born, he was so soft with them. So gentle. Rose spent such a long time telling herself he could be different from all the other shitty men in his family. He could be a good husband, a good father. He could love her and the kids in the way they deserved to be loved.

"You can't be here right now, Tommy," she says, keeping her voice soft. "Not like this."

"This is my house."

"Not anymore."

"I lost everything."

"Not yet," says Rose. "Go home, sleep it off. We can talk tomorrow."

For a few moments, she thinks she's done it—convinced him there's something left to salvage, something they can work out after he's sobered up. His face softens, and he looks at her almost like he used to, back when they were teenagers.

Then the phone rings.

Tommy stares at Rose, unblinking as it goes on ringing.

Finally, the machine beeps on—*Hi, you've reached Rose and the boys, call us back if you want*—and Tommy keeps staring at her as Nate's voice fills the trailer. She wills herself to stand still even though every nerve under her skin is stretching toward the phone.

"Rose, if you're there, pick up. It's important. I need you to call me as soon as you get this."

The machine beeps, and he's gone.

When Tommy speaks, his words are thick and slow. "How long you been screwing him?"

"You need to leave, Tommy. You need to leave right now."

"I told you I ain't leaving. It's my fucking house."

"You haven't paid rent here in years. This is our house. Mine and the boys."

"Yeah—but the boys belong to me so this does, too."

He points a shaky finger around the room as if claiming every piece of furniture, every toy on the floor, every inch of wood paneling. Her.

"You don't own anything here, Tommy."

He teeters on his feet, swaying like a sapling ready to break. He looks pathetic, mean. Small.

"I done my best," he says. "It ain't fair."

He sounds so much like a kid that Rose's first instinct is to wrap her arms around him and promise him everything will be okay. There was a time she might have done just that—anything to make him feel better, anything to make him feel loved.

But she was another person then. She barely even knows that girl anymore.

"If you don't leave right now, I'll call the cops."

The same rage that was on Adam's face just a few minutes ago flashes across Tommy's now, and it's so much bigger and so much worse.

But Rose is ready for this, too. Ever since he kissed her when she was fifteen, some small part of her has always been ready for the inevitable ending of a terrible romance. This is what you get, she thinks as he comes closer, bringing his reek along with him. This is what you get when you fall in love with a boy like Tommy. This is the fate that waits for any woman stupid enough to spread her legs to create even more of them, boys who turn into men who hurt more women. Over and over and over again. Here she is, waiting, as he raises his fists.

They hear it at the same time, a click and a shushing of feet on carpet, and then—she isn't ready for this, she could never be ready for this—Rose turns to see Adam and Brandon standing in the hall, and they are both staring at their father, and what the hell is wrong with Rose that she isn't rushing toward her children to protect them from this psycho in her living room?

"Dad?"

Tommy lets out a shivery breath, takes a staggering step backward, and crumples to the carpet like a bird struck by a stone midflight. He remains there, cradling his head in his hands, as Rose ushers the boys back to the bathroom, where Brandon, snowsuit still tangled around his ankles, climbs into the tub.

"What now, Mum?" asks Adam.

"Now we wait," says Rose, shaking so hard she's afraid she might puke. "We wait."

"What are we waiting for, Mumma?"

She should hold them both close, apologize for what they just saw, what they could have seen. But she can't make her body move. She can't do anything other than sit here wedged between the bathroom door and the tub, hoping the weight of her body will be enough to keep Tommy out if he tries to follow after them.

"Mumma, why's Dad so angry?"

There isn't even a window in here they can use as an emergency exit. The only way out is past Tommy. So there is no way out.

Then Rose hears the creak of the front door, followed a few breaths later by the sound of Tommy's truck roaring to life. As it idles in the driveway, she imagines Marian peering out her windows, angry about the noise, and she's suddenly desperately fond of the old bat, the dedication it takes to watch over Larch Street hour after hour, year after year, cats brushing up against her ankles as she fantasizes about tearing down children's Christmas lights and slashing drunk men's tires. Which Rose is pretty sure Marian did one time when Brandon was still a baby, and Adam had the flu, and Tommy was in such a fury one night he locked Rose outside in the pouring rain. No other way to explain the ruined tires on Tommy's truck the next morning. No other person on Larch Street would care enough to do something as petty as that.

Rose waits until she hears the truck back out of the driveway and head down the street. Then she waits a little longer, just to be sure.

"Stay here," she tells the boys. "Don't come out till I tell you."

The living room is empty—he's gone. And that would be a good thing, except Rose has a pretty good idea where Tommy is going.

She picks up the phone and dials Nate's number, praying to all the gods she's never believed in that she hasn't waited too long.

Negotiations

I'm okay," Rose says. "Me and the boys, we're fine. He's heading your way, though. He didn't tell me, but I can just feel it."

Nate presses the phone to his ear and stares out the kitchen window. Not long ago, the clouds that had been hanging low over Dalton for days finally cleared enough to reveal an inky night sky, which he sat here watching as the good news rolled in, one call after another—Greg and Angela, found safe. Alive.

"Nate?"

He can hear the boys in the background, Brandon crying, Adam offering him a cup of juice. Every second, Tommy's getting closer. One mile, maybe two.

"I'm going to hang up now, okay?" says Rose. "I'll call the station and have them send someone your way. I'm so sorry, Nate."

"Don't," he tells her. "None of this is your fault."

Maybe the sane reaction would be to lock all the doors, hunker down in a dark room, and wait for the cops on duty to show up and handle the situation.

But from the moment Rose tells him Tommy is driving out to Davis Road, Nate feels something closer to relief than fear or even dread. He has been waiting for this ever since the summer night he arrested Tommy—the night Bridget died; the night everything stopped and everything started, too, all at once. A few one-sided punches in the gravel after her funeral wasn't enough to finish this story they have fallen into together. It was always destined to end something like this.

Nate unlocks the doors. Then he goes from room to room, turning on every light, letting that brightness spill over snowy fields and forest, guiding Tommy straight to him.

Soon after, headlights cut two yellow lines down the road, then slash across the driveway as the truck pulls in. Nate steps out onto the porch, into the cold.

When Tommy climbs out of the truck, he slides on the ice, righting himself with the butt of a shotgun, the barrel pointed toward the sky like it might start blasting down the stars.

"Fucker," he shouts into the night.

"Let's go inside," says Nate, relieved he doesn't sound as terrified as he feels. He wasn't expecting the gun. Sophie can't lose another parent; he's the only one she has in this world, and here he is, inviting the danger into her own house.

"Dumb prick," Tommy says, his words sliding into and around each other. "You think we're about to have a fucking cup of tea?"

The world is lit by the moon, all the fresh snow sparkling.

"Come on," says Nate, as he steps toward the door. "It's warm in here."

Tommy lifts the gun, cradles it in his arms.

They sit across from each other at the table. Tommy's face is covered in a sheen of sweat. He smells like vodka and puke and something worse, something feral.

Nate doesn't understand why Tommy hasn't already shot him—instead, he holds the gun in his lap, fingers caressing the polished wood stock. His shakes and shivers are painful to watch.

"You're freezing, man. Let me get you a blanket."

"Piss off."

"Coffee, then."

"I don't want anything from you."

"At least let me throw more logs on the fire."

"It's your damn house."

Careful to keep his hands in plain view, Nate crosses the room and fills the woodstove, grateful for the orange sparks—there's comfort in those embers, even now.

"So Rose called you, then," Tommy says when Nate returns to the table. "That's how you knew I was coming."

"Let's just leave her out of it."

"Bet she called all your fucking cop friends, too, didn't she? How long till they show up and start busting down doors to get at me?"

"No one's busting down any of these doors if I have anything to say about it. Not after the work I put into them."

"You should be scared," says Tommy, finger moving closer to the trigger.

"Sometimes," says Nate, desperate for any sort of distraction, "I wish I'd painted all the doors green instead of red."

Every muscle in his body is wound tight, and his spine feels like all the bones have been replaced by cords that refuse to bend in any direction. Is this the kind of pain his father sits in every minute of every day? If that's the case, Nate has no idea how the man can stand it. A person could go mad from so much relentless hurt.

"I should've known she'd call you," Tommy says after a few minutes of silence. He jiggles one leg up and down with enough force to make the table quiver. "She wouldn't tell me, so maybe you will. How long you two been screwing?"

"I mean it," says Nate. "Leave her out of this."

"Don't you get it, asshole? She's part of this. This whole fucking thing."

Nate understands. For Tommy, *this* isn't just right now, or this room, or this house; it is and always has been everything—his family, Rose, his kids, his inherited thirsts and impulses. *This* goes far beyond Dalton; *this* ripples all the way out to a world too big and too cruel for anyone to feel anything other than defeated.

It's exactly how Nate felt after Bridget died.

"Come on, man," he tells Tommy. "Let's have some coffee."

"That won't help."

"It won't hurt."

The house is filled with the same stillness he feels inside his dreams. Like every room and wall and floorboard is holding a collective breath. Waiting to exhale.

As Nate scoops coffee into the pot, he glances out the window and spots the DPD cruiser heading slowly down the road, lights and siren off.

Bruce will know better than to barge in here and make a mess of things—he will park close enough to the house to keep an eye on everything but hidden enough so Tommy can't see him. For all his crassness and questionable hygiene, Bruce is a good cop. A good man. And with him nearby, Nate feels like maybe there's a chance after all. Maybe this story between him and Tommy could have a softer ending.

"Why the fuck," asks Tommy, "would you paint a door a color you didn't want?"

Nate thinks back to those autumn days on the porch, the smell of ripe apples lifted on the breeze. Bridget, fingers laced over her pregnant belly, watched as he rolled the brush into the tray of paint. Royal Red. He thought a muted green might be better. But Bridget, who had grown up in a house with white walls and white carpet, wanted something bright and bold to welcome people into their home. So Royal Red it was.

"I can't explain it," Nate says. "It just sort of happened that way."

After a few sips of coffee, Tommy stops shivering.

After a few more, he lifts the gun from his lap.

A jumble of images and memories: The river after ice-out, cold spray kissing his face as Sophie squeezes his hand, shrieking with delight. His father lifting a trout from the lake. His mother's hands covered in the fish's iridescent scales, like flakes fallen from a rainbow. His mother on the porch with Trudy beside her, both of them laughing as lightning streaks across the sky. Clean canvas. Smell of turpentine. Taste of wine coolers. Bridget. The tight round drum of Bridget's belly. A flutter. A kick. A beating heart. Pink and yellow flowers. Heliopsis. Fire. Fire hydrant gushing a river upward, straight to the sunny sky. Rose smiling. Rose. Scent of freshly dug earth, flutter of wings, drone of bees. Sophie in the garden. Sophie climbing trees. Sophie on the swing. Sophie spinning circles in the grass, claiming herself queen of all the wild things—birds and woods and clouds and rivers. *Mine*, she says. *Mine, and mine, and that's mine, too.* And Nate can't remember what he told her in that moment, but he hopes he said yes. Yes, my girl, it's yours; reach out your arms and take it.

Tommy sets the gun on the table between them, barrel aimed toward the window across the room.

"Decent coffee," he says.

"Maxwell House," says Nate. "Buy one get one free at Bergeron's."

He is shocked by it—the uncontestable fact his heart hasn't been blown out of his chest, that it is still there, held safe, each beat proving him alive.

He has often wondered about Bridget's thoughts that final night. The first few months after she died, he obsessed over what must have been looping through her mind as she sank into the tub with his razor. Did she consider him or Sophie or anyone else she loved? Was she cogent enough—Bridget enough—to think at all?

He searched every pocket and drawer and closet for a note after she was gone. Something that would explain why she chose to leave like that, why she was hurting so badly, why she didn't ask for help. One time, he thought he found the explanation at the bottom of her purse on a neon pink Post-it. *Tell N,* the note began, and his fingers shook as he rushed to unfold the paper. *Out of dish soap.* He couldn't recall any specific instance when she had asked him to bring some Joy home. Maybe she forgot to ask. Maybe she did ask, and he forgot. Whatever the answer, it wasn't the one Nate was looking for.

He kept the note, anyway. It lives in his wallet, nestled behind Sophie's kindergarten picture. He imagines he will keep it there for years to come, Bridget's words fading little by little as their daughter's face grows older, wiser, more beautiful.

Tommy stares at Sophie's latest artwork on the fridge—a house with a triangular roof, a snowman wearing a hat bigger than his head.

"It's fucking useless," he says.

"What is?"

"Everything."

"You've got kids, man. Adam and Brandon aren't useless."

Tommy pushes his empty mug aside. "They'd be better off without me."

Nate has thought the same thing many times before, and he knows Rose has, too.

Tommy squeezes his eyes closed and presses his fingers into his temples. "I should've never come back to this damn town."

"But you did," says Nate, knowing there's not much left to talk about. Wondering how long they can keep pretending there is.

The house is silent. Waiting.

The gun is on the table. Waiting.

It really is strange, Nate thinks as he watches Tommy's hands float down from his face and back to the gun, how much of his life has been spent holding his breath, getting ready for the next thing, and then the next, and the next.

"Fuck it," says Tommy, pulling the gun closer.

Nate sees it as though it has already happened—one swift

movement, barrel to mouth, trigger-pull, spray of crimson over everything he has built here. More grief spilled in a house that has already seen far too much of it. More loss for more people who don't deserve to suffer. It will change Sophie, the echoes of another suicide executed in this place that's meant to be her sanctuary. It will destroy Adam and Brandon. It will ruin Rose, crush her spirit until eventually she gives up, too, and on and on it will go, sorrow after sorrow rippling out to touch everyone in this entire town.

He leans over the table, covering Tommy's hand on the stock of the gun. Even though Tommy's clammy knuckles harden at the touch, Nate holds him there, steady, until he sees something in Tommy's eyes he has never seen there before. This expression isn't the usual hate or resentment. It's something else. A letting go.

"None of us," says Nate, "would be better off."

This

Just a few hours ago, if anyone had tried to hold his hand the way Nate is doing right now, Tommy would have decked him in the face. But here they sit, hands locked together over the shotgun.

Maybe it's how hot it is in here. Maybe it's a lack of food—he hasn't eaten anything other than peanuts since Tanya served that sad excuse for breakfast this morning. Or maybe it's the way Nate is looking at him, which is nothing like the way anyone else has looked at him before. Whatever the reason, Tommy's got no fight left in him.

Earlier, as he sped over icy hills, he was ready to blast Nate's head off his shoulders. If he couldn't have Rose, that bastard shouldn't get to have her, either. His father's voice echoed through his brain. *Don't let another man take what should be yours. What you got a right to.*

He doesn't know when he decided not to shoot. Maybe it was when Nate made coffee. Or added more wood to the fire. Or maybe it was when he opened the door to the house that could have belonged to Tommy's father and invited him inside.

He also doesn't know when Nate started thinking Tommy wanted to pop the gun into his own mouth. Maybe he assumes a self-made ending is another fate that's been waiting for Tommy since he was born. Before that, even.

None of us would be better off.

Sometimes Tommy gets jealous of dead people. The distance they have from all the bullshit here on earth, hassles like construction and bad music; and other, bigger things—money, work, family.

Right now, the thing he envies most is how the dead don't have to see the hurt they leave behind. He can't stop remembering it—the betrayal on his kids' faces. Seeing them like that made him feel as if he was splintering into pieces, ricocheting off walls, slipping through uninsulated cracks and swirling away on the breeze.

Tommy doesn't actually want to die, though. He doesn't want to leave his kids to deal with something like that the way his own father did to him. Like what Nate's wife did to their daughter.

Mostly to get Nate to stop staring at him—it was almost comforting at first, but now it's giving him the creeps—Tommy lets go and sits back, watching as Nate takes away the gun, propping it against the wall beside him after checking to make sure the safety is on.

They sit for a while not saying anything. The kitchen smells like coffee beans. The house makes ghost-like noises as it shifts and settles in the cold. Tommy is stuck inside a familiar post-binge feeling, all sour-bellied and cotton-tongued. He'll never drink again. He would take a drink right now, if Nate offered him one.

Will Adam and Brandon turn into drunks just like him?

"I screwed up," Tommy says, unsure why he's talking but unable to stop himself. "Rose is never gonna let me see my boys again."

"You don't know that for sure," says Nate. "People can surprise you."

"Never in good ways."

"Sometimes."

Outside the window, Tommy catches the flash of moonlight off a car—squinting, he sees it's a police cruiser. Not that he didn't think the cops would roll up to what they're probably calling a hostage situation. He was hoping, though, to get out before they got here. That's what he wants more than anything. Just to get out. Drive away. Go back to his shitty apartment and sleep for two or three days.

"What happens if I try to leave right now?" he asks. "Will all those frigging pigs out there come swooping down on me?"

"It's just Bruce out there. And he won't do anything unless I ask him to."

"But if he sees me with a gun . . . "

"How could he, when you didn't bring one?"

It takes a minute for Tommy to understand. Pansy-ass Nate Theroux, who probably picks up litter from the side of the road and visits classrooms to tell ten-year-old kids to Just Say No to drugs and alcohol. In high school he was a total drag—honor roll, varsity basketball, never went to a pit party like everyone else. Mr. Good Cop, even back then.

"You'd do that?" Tommy asks. "Just let this whole thing go like it never happened?"

"Like I said. People can surprise you."

After Nate locks the shotgun in the hallway safe—shielding the combination with his body like Tommy plans on coming back later to rob him—he asks Tommy to stay put while he goes out to talk to Bruce.

"What will you tell him?"

"That we had coffee," says Nate. "It's not exactly a lie, is it?"

For a second, Tommy thinks the guy is asking permission to break the rules. Then Nate shrugs, slips into his DPD jacket, and steps outside, the cold blasting through the door before he pulls it shut behind him.

Alone in the house, Tommy feels an urge to wander every room. See what kind of life he and his father and his mother might have lived, if things had gone their way.

The living room is small, cluttered with toys and books. In the downstairs bathroom, the faucet drips into a stained cast-iron sink. Upstairs, Nate's bed is perfectly made—no surprise there—and his kid's room is so yellow it makes Tommy's eyes hurt.

By the time Tommy finishes with the last room, which is crammed with paintings, some finished, others barely started, Nate and Bruce are waiting for him at the bottom of the stairs, and Tommy has a flare of anger and panic, sure the fat cop is about to whip out a pair of handcuffs. At the very least, they'll ask him to turn out his pockets, reveal whatever they assume he stole from Nate and his daughter.

"Okay then," says Nate. "Bruce here is going to follow you back to your place. Make sure you get home safe."

Tommy starts to say no, he doesn't need a babysitter, he's been driving his whole damn life. Then something—a ripple of movement out of the corner of his eye, or a sound like muffled footsteps behind him—changes his mind.

"Whatever."

"I'm going to give Rose a call, too," Nate says. "Tell her everything's okay."

"Fine."

Outside is colder than he left it a few minutes or a few hours ago—he has no idea how long he and Nate were in that kitchen. How much the world changed or didn't change while they were in there.

Before he gets into his truck, he glances toward the porch, where Nate is standing under the light with one hand held up in a motionless goodbye, as if he knew all along Tommy would turn to look.

The drive home is long and slow. The stars are out and the moon is high, and Bruce's headlights shine bright in Tommy's rearview mirror all the way back to town.

IV.
Choice

Overnight

The last time Angela and Greg were in a hospital room together, she couldn't look at him. Now, she can't stop. At fourteen, she had been humiliated by the scene she caused at the river, ashamed to think what could have happened to Greg if one thing had gone wrong when he crawled across the ice to rescue her. Now, nearly twenty, she feels crushing waves of gratitude for this boy—this man—lying in the bed next to hers.

After the doctor—who might be handsome if it weren't for the arrogant set of his mouth—says they want to keep Greg overnight for observation, Angela insists on staying with him.

"No, we can't do that. You're not family."

"Define family," says Momma, who hasn't left Angela's side since she came bolting into the ER with a drippy nose and red-rimmed eyes.

"It's against hospital policy."

"I don't give a shit."

"It's inconsiderate of our staff," says the doctor, looking at the nurse, who is replacing the IV bag of fluids next to Greg's bed as he sleeps.

"It's no trouble," she says. "She can stay as long as she wants."

With three women against him, the doctor finally gives up. As soon as he's gone from the room, the nurse winks at Angela.

"Glad you gave him hell, honey—none of us can stand that pompous little prick." Then she turns to Cindy. "Not a lot of young women come in here with that much confidence."

"My Ange is tough, that's for sure."

The nurse, who wears one of those rings with all the different birthstones of her kids or grandkids—red, blue, yellow, green—cups a hand on Angela's mother's elbow and guides her to the door.

"Come on," she says. "Let me get you some coffee—the shit in the cafeteria is a tragedy, but we've got a decent pot in the staff lounge."

About a half-hour later, the nurse comes back into the room, alone this time. "I sent your mom home, honey. I thought you might like some quiet time."

"Thank you," says Angela, so grateful and exhausted she nearly starts crying.

"My name's Brenda, by the way. I'll be coming in to check on your friend every hour or so. You need anything in the meantime, just buzz me out at the nurse's station."

"Is he . . . " Angela lets the worry float unspoken in the air as she stares at Greg, the rise and fall of his chest, the slight trembling behind his closed eyelids.

"He's going to be fine. He's doing what you should be doing. You settle yourself down and get some rest."

After Brenda leaves, Angela sits propped up on the bed surfing through muted channels on the TV mounted in a corner of the room—something about nearly-extinct animals, something about shipwrecks. Mostly, she just watches Greg as he dreams.

For a while, there had been a question whether he would lose one or two of his toes to frostbite. Small price to pay, the doctor told them, for a couple hours barefoot in the snow. But slowly the color started to return to his feet, blood flow restored. The nail on his pinky toe might never grow back, though, the doctor said. Sometimes you can't save everything.

"I can live with that," Greg said. "Maybe I'll even ask for a nine-for-ten discount at my next pedicure."

He had stayed mostly silent on the ambulance ride over to

Prescott and in the emergency room as nurses covered them with blankets and flushed warm saline through their veins, and Angela feared he would never forgive her for their second near-death experience together. But when he grinned at her, she knew that they were okay.

She had wanted to do it right then—throw her arms around his neck and kiss him. But before Angela could even smile back at him, there was a burst of sound from the hallway outside the room and then the door was flung open, Momma running in to hug her so hard all the air was squeezed from her lungs. Greg's parents came in right after, Cheryl wild-eyed and Jim almost eerily quiet as he stared at his son from behind glasses that kept fogging.

It was so much like what happened six years before that Angela felt rootless, disoriented. Their parents with them in the hospital under too-bright lights, the crinkle of tinfoil blankets, the desperate thud of her heart . . . She couldn't shake the sense that this was what life boiled down to, an endless string of moments mirroring other moments, a constant ripple outward and inward, backward and forward. Maybe some people would call it déjà vu or fate. To her, though, it felt less like kismet or coincidence and more like collision—and she was surprised to find herself reassured, rather than pulverized, by all those fractured pieces.

"Thank God," Momma kept saying. "Thank Jesus."

"You two got lucky," Greg's mother said. "If Molly hadn't found you when she did . . . "

Greg's parents had left not long after that, his father claiming he had to go home and get some sleep so he could open the store early the next day.

"It's fine," Greg said after they were gone. "They're allowed to be pissed at me for this one."

"You can be furious at your dumbass kid," said Momma, "and still stick around to tell them about it."

Then her mother had asked Angela if she wanted to call her father. "I've been keeping him posted on everything, but he'd probably like to hear your voice."

"No," said Angela.

Now, however, with Greg lightly snoring across the room, she rethinks the decision to talk to her dad. It's not like she owes him anything—he's called Angela only a handful of times since she got back to Dalton—but getting in touch with him after what happened today feels like the considerate thing to do. The adult thing.

She stretches the cord of the phone into the bathroom, shutting the door behind her. She's surprised when her father answers before the first ring has gone all the way through.

"Angie?"

"Hey, Dad."

He lets out such a big sigh of relief she can practically feel the air blow against her face. "I'm going out of my mind down here, worrying about you."

"It's okay. I'm okay."

"You could have—"

"But I didn't."

"You're a tough kid, you know that?"

"I get that from Momma, I guess."

Her father goes silent. In the background, Pam is laughing with JJ and Colie, dishes clattering. Maybe she's teaching them to bake macarons. Maybe she's letting them taste-test her millionaire's shortbread. A day ago, Angela might have been envious of her half-sisters. Today, she only feels a detached affection toward them, remembering the times she and Momma used to sit around in their pajamas eating raw cookie dough right out of the bowl.

When her father speaks again, his voice trembles. "I'm sorry, Angie. You . . . deserve better."

Now is the time to hold him accountable for every mistake

he has ever made, every way he has let her down. She can tell him about the father/daughter dance she had to skip in third grade. The Christmases and birthdays that always left her depressed, because no matter how nice a present he got her—the pink toy Jeep, the Barbie dreamhouse—he was what she really wanted but could never have. She can confess the truth of what Mason did to her on his watch, wreck him with the guilt of it.

"I don't have an excuse," her father says before she can tell him anything. "I wish I could make it better, but I don't know how."

Her irritation fades into a resigned sort of pity.

"Maybe we can talk about it the next time I come for a visit," says Angela, just as unsure as he is if she's lying.

On her way back from the bathroom, she pauses to look out the window, hoping to see the snow twinkling under the lights in the parking lot.

"You put the moves on me."

Startled, she turns to see Greg sitting up in his bed, staring back at her. He looks as wide awake as she feels.

"What are you talking about?"

"In the woods. You kissed me."

"That wasn't a kiss." She remembers the breath she blew into his mouth, the warmth she tried to lend as they stood under all those trees. "It wasn't romantic."

"You don't think so?"

They are speaking in hushed voices, as if afraid of disturbing some invisible third person haunting the room.

She moves over to Greg's bed, questioning him with a silent glance and receiving his silent, nodded yes before settling beside him. He makes as much room for her as he can, but it's a narrow mattress, and their limbs overlap in a comfortable tangle.

"Sorry for almost killing you," says Angela, nestling her

head into the space between his jaw and shoulder. He smells like snow and saline. "Again."

"It's just your thing." Greg's laughter hums into the back of his throat.

"We were close to death, weren't we?"

"No more than any other day, maybe."

"You think?"

"Honestly, Angie, I have no idea what I think."

"About what?"

"Anything," says Greg. "Usually."

Out on the hall, or in another room, a monitor beeps several times, then goes silent.

"You really didn't think it was romantic?"

"Did you?"

"Hell yeah." Greg shifts so he's lying on his side, his face a few inches away from hers. He looks nervous but determined. "Honestly, though, it wasn't the way I always imagined it."

He strokes his fingers along Angela's arm until goosebumps rise up over her whole body. So there it is, her definitive answer: he's not gay. At his touch, she waits to hear the familiar chorus of crickets haunting her. But the building is as quiet as the woods they left behind.

Watching Greg's face in the flickering glow of the muted television, she feels it again—all her fragments falling together. She sees him as he is now, nearly an adult and lean with muscle; she sees him as he was in grade school, her pudgy friend obsessed with four-leaf clovers, certain he could pluck good fortune out of the ground. When he kisses her, it is nothing desperate or wild, but a soft and steady smolder. And when he closes his eyes, she remembers him sleeping earlier, dreaming dreams she could clearly imagine for herself—trees tall as church steeples, limbs laced under endless sky, and fields bright with color, and slate gray oceans cold enough to steal your breath and shock it back into you at the same time. She's never seen the ocean. But one day, she thinks, as he cups her face with both hands, IV line tinkling against the metal frame of the hospital bed—one day, she will stand at the edge of a sea and watch the water rolling toward and away from her. Over and over. And when she can't resist the pull any longer, she will run as fast as she can and throw herself in, let the salt and the chill pummel her, wash her clean of everything she left behind, far off in some nameless place.

Morning After

When Greg wakes up, a stream of sunshine is pouring through the window, glinting off the rails of his bed, turning the saline in the plastic pouch above his head into molten silver. Beyond the closed door, he hears the shuffle of nurses' feet, the beep of someone else's heart, an intercom asking Dr. Merrill to report to the nephrology wing.

"What the hell's nephrology?"

Greg looks over at Angela, who is lying on her side in her own bed and smiling sleepily back at him.

"Kidneys, I think." He rolls over so they're face to face, only a few feet apart. Part of him wants her to vault over here, tangle herself around him. But another part, more conscious of his unbrushed teeth, is grateful for the distance.

"Did you sleep at all?" he asks, even though he already knows the answer, because he stayed awake for hours listening to the rhythm of her breath.

"Better than I have in a long time."

The kisses were perfect. Beyond anything he ever thought they might be. As it was happening, he wanted to sink himself into Angela. But neither of them had to say it out loud for both to understand it was too soon for anything like that.

"Want to watch TV?" he asks.

She flips through channels before settling on the local news, which can't talk about anything other than the storm. Some places saw up to twenty inches of snow; Dalton received seventeen. "A real ripsnorter," the jowly weatherman says. A lot of car accidents. Two heart attacks while shoveling. A group of widows made the best of it, sledding down the hill in Ethel's backyard all afternoon.

When a different nurse from yesterday comes in, she brings breakfast with her, two trays of toast, cantaloupe, oatmeal, and tiny boxes of apple juice. She tells them the doctor should be discharging Greg soon, that one of their parents will be in to bring them home.

"What if we want to stay?"

"Yeah, can't we get a late checkout?"

The nurse's expression never changes as she disconnects Greg's IV. "You haven't tipped us well enough for that sort of special treatment."

After she leaves, Greg and Angela look at each other, grinning like kids, and lift their juice boxes in a salute. They almost died yesterday. They kissed for hours in ammonia-scented darkness. Neither of them has any idea what comes next.

Their high spirits come crashing down about an hour later when Greg's father walks into the room. He's dressed in his usual Wranglers and corduroy shirt, but he looks like a stranger as he hovers near the door.

"Where's Mom?" asks Greg.

"At the store. One of us had to be."

"Did she make you come here?"

"I volunteered."

Each word is spoken softly, but there's something threatening about it. All Greg's life, it has always been his mother who dealt with doctors and dentists, chauffeuring him and his sisters around while their father reported for duty at the hardware store. *It's just so grossly old-fashioned*, Aimee said after their mother had to fight against the stomach flu to take her to the orthodontist because their father refused to leave the store unattended.

Angela, knowing enough about Greg's family dynamics to understand how weird it is for his father to be here, stays quiet and lags behind as a nurse pushes Greg in a wheelchair to the hospital entrance and then follows him and his father at a distance across the freshly plowed parking lot. Greg is desperate to comment on how much nicer the weather is compared to yesterday that he feels the words climbing up his throat. But one look at his father's clenched jaw tells him to keep his own mouth shut.

The ride to Dalton is endless. Angela sits in the backseat; Greg beside his father, who steers with his hands in a perfect 10-and-2 position, elbows locked, eyes regularly sweeping the road before them, the rearview, and the side mirrors. Every rule followed. Every movement calculated, precise.

At Angela's house, they're barely in the driveway before she's opening the door and jumping out of the car. "I'll call you," she says, then she slams the door shut.

And now it's just him and his father, alone.

Just one more minute, Greg tells himself, then they'll be home, and they can retreat to their separate spaces; their separate stories.

But instead of heading toward High Street, his father turns left on Main, and they drive south down Route 11. It's not until they're nearly at the Lannigan property that he understands where they're going, though he still can't figure out why.

His father turns onto the logging road, careful to position the car precisely between the man-high snowbanks that flank either side. Trees tower around them, an evergreen city. The sunlight, bright on the open road, seems dimmer here, as if they are driving into some sort of permanent dusk.

"Dad, we don't need to—"

"We do."

He drives until the road abruptly ends at a large hummock of snow, then throws the truck in park with the engine on so warm air can keep blowing through the vents.

For a minute or two, they sit not saying anything, Greg so anxious he could puke. He feels like his body is collapsing cell by cell. Usually, trees mean comfort and safety, but right now, they are bars in a prison cell reaching all the way to the clouds. No hope for escape all the way down here at the bottom.

Finally, his father speaks, staring out the windshield. "You see that?" he asks, pointing at the mound of snow.

"I mean, yeah. I'm not blind."

"What do you think it is?"

Sensing this is a trick, but unable to come up with an alternate answer, Greg says, "It's a snowbank."

"No," says his father. "It's not."

It takes a few seconds before Greg traces a subtle shape under all that snow.

"Angie's truck?"

His father nods, then turns to look Greg in the eyes for the first time all day.

We wouldn't have found you," he says, his voice cracking. "They're about to close this road to logging trucks for the winter. The only reason it's clear today is because I asked Bert Junkins to come plow it out."

Greg has never been able to decide if he wants to have kids someday in the far future. On one hand, he's always loved being Aimee's big brother, watching her learn to walk and talk and toss middle fingers to whoever she thinks deserves them. On the other, he grew up seeing how tired his mother was all the time, the constant work and worry that went into raising children.

Now, seeing the feral grief in his father's eyes, Greg is almost certain he will choose to never be a parent. It could ruin a person, he thinks, carrying around so much fear all the time. Knowing all sorts of terrible things could happen to the people you love most in the world and not being able to do a thing to stop them from happening.

"I'm sorry, Dad. I was stupid. I'm sorry"

"No," his father says. "I mean, yes, you were stupid as hell, driving out in a storm like that. But I brought you out here so I could apologize to you."

Greg, stunned into silence, waits for the next words, which he knows won't come easy to this man, who can talk to random people for hours about hose nozzles and PVC pipes but can barely manage to ask his own family how they think or feel, what they're afraid of and what they hope for.

"It wasn't fair of me to assume you'd want the same life as me. I never should have put that burden on you. So I'm sorry, son. I'm sorry."

Greg wants to roll down the windows and shout it to the forest—he is forgiven.

"I can't imagine studying plants for a living," his father continues. "But if that's what you want to do, your mother and I will make it happen."

"Are you sure?"

"Of course. You're my kid."

Greg could say a lot of things. Instead, he says the one thing that matters most.

"Thank you."

His father lets out a sound that could be the start of a sob or a sigh, then turns to look out the window, craning his neck to see the treetops.

"Crazy, isn't it?" he says. "How far they grow away from where they start?"

Usually, Greg would think about all the roots that extend below earth, mirroring the limbs that stretch above. But here beside his father, all he can think about is a dim hospital room and a dance club pulsing with neon lights.

The only person in his family he has ever wanted to tell is Aimee. Now, however, something feels settled. Something feels right, or at least not completely wrong. There may never be a better time.

"Dad?"

"Yeah?"

"I kissed Angela."

When his father grins, he looks like the high-school-yearbook version of himself. If it weren't for the crinkle lines around his eyes, he could be eighteen again.

"That's great, I'm so glad to hear that. Angie's a wonderful—"

"I've kissed guys, too."

The lines around his father's eyes deepen; the grin slips away. "What . . . are you trying to pull some kind of prank on me? Why would you do that? Was it some kind of dare?"

"It's not a prank, Dad. And it wasn't a dare. I wanted to kiss them."

"I don't get what you're trying to tell me."

"I'm bisexual. I like guys and I like girls."

His father stares out the windshield. "For how long?"

"Forever."

The elation Greg felt only moments ago is gone, replaced by the thing he has always feared: a certainty that he is unlovable. Unacceptable. Though his father doesn't go to church anymore, he was raised Catholic, taught to believe anything other than heterosexuality was a trick of the devil.

What the hell was Greg thinking, spilling this sort of confession?

"Let's just forget it, okay?" he says. "Pretend I never brought it up. It's all right; I know you don't understand."

"No, I don't," says his father as he stares at the mound of snow burying Angela's truck, his fingers gripping the steering wheel hard enough to turn his knuckles tight. Behind his glasses, his eyes are round and wary. "But I could try."

Deal

Tommy is a prisoner in his own apartment. After a few hours of shitty sleep, he woke up with his face smashed into the pillow.

Since then, he's been pacing the apartment and smoking one cigarette after another. He can't stop looking out the windows, sure he'll see a police car out in the parking lot waiting to haul him off. No way you can threaten a cop with a gun and get away with it. Nate and Bruce were fucking with him last night, telling any lie they could think of to get him out of that house. Making promises they didn't mean to keep.

Now it's just a matter of time—they're coming for him.

Any second now.

It's been any second now for a long time, and Tommy is nearly out of cigarettes. He's hungry, too. And he could use a drink to calm the nerves, but he won't do it. Not today. Maybe not ever again, not after seeing the fear on his kids' faces last night.

Earlier, in the middle of a restless pass through the apartment, Tommy hadn't been able to take it anymore—the waiting—and he picked up the phone. Rose answered halfway into the first ring.

"Aren't you going to ask what happened out at your boyfriend's house?"

"I don't need to ask you," said Rose in a heavy voice. "Nate called me as soon as you left last night."

"What'd he tell you?"

"All of it—the coffee, the gun, your little deal not to talk about the gun." She paused to take a deep breath. "Lucky for you, he can be pretty convincing. I won't tell anyone about it, either."

Tommy wanted to know what Nate said to convince her. But he sensed it was better not to push his luck.

"When can I see the boys? I need to see them, I need to tell them—"

"They don't want to see you," she said. "They kept me up half the night, scared you were going to come back here and finish what you started.

"I'll fix it."

"I kind of doubt that."

Since then, Tommy has had to stop himself a dozen times from calling her to ask if she's ready to forgive him now, or now, or now. What's even harder to resist is the urge to go over to the school and get Adam and Brandon dismissed so he can take them for a drive, explain everything. He'll tell them it's okay to be mad at him, he deserves that, but they need to know how much he wants to be their dad; how much time he spends thinking about all the little things that make them who they are—the cowlick in Brandon's hair, the freckles on Adam's nose. How serious Brandon gets when he's drawing, his bottom lip caught under crooked teeth. How hard Adam laughs when he watches cartoons that aren't even that funny.

He fucked it all up.

After his last cigarette is gone and he comes close to passing out from hunger, Tommy decides he has no other choice. He's got to leave the apartment.

Luckily, it's late morning on a Tuesday, and there are only two other customers in the Diner, an older couple sitting in a booth by the window. As he passes them, he catches a bit of their conversation.

"Gretchen, I'm telling you, there's no way a shark could actually get that big."

"I know that, Jerry, I'm just saying it would be terrifying if one *could*."

"Coffee?" asks Arlene, pouring a cup before Tommy can say yes or no as he sits down. "How about some waffles? Bacon or sausage?"

"I don't—"

She's already walking back to the kitchen to tell George to make waffles. And bacon. And sausage. If Tommy had more energy, he'd tell her not to assume she knows what he wants or needs. But he's so tired he can barely sit up straight, and it sounds all right, this breakfast she's demanded her husband cook for him.

While he waits, Tommy listens to the couple in the booth—they look familiar, but then again, all old people pretty much look the same, with their wrinkles and white hair and liver-spotted hands.

"Vera won't want steak, she'll want something healthy."

"Steak has protein. Protein is healthy."

"You don't have to tell me. It's your daughter who's so damn stubborn."

"Wonder where she learned it from."

Arlene comes out of the kitchen and sets a plate down in front of Tommy, as well as a bowl of mixed fruit. "You look like you need it," she says

Tommy doesn't bother arguing. Just sits there and shovels it all in as she busses a few tables and flits back to the kitchen to rinse dishes and then comes back out again to make a fresh pot of coffee.

"Do you ever stop moving?" he asks as she writes out new specials on the chalkboard. *Meatloaf, mashed potatoes, & slice of pie, $5.99: Helluva deal!*

"This is a restaurant," says Arlene, raising her eyebrows and shaking her head at him like he's supposed to know what she means.

"It's dead in here."

"Won't be for long."

"But for now it is. So shouldn't you take a break or something?"

"You see anyone here ready to spell me if I want to take a break? You see anyone ready to cover for poor Georgie back there so he can take a break?"

"You should hire some help."

"Like it's that easy."

"It can't be that hard."

"You volunteering?"

It takes Tommy a second to understand she's offering him a job. But he's got no interest in wearing an apron and carrying coffee around to snobby assholes who look at him like he's no better than the scuzz covering the top of the ceiling fans.

"I don't exactly have people skills," he says. "You don't want me waiting tables."

"No, I sure as hell don't," says Arlene. "But we could use you in the back. You opposed to washing dishes? Maybe learning to flip burgers?"

George is peeking out from the kitchen, his apron splotched with grease and what looks like strawberry juice. Or blood. Tommy has never heard the man say more than a dozen words, and he doesn't know much about him other than that he fought in Vietnam. That's the last thing he needs: a shell-shocked veteran with easy access to meat cleavers keeping track of his every move.

"I don't think so," he tells Arlene. "Sorry."

"Don't be sorry for me," she says. "It's your loss."

Usually, Tommy would go to the Store 'N More for cigarettes. But Bev Theroux works there, and he doesn't want to run into her, because fuck only knows what Nate might have told her by now. What he might have told everybody.

Wandering the aisles at Bergeron's, Tommy decides to pick up a few things for the apartment—if no one arrests him today, he'll need to feed himself again later. He spends too long picking out bananas, pretzels, bread, a giant tub of peanut butter.

He pauses in front of the coffee, staring at the display for the brand Nate served him last night. It was good, well-balanced, not too bitter, and he'd like more of it. But Tommy can't bring himself to pluck a can from the shelf.

In the cold aisle, he glances from the gallons of ice cream to the cases of beer. He could have chocolate or PBR. Budweiser or rocky road. Before he can decide, Tommy feels a punch on his shoulder and turns to see Uncle Stu grinning at him.

"Hell of a game the other night," he says. "Surprised you got money left to buy groceries at all."

Tommy hates it, the way he feels like a little kid every time he's around Stu or Daryl or any of these men who know they have total control over him.

"I might have a way you for to make that money back. Unless you found yourself a job since I last seen you?"

The way Stu is looking at him makes it clear he knows all about yesterday morning's failed interview. Tommy is supposed to either laugh it off or throw some equal insult back. But he can't find any words, and it's so exhausting, standing here under tinny speakers playing some kind of elevator music, pretending he doesn't want to knock his uncle's teeth out of his face, one by one.

The idea of money, though . . .

"You saying I could come back to the shop?" Tommy asks. "Because I'm a little out of practice, but I can learn again easy."

"No, I got plenty of help with the cars. It's something else. You know," says his uncle, lowering his voice as an old lady walks past them, pushing a cart loaded with all the fixings for a boiled dinner. "What you were doin' before."

Tommy's mind flashes back to it, that life he led for a while. Baggies and damp cash exchanged in parking lots. The rush of coke and speed and whatever else he could get his hands on, and the high of not getting caught for any of it. Until he did.

If he hadn't gotten caught, though—if Nate hadn't arrested him that night—where would he be right now? What would have happened to him and Rose and the kids in the years between then and now? Would they all be a happy family like he always wanted and never had? Or would Rose have eventually gotten tired of Tommy's bullshit and left? Maybe she would've ended up with Nate no matter what. Or maybe she would've found another guy, one who could treat her better than Tommy ever had. Maybe she always would have found someone better, someone who could raise Adam and Brandon right.

"Thanks for the offer," Tommy tells his uncle. "But I'm gonna take a pass."

Then he grabs a rack of Bud and a gallon of chocolate ice cream and heads for the register.

Back at the apartment, he locks himself inside. He puts away the groceries, pulls down the blinds, and collapses on the couch, which smells like old Cheez-Balls even though he's never sat here eating them.

Staring around the room, he thinks maybe it could be a decent place, if he knew anything about decorating. Maybe curtains would cheer things up in here. Or some of those braided rugs he saw at Nate's house, lots of colors woven together.

He closes his eyes and listens to the sounds from downstairs. Clatter of silverware, sizzle of grill, annoying bursts of Arlene's laughter. Weird, he thinks before he drifts off, the things that become so familiar.

Several loud bangs jolt him awake, and even before Tommy opens his eyes, he knows it's the sound of gunshots. Nate decided to bypass any sort of police intervention and is going for this sort of justice instead. This will be how he goes, Tommy understands, blasted away by his own dead father's gun.

Then a calm voice comes through the cracks around the door. "It's George."

Peeking through the window first to be sure this isn't some kind of ruse, Tommy unlocks the door and opens it just wide enough for George to slip his skinny body inside the hall. He's still wearing his grease-stained apron, even though Tommy can now hear the whir of the vacuum that Arlene always pushes through the restaurant after they've closed up for the day.

Even though George is technically his landlord, they've never stood in this place alone together before. It was Arlene who led the apartment tour back in the fall, Arlene who collects the rent check on the first of every month. Tommy has no idea what to say, where to stand, how to act.

"Don't get worked up," says George, holding out two hands like you might with a dog trying to decide if it should bite. "You're not going to get any trouble from me. I'm just here to tell you something—just one thing, and then I'll leave you alone, okay?"

Still suspicious but strangely desperate to hear what this man has to say, Tommy nods for him to keep talking.

"You should take Arlene up on her offer. We could use the help. I get pretty sore, standing at that grill all day. Be nice if someone could spell me when I needed it."

"I don't know how to cook."

"You can learn. I can teach you."

"I'm not so quick on my feet. Don't you have to be quick, working in a restaurant?"

"Maybe other places."

Tommy doesn't want to be stuck in a hot kitchen all day,

cooking other people's food, cleaning up other people's dirty plates. Just the idea of all the townies coming in and seeing him behind the line, one of those hairnets slicing into his forehead, makes him feel as humiliated as if he got caught with shit on his pants.

"I'm not—"

George holds up his hands again, and even though his eyes are soft—nothing violent there, nothing threatening—Tommy falls silent, understanding he is expected to shut up and listen.

"Only assholes and morons," says George, "turn down second chances."

Breathing Room

If one more person acts like it's her fault they owe a copay, Rose will start screaming right here at her desk. No words, just a high-pitched shriek that sends everyone running from the waiting room and out of the clinic. She doesn't care where they go, as long as it's somewhere far away from her.

"What is up with you?" Vera asks after Rose snaps at Jay LeClerq to invest in some new hearing aid batteries.

"I'm fine," Rose says. "It's just that I don't know what Dr. Haskell did yesterday when he sat at my desk, but none of my stuff is where it should be. Look—he pushed my pencil cup over by the phone when it should be beside the appointment book."

"The nerve."

She wants to tell Vera what happened the night before. But even though it was Tommy who was drunk, Tommy who took that gun out to Nate's house, it was Rose who woke up this morning feeling guilty and humiliated, as if the whole thing were her fault. Talking about it right now would unravel her.

She settles on telling Vera a half-truth. "I'm just tired. The kids had some stomach issues last night, and none of us slept a whole lot."

Last night was the first time either of the kids had witnessed the damage their father could cause, the fear he could inspire. It took a long time to calm them down after Tommy left, and even then, they wouldn't crawl into their beds until they were sure Rose had locked all the doors and windows. She stayed up for hours, even after Nate called to assure her everything had turned out okay, watching the street for any sign of Tommy. This morning, she almost called out of work and kept Adam and Brandon home with her, but they seemed better in the daylight—not exactly well-rested, but not in complete terror, either. They both swore they wanted to go to school. And Rose was secretly glad for it, glad to get out of that trailer and to deal with whatever mess Dr. Haskell had left for her here at the front desk.

"I know you're lying," says Vera, handing Rose a fresh mug of coffee. "Whatever it is, tell me when you're ready."

The day passes. She manages to stop herself from screaming and from jamming her stapler down on Harvey Trinko's balls when he sneaks a peek down her shirt as she leans over to take his insurance card. *Just a little bit longer,* she keeps telling herself. Just a little bit longer, and then she can leave, pick up the boys, maybe surprise them with an after-school trip to Prescott. They could go to the mall, walk around and look at all the clothes and toys they can't afford. Or maybe there's a kids' movie playing at the theater—that might be nice, sitting together in the dark with hot butter coating their fingers.

When the phone rings just before her lunch break and she sees the number for the police station flash across the ID screen, she almost stops breathing, sure she is about to hear that her children have been kidnapped by their psychotic father.

"Everything's fine," Nate says before she can sputter out a greeting.

"Why are you calling from the station?" asks Rose, willing her heart to slow. "Don't you have the day off?"

"Thought it'd be good to come in, debrief with Halstead after everything."

"And how'd that go?"

"I think I gave the poor guy another ulcer."

Despite herself, Rose laughs. "Maybe it's the push he needs to finally retire. Give Bruce the job."

"Then we'll all have ulcers."

In the waiting room, Althea Morse unleashes a string of wet, hacking coughs into a Kleenex.

"So listen," says Nate. "I was wondering if you and the boys wanted to come out to the house this afternoon. I thought we should all . . . "

"Debrief?"

"Something like that."

Judging by the weariness in his voice, he didn't get much sleep, either. Part of Rose is livid about his truce with Tommy, which he had explained to her when he called last night. But most of what she feels is relief that no one was hurt.

"We can come over," she tells Nate. "If the boys are feeling up to it."

When Rose gets to the school that afternoon, Adam comes across the snowy parking lot with a paper held high, waving it triumphantly as he slides into the back of the car.

"101 on my math test, Mum. One hundred and *one*. I got the bonus question."

"I'm not surprised," says Rose, twisting awkwardly in her seat to hug him. Normally, he'd squirm away. But he wraps his arms around her and nuzzles his forehead into her neck for a couple seconds before pulling away, still beaming.

"Where's your brother?"

"I dunno."

Rose is about to go find him—maybe he's still in his classroom, looking for his hat—when the Lower Wing doors open and Brandon steps outside. He's carrying a paper, too, and it hangs limply by his side as he trudges his way over to the car.

Throwing himself into the backseat beside his brother, Brandon wordlessly passes his spelling test to Rose. She tries not to react when she sees a red X circled at the top and a red line drawn through all the words he knew how to spell yesterday morning.

"It's just one test, buddy," she says. "Try not to worry about it."

"Everyone's going to think I'm stupid now," says Brandon. He stares at his hands, misshapen in Adam's hand-me-down mittens.

"No one could ever think that."

Even on a good day, Brandon always takes himself too seriously when it comes to getting good grades. He has never failed anything before. Rose has no idea what she could say to make him feel better. She should talk to them about what happened last night—but she has no idea how to do that, either. So she gives them another sort of offering instead.

"You guys want to go hang out with Sophie?"

A few hours later, after Rose and Nate have helped the kids build a snowman five feet tall, they go inside to get supper ready. While Nate starts shaping hamburger patties, Rose chops veggies for a salad, grateful for something to focus on other than how exhausted Nate looks. The guilt she woke up with this morning is somehow stronger now, even though this afternoon has seemed to prove that Tommy's rampage hasn't necessarily ruined everything. As soon as Rose pulled into Nate's driveway, Adam and Brandon had shot out of the car and run straight toward Sophie, who waited for them on the front porch in a puffy blue snowsuit. Both tests—the success and the failure—lay forgotten on the backseat.

"Ro."

She looks up to see Nate nervously folding a dishtowel, the patties heaped in a neat pile on the counter behind him.

"What is it?" she asks, even though she knows this is the conversation he's been waiting to have with her all afternoon.

"I just want—"

Before he can finish his thought, the front door bursts open and Sophie comes running into the kitchen. When they saw her outside just a few minutes ago, she was wearing a hat with a giant pom-pom on it. Now the hat is gone. She's not crying, but she looks like she might start any second. Half-frozen snot trembles from her nose.

"What is it, Soph?" asks Nate. "What's wrong?"

Her eyes flick between her father and Rose. "If I tell, he'll get in trouble."

Throat tightening, Rose glances out the window to see her boys huddling together on the porch steps, Adam shaking his head and mouthing a strand of frantic words she can't hear—but she has no doubt he's trying to defend whatever he did.

"No one will be in trouble," she promises. "Just tell us what happened."

Sophie sighs and pushes a mass of red curls away from her face. "So, what happened is this. We were on the snowbank, and I was queen, but then he got mad and said *he* wanted to be *king*, and then he pushed me and I fell off the snowbank. All the way to the moat."

Rose looks to Nate for a translation.

"The space between the snowbank and the porch. She calls it the moat."

"Yeah, so I got stuck there because the snow was slippery so it was hard to climb, and I couldn't move. I was *trapped*."

"Were you hurt?"

"No, but I was down in the moat, and he was up on top of the snowbank, and he said, 'If you come out of there and make yourself queen, I'll push you back down again.'"

"Adam said that to you?" Rose asks.

"No, Brandon said it."

"But why would Brandon say it?"

"Because he's the one who pushed me," says Sophie, looking at Rose as if she might be the dumbest grownup in the world.

It doesn't make sense.

It's Adam who laughs when cartoon characters get punched in the face or kicked in the crotch. Adam who shoves other kids off slides. Adam who has his father's eyes. Brandon is the good one—and she knows it's wrong, thinking of one kid as Good and the other as Not So Good, but Rose can't help it. Brandon is her sweet boy. He's afraid of a lot of things, but he's never shown any sort of anger or aggression toward anybody.

While Nate goes to bring Adam and Brandon inside, Rose dabs the dishtowel on Sophie's face, wiping away the snot now pouring freely from her nose. "It's all right," she says. "It's okay."

Nate returns with the boys. Brandon is crying so hard it sounds like he's choking. Rose holds him while Sophie, Nate, and Adam try not to stare. The oven beeps, preheated long enough for the frozen tater tots to go in. But food is a faraway thought.

Finally, Brandon calms enough for Rose to talk to him. "Why did you push Sophie?"

He shrugs. Whimpers.

"It's not okay to hurt people like that."

"But I wasn't hurt, though," says Sophie. "I wasn't even scared, not really. Brandon was just being a boy."

"Being a boy is never an excuse for bad behavior. All three of you need to understand that."

Nate says it so gently that it sounds like he could be asking the kids what kind of ice cream they want. Adam is staring at him with the expression he usually saves for the superheroes in his cartoons. Part wonder, part disbelief.

"I'm sorry," whispers Brandon.

"It's okay," Sophie says. "We can share the snowbank next time."

"Are you mad at me, Mumma?"

"I don't like what you did," says Rose. "But I'm not mad at you."

Brandon takes a shuddering breath before looking up at Nate. "Do you hate me now?"

Nate kneels down so he is eye-level with her son. No anger in that face. Only kindness and the sort of tenderness that comes from knowing deep hurt.

"Never, Brandon. I could never hate you."

"Can I keep being Sophie's friend?"

"Of course."

"Can me and Adam keep coming out here to play?"

Nate doesn't hesitate. "You're always welcome in this house."

By the time supper is over, the kids have moved on from the snowbank incident and retreated to the living room to make a blanket fort. Nate and Rose stand shoulder-to-shoulder at his kitchen sink. He washes the dishes. She dries. They don't talk much, but sometimes their hands touch, a quick exchange of warmth and soap suds.

"Thank you," she says.

"For what?"

"Talking to Brandon, being so calm. You had every right to be angry with him." Rose wipes a glass longer than necessary. "You're good at it, you know? Talking to people when shit's hitting the fan, keeping everyone calm. I have no idea how you got through to Tommy last night. I thought for sure . . . "

"Hey." Nate drops a bowl into the water, where it settles on the bottom of the sink with a muted, ceramic clunk. "Let's not think about what could have happened, okay? Let's just be glad it didn't."

They continue with the dishes, wordlessly now. In the living room, Sophie is trying to teach Adam and Brandon the words to a song she's made up about rhinoceros feet. *Gray and FLAT; heavy and FAT.*

"We should go soon," says Rose once she's put away all the silverware and Nate has wiped down the countertops. "It's getting late, and it's a school night . . . "

"They're having fun in there. Let's leave them for a bit."

"Are you sure?"

"I'm sure. And anyway, I want to show you something."

Rose follows him up the stairs and down the hallway. They stop at the closed door of the only room in this house she has never stepped inside before.

"Nate, you don't have to—"

"I want to."

They smile shyly at each other under the shine of the hallway lamp, then he pushes the door open and they enter, into darkness that smells like paint and canvas.

"Hang on," says Nate, flicking on the lights to reveal a room full of color.

Bridget's paintings are everywhere, hung on the walls, propped on easels, stacked on the floor. Blue and green and orange and red; purple and teal and silver and gold. Potato fields in blossom, meadows dotted with sunflowers and autumn leaves, crumbling barns, sunsets over Portman Lake, the gentle bend where the Aroostook and Machias Rivers meet—their entire town brought inside and close enough to touch.

"Oh," breathes Rose, wanting to touch every landscape. She spins in slow circles, trying to take it all in, seeing something new with each rotation. The Diner. The Store 'N More. Even The Shanty, advertising Orange Creamsicle Twist on the board out front. Somehow Bridget captured it all, transforming it into something more beautiful than it really is.

When Rose pulls her gaze away from the painted universe around her, she's surprised to see Nate watching her. There's an intensity in his gaze she has dreamed of countless times during lonely nights when she has soothed herself to sleep with the thought of his hands exploring all her hidden places.

"Why did you show me this, Nate?"

"I wanted you to see everything."

She knows the next part is up to her. He's not the kind of guy to make the first move; he will wait for an invitation. And she understands that bringing her to this room is probably more intimate for Nate than sex itself.

She steps toward him. He doesn't move away. When she lifts her arms to his shoulders, moving in so close her breasts brush against his ribs, Nate tentatively places his hands on her waist. It reminds her so much of her middle school Spring Fling with one of the Bergeron boys that she can't help but laugh.

Nate laughs, too. "Little out of practice."

"Same here."

Rose will never be able to figure out, later, who started it first. All she knows, and all that really matters is that suddenly her lips are on his lips, and his fingers are brushing along her jaw and up into her hair, and they're both melting, here in a room filled with color.

And downstairs, all together, their children are laughing.

The past twenty-four hours have been like one long, unbroken dream. First Tommy in his kitchen with a shotgun, and then a sleepless night watching the road in case he came back, and then a morning spent at the station explaining the whole mess to Chief Halstead, Bruce standing beside between them as a buffer.

And now this—Rose's body pressed against his. Her tongue, warm and sweet, inside his mouth. And all of it happening in a room that belonged to the first woman he loved. The only woman, he used to think, he could ever love.

He'd had no plans for this, no intention of showing Rose the studio where Bridget poured so much light. It was just another part of the dream, as if invisible hands and voices were guiding him on what to do and what to say.

I wanted you to see everything.

Nate didn't know until he spoke the words how true he wants them to be. But how can he show Rose anything when there is so much he continually fails to see for himself? He should end the kiss and confess to her how he always seems to be looking in the wrong direction.

He doesn't end it.

What ends it is a crash from downstairs, followed by a chorus of kids shouting not to worry, nothing happened.

Rose and Nate fall away from each other, though she holds onto his hand for a moment before they hurry down to the kitchen, where Sophie is standing above Adam and Brandon as they push a pile of broken glass into a dustpan.

"It's okay, Dad. It was just the Road Runner cup."

Nate, who has an embarrassing attachment to that jelly jar, a relic of his own childhood, is grateful nothing worse was broken. Earlier, he had felt worried about Brandon in a way he's never felt for a kid before. There was something about the look on his face when he shamefully apologized—the set of his mouth, maybe—that made Nate feel that dreamlike strangeness again. Because suddenly Tommy was there with them in the kitchen. And Nate felt a ripple of what could come later, as Brandon grows older and has to start deciding what kind of man he wants to be. Anything could happen between now and then to change what and how he chooses. But Nate saw in that second that the potential for wreckage would always be there, under the surface.

After they've made sure no glass remains on the floor, everyone stands around the kitchen as if unsure what happens next. Rose, Adam, and Brandon should get going—the kids have school tomorrow; Rose has work; Nate plans to take advantage of his last day off shift and shovel his father's roof.

He doesn't want them to leave.

But if they stayed, he wouldn't be able to stop himself from kissing Rose again, or from asking her to sleep beside him. Something that can never be taken back.

When he and Bridget bought this property shortly after they got married, it seemed both fated and impossible to Nate that he should get the house he had loved from the first time his father drove him out to Davis Road to watch thunderstorms roll across the valley. That he should get to marry the girl he'd loved since second grade. Those first few weeks here, he would stand in rooms that felt alive and stare out the windows at the new green grass in the fields, wondering what he had done to deserve so much goodness.

Now this house belongs to him and Sophie, the life they have built here together, in Bridget's absence, one minute to the next. And it might not have enough room to hold anyone else's dreams. Or ghosts.

"Okay," says Rose. "Time to say goodbye, get your coats and boots on."

As Adam and Brandon protest that it's not fair, they want more time with Sophie, Nate looks at Rose and sees her looking back at him, unblinking, and knows she did it on purpose—played the role of bad cop so he could be the good guy. Made the choice to go so he wouldn't have to feel guilty about not asking her to stay.

In the middle of the night, in the middle of a dream, he wakes as suddenly as if someone were standing over his bed, calling his name. He squints into the darkness, all the edges of his furniture made unfamiliar. His jacket, slung across the back of a chair, looks like the hunched form of a small but determined monster.

Heart thudding against his ribs, he tries to understand what woke him. Was it a sound, a smell, a feeling? What was he dreaming? He can only catch glimpses of it, like gossamer curtains blowing in a breeze, and he can only hold onto the feeling of it, a vague sense of claustrophobia.

He gets out of bed and slips down the hall. He's sure he closed the door to Bridget's studio before he and Sophie said goodnight, yet here it stands, open. He steps into the room, placing himself in a square of moonlight shining through the window. Her paintings surround him, all the colors invisible in the night.

The dream comes back in a rush. He was standing in an attic, the floor and ceiling a latticework of intricate pine that glowed like melted honey. He was at one end of the room, and he had to get to the other, but with each step he took, the floor and ceiling pressed closer together, pushing up against his feet and down on his skull, steadily and slowly, until he was squeezed into a version of himself no taller than the tiny plastic fairies Sophie sometimes plays with, the ones so small they slip through the cracks between the floorboards. The more he shrank, the less he could breathe.

Enough.

The word is so clear Nate turns to look behind him, sure Sophie must be standing in the doorway of the studio. But there's no one there, only the open, dark throat of the upstairs hall. He is alone in the room.

But also not alone, because here in the air around him is the smell of Bridget's skin right after a shower, and the feel of her cool fingers against his temples.

Enough, she says again.

He wants more than that one word; he wants to know everything—why she left, what he could have done to make her stay. He wants to tell her everything, too—how he still sometimes forgets to drain the dishwater, and how the flowers bloomed with such vibrance last summer, and how Sophie's eyes shine whenever she talks about animals. Otters, she told him recently, hold hands when they sleep so they won't float away from each other.

But then he hears it again, fainter this time—*Enough*—and he understands there's no need for any other words. She doesn't need him to show anything to her. She's still here, still somehow seeing all of it for herself.

Late the next morning, Nate stands on the roof of his parents' house, pushing snow in neat lines off the roof and into the backyard. His shoulders ache from the repetitive motion, and his eyes won't stop watering in the wind that whips through the pine trees. They're still digging themselves out of one storm, and another one is predicted for next week. Anywhere else, that sort of relentlessness might feel personal, but here in the County, it's just the way it goes. Winter lasts until April, sometimes May.

At noon, after the final strike of the bells down at the Congregational Church, Nate hears his name being called. He steps to the edge of the roof and looks over to see his father standing in the driveway, staring up at him.

"Good enough. Come on down."

"I'm not finished."

"It's lunchtime."

"Just one more pass, Dad."

A few minutes later, Nate throws the shovel off the roof and into the snowbank. He has an urge to jump down after it, just like he used to do when he was a kid—it's a one-story house, the distance isn't great, and the landing would be soft. He chooses to descend the ladder instead.

In the kitchen, his father is cutting ham and cheese sandwiches into triangles, just as he does for Sophie. Between the slices on each plate, he places three baby carrots and a handful of Humpty Dumpty chips.

Most of his father's routines, like this one, haven't changed in Nate's entire life. Every morning, he brushes his teeth twice—once after waking up, and again after his second cup of coffee. Every night, he watches the local news but skips the broadcast that comes after, the news of the world. Every Saturday morning, he drives the garbage out to the dump. On the first day of every month, he goes through the house and checks the batteries in the smoke detectors.

Nate loves knowing he can guess at any given moment exactly what his father is doing. It's nice to know some things stay as you leave them. But there are times he worries his father's need for structure is indicative of something wrong in his wiring, like the people who need to close and open a door three times before leaving a room. And Nate worries that obsessive instinct is alive in his own blood—his need for rules and order.

He and his father settle at the table and start to eat. Nate feels wobbly-kneed and dizzy, as though he were still on the roof. Or maybe the disoriented feeling comes from the way he can't stop thinking about Rose, or about Bridget. The feel of Rose's mouth against his. The clear sound of Bridget's voice in the moonlight.

"Okay, then," says his father. "What's bugging you?"

"It's nothing."

"Just tell me."

Nate and his father's relationship is good, but it is based mostly off silent understanding. The deepest thing they've ever discussed is the choice between vinyl siding or wood, and the closest they have ever come to any sort of heated argument was the time when Nate, as a teenager, missed an easy shot on the last day of moose season. They'd spent so long in the woods, and to leave without anything was a kind of failure, his father said. But even that was forgiven by the time they drove back into town, his father apologizing for the way the pain in his back made him so cranky.

Now, though, Nate is filled with countless conflicting desires and allegiances, and if he doesn't find a way to sort them out, they might drive him mad.

"Do you think," he asks, "that it's ever possible to be in love with more than one person at one time?"

Other than a slight upward flick of his eyebrows, no expression on his father's face gives away what he has on his mind.

"I think," he says, "you should talk to your mother."

It feels like a dismissal. A rejection. Nate wants to apologize for putting the man on the spot, asking such a personal, impossible question.

Then his father continues.

"What I'm saying is that your mother knows a little something about this. And I think maybe it's time you know, too."

For many years after, Nate will remember it perfectly: The somber yet resigned look on his father's face. The way he looks out the window and nods approvingly at the heap of snow Nate has pushed into the yard. *Pretty darn good.* The way the sun throws strange shadows through yellow curtains made by his mother's hands, curtains his father has always claimed to hate but has never, not once, asked her to take down.

How We Talk About Love

When Bev gets home from work, her feet aching and her throat sore from all the conversations she had with customers about Greg and Angela's rescue, she's greeted by the smell of baking cookies. For a second, she wonders why Bill would try to bake anything after the lasagna fiasco of '92. But when she steps into the kitchen, she sees Nate bending down to take a tray out of the oven.

"Chocolate chip, Ma."

"Sounds good," says Bev, collapsing on a chair without taking off her shoes. She shrugs out of her jacket, lets it drape behind her. "Why are you making them?"

"I was waiting for you. Wanted to keep myself busy."

She's always glad to see her son, but she wasn't expecting company. All she wants is to take a long bath and curl up on the couch with the novel Trudy keeps insisting she should read.

"Where's your father?"

"Left early for the bus run."

Nate leaves the cookie tray to cool and joins Bev at the table. She can tell by the look on his face there's something on his mind, and she feels panic twist inside her stomach. It's the same way she felt when he asked her and Bill, after Bridget's funeral, to take Sophie home with them. *Keep her safe*, he said, and Bev didn't know what was worse—Bridget buried underground, or Nate wandering alone out in that farmhouse.

"Was work okay?" he asks, setting the rhythm she understands he needs her to follow.

"Not bad."

"How many pastries did Larry buy?"

"Three donuts, one turnover, and a chocolate muffin."

"Must be something brewing at the mill."

"He mentioned more layoffs."

"Marshall would be devastated. Seeing that place fall apart so fast."

Bev nods but doesn't answer, already tired of this game. If she doesn't push a little, neither of them will say anything meaningful at all.

"What's going on, Nate? Are you having doubts about work again?"

"I always have doubts. But no, I'm pretty sure I'm where I'm supposed to be, doing what I'm supposed to be doing."

"So it's about Rose, then?"

The question throws him off guard, just as Bev hoped it would. She learned early on with her son that the best way to get to his true feelings was to sneak up on them from the side. Even when he was a kid, he never wanted to admit when he was hurt or anxious; she always had to go in covertly, surprise the true answer out of him.

"How do you know about Rose?"

"We all know."

"Who is we?"

"Me, your father, Trudy, Richard—we all see it. The way you two are together. The way you could be."

The first time Bev imagined the possibility of Rose Douglas, she wasn't sure. She didn't want Nate taking on the responsibility of another person's children or the pressure of trying to heal a woman who had been mistreated since she was a child herself, first by her mother and then by Tommy. It was too much grief, and Nate had already had enough grief. Much as she loved Bridget, Bev sometimes felt she relied on Nate too much for her own emotional stability. She was a good person, smart and kind and talented, but her gregariousness and charm masked a vulnerability that appealed to Nate, who wants to help others so badly he often forgets himself in the process. And Bev had always worried about that imbalance, which she feared would be even more pronounced between Nate and a woman like Rose, who has seen some of the worst life has to offer.

But the day Rose came over here for a barbecue last summer, Bev changed her mind. It was several little things strung together—the way Rose wordlessly handed Nate the last hamburger, passing the ketchup along with it before he could ask, the way she knew what song he was talking about when he couldn't remember the title. Nothing momentous, but nonetheless profound. Enough to convince Bev that Rose would take care of her son just as much as he would take care of her. A life shared between those two would never be one-sided; it would be an even exchange, one strength for another.

"The way we could be," says Nate, twirling the wedding band he still wears. "How's that possible, Ma? How can I be loyal to Bridget—and Sophie, for that matter—and still have enough space left over for Rose and Adam and Brandon?"

"Trust me, sweetheart. You can make room."

"I don't know." Nate stops fiddling with the ring and folds his hands together. "Listen, Dad said something weird today. Something about how I should ask you about loving more than one person at one time."

She has been waiting for this moment since Nate was nearly thirteen, the night she and Trudy finally kissed and understood what was meant to be and how their lives would go from then on. Countless times in the years since, Bev has wondered how Nate didn't question the extent of her relationship with Trudy, why he seemed to have no suspicion of her double-life. She usually sensed he was oblivious, and she was relieved for his lack of imagination. On occasion, though, despite how discreet she and Trudy tried to be, she thought that Nate, like his father, must have at least suspected but perhaps chosen not to acknowledge it.

Maybe not telling him sooner has been her biggest failure as a mother. Perhaps if she had been open with him as a teenager, giving him no option but to face the complicated truth, he would have grown up understanding more about the world. Or at least understanding the world in a different, more colorful way.

If anyone were to ask her why she kept it silent for this long, Bev doesn't think she could give a satisfactory answer. She's not ashamed of herself, or of Trudy. She is at peace with the compromises they have each made within their marriages, the ways she, Trudy, Bill, and Richard have all adjusted to make space for each other. The best explanation she can come up with is that she has been waiting for Nate to ask. For him to be willing to see.

"Trudy," she begins, "is a hell of a lot more than my best friend."

And then she tells him. Not the gritty details—those are for her and Trudy alone—but enough for him to understand what their relationship really is, how long it has existed, running like an invisible current beneath every joy and tragedy in his life for nearly twenty years. She tells him enough for him to be unable to look away.

As she talks, Nate listens carefully, his face betraying little, though every few minutes, his blue eyes widen or blink rapidly.

"So," says Bev after she has shared all she is willing to. "There you have it."

The oven fan shuts off, leaving only silence and the smell of baked sugar as Nate stares out the window, gathering his thoughts.

"Jesus," he exhales. "I wasn't expecting that."

"You never suspected?"

"Bridget did." Nate twirls his ring again. "She tried to tell me once, a long time ago. But I told her it couldn't be true, and she dropped it."

"What about it was so hard to believe?"

"I don't know. It's just . . . this is Dalton, you know? You don't really hear about that sort of thing here."

This town, thinks Bev. This picturesque, neighborly, silent town.

"Are you ready to disown me now?"

She doesn't realize until she asks how terrified she is he might say yes.

"Ma, I could never disown you. It'll take some adjusting, though. I mean, it's a lot. It's a lot to process.

"I understand that."

Nate sighs as he folds his hands on the table. "And it's just one more thing, you know? One more thing I got wrong, even though the proof was right there in front of me."

He may never stop blaming himself for Bridget's death, and as much as that tears her up, Bev knows there's nothing she can do about it. *You can't direct another person's healing*, a therapist once told her. *You can't tell anyone how to carry their hurt.* But she'll be damned if she lets this next thing go silent.

"Nate, look at me. Listen."

He looks at her. He listens.

"Life is too damn short," she tells her son, "to limit yourself to one kind of love."

Trudy is sitting on the couch surrounded by stacks of gardening books when Bev calls. Curious why she's calling now rather than after supper like normal, but also irritated by the distraction, she answers.

"Bevy, I'm right in the middle of my garden plans."

"It will be months before you can plant any flowers. Just give me ten minutes, I need to tell you something."

"Five minutes."

"I told Nate."

"Okay, then. Ten minutes."

While Bev relays the conversation, Trudy has to stop herself from interrupting several times. From the very beginning, she has wanted to tell Nate the reality of her relationship with his mother. But Bev always said she would address the issue if and when it came up organically. And even though Trudy thought this was ridiculous, she also accepted it wasn't her call—she may think of Nate as her own son, but there are things only a man's natural mother can tell him, and this is one of them.

Now that he finally knows the whole of it, Trudy feels the same sort of relief as when she pushes Mycroft off her chest every morning—a weight lifted; a burden gone.

"I just can't believe it," says Bev. "How kind he was about the whole thing."

"What did you expect? Some sort of homophobic bullshit?"

"No, of course not, I know he's not that sort of person. It's just—the fact that his father brought it up to him . . . "

She doesn't need to explain this. Not long ago, Richard described Bill as a duck—sturdy and lovable, but content to float along with his head underwater. The fact that he popped up against the current, however briefly, to suggest Nate ask his mother about the truth of who she is suggests a strength Trudy has never believed Bill capable of possessing.

"It's a good thing, Bevy. For all of us."

"I hope so."

"And I can't wait to tell Nathaniel he owes you and me over twenty years' worth of those stupid anniversary cards he buys you and Bill every year."

"That's right," says Bev, laughing. "We'll have to hold him to it."

Later, after Richard comes home and they have supper together—cheddar broccoli soup, slightly scalded but still perfect—Trudy brings her gardening books into the kitchen so she can sit with him at the table while he researches his summer birding adventure. She flips through glossy pages, marveling at all the heights and textures. She's been gardening for over half her life, and she still can't believe how many ways there are to grow one, all the ways you can fill a plot of land with color.

"How would you feel if I took two weeks off instead of just one this summer?" asks Richard. "There are so many sanctuaries down on Cape Cod, and if I had more time, I could really take advantage. I could see swallow-tailed kites. Sandhill cranes."

"If you're prepared to deal with Massholes for two weeks in the middle of summer, I'm not going to stop you."

"You could come with me."

It's a nice offer, but they both know Trudy will choose to stay here. When they were younger, before Bev came along, she would have said yes. For a brief, bright period when they were just starting, she and Richard dreamed of all the places they might one day go, places far from Northern Maine. They were so different back then from who they are now. Hard to believe a person can go through so many iterations of oneself—all the infinite, tiny changes that occur minute to minute, day to day, year to year. But that's life, Trudy supposes, a constant evolution, everything moving always onward.

She flips a page of her book, feeling her breath catch behind her ribs when she sees the array of purple flowers bursting and blooming on the page. Globe thistle, cosmos, lavender, salvia, catmint, liatris . . .

"Which one of these should I plant this year?" she asks, spinning the book around so Richard can see what's possible.

He studies the page as seriously as she has seen him read the charts of his patients. "Any of them," he says. "Any of them would be good."

"Momma?"

"What is it, baby girl?"

"Can you help me get ready for my date with Greg?"

Her mother's squeal is piercing. She stubs out her cigarette in the ashtray on the kitchen table before jumping up to wrap Angela in a rib-splitting hug.

"You and Greggie! Why didn't you tell me you two's are an item now?"

"We're not an item, Momma. It's just a date."

"Tell me everything. Who asked who? How? When? Where are you going, what're you going to do?"

The reaction is exactly what Angela knew would happen as soon as she dropped the news on her mother. It's also why she's been waiting to tell her, and why she's glad no one else is around to witness this teenage level of excitement coming out of a grown woman.

"He asked me," Angela says. "Yesterday. And I don't know where he's taking me, so I need you to help me pick an outfit that could work for anything."

When she called Greg last night to check on him, Angela felt giddy waves roll through her as soon as she heard his voice. She didn't hesitate to say yes when he asked if he could take her out. Even though she asked for specifics, he refused to give anything away.

Her mother clasps her hands under her chin and fixes Angela with a moony stare. "You got no idea how long I been waiting for this."

"Calm down, Momma."

"He's a good one, Greggie."

"I know, Momma."

"How long till he picks you up?"

"An hour."

"Shit. No time to waste."

They start in the bathroom, Angela sitting backwards on the closed toilet seat so Momma can work the curling iron through her hair. The room smells the way it always has, a blend of strawberry shampoo and vanilla perfume. A bit of Angela, a bit of her mother. There are hair accessories and makeup strewn over every surface, boxes of pads and tampons, a facial bleach kit left out for anyone to see.

At her father's house, Angela couldn't believe how clean the bathroom was. The only things out were the family's toothbrushes—a different color for everyone; she was assigned blue—and a glass jar of hand soap that never dipped below the halfway point. A few months after she moved in, Angela dug through every drawer and cupboard until finally, on the top shelf of the linen closet, tucked behind a stack of guest towels no one ever used, she found proof of her stepmother's humanity—pantyliners, yeast infection cream, bikini wax strips. Growing up in Momma's house, Angela never stopped to consider those products would be something a woman might need to hide. When she found that trove of feminine shame, she missed her mother more than ever before.

"Momma, how did you and Dad meet?"

"I was visiting my cousins in Bangor," says her mother, wrapping a tendril of Angela's hair around the barrel of the curling iron. "We went to a party, and he was there. I was supposed to come back north the next day, but I ended up staying on the rez a couple years. Maybe you can't tell nowadays, with that little potbelly of his, but your dad was a looker back then."

"What was he like?"

"Real sweet, in a quiet sort of way. When I was pregnant with you, I couldn't stop craving maple syrup. So he'd make me pancakes every morning and just drown them in it. This was the real shit, tapped from his own trees. And I had a lot of real syrup before that and I've had a lot after that, but nothing ever tasted so good as his."

Angela can't help but imagine her father boiling off sap, letting it cool before bringing a ladleful of it to her mother's lips.

"Why didn't you stay together after I was born?"

"Oh, a lot of reasons. Mostly what it came down to was he wanted to stay there and I wanted to come home."

"And he just let you go? Even though . . . " Angela lets the thought hang in the air as she remembers his defeated voice when he apologized for being a crappy dad.

"Thing is, I didn't give him much of a choice." There is regret in her mother's words, but also resolve, as if she has been waiting for this conversation for a long time. "One day while he was at work, I packed my stuff, put you in the car, and drove north. Your grandma took us in until I saved up enough money to buy this dump."

Angela's first instinct is anger. What right did her mother have to steal her away from her father? But in a few breaths, the resentment fades. Momma was only eighteen when she met and married Deacon, twenty when Angela was born, twenty-one when she filed for divorce. In many ways still a child herself, homesick. Angela barely remembers Grandma Pearl, who died when she was in kindergarten, but she understands that pull back to one's mother.

"Your father tried," says Momma. "In his own way. But communication has never been his strong suit."

Maybe in this one way, Angela takes after her father. All those failed conversations; neither of them knowing what to say or how to start. An inherited inclination toward silence.

"Now," says her mother. "We gotta shift focus, all right?"

"Okay."

"What do you think?"

Momma holds up the handheld mirror so Angela can see the way her hair spirals down to her waist. She knows from experience how exhausting it is to curl so much of it; when she does it herself, she has to take frequent breaks to rest her arms. But her mother doesn't seem tired at all when she grins at Angela in the mirror, freckled with hairspray. In fact, Momma looks younger than ever, like some bright light is dazzling out from under her skin. Like her blood is made of stars.

On the drive to Prescott, Greg and Angela don't say much. She can't stop glancing at him in the glow of the dashboard lights, remembering the drives she took with Henry along this same road in high school. She never felt with Henry the way she does now, a mix of insane nerves and complete peace. A mixed tape plays, serenading them with the Cranberries, Dylan, the Kinks, Mariah Carey.

"A little old and a little new," says Greg.

She likes the way he sings along with it all, knowing every word and every rhythm. He has a nice voice, quiet but strong, and he doesn't seem embarrassed about letting her hear it like most other guys would be.

When he pulls into the parking lot of the mall, Angela can't help but laugh. It's where every Dalton teenager goes for a date, which is why she figured it would be the last place he would take her.

"Would you prefer the bowling alley?" asks Greg, grinning. "Pizza Hut? Tim Horton's? Prescott is nothing if not a hotbed of romance."

"I don't know why more people don't honeymoon here."

"Rumor is it's slated to be the next Niagara Falls by 2010."

On their way across the lot, Greg walks close enough to catch Angela if she slips on the ice but far enough away for her to feel free. Unencumbered. She wonders if that's what all the best relationships come down to—independence and togetherness in equal measure, the promise of support without the weight of expectation.

The mall smells just how she remembers it, an eye-watering assault of cucumber-melon body spray, fried rice, and new sneakers. They wander each store, starting with K-Mart and working their way down to Sears. In B-Dalton (when they were kids, they believed the store was named after their town), Angela buys Greg an illustrated book about perennial flowers. He returns the favor at Claire's with a gaudy rhinestone bracelet, which she wears the rest of the night even though it turns her skin green.

Sometimes they walk close enough for their fingers to graze briefly in the space between them, which is a kind of melting ripple, a want for more. But as much as she wants to kiss Greg and run her hands under his shirt to feel the muscles of his chest, that's as far as Angela's imagination can go.

Before Mason, she loved sex and all that went along with it—the kissing, the touching, all that blurry buildup. After Mason, she can barely bring herself to touch her own body anywhere below her collarbone.

If this were any other guy, Angela would feel the pressure rolling off him like heatwaves. Even Henry, who always followed her lead in these sorts of things, had a way of making her feel like he was only pretending to listen to whatever she was saying so he could rip her clothes off. And usually she didn't mind, because that was what she wanted. But there were times she wondered what it would be like to have a date that didn't end in an abandoned parking lot or back road. One that ended at the front door, like in the movies.

After their second loop through the stores, they head for the food court.

"So many choices," says Greg, pointing between the Dairy

Queen and the Chinese place. "How can we even narrow it down?"

They settle on veggie lo-mein, chicken-on-a-stick, egg-rolls, onion rings, and Orange Julius, bringing it all back to one of the plastic tables near a fountain that only pushes water out sporadically, the air hissing through the pump in pitiful bursts.

"I see it," says Angela, nodding toward the weak bubble of water. "Niagara Falls."

"I'm telling you. Fifteen years from now, this place is going to be on the map."

The food is greasy, barely warm, perfect. As a stream of families and other young couples move past them in a blur, they talk about Greg's classes, Angela's job at the store. Their families. Old Town and Orono and Bangor, the way things feel so different there, even though it's not so far away from here.

"Do you think you'll go back?" Greg asks. "To your dad's, I mean?"

Angela can tell by the hopeful tone of his voice that he's thinking of other dates they could have down there. Better Chinese options, for one thing, other cafés and restaurants. Tours of his greenhouses on campus. Clubs where people their age dance all night.

"I don't know," she says. "Maybe if I had a good reason to."

Greg nods, his brown eyes alight with thoughts he leaves unspoken. And then he moves on, asking her if she's seen *Toy Story* yet.

Not long after, an angry-faced manager shouts at them to get their asses moving. The mall is closing in ten minutes. Angela looks away from Greg, stunned to see half the lights are off and they are the only customers left.

"Shit. That went by fast."

"Too fast."

"It's only nine. Do you have to be home soon?"

"Momma told me if we were back before midnight, she'd kick both our asses."

They talk the whole way back from Prescott, all sorts of different music flowing under their words. The familiar landscape slips by outside, trees and hills and fields.

It isn't until they're nearly to the water tower at the edge of Dalton that Angela asks Greg what they should do with the rest of the night. As soon as she says it, she's afraid it sounds like a rehearsed come-on line. But he grins as a truck passes them, headlights flooding the car.

"I might have an idea. Do you trust me?"

"Dumb question."

He drives down Depot Hill, then turns into the lot of the Aroostook Lodge. The cabin looks small and sad against all the snow surrounding it. The path along the river has been plowed, and Greg coaxes the car through ruts and potholes, not stopping until they're at the boat launch.

He leans over the center console and kisses her, cupping her face in both hands. Soft and slow. He tastes like Orange Julius. She takes his hand down to her breast, curious about her own reaction as much as his. He groans against her lips, and Angela feels dizzy from it all, her skin a wash of shivers.

She pulls away. "I'm sorry. I need to stop. I'm sorry."

"You have nothing to apologize for," says Greg, sitting back against his door to give her room. "Are you okay?"

She hasn't talked about it with anyone, not even Momma. The shrink at rehab tried to get her to tell about it, to assure her that something a man did to her against her will shouldn't be her shame to carry. Up until now, though, Angela didn't really believe it.

"There are things I want to tell you," she says to Greg. "But I don't think I'm ready yet."

"That's okay," he says. "There are things I want to tell you, too."

They sit with that for a minute, each wondering what stories the other has to share. Both of them knowing they can talk about all of it later.

"Do you trust me?" asks Angela.

"Dumb question."

She reaches over and turns off the ignition so the headlights will disappear. Then she steps out of the car and makes her way down the slope toward the frozen river. She doesn't have to look back to know Greg is following.

"Don't worry," she says when the reach the boat launch, a concrete ramp that leads from the path to the river. "I won't make you go all the way out on the ice this time."

"Good to know you're not a total maniac."

It's a cold night, but not nearly as freezing as the County can get. They take off their jackets so they're down to their sweaters and fleeces, and then they use the coats as cushions on the snowy ground.

Both at the same time, as if agreeing beforehand this is exactly what they meant to do and where they meant to end up all along, they lie down so they're side by side, facing the sky that blinks stars back at them. A pure white moon. And down below their feet, hidden under ice, the river flowing on as always, east toward the sun.

Soon after, Greg walks Angela up to the front porch where they spent so many hours together when they were kids, watching people come and go from the Tavern, imagining adulthood as something far away and unattainable. He kisses her cheek. Nothing is expected, and anything is possible.

Even before she pushes open the door, she knows Momma will be waiting for her on the other side.

Invitations

The morning after his date with Angela, Greg walks to the library with a stack of overdue books in his arms. It's a mild morning, cloudless, temperature hovering around thirty-five degrees. Something about the quality of light falling from the sunny sky to the snowy ground makes it feel like winter is loosening its grip. It's a trick, though. There are months to go before ice turns to mud turns to grass and budding leaves.

In the library, Greg sets the books on the desk and hangs back while Trudy reads to a group of grade schoolers. It's slightly unsettling to watch her read so animatedly, her usual frown replaced by exaggerated expressions. She even does voices for each character like Greg's father used to do when he read *The Hobbit* to him and his sisters.

After she's turned the last page, Trudy stands and tells the kids to spread out, look through the books, have fun. When she gets to the desk and sees Greg grinning at her, her frown returns.

"For Chrissake, wipe that smirk off your face. I'm paid to entertain them like that."

"Paid to read, sure. But all that pizzazz you threw in?"

"Little shit. And what's this? All these books?"

"Aimee asked me to return them."

He scans the books his sister has been hoarding in her room for who knows how long. Joan Didion, Sandra Cisneros, Ruth Moore—not a single one of the Dalton High curriculum-approved titles like *Huckleberry Finn* or *Lord of the Flies*. Little rebellions like this assure him Aimee is going to turn out just fine, though he may need to sit down with her and have a frank discussion about her wardrobe choices.

"So," says Trudy as she tucks date due slips into the back of each book. "You survived."

He knows she was the one who called Nate to report him and Angela missing three days ago. He knows how worried she must have been, even if she will never admit it. And he knows it would have shattered something irreparable in her if he hadn't come out of the woods.

"Who the hell goes into the forest during a snowstorm? An idiot, that's who."

"Yup. That's true."

Across the room, Mrs. Perkins is lining up the second graders to make the short walk from the library across the parking lot to the grade school. One of the kids, Brandon Merchant, gives Greg a shy smile as he walks past.

After they're gone, it's just Greg and Trudy in the library. It's a small building, only one floor crammed with thousands of stories. Sunlight shines off dust jackets; the place is filled with the scent of old ink and paper.

"When do you head back to Orono?"

"Day after tomorrow. Classes start Monday."

"Any big plans before you leave?"

"Family supper tonight." Greg pauses for dramatic effect. "I came out to my dad."

"Well, shit." Trudy gives him a look half-shock, half-pride. "How'd that go?"

"Not great. But not terrible, either."

"Sometimes that's the most you can ask for."

They chat a bit longer—he tells her about his date with Angela, to which Trudy says it was about damn time—and then they say goodbye, for now.

Outside, the sun is shining so bright Greg takes off his jacket to let the warmth soak through his sweater. He tilts up his face, closes his eyes, and imagines the light soaking all the way down through his skin and into his bones, becoming part of his cells. His own version of photosynthesis.

With Sarah and Ian, it's a full house that night. Greg's mother makes lasagna and garlic bread. It's crowded around the table, everyone talking over each other. Ian, as usual, wants to talk potatoes—predictions for the growing season, estimates of profit. Aimee and their father get everyone laughing with their impersonations of Helen McGreevy shopping for a new plunger. Their mother and Sarah discuss curtains and tablecloths, their words circling around like frantic little sparrows. Greg talks about the landscape design course he's most excited about for this semester.

"And what about summer?" asks their mother. "Will you stay in Orono, or do you think you'll come back home?"

Three weeks ago, the question would have been easy to answer. Now, though, Greg can see all sorts of different possibilities spooling out before him. Down there, he could get a work-study job at the greenhouses. He could spend some time on the road, driving around to some of the places he didn't get to see last year and still wants to discover. Beaches and wildlife preserves, inland hills and forests.

But if he came back here, he could spend the summer with Angela. They could paddle the river, go swimming at Portman Lake, drive around backroads they have known forever. Talking about nothing. Everything. Greg could even take her on a trip down to the coast, and they could stand on the shore as waves roll in, sun rising over the water, washing the world in light.

"I'm not sure," he tells his mother. "I guess I need to think about it."

For dessert, they each make their own ice cream sundaes.

"Maybe it's childish, but I just thought . . . "

"It's perfect, Mom," says Sarah, spraying whipped cream into her bowl.

Greg sits back in his chair and lets it flow over him, the conversations and laughter. He knows every word his mother will say before she says it. He knows exactly how hard Aimee will roll her eyes the next time Ian uses the term *spud projection.* And he knows without having to ask Sarah that she will try again to be a mother. Maybe by this time next year, Greg will be an uncle, or on his way to becoming one. Maybe one day he will teach his niece or nephew how to plant a garden. How to survive a snowstorm. How to avoid their Aunt Aimee's fashion mistakes.

Greg still hasn't come out to his mother, but he suspects his father has told her. She's been different with him the past couple days. Not in a bad way, and not anything too obvious—more of a subtle shift in the way she looks at him, speaks his name.

Later, after Sarah and Ian have left and Aimee has retreated to her bedroom, Greg's parents tell him they want to show him something. They have that look they always used to get on Christmas morning, faces shining at the thought of what their kids were about to find wrapped under the tree.

"Should I be scared, Mom? I feel like I should be scared."

"Honestly, Greg, I don't know why you always have to be so dramatic."

They lead him to the basement, where his father keeps his model railroad. Greg hasn't been down here since late last summer, the night he told his father he didn't want to inherit the family business. The night they found out Sarah had lost the baby. All sorts of legacies erased within the span of minutes.

"Show him, Jim."

"Cheryl, I will. I'm about to."

The three of them kneel in front of the little world his father has created, an exact replica of the world they already live in. Frenchie's, the Store 'N More, the Diner. The grade school and the high school, the post office, the Rec Center. All three churches. Tiny people speckle the sidewalks. Tiny cars drive through the streets.

"Do you see it, son?"

"What should I be seeing?"

"Look."

Inching closer, Greg notices a spray of color behind the hardware store. Little shepherds' hooks overflowing with pink and red. A section for saplings. There's a greenhouse, too, complete with a miniature rubber hose curled outside of it.

"Dad, what is this?"

His father is beaming in a way Greg has never seen before.

"Your mom and I thought it was time to make some improvements to the store," he says. "This spring, we're going to add a plant shop. Something more substantial than the shitty inventory I've been selling the past few years."

"That's right," adds Greg's mother. "Something we can really be proud of."

He pulls his eyes away from the model and looks at his parents. His mom is chewing her bottom lip the way she always does when she's nervous, and his dad keeps pushing his glasses further up his nose. They've talked about this together. They planned this together.

"Is this your way of trying to get me back to the store this summer?"

"We hoped you might help us figure out what to buy," his mother says. "Teach us how to take care of everything. But no, this isn't an obligation."

"That's right," says his father. "We just want you to do what makes you happy."

Greg can tell by the looks on their faces they really mean it—he can come home, or he can stay away.

The choice is his.

Your Own Understanding

After George teaches him how it all works, it doesn't take long for Tommy to find his rhythm in the kitchen. Accept dirty dishes and silverware from Arlene, rinse with hose-like sprayer, dip in soapy water, rinse again, put through the dryer, turn around and accept more dishes and silverware from Arlene, do it all again. Again. Again.

He finds a way to stand so his feet are planted but his upper body can swing freely in whatever direction necessary. Bits of other people's food touch his fingers, stick to his apron, clog the sink. The water scalds his hands, and the heat from the grill turns the kitchen into a stainless steel sauna. It's loud in here, a constant sizzle of grease, rattle of dishes, spatter of water. There's hardly any time for Tommy to think—all he can do is keep moving, keep turning dirty dishes into something clean.

He's only been at it a few days, but it might be the best job he's ever had. Or maybe just the one he's hated least.

But the restaurant is only open for breakfast and lunch, leaving a chunk of time from late afternoon until the moment he goes to bed when Tommy can't think of anything other than how much he wants a drink and how much he wants to see his kids.

On Tuesday night, a few hours after he and George made the deal for him to start working at the Diner, Tommy called Rose at suppertime. All he got, though, was her machine, and it was torture, trying to decide if she, Adam, and Brandon were there eating Shake-n-Bake chicken and ignoring him or if they were out at Nate's house, not thinking about him at all. And so he nipped out to the store and bought one tall boy, and he drank it by himself in the dark while he watched cars drive up and down the street outside the Diner.

On Wednesday, he called when he figured the boys would be taking baths and getting ready for bed. That time, the phone didn't ring at all, in a way that let him know Rose had unplugged it from the wall. Once again, torture, and he almost drove down to Frenchie's. But he was so tired from his first shift he decided it'd be better to crash early.

Yesterday, Rose finally answered the phone—only, though, because Tommy called her at the clinic, and she was obligated to answer. Maybe it was a low-ball move, but he couldn't think of another way to make her talk to him.

"You can't call me at work," she said.

"But I got a job now, too. They hired me here."

"I know. Arlene told me."

When she hung up, Tommy didn't bother calling back. He did, however, go to the store for two more tall boys. He drank the first one in about five long swallows. He didn't finish the second one. Every muscle hurt, and he could barely keep his eyes open. Like an old man, he fell asleep by nine.

Today, as he sprays dishes, he tries to come up with a new plan. Maybe he should just show up at the trailer. All he wants to do is tell Rose that what happened the other night won't happen again. Not ever. And then she'll finally let him talk to Adam and Brandon, tell them he's sorry. He'll never try to hurt their mother again, he'll say, and he'll never hurt them, either. Not ever.

But he doubts Rose would be okay with him appearing unannounced at the trailer. As soon as she saw his truck rolling down Larch Street, she'd probably call in Nate and the whole goddamn police fleet.

"Hey, you."

Tommy turns from the sink too fast, losing his grip on the nozzle so water sprays all over the floor, soaking his sneakers.

"Shit," he says, torn between irritation at Arlene for jumping him and worry that she'll be mad at him for the mess he's made. "I didn't see you there."

"Don't worry about it." She's holding a stack of menus in one hand and a coffee pot in the other. "Someone here to see you."

"What should I—"

"We're heading into our pre-lunch lull. Go ahead."

Wiping his hands on his apron, he steps out of the kitchen and into the dining room. Only a few customers are left at the tables, one older couple and a mom with a baby asleep in his car seat next to her. When Tommy sees Rose sitting at the booth in the window, he's surprised both by the fact that she's here and by the way his stomach doesn't perform its usual flip at the sight of her. It's like his body has let go of the idea he might ever get to hold her or kiss her again, let alone anything else.

"What are you doing here?" he asks as he sits down across from her.

"I'm on lunch break," says Rose, pointing at the uneaten BLT on the table as if he might not believe her. "And I figured this is as good a time as any to talk."

He understands this is her saying she won't see him in a place that isn't public. She thinks she needs witnesses.

"Are you just here to tell me what a piece of shit I am?"

"No."

"Show me some restraining order you have against me?"

"No."

Midday light comes through the window, making her eyes sparkle. She looks so much like she did as a teenager, but there's something different about her now. Something softer and harder at the same time.

"I'm here," she tells him, "to say thank you."

He feels the same sort of breathlessness he's gotten before after a kick to the balls.

"What are you talking about?"

"You could have hurt me. Or the kids. Or Nate. But you didn't touch any of us. And I'm thankful for that, Tommy. I really am."

"You get that I showed up to his house with a gun, don't you?"

Rose winces, the tendons in her neck showing briefly. "I know."

"I wanted to shoot him. I could've."

"But you didn't. You chose not to."

He doesn't understand what sort of trick she's trying to play on him. It would be easier, or at least less confusing, if she'd shown up here with a gun of her own and pointed it at his face. The couple gets up from their table and walk out the door, letting a blast of cold air in behind them. The baby in the car seat fusses, and the mom pats his chubby hands, hums a song that lulls him back to sleep.

"I'm too tired for any bullshit mind games, Rose. What are you saying?"

She chews on the straw in her water as she stares out the window, where the old people who just left are hovering on the sidewalk. When the man isn't looking, the woman scoops up a palmful of snow and tosses it at his back, the snow scattering against his jacket. He turns and lunges toward her, faster than Tommy thought an old guy could move, and wraps his arms around her waist. Both of them laugh as he plants a bunch of kisses all over her face. And then they walk off arm-in-arm toward the parking lot.

"It's so weird," says Rose. "For so long, I thought that could be you and me."

He doesn't have to ask if she still thinks that. He doesn't have to tell her he doesn't think that anymore, either.

"When can I see Adam and Brandon?"

"They still don't want to see you, Tommy."

A week ago, he would have been sure she was lying just to pull one over on him. But he's the one who fucked things up. No one else to blame this time.

"What can I do to make it better?"

"You'll have to ask your kids. When they're ready."

"How will I know when they're ready?"

"I'll tell you. Just as soon as they tell me."

Part of Tommy doubts she'll ever let him see those boys again. But there's some sort of promise in her eyes—maybe nothing that says she forgives him, but something that says she'll give him another chance if he's smart enough to take it.

One thing is still bothering him, though, and he's not sure he'll ever be okay with it—that pantywaist cop helping raise his sons. Doing all the things for them and with them that Tommy should be doing.

"So," he says, "is Nate your boyfriend for real now?"

Rose starts to chew her straw again, then pushes it away. Outside, a cloud shifts, and the light hits her brighter than ever, picking up the reddish undertones in her dark hair.

"Whatever Nate and I are to each other is between me and him. You don't get to be a part of that."

There are a lot of things he could say, so many names he could call her or threats he could make. But what would be the point? He needs a drink. He needs his kids. He needs to get back to work before George and Arlene decide to fire his ass.

"Okay," he says. "I guess that's that, then."

"For now."

Tommy leaves her there with her uneaten sandwich, almost bumping into the mom as she hefts the car seat off the table. She apologizes, then heads for the exit. He turns back to see Rose get up out of her seat, holding the door open for the girl. "What a cutie," she says as she squeezes the baby's toes while the mother stands there grinning. "So irresistible."

He goes back to the kitchen, where George silently watches as he returns to his station at the sink. There are dishes to wash, and he's getting paid to wash them. Best not waste any more time.

After the Diner is closed for the day and Arlene has disappeared into her office to work on bills, George asks Tommy if he can bum a cigarette.

They step into the alley between the restaurant and the dumpster. It's mid-afternoon, and the light has gone the sort of pinkish-gray that means more snow could be coming tomorrow, or maybe the day after. Sometime soon.

"Plans for the night?" George asks.

"Not really."

He can see Frenchie's in his mind like he's already there. He can taste the vodka, feel its slow burn down his throat and into his belly, his blood, his brain. A man deserves a drink after a day of hard work. A father whose sons don't want to see him deserves a dozen drinks anytime he wants.

George blows out a ring of smoke and watches it roll away in the breeze.

"Few old buddies of mine," he says, "they're meeting at the library tonight."

"Book club?"

"AA."

So it's a fucking trap. The man trapped him with a place to live and money to pay the bills, and now Tommy is stuck here with half a cigarette to go, about to hear some bullshit about the evils of booze and the wonders of a higher power.

"Never would've pegged you as a drunk, George. Or a Jesus freak."

"I'm neither of those things. And I don't go to the meetings myself. But I support what they're doing there."

"Brainwashing each other?"

"Trying to better themselves. Trying to clean up some of the messes they've made."

George flicks his ash onto the ground, a few embers going along with it and sizzling in the snow. He's gazing across the street at the band stand, boarded up for the season, but Tommy feels like the man is staring right into his eyes and down somewhere far inside him in a way no one ever has before. Not his uncles or cousins or friends. Not his mother. Definitely not his father.

He thinks back to what Rose said about how thankful she was that he chose not to hurt her or shoot Nate. *You could have,* she said. *But you didn't.*

It easily could have gone the other way, though. One breath different and he would have wrapped his hands around her throat. Or pulled the trigger and watched Nate fall to the floor. Tommy knows what stopped him from hurting Rose, but it's not so clear why he left Nate whole. It made sense at the time. Or maybe it didn't.

"I don't think I'll be going to the library tonight," he says.

He expects George to lecture him, give him some kind of ultimatum. *Get clean or you're out on your ass. Get right with God or watch me take away everything from you.*

Instead, George shrugs and stubs out the remainder of his cigarette on his boot. "Up to you," he says. "They meet there every Friday at 7:00."

Then he goes back into the kitchen, leaving Tommy outside. He stands alone in the chill for what feels like a long time, his gaze flicking from his truck, which will take him down to the Store 'N More or Frenchie's for whatever kind of booze he might want, to the stairs, which will bring him back up to his apartment, where the only thing he has to drink are cans of Coke and old coffee.

In the end, the decision seems to make itself.

Here

Back at the clinic after her Diner chat with Tommy, Rose steps into Dr. Haskell's office with her mostly uneaten lunch. Usually, he sticks to his post-heart-attack diet, but sometimes he'll break his own rules.

"Sandwich, Dr. H?"

He looks up from a pile of paperwork. He's been wearing reading glasses more and more lately, and his hair is thinner than it used to be. But his face is mostly unwrinkled, and he smiles a lot more than he did when Rose started working here a few years ago.

"Think I'll pass," he says. "Trudy's making chicken stew tonight."

She pops the takeout box into the mini fridge near the window, just in case he changes his mind. She has a few minutes before her lunch break is over, and she has an overwhelming urge to sink into one of the cushy chairs across from Dr. Haskell's desk. Before she can ask, he gives her a knowing look and nods.

"Go ahead. Stay for a bit."

He caps his pen and leans back in his own chair, smiling, as she gives her weight over to the fake leather cushions.

"Long week."

"So damn long."

Neither of them has to say anything else for Rose to know they're thinking of the same things—snowstorms and teens lost in the woods, dozens of patients with endless sicknesses that may or may not be curable. She also suspects Dr. Haskell's mind keeps floating to all the birds he's fallen in love with these past few months. On one of his walls, he's replaced a bunch of medical charts with a series of his own sketches of cardinals and blue jays and chickadees—the one Rose likes best is a pair of goldfinches sharing a pine branch.

Sometimes it's hard for her to wrap her head around the fact she has known Dr. Haskell most of her life. When she was a kid, she thought he was ancient, but now she recognizes he's only fifty. Just twenty-four years older than her, which means he wasn't that much older than she is now when he took over this clinic. She can't imagine bearing that kind of responsibility at such an age. It's hard enough to keep her own two kids alive and safe.

And then there's Nate, another man who voluntarily takes on the burdens of everyone else, even though he has so much grief of his own. What makes a man like that? What makes a man—or any person—so deep-down decent despite all the thousands of reasons there are to be angry and bitter?

Rose stares at the skeleton across the room. The skeleton stares back.

"Who do you think this guy was?" she asks.

"You have no idea," says Dr. Haskell, "how often I've wondered that same thing myself."

"Do you ever make up little stories for him?"

"When I was a kid, I liked to imagine he was a bandit from out west, that he escaped the law and got the last laugh by living forever in some Northern Maine clinic where no bounty hunter would ever find him."

Rose laughs, imagining the bones dressed like a cowboy, riding a horse through a desert. Then she feels guilty—the skeleton was, after all, a real person at some point, and who's to say the soul attached to these bones isn't with them right now, witnessing her disrespect?

"Do you think," Rose asks, "that people stick around after they die?"

"Are you asking my medical opinion or my personal one?"

"Are those things different?"

He twirls his pen in his hand as he stares out the window, where sunlight glares off the snowy ground.

"Medically speaking, once a person's heart stops beating and their brains cease to function, we consider them gone. It's remarkable, how suddenly after death a person turns into just a body, a shell. Like something empties out. You'd be surprised how unhuman a dead human body appears."

Rose, who has only seen corpses of animals, doesn't actually find this surprising—you know when something that used to hold a spirit doesn't hold one anymore. But she doesn't want to interrupt.

"Now, personally speaking . . . Sometimes out of nowhere, all these years later, I'll feel the weight of my father's palm right here, right on my shoulder."

"But couldn't that just be memory?"

Dr. Haskell fixes Rose with the same kind stare he used to give her when she would come in after-hours for him to clean up whatever mess Tommy had left on her body.

"Do you think," he asks, "there's a difference between a ghost and a memory?"

An hour before she's supposed to go pick up the kids from school, the clinic door opens, and Nate, dressed in his uniform, steps into the lobby. It's a slow day; only Marnie Stephens sits in the waiting room, reading the *Bangor Daily.*

Nate and Rose haven't talked or seen each other since the kiss. She has been living in a weird limbo of confidence that he would seek her out, once he had processed all of it, and nervous certainty that he would never speak to her again.

Rose, aware that Vera is standing behind her at the fax machine, can only wait for Nate to make his way across the lobby and up to the desk. He smiles as she slides open the glass window, but that's still not enough to assure her he's here with good news. He might just be trying to be polite.

"Hey," he says. "Would you like to come out to my place for dinner tonight?"

"Definitely." Then, afraid to hope for what she thinks he's asking, Rose adds, "The boys would love to see Sophie."

"Well, sure, you know the boys are always welcome. But Sophie's actually staying with her grandparents for the weekend, and I sort of thought . . . "

Vera, no longer pretending to send faxes, pipes up. "I could watch Adam and Brandon. They can come help me set up the Nintendo I bought for them."

"Great. My shift ends at 4:00, so if you come out around 5:30, Ro, that should give me time to get everything ready."

"She'll be there," says Vera. "Should she bring anything?"

"Only herself."

It's not until after Nate has left the clinic that Rose turns to Vera, who's staring back at her with a look of mock innocence.

"That was humiliating."

"It was necessary."

"Did you seriously buy a Nintendo for my kids?"

"How else am I going to rack up those Cool Aunt points?"

"Maybe we need to talk about boundaries."

"Maybe we need to talk about what you're going to wear."

On the drive out to Davis Road that night, Rose can't stop thinking about what Dr. Haskell said about memories and ghosts. Is one any more or less real than the other? It seems impossible to answer, but the process of trying is a good distraction from the twisting nerves in her belly.

Not far from here, Nate is waiting for her. He's in his kitchen, tending something on the stove, listening for the sound of her car. She knows this the same way she knows even before Adam or Brandon shakes her awake that they have had a bad dream.

It is also this same way of knowing that tells Rose that Tommy will haunt her and the boys the rest of their lives. No matter if he stays in Dalton or moves away; if he gets sober or stays drunk—all he has done and all he could do will always be lingering at the back of their minds. She wants to believe he'll keep this job and straighten himself out, if not for his own sake, then for Adam and Brandon. There's a difference, though, between hoping for something and believing it could actually happen.

But enough of Tommy, Rose thinks, as she rounds the final corner and sees the house, all lit up.

Nate greets her at the door, smiling as she takes off her coat and hangs it on a hook in the hallway, next to his jacket. She's glad Vera convinced her to wear her turquoise sweater dress—rather than his usual jeans and sweatshirt, Nate is wearing nice slacks and a navy sweater with a checked Oxford shirt underneath. No shoes, though, just a pair of thick wool socks.

"I'm sorry," she says, glancing down at her snow-covered boots. "I don't know what I was thinking. Your house is so clean . . . ."

"A little dirt won't hurt this house."

They head into the kitchen, which smells like warm, buttered bread. He's laid everything out on the table, and he points out every item to her, along with an explanation: One bottle of sparkling cider, one bottle of wine—he wasn't sure what she'd like. One green glass vase containing a spray of carnations and baby's breath—the best Bergeron's had to offer. And two mismatched plates, each bearing a perfectly toasted grilled cheese—because the chicken didn't thaw like it was supposed to, and there's only so much you can throw together in such a short amount of time.

"I'm sorry. I wanted to make you something nicer."

"It's perfect, Nate."

They each opt for the cider with a splash of wine mixed in.

Eating their sandwiches in no hurry, they talk about little things, boring things: Rose's frustration with patients who cancel appointments last minute and then get snippy when she can't get them rescheduled right away. Nate's frustration with Bruce's bad penmanship. Weather. Taxes. Nate is thinking about enrolling Sophie in Molly Lannigan's horse riding classes this summer. Rose is hoping Adam decides to play baseball with the Rec team in the spring.

"What about Brandon?" Nate asks. "Do you think he'll want to try any sports?"

"I kind of doubt that. I see him as more of an artist."

For a second, Rose is afraid she's ruined the night with just one word. Because, of course, Bridget was an artist.

But Nate looks unbothered as he refills her glass. "I see that for him, too."

"Can I tell you something?"

"Anything."

"I worry about him."

"Because of what happened with Sophie the other day?"

"Because of his whole life."

Both of them know she's talking about Tommy—he found a way to sneak in here tonight after all—but Nate sits back, waiting for Rose to continue.

"I've been thinking," she says, "that with all the shit he and his brother are up against, maybe it would do them both some good to go talk to somebody. Dr. Haskell says there's a child therapist over in Prescott he could refer us to."

It isn't until the words are spoken out loud that Rose really starts to fear them. Isn't sending your kid to a shrink proof that you think something is wrong with him? A screaming announcement to the world that you are a failure as a parent? She can't think of anyone else in Dalton who willingly goes to therapy—Annette Frazier was a special case.

"I don't know. Maybe it's a stupid idea"

"No," says Nate. "It's a good thing, Rose."

He reaches across the table for her hand, grazing his thumb across her knuckles in a way that sends tingles tumbling down her spine. She realizes he is no longer wearing his wedding ring.

"Now can I tell you something?" he asks.

"Of course."

"My mother's gay."

"Say that again?"

"She and Trudy are, you know, lesbians. Together."

At first the idea is crazy to Rose. After the initial shock, though, the revelation not only seems possible, but completely right. She's seen the way those two look at each other during parties and barbecues. The way they always seem to find each other in a crowd.

"Do your father and Dr. Haskell know?"

"Apparently, yes. It's like an open secret between all of them."

"And how do you know all this?"

"Ma told me the other day."

"Are you okay with it?"

"With lesbians in general? Or with my mother?"

"Both."

Nate releases her hand and settles back in his chair. "I want Ma to have the same things I want," he says. "And if Trudy is part of that, even though it will take some getting used to . . . Yeah. I'm okay."

Rose's heart could belong to a hummingbird, the way it's beating so hard inside her chest. Look at him, she thinks, just look at this man sitting across from her. He learns his parents' marriage is a sham, and instead of bitterness, he opts for understanding.

"What are the things you want?" she asks.

"All of it," says Nate, his blue eyes steady on hers. "Everything."

And they let that linger for a while, in the warm space between them.

Then he asks, "What about you? What do you want?"

"This."

And they know, without her having to say it, that *this* means Nate and Sophie and Brandon and Adam and all that comes along with each. The hurt and the healing. This room. This house. This land. This life.

"Ro?" His voice a question.

"Nate." Her voice an answer.

"Please don't drive back tonight," he says. "Stay here with me instead."

A few hours later, Rose, laughing, convinces him to bundle up and go outside with her. She wants to see the sky.

Their breath blows back toward their faces as they walk out of the driveway and into the middle of the road—this time of night, this time of year, it's completely empty except for the two of them. No danger here.

"Look," says Nate, and Rose tilts her face up to see what he sees—the silver-blue moon, and all the stars surrounding it. Then he tells her to look again, in a different direction, and she adjusts to see this other view he is pointing her toward.

Down below, beyond miles of woods and fields and the frozen river, is Dalton, the town revealing itself in a smattering of dim streetlamps and porch lights. Most everyone they know out there is probably asleep right now, dreaming dreams Rose could never imagine. Maybe some of them pace their houses sleeplessly. Maybe some will wake in their trailers before the sun is out and drive to a job they hate to feed a family they never wanted. Maybe a few will greet tomorrow with a smile, knowing they're exactly where they're meant to be.

It really is something, she thinks—all those untold stories. All those little lives spread out beneath the sky, across that distant valley.

Epilogue
December 31, 1999

Nate drives through Dalton, the same round he makes during every patrol shift. High Street, Main, Old Prescott Road, Howard Street. Turn around at the water tower. Larch Street—no need to slow at Rose's trailer; she hasn't lived there in two years, not since she gave the keys over to Tommy.

On Rich Fucker Road, near a For Sale sign pocked by snow and grime, Nate pulls over and lets the cruiser idle, the radio playing the same Britney Spears song Sophie belts out a dozen times a day. He stares at the house where Bridget grew up, the massive windows reflecting the few clouds in the early afternoon sky. The driveway is unplowed; the place abandoned since the last prospective buyer got cold feet and backed out at the last minute. When Marshall called the other night for his weekly check-in with Sophie, he told Nate their realtor has suggested he and Annette lower the price again. But even at a lower price, it would have to be someone with deep pockets, probably from away, who could afford a place like this.

Nate drives on without looking back.

Down Depot Hill, over the railroad tracks, all the way to the river that shines like a silver ribbon under the sun. If he parked the cruiser here and walked a few miles upstream, he would emerge at the edge of his property, his roofline peeking over the tops of evergreens and trees left bare for the winter. If he walked further, through the woods and the fields, he would arrive on his porch, and Rose would be there, opening the door for him as she does at the end of each of his shifts.

On his way back up Depot Hill, Nate notices a flurry of movement outside the yellow ranch that used to belong to the Gilberts, until they moved up to Fort Kent a few months ago. Slowing, he sees a woman in a blue bathrobe running down the driveway, flapping her arms in his direction, yelling something he can't hear.

Nate can imagine all sorts of things: Someone inside the house is hurt or sick or dying or already dead. The woman is being threatened by her partner. There's a smell of something sinister in the kitchen, a gas leak that will blow the place up if he doesn't act fast.

He stops and steps out of the cruiser, pulling in deep, winter-scented breaths in an attempt to ready himself for any terrible possibility. Then he strides down the driveway, meeting the woman halfway.

"Thank God," she says. She looks vaguely familiar, but Nate can't put a name to her face. She doesn't seem much older than him, ten years at most. Under her robe, she's wearing a pair of pajamas flecked with bleach stains.

"What's going on? How can I help?"

"I'm so sorry to flag you down. No one's hurt; it's just that it happened, and I saw your car, and I thought . . . Well, come on. I'll show you."

Confused and off balance—the only emergency he wasn't ready for was no emergency at all—Nate follows as she hurries toward a porch off the back of the house. She crouches beneath a picture window and scoops something into her hands.

"I was unpacking boxes in the living room, and out of nowhere I hear this awful thunk, so I run to the kitchen, over to this window, and I look out and there he was. He's just the sweetest little fellow."

She stands and extends her arms toward Nate; by instinct, he cups his palms to accept whatever it is she's offering. Looking down, he sees a rumple of feathers, a black cap on a head no bigger than his thumb. The chickadee weighs almost nothing in his hands, and something about all those hollow bones triggers a faint sense of déjà vu.

"Is he hurt bad, do you think?" asks the woman, laying one slender finger on the bird's back. Her wedding band glints under the sun.

"I think he's okay," says Nate. The bird's claws prick into his palms, and he can feel the quick vibration of its heart. "Just a little stunned."

"You'd think I'd have some idea what to do—I work at a veterinarian's office. But then again, I'm just the secretary. It's not like they trained me in wild bird emergencies."

The bird chirps as he fixes his black eyes on Nate's. Pecking its beak once into the heel of his palm, it then stretches its wings and lifts off, pushing its talons against the pulse point on his wrist.

Nate and the woman watch as the chickadee flies away, up toward a hemlock at the edge of the yard.

"Guess I made a big deal over nothing. Come on, I'll get you some coffee."

"That's really not necessary—"

But she's already opening the door and beckoning him inside. Nate follows her into a kitchen that smells like fresh-baked blueberry muffins and dish soap. Every surface is so clean. Several glasses rest upside down in the dish drainer, catching rays of sunlight that pour in through a window on the opposite side of the room. The fridge is uncluttered except for one picture, held in place by a magnet shaped like a maple leaf.

"May I?" asks Nate, waiting for her nod before stepping closer for a better look.

In the photo, two teenage girls with matching blonde hair, brown eyes, and short noses stand close together under dappled shadows of a birch tree. One wears a blue cap and gown; the other wears a pink sundress. Beside the younger girl stands the woman, her hair pulled back in an elegant twist. And next to the older girl is a burly man with a grizzled beard who is grinning so hard his eyes nearly disappear.

Nate feels like some kind of god has reached down from the clouds to put a hand on his chest and push him all the way back to that December day nine years ago.

He was driving back from Prescott. He was desperate with grief, ready to give in to the urge to drink the coffee brandy in his glovebox. When he saw the red Cavalier on the side of the road, he pulled over to help the two girls inside it. They were young—one was thirteen, the other six or seven. They were so small. The older one didn't want to trust him, but somehow, he convinced her they were safe with him. He brought them home, to that man and woman in the picture, this woman who back then barely spoke a word and swayed where she stood in another perfectly clean kitchen. In the end, outside that other house, Nate handed his own booze to her against his better judgment, not wanting to condone her behavior but unwilling to punish her for whatever had driven her to that thirst in the first place.

"Deb?" Nate says now. "Is that your name?"

The woman, startled, looks up from the tray of muffins. "That's some good cop ESP right there. Or do I know you?"

"Not officially. We only met once."

He wasn't wearing his uniform that day, and she was so out of it back then—maybe that's why she didn't recognize him when he came walking toward her down the driveway a few minutes ago. And then she was so intent on the bird, she barely looked at him. But now, stepping closer, Deb's eyes widen in shocked recognition. She smiles.

"Oh my god, it's you . . . Nick, is that your name?"

"Nate."

"Shit, it's good to see you again. You have a few minutes?"

They sit at the table in front of the window where the bird struck, mugs of coffee in front of them. Nate doesn't want to be rude, but he can't stop staring at her. She looks so different than the day they first met. Like an entirely different person.

Catching him looking, Deb smiles. "Crazy what sobriety can do for a person."

"How long?"

"It'll be six years in April."

"Congratulations," he says, raising his mug.

Deb clinks her cup against his.

"You know," she says, "you saved my life that day."

"That's not—"

"No, please listen." She fiddles with the sash of her robe. "When you brought my girls home to me . . . and then the booze . . . I was in bad shape. Don't get me wrong, I didn't stop drinking that day, or even the one after. But what helped me eventually give it up was the thought of you. The way you looked that day. Like you were letting me take the last lifeboat off the ship even though you might drown yourself."

She pauses to take a sip of coffee. Nate, uncomfortable as he is with this sort of talk and this sort of credit, understands this is about her, not him. And so he stays quiet.

"Few times," she says, "I thought of tracking you down. But it was the damndest thing—none of us could remember where you said you lived. And we had no idea you were a cop. Jesus, if we'd known, I would have been scared shitless, thinking you were going to report me to child services."

He remembers the choice not to tell Tina and Courtney. It was a sad, strange time; he had left the force shortly after Bridget's funeral, and he didn't know if he ever wanted to go back to it. But there was more to the decision not to reveal his vocation to those girls, an intuition that it might scare rather than comfort them.

"Anyway," says Deb. "I guess what I'm trying to say is thank you."

Nate, still unsettled by this praise but grateful she's better now, can only nod. They sit in comfortable silence as the furnace kicks on down in the cellar—it's the same sound his parents' furnace makes, the same sound he heard all throughout his childhood winters.

"So," he says, "are the girls here? Hiding somewhere in the back of the house?"

"No, they're over in Prescott today. Shopping spree."

"Ah. And how are they?"

Deb's eyes brighten. "Tina works for ACAP, helps people find housing and jobs and childcare. Connects them to services they might not have found on their own. It's perfect for her—she's really blossomed since she started there."

"That's fantastic. What about Courtney?"

"Your typical seventeen-year-old girl—all boys and makeup and *dying* to head off to college next year. Gary and I feel guilty, pulling her out of her old school mid-year, but she's already made a couple friends here in town."

"And how's Gary doing?"

"Doing all right," says Deb. "He took a forklift operator job at the mill a few weeks ago. That's why we moved here. He's actually there right now. Seems to like it so far."

Nate decides not to mention the rumors circulating around town that Acadian Lumber is thinking of selling the mill to another company, this time out of New Brunswick. Hopefully nobody will get laid off in the transition, but you never know.

"What about you? What do you do when you're not policing?"

"Oh, nothing too remarkable. I have a daughter, two stepsons." Nate pauses, still emotional, a year after the wedding, by the fact that he can officially claim Adam and Brandon as partly his own. "And another on the way. Due in February."

"If we make it that far," says Deb with a sardonic smile.

According to everyone on TV and in magazines and all around the globe, the world is going to end tonight.

Adam, thirteen, believes that at the stroke of midnight, clocks will stop, computers will crash, and planes will come tumbling out of the sky. Brandon pretends not to buy that story, but Nate and Rose can tell he's worried. He's usually worried about something, whether it's ropes of lightning that whip across the sky or the clunky sound the logs make when they shift inside the woodstove. Nothing like Sophie, who at ten years old appears to be afraid of nothing, not even the idea of an entire civilization wiped out in one second.

Nate doesn't believe in any of the Y2K madness. Because whenever he places his hands on Rose's belly and feels their unborn child kicking away, rippling up from unseen depths, he knows there is no way this world could come to an end. Not now, when everything is just beginning.

Back at the station, as soon as Nate has walked behind the desk, he's greeted with a giant hand slapping down on his shoulder. "Get into trouble out there?" asks Bruce, his beard spackled with cake crumbs.

"Quiet day," says Nate. "Question for you, though. Do we need to fill out incident reports for avian rescues?"

"What the hell are you talking about?"

"I rescued a bird. Sort of."

"Did you give this bird mouth-to-mouth? Or should I say beak-to-beak?"

"Thankfully it didn't go that far."

Bruce throws his head back to roar with laughter, big belly shaking. Then he fixes Nate with a serious expression.

"I walked a cow home one time."

Sure this is the beginning of a crass joke, Nate tells Bruce to stop talking.

"This isn't bullshit, Boss. This was twelve, thirteen years ago. I was on patrol on Poor Man's Road, and I found one of Eddie Dawson's milking cows wanderin' all by her lonesome.

What was I s'posed to do? Leave her there? Shove her in the back of the cruiser?"

"How'd you get her back to Eddie's?"

"Well," says Bruce, hitching up his gun belt. "I was a little more svelte in those days. A little more handsome than I am now, if you can believe it. So I just sorta sweet-talked the girl and herded her in the right direction. Took a while, but we got there eventually."

It's a great mental image—Bruce and a heifer on the side of the road, taking in the scenery—but Nate isn't sure what the moral of the story is.

Bruce sighs like a father tired of having to repeat an answer countless times. "What we do here ain't always glamorous. But sometimes we get to do some good for people."

"Or cows?"

Bruce's laugh thunders around the station, turning the heads of half a dozen EMTs and firemen who have stopped in to wish each other a Happy New Year and to congratulate Bruce on his new title of Chief, now that Halstead has finally retired.

"That's right, Boss. Or birds."

As Nate fills out the paperwork—*Depot Hill, bird strike, no resuscitation needed, all survived*—he thinks about what Bruce said. How the work they do here skirts the line between tedium and terror. Chasing speeders, ticketing people for expired registrations, trying to mediate domestic disputes that range from almost-funny arguments to full-blown violence. There are still moments when Nate wonders why he has signed on for a lifetime of this job.

But it's not all disaster or drudgery. It's also small birds that kiss your hand before flying off into an existence you can't imagine. It's mothers who stop drinking and men who, sometimes, choose surrender over violence.

Things with Tommy haven't changed much over the years—he has stretches when he's sober and stretches when he's not.

He doesn't have a lot to say to Nate on the occasions when he comes out to the house to visit Adam and Brandon—they don't like to spend time with their father at the trailer on Larch Street—but Nate can live with that. They can all live with that.

Shortly before his shift ends, Rose calls Nate on the main extension to tell him Adam changed his mind and wants pepperoni pizza instead of plain.

"No problem."

"And Sophie told me to tell you not to forget the cheese breadsticks."

"I wouldn't dare."

"And I know Brandon said he wants orange juice, but he doesn't actually mean orange juice. He's talking about that nasty sugar-water stuff. You know, in the coolers down by the deli."

"You got it."

There's a brief silence between them, and Nate smiles into it. Settles into it. He can see Rose in the kitchen, resting her hand on her belly. Leaning against the doorframe as she gazes at the kids in the living room, curled in front of the television, all of them giggling together as they watch the crowd in Times Square.

"I promise."

After he hangs up, he places the order at the store and gathers his things. In the break room, there's a swirl of voices, everyone talking about the snowstorm that's predicted to come rolling in tomorrow—if tomorrow ever comes.

Just as Nate punches his timecard, Bruce steps into the lobby.

"Joining the party, Boss? Pretty good cake back there."

"Save a little for me," says Nate, already reaching for the door. "I'm going home."

ACKNOWLEDGMENTS

For my family, my friends, my Fella, and the many writing mentors and colleagues I have been lucky enough to find along the way: Thank you all. This book, and the others before it, could never have been written without your love and support.

For Judith Weber and Nat Sobel: I will always appreciate everything you have done to get my words out into the world. Thank you, thank you.

For everyone at Europa Editions: I feel so fortunate to have worked with you these past few years. Special shout-out to Ginevra Rapisardi for the beautiful covers she has created for The Dalton Novels—no matter how many times I look at these books, I am blown away by how she captured the essence of this small town at the crown of Maine.

For Autumn Toennis: To say how much our editor/author journey means to me would fill another book (full of repeated words and parentheses). The phrase "Thank you" seems so laughably insufficient. SSDGM.

For my fellow library workers, near and far: Thank you for sharing the power of stories and for creating environments where everyone is welcome, whether they're a Merchant or a Frazier, a Trudy or a Greg.

For all the incredible booksellers: Thank you for everything you do for writers and for the communities you serve. The world is better with you in it.

For everybody reading this: Thank you! Please support your local library. And your local bookstore.

Finally, for my cat, Rosie, who keeps me company—often begrudgingly—while I write: I see you. I hear you. I know you were the one who opened all the kitchen cabinets.

In a Distant Valley Reading Guide

1. Many characters in this novel struggle with addiction, violent impulses, and mental health issues. What role does generational trauma play in the lives of people like Tommy Merchant and Rose Douglas? How does the community of Dalton foster or perpetuate that trauma? Does any character succeed in breaking the cycle?

2. A recurring theme throughout *In a Distant Valley* is that of choice vs. fate, or nature vs. nurture. Which characters feel most conflicted about these ideas? Who believes life is shaped by destiny? Who believes their story is dictated by their own actions? Do any of the characters change their perspective by the end of the novel?

3. Since the death of his wife five years prior to the events of *In a Distant Valley*, Nate Theroux has been torn between staying loyal to her memory and moving on to a life no longer defined by grief. What steps does he take toward healing? How do the people around him encourage or complicate his trajectory?

4. Though Bev Theroux and Trudy Haskell have come out about their romantic relationship to their families, they remain fairly closeted within Dalton. Might they ever seek to live together openly as a couple? Or will they forever be defined by the limitations (perceived or real) of their community?

5. Considering the lives of young characters such as Adam and Brandon Merchant and Sophie Theroux, how might their experiences as they grow up in Dalton mirror or differ from those of their parents? How might these kids be better off? Or worse?

6. Along their individual journeys to understand themselves and their place within their families, Greg Fortin and Angela Muse continue to cross paths, culminating in a tentative romance. How do you think their relationship might, or might not, evolve? What futures do you imagine for these two characters?

7. *In a Distant Valley* wraps up the Dalton trilogy at the end of 1999. As the residents of this town continue into the twenty-first century, how might their lives change or stay the same? Which characters might flourish in a better connected world? Who might prefer the isolation that is so often a staple of far-flung, rural communities like Dalton?

About the Author

Shannon Bowring's work has appeared in numerous journals and has been nominated for Pushcart and Best of the Net prizes. Her debut novel, *The Road to Dalton*, was chosen as one of *NPR*'s Books We Love in 2023 and won the Maine Literary Book Award for Fiction. Her second novel, *Where the Forest Meets the River*, was featured in *Oprah Daily*'s Best Books of Fall in 2024. Shannon resides in Maine.